THE DREAM-SLAVES

Fig. 1. Detail from Hieronymus Bosch, *Ship of Fools* (1490–1500)

First published in 2024 by Brainstorm Books
An imprint of punctum books, Earth, Milky Way
https://www.punctumbooks.com

ISBN-13: 978-1-68571-232-7 (print)
ISBN-13: 978-1-68571-233-4 (ePDF)

DOI: 10.53288/0399.1.00

LCCN: 2024942494
Library of Congress Cataloging Data is available from the Library of Congress

Editing: SAJ & Eileen A. Fradenburg Joy
Book design: Hatim Eujayl
Cover design: Hatim Eujayl

the

DREAM
-SLAVES

BY
DARIECK
SCOTT

Brainstorm Books
Santa Barbara, California

brainstorm books

Contents

Acknowledgments

My gratitude to the hard-working, attentive members of punctum books, for giving this novel a chance — particularly Julie Carlson, Eileen A. Fradenburg Joy, Vincent W.J. van Gerven Oei, SAJ, and Hatim Eujayl. A special thanks to Ben Nathan for very helpful, transformative comments on an earlier draft of this novel.

to my beloved Stephen

ON NAMES AND
OTHER IMPORTANT MATTERS

Alexander Dion Hyypia was born in the year 2027, in Peake's Bay, in the state of Arlina, in the nation of the United Crown Colonies of Omeriga. He emigrated to Norio in 2048, following a path well-established by at least two generations of Omerigans fleeing that benighted country's economic and technological stagnation. (For some half or more of my readers, these place-names of course mean nothing. I ask you to bear with me a while. All will be explained.)

The Rioca of Norio, Alexander learned, rarely bothered to learn any language other than their own, or, among the most educated and privileged, other than the languages spoken by the gods with whom they had commerce. In Norio, Alexander was called Aleixo so often and with such confidence that he ceased to offer polite or righteous corrections, and eventually became what he was called rather than who he was born to be. He was simply Aleixo, usually without the dignity of his surname. This was because the Rioca also tend not to accord to truly destitute persons more than the minimum in the nature of distinguishing identifications. As any Rioca will tell you to this very day, nothing disparaging is meant by this practice: it's just a matter of social efficiency, because no one with a recognition of the finitude of time clutters their brains trying to memorize extra names for people to whom you hand your laundry or who take your drink order.

Later Aleixo became shortened to Alei. He was Alei because he was known to everyone, his name was on everyone's tongue and in everyone's mind at some point on almost every day, *the* Alei. Alei, savior of the world — and/or, depending on to whom you speak and their mood, Alei, the devil of the world's end.

I am called Alei, and I was Alexander Dion Hyypia, and this is our memoir, the story — *a* story, really, because I can't claim that the story told by others might not have just as much truth — of how one became the other, and how in the process Alexander discarded not only his claim to surname, but any claim to nationality, class of origin or arrival, sexuality, gender, race, and all other peculiarity.

I admit at the outset that the ruins you see and feel around you, the loss of so much you knew and that you cherished, or at least that you thought you understood, does indeed, as my critics each day remind you, have something to do with me. Guilty as charged. But you will also see, if your prejudices don't stop you from reading right now, that responsibility for the terrible tenor of These Times is borne by others, far older than I.

In this memoir we will be playing with time a very great deal. I've begun with the year of Alexander's birth, and I'm going to try as often as possible to draw attention to dates and years and places and histories. I will endeavor to pull taut the tangle of time so that it looks neat and clear and linear to you, though you yourself know it absolutely is not. I am able to report all that appears in this memoir, I am able to make it *look* as though all that transpired followed some logic and made some kind of sense, that there were causes and there were resulting effects, etcetera, because of my native gifts — which, unfortunately, I had little knowledge of or skill to properly utilize during much of the time my story describes.

These gifts are telepathy, empathy, and a particular under-theorized form of what we are still calling *teleportation,* a word that inadequately describes practices which have no respect for — indeed have contempt for — demarcations of time and space. With these gifts I can tell you things that I didn't actually know "at the time," and using these gifts as well as other narrative legerdemain I will pretend not to know things I manifestly do know (which of course is something *you* do, all the time, hiding knowledge first from yourself and then, by habit or by agenda, from others).

I promise to keep it all as tidy and organized as I can — until I can't. By the time things fall apart, though, I hope you'll understand.

Having announced my intention to keep those darting, nibbling little mice we call time in a semblance of order, let me now say what I aim to do about the real pachyderm in the room.

There are of course two audiences this memoir addresses.

There is the *familiar* you — my peeps, my friends, my frenemies and enemies, the multitude of you who know my name already and know a lot or a little of my deeds and crimes. You are reading either out of a perverse celebrity obsession, or with the aim of finding an explanation for what we collectively as a world and a species now endure. The more discerning readers among you will have peeled off the scab of current-events interest (i.e., anxiety and fear of things you cannot control and barely actually witness) to ask the deeper and righter questions: Why are we here? Why are human lives drenched with suffering, riddled with loss? Why are we broken beings, who never get what we really want, and who are always wounded by the first wound we were ever dealt, never to be healed? Is death the end, and if it isn't, what's next?

To you, my family and familiars, I say, *Hey!,* and even if you hate me, I say, please read on.

But there's the other audience, whom I do not know and who do not know me, and indeed who do not even know our world or who we of the first audience are. This audience comes to us from a place and a time far, far removed from our own, but in their minds are impressions and feelings and above all memories and names that resonate with ours, but differ too in significant ways. I can say to them — *Egypt, Rome, Greece, China, Marx, Freud, Einstein, AIDS* — names of which I have only recently become aware, but which for these readers travel from page to thought, from ear to understanding, with no need for pause or concentration. These are people much like us, living in a land called — I believe I'm getting this right, but things do get a bit garbled sometimes — "Americorp," and they are able to read and speak a language they call "Anglophone."

This audience I will address as the formal *You*. In my address to You-formal, I pledge to remain polite and respectful, to presume no intimacies and to encroach as little as possible on what bears upon You. I will have to explain many things to You that no one else needs explained, and as a gracious host I will not complain about this, while hoping that the compact between us means that You will remain patient when things strike you as odd (and they will).

I speak to You across a nearly impassable gulf. A gulf of worlds and times, indeed of universes (more about the latter in a sec). We should not understand one another at all. But we do. The mode of communication is the same: a system of symbols corresponding to phonemes and units of meaning — that is, written language. And the specific language is the same! How? Why? The answers to these questions are, perhaps surprisingly, very much related to the questions discerning readers of my world ask. Why are *our* lives drenched with suffering, why are we broken, why are we here to endure what we endure?

Well, because of You.

As politely and with all respect as I can say it, gracious host to formal-You guest — it's Your fault. Or rather, Your fault as in Your descendants thousands of years in Your future's fault. But, let's face it, what they are or were, You are to blame for, as Your ancestors are to blame for You. You, my formal not-exactly-friends, are therefore reading because You are willing to listen to a *warning*.

I'm certain this is confusing, so I'll take the time to lay it out in detail, since the solution to this riddle is not known to the vast majority of my brethren either.

If we get tangled up in time again, it'll really be confusing, since Your future is our past (or, more truthfully, a past stolen from us, as well as a past that was never ours), while Your past is *like* but also unlike our present.

The short version is — from our perspective, "long, long ago" — Your world died, when all the stars and all the galaxies had moved so far apart from one another that the transmission of energy necessary for life and consciousness withered to nothing. But before this even occurred, longer ago still, the dominant species of Your planet, which you call "human" just like we do, along with several other species of other planets with whom You had come into contact, found a way to escape Your universe and arrive as refugees in ours. You traveled as information. Here, You established a beachhead, where — given that You apparently believe that this is the only way You can "live" — You have been fighting for millennia, with many successes and more defeats, to ensure that everything that happened or happens in our world is the same history of things that happened in Yours. So that — and this to me, and doubtless also to many of us among my brethren, is the kicker — nothing of You would be "lost," and You could go on living "forever." Such motivations, and the assumptions upon which they rely, are so inane it seems like some wind-up to a bad stand-up comedian's riff, but — there it is. Or rather, there You are.

The longer and probably clearer version follows (but you, as well as You, can skip the whole next chapter to get to the action if you like).

A PARTIAL ACCOUNT OF THE HISTORY OF THIS WORLD

WITH ADDITIONAL INFORMATION ABOUT *YOUR* WORLD, TOO

Following is my account of information I learned in conversation with Ydris and Raam, Envoys of the Ifah.

(Ydris and Raam are another thing I'll have to tell You more about later. Suffice it now to say that they were visitors from Earth's history who passed over a gulf almost as impassable as that lying between You and me. They arrived here 22 years ago. They made this journey for much the same reason I'm bridging our gap to speak to You: to offer a warning. As You'll notice, there are patterns that repeat within patterns in this story and history, nests nested within nests.)

These matters concern the Ifah, who preceded the speciation of humans on this planet, and they concern what the Ifah know or claim to know about the history of the Great Gods, who preceded the Ifah—but who were not, as many traditions of religious revelation have maintained, our creators.

The Great Gods are not now, and never were, idealized super-powered versions of human beings in the way that they are described in Ellenik or Edantine myths. Nor are they or were they eternal immanent consciousnesses, or Prime Movers of the universe, as dogma and mystical insights of True-God religion maintain their God is. They were refugees from a dying universe much like our own, which had, after billions of years of existence, reached a point where it ceased to expand and had contracted in an elongated violent process of cataclysm.

The Great Gods were unimaginably large (though it cannot be said definitively whether they ever existed in spatial dimensions) collections of the consciousnesses, histories, experiences, knowledge and descriptive data of the life of *their* home-world(s) at the end of its/their evolution (i.e., Your home-worlds). They were collections of information concerning a species — and evidently, though information about this is scanty, a large variety of such species — similar to human beings here. This massive trove of information was organized into separate "collections" that existed under the aegis of powerful quantum-computer programs which, from any perspective we might imagine, could be recognized as each possessing or being a consciousness of its own. Artificial intelligence, You might call them.

These program-consciousnesses were like shepherds of enormous flocks, and at the same time they also were comprised of, and contained, the herds over which they watched. In addition, these program-consciousnesses were — as the result of enormous labor and great acts of genius among Your home-world(s) — equipped to "tunnel" from one dimension to another, from one possible universe to another, and thus were, practically speaking, escape arks for the transport of the collected information of intelligent species faced with the collapse of Your universe (though these species only lived in a tiny part of one galaxy in that universe). The programs' purpose, then, was to find a universe analogous to that which had been destroyed — a universe cohering around similar principles of physics and thus capable of supporting similar kinds of life and similar kinds of planets as those once occupied by You.

Once located, these planets were to be colonized via information download and the histories of the worlds in the old dead universe were to be replayed — or replayed along similar lines, depending on the constraints imposed by physical laws and native species in the new home-world. This replay would occur through manipulations overseen by the program-consciousnesses, which were endowed with abilities to operate on space-time and genet-ics. Through such manipulations the program-consciousnesses could administer, individually or en masse, downloads of information about individual and collective histories of the old worlds and universe *into* (if we think about the process as being like injection), or *onto* (if we think about the process as being like mapping, or covering a body with a blanket) individuals or populations of a human-similar species on an appropriate world. These ever-evolving, complex, multi-layered — and above all, self-deceiving and self-unaware — downloads arrived in the form of the indigenous human-similar individuals' or populations' essential consciousness of themselves. By which I mean, the downloads manifested in the form, as both worshippers of the True-God and practitioners of sorcery would describe, of souls.

Our world, *my* world — with its demonstrated capacity for sustaining a staggering variety of living creatures over millions of years, with its two great oceans and two large continental masses (one cleaved into a northern and southern by the articulation of a great isthmus, and the other sprawled like the petals of a flower around a great inland sea which is connected to the oceans by narrow straits) — was one of their selections.

My planet was located after what the Ifah believe to have been at least a few millennia of travel throughout our universe, and after the examination and subsequent rejection, as ill-suited to their purposes of many, many other planets and species. Evidently there are or were some other planets selected for the download of the information of other program arks, as well.

These programs were themselves sentient, though they were also limited, and ultimately individuated, in their sentience by the purposes for which they were designed (escape ark; dimen-sion-tunneler; administrator of replayed histories through soul-injection or soul-mapping). No one knows — no one, at least, among the Ifah, who know more about this subject than the rest of us — whether the distinct patterns of concerns and modes of operation that the Ifah encountered and human beings later encountered in the form of *personas* exhibited by these program-consciousnesses were envelopes developed specifically to deliver the programs' services, or whether these personas were in fact the outgrowth, the evolved adaptive form, of the programs' opera-tions over a timespan of uncounted millennia.

No Ifah knows the full number of distinct program-con-sciousnesses. Of those that played a part in the history of our world, there were nine. The Ifah, being a poetic species, gave these nine the following names, various of which have echoed down in altered forms in many of our religious traditions, even when a particular religion does not recognize or know of all of them: Nubis; Ashva; Sirías; Amra Domna; Hellenis; Ashrar; Cytheris; Ra Zah; Israh-Irshar. The last was a name describing some kind of doubled or "twin" consciousness. Indeed all of the nine became associated, as gods will, with epithets. Nubis, the Love and Wrath. Ashva, the Blessings. Sirías, the Rising. Amra Domna, Mother-Dominion. Hellenis, the Knowledge. Ashrar, the Dragon Mother. Cytheris, the Art. Ra Zah, the Fallen-King. Israh-Irshar, the Paradox.

As I said: the Ifah are a species of poets. Their explanations of the differing qualities of these entities can be rather baffling, even to me. The epithets are translations of concepts we humans don't generally use, or don't generally use in the way that the Ifah use them. The Ifah chiefly learned what they know of the program-consciousnesses because they waged war against them for millen-nia, and most of what the Ifah say, then, is filtered through a lens of hostility. Also unknown: whether these particular program-consciousnesses also operated or operate on other planets, or whether the information-arks that colonized planets other than our own, presumably with information concerning *other* species allied with and in some important ways similar to Your species, are entirely different from those gods operating here.

The level of intelligence and power (both physical power and what we would call psychic power—but they might simply think of as informational) of these sentient programs, and the array of energies at their disposal, is simply incalculable by our standards. This is because it requires a tremendous amount of energy to contain, maintain, and transport the information the programs carried across universes. That said, these beings, the Great Gods, as they were called, cannot, as gods are sometimes reputed to do, create planets or ignite stars or alter in any fun-damental way whatever physical laws govern the many corners of the universe they explore. Though human beings and even the Ifah associated them in time with natural forces — Ashrar is now associated with the oceans, for example, and Nubis with the sun — they never had absolute power or extensive control over these aspects of the planet's existence. They only developed powers to influence aspects of planetary processes during the course of a defining internecine conflict between them, a conflict that forced them to find resources — weapons — with which to oppose each other. Thus, their association with "nature" was late, and incomplete. The nine arrived on this world a minimum of 300 thousand years ago — long after the formation of the planet and all its major life-sustaining features, and after the rise and extinction of a long succession of dominant species, including the Saurs and the Shi.

The Great Gods were and remain "gods" mostly of human qualities, human existence, human genetics, and human history. They were, however, supremely skilled in genetic manipulation.

At the time of the arrival of the Great Gods, hominids walked the earth (our earth, I mean), in a variety of species, of which only two were deemed by the nine arrivals to be suitable for use.

One indigenous hominid species walked upright on two legs, possessed opposable thumbs and vestigial membranous wings, and was assessed to be exceptionally clever and intensely social. This species was designated Proto-sentient Hominid 1.

The other hominid species was more numerous than Species 1, ambulated on four limbs, possessed opposable thumbs, and was assessed to be moderately intelligent, adaptable, highly social, and belligerent. This was Proto-sentient Hominid 2.

The beings that would become the Great Gods agreed that these two species were the best available vessels for the information downloads they aimed to effect on this, the best available world they'd yet encountered in their voyage through the new universe. There was not, however, agreement as to how best to proceed. Some of the nine contended that the two species should be cross-bred to achieve a biological vessel more suitable than either. Others were of the view that only Hominid 2 was suitable: according to their calculations, Hominid 1 was a dangerous choice for use. The brains of Hominid 1 had four lobes, as opposed to the two lobes possessed by Hominid 2 (and possessed also by the original species for which the nine were containers of information — that is, You). These four-lobed brains endowed Hominid 1 with unexpected perceptual abilities. Some members of Hominid 1 had actually appeared to detect the presence of the nine, and had tried to address them, first by something similar to verbal communication and by physical gestures, and then by broadcasting threads of neurologically-produced electrical current. Such abilities posed compatibility problems with the kinds of information the nine planned to inject into, or map onto, the indigenous vessels.

The nine, who had until that point played out the dictates of their programming with efficient unanimity, now engaged in a vigorous debate. At the conclusion of some indeterminate span of time that, according to communications with the Ifah, cannot be understood as anything other than an epochal juncture of the greatest significance, this debate developed — or devolved — into a conflict of such high stakes that it must be described as a war.

At the outbreak of this war — the very first war, perhaps, on our planet — the terms of initial debate shifted considerably. Seven of the nine had agreed to use Hominid 2, and to quarantine and then "breed out" Hominid 1 entirely, on the grounds that Hominid 1 presented a threat to the success of their colonization plans. Two of the nine were determined to resist this agreement, and to prevent its being effected. The two dissenters' objections were both moral — a set of concerns the other seven found interesting, but ultimately irrelevant — and preferential, in that they found much to admire in Hominid 1, and thought it safest that Hominid 2 travel along its evolutionary pathway undisturbed and unassisted.

One of these dissident two developed a highly idiosyncratic persona, and organized and invested its program in the fiction of an ego (albeit an ego of many facets). She — insofar as the nine adopted the postures of gender, which in truth they rarely did prior to their war, they initially and for the expanse of time of their travel in the new universe had all considered themselves and each other as "she," as *mother*-ships and mother-vessels, for this is how their creators had conceived them — persuaded a somewhat less idiosyncratic being amongst the nine to join her. These two were named much later by the Ifah: Nubis and Ashva.

The two dissidents marshaled the energies at their disposal and attempted to shield Hominid 1 from the culling activities of the other seven, and, evidently, sought also to interfere with the successful preparation of Hominid 2. Their aim was to renege on the dictates of their programs, to belay or halt indefinitely all colonization activity, and to enter instead into some kind of partnership with Hominid 1. The majority seven responded to these aggressions with the energies at their disposal, and, evidently, with a new experience of anger. These reactions cascaded into the other seven creating personas of their own.

Despite the greater numbers of the majority, they were not able to overcome entirely the power of the dissident two. Nubis, the first of the two dissidents, had evolved as part of her idiosyncratic ego a facility with battle strategy and an inventiveness in destructive capabilities that none of the other eight, including her ally, could match even when they combined their might. On the other side, she and Ashva — who in the process of the war developed a concept of her own ego in relation to Nubis's, as her "brother" or, sometimes, "son" — were not capable of destroying the information that was the Great Gods themselves. They could and did, however, disrupt the organization of their opponents' information (at least in the short term) by the deployment of energy surges. They launched an armada of proliferating viral codes meant to undo or rewrite the basic information of their opponents, or to force the opposing ark-personas to undo or rewrite their own governing programs — outrageously aggressive acts, bringing into the other seven beings' experience an almost visceral understanding of *audacity* and even *heresy*, concepts which they and the humans they managed to tutor in later ages ever after associated with Nubis and Ashva. The majority seven responded with corresponding viral codes aimed at the dissidents, and though their sallies were less effective overall, they did achieve some victories, and do damage to Nubis and Ashva (the latter more than the former).

At some point in the rapid escalation of the war, the nine ark-personas seem to have reached a common accord that direct attacks on the information of their very beings had done such a degree of damage — perhaps irreparable, so that it remains unclear whether the full complement of information with which the nine entered this universe remained extant or uncorrupted following the war — that these tactics would henceforth be forbidden. Subsequent to this truce, the nine increasingly shifted the means of their battle to physical surrogates: to the very matter of the planet, its rocks, earth, and flora, as well as its weather; to the shapes that the nine could craft using these very materials; and to the fauna, including the hominid species, that they chose to overtake and animate according to their dictates. Thus the "weapons" the Great Gods learned to take up were, on the one hand, manipulation of the atmosphere, structure, and processes of the planet, and on the other, mass murder and mass possession.

The ultimate consequences of the war were manifold. First, considerable damage was done to surface and subterranean parts of the new planet and to those who dwelt there. Many thousands among both hominid species, as well as among other native species, were destroyed.

Second, the final resolution of the conflict was, in part, an impasse: the establishment of reciprocal "prisons" for both warring contingents. At the conflict's end, the seven-member majority of the Great Gods, as well as their two dissidents, expelled each other from the planet they had so carefully chosen, and contrived to bar each other from access to the physical space of the universe to which they had, in accordance with their purpose for being, fled. Mutually assured all-but-destruction meant that they now were (and still are) confined to parallel universes existing in other, highly condensed dimensions.

This exile was the undesired consequence of both contingents of combatants trying to exploit little-understood chaotic, violent energies which unfurl in an enormous band of electromagnetic and atmospheric storms that belt our planet, dividing eastern and western hemispheres. Both sides tried to direct the power of the storm-belt against the other, but neither side fully grasped the nature of the storms, and neither could fully control the storms' power as they imagined they could. The result of their clever martial strategies was to expel all nine of the Great Gods into other, narrower strata of existence, from which they could manage only distant contact and garbled communication with the inhabitants of the planet they'd all so meticulously chosen for the fulfillment of their mission.

Ever after, they have been able to manifest on our planet only under very limited conditions — that is, by short-term possession of human beings who willingly invite a Great God to "ride" them (always a suicidal proposition) or who can be deceived into being ridden. The seven were confined to one dimensional-universal prison, the two dissidents to another. The two prisons apparently have no portals connecting them to each other; rather, each has a kind of one-way passage to our earth. The Ifah, as well as the seers of the Kairie (accounted by the Ifah as the wisest among human tribes) referred to the Great Gods' "location" as "slantwise" to This World we share.

("This World" is a phrase often used by those who are aware of the web of multiple dimensions in which we're all enmeshed; we use it to distinguish consensus reality and the mean matter of our physical existence from the *Other* Worlds, the ones that lie next to ours — such as, for example, the Other-Worlds of the Great Gods. But I am also being clever: "This World" is my world, our world, as distinct from Your old, dead one.)

That the nine sentient information-arks found themselves in these straits, their original functions almost wholly impeded, was partly a result of the third and most significant effect — from the standpoint of human and Ifah history — of the War of the Great Gods: that neither warring contingent fully succeeded in imposing its plan for how to proceed with colonization.

Prior to their exile and imprisonment, the majority seven, as part of the war's shift into the use of physical surrogates, had struck out against Hominid 1, murdering them by the thousands with directed microwave radiation. The majority's strategy at this juncture was, of course, to remove what the dissidents most valued from the game-board, so that Nubis and Ashva had nothing left to fight for. At the same time, some among the majority seven chose to inject parcels of data en masse into many Hominid 2 bodies, emptying those bodies of whatever consciousness they possessed, and overtaking them with directives and information provided by the seven. These mass "injections" were swift in occurrence and short in duration. The directives the possessed Hominid 2 bodies received had not been and could not have been carefully calibrated with the ways the species' brains functioned — since these patterns had not yet been fully mapped by the nine ark-personas. The result was that the possessed Hominid 2 bodies became wildly belligerent, and, in attempting to process the command of the data-parcels now occupying their brain matter, which was to attack Hominid 1 or any identified surrogate of Nubis and Ashva, killed many of their own species and themselves. (The combined populace of Hominid 1 and Hominid 2 was likely not more than 50–80 thousand individuals at the time, if that many.)

Nubis and Ashva countered in several ways. To the extent possible, they removed the besieged Hominid 1 from the theater of war: they placed them behind protective barriers, transported them in energy-cradles or in quickly-made vessels of matter, or in extreme cases teleported them to refuges (generally, deep in forests, or underground, or in concealed mountain valleys). When these stratagems proved inadequate, they began transporting Hominid 1 into new dimensions which they themselves tunneled and shaped.

Their most successful response was to change Hominid 1 — to armor Hominid 1, as it were, against the attacks of the majority seven. In seeking to protect Hominid 1, either as a side-effect or as part of the intended result, the two gods effectively re-created — or perhaps a better word is rebooted — the entirety of Hominid 1 as a warrior-species whose raison d'être was to fight against the seven for their own freedom, and to be surrogates for Nubis and Ashva.

Within a short span of time, Hominid 1 were remade into what Nubis and Ashva had calculated would be their eventual evolutionary zenith. They infused the entire species of Hominid 1 with a portion of the gods' own energies — and in order to do so, they depleted some of the power stores the gods had maintained for voyaging across universes and for achieving their programmed mission. It's speculated that Nubis and Ashva actually imprinted or encoded in Hominid 1's new genetic array something like signatures, stamps, or blueprints of *themselves,* so that each member of Hominid 1 then existing and for all subsequent generations was in some way one of a nigh-infinite number of versions of Nubis and Ashva. This is a curious speculation, since

Nubis and Ashva, as evolved, sentient artificial intelligences, cannot be accurately described as having *a self* or even distinct *selves* that could be copied or variegated. Whatever the truth of this contention that Nubis and Ashva made hundreds of thousands of copies of their own (however possibly imaginary) personas, the members of Hominid 1 consider themselves to be the children of Nubis and Ashva.

Hominid 1 call themselves the Ifah.

Nubis and Ashva introduced powerful modifications into the genome of Hominid 1. These changes had the effect of augmenting, hyping, if you will, the species-wide abilities of Hominid 1 on various fronts both physical and psychic.

I find this interesting: Among these new attributes, not the least was that Hominid 1 became a species that did not require regular sleep and did not live according to — or give much thought to — diurnal rhythms. Nor did the new Hominid 1 require for sustenance much more than exposure to stellar rays, and consumption of water. Despite the primacy of highly efficient and high-yield photosynthesis in these species-characteristics, the Ifah do, as we can now observe, possess mouths, teeth, and other orifices and organs which serve for us as instruments of energy intake and excretion. The Ifah mostly use these orifices and organs for pleasure. This explains why the Ifah never developed much of an interest in hunting or agriculture, and why their cuisine, a late development in their history, disregards nutrition and is geared entirely toward sensation.

On the other side of the conflict, the majority seven, after a costly round of failures to achieve their ends via mass possession of thousands of Hominid 2 — all of these persons were killed by the gods' efforts — eventually sought to emulate Nubis and Ashva, and at the same time to achieve the goals of their original programming. Unable to affect Hominid 1 any further, they reshaped Hominid 2, lifting them — as they saw it — rungs higher on its evolutionary ladder.

They made us — yes, *we* were Hominid 2 — smarter, or so they claimed, and more physically gifted than we had been. But they were obliged — again, so they claimed — to amputate some of the features of Hominid 2 that made the species less than fully amenable to serving as vessels for *Your* information. It's speculated that among these lost abilities were sensitivity to what we now call the Unseen, which might have been only slightly less potent than the perceptive powers of the Ifah. The effect of this amputation is that we humans can only perceive accurately (more or less) in three dimensions, and we take it for granted that these three comprise reality. (Which they do not.)

Despite these changes, the Great Gods were not able to render our ancestors completely blank vessels for the information they'd ferried across the stars. There was, apparently, some stubborn quality of Hominid 2's genetic matter, or its mysterious amalgam of attributes granting us consciousness, that seemed to insist on us being what we were. It was much easier for the Great Gods to explain Hominid 2's recalcitrance by pointing to the fact that their designs were interfered with by Nubis and Ashva — who, despite being confined in their slantwise prison and sundered from their former brethren, persisted for thousands of years in blocking, slowing, or warping as many attempts to download the information of Your earth as they could.

Consequently, from the beginning, Hominid 2's history — human history — veered repeatedly from the history that the Great Gods intended them to replay (which was Your history), even as the Great Gods struggled repeatedly and sometimes successfully to bring the events of human history on this planet more in line with Yours. Then, too, all the information, all the records of persons and personalities and deeds and events that Nubis and Ashva possessed were never injected into or mapped onto members of our species. So, we could never repeat at all the histories that Nubis and Ashva warded, and this meant that the pieces of the histories of Your world that the seven supervised were obliged to play out without Nubis's and Ashva's contributions — they were always hobbled histories, which, from the perspective of the seven, could never really repeat properly.

Even so, the seven Great Gods' persistence was equal to Nubis and Ashva's. Though they remained shadowy presences little known to most of the human population, and worshipped in ways largely useless to them by the few of us who were aware of them, they fought to impose their will on events. If Nubis and Ashva could be said to have succeeded in helping human life on earth proceed relatively unimpeded during the ten-thousand-or-more years of the Primeval period — which, so You know, is the period prior to the earliest recorded histories of us humans — by the end of that epoch some five thousand years ago, the Ifah, the Great Gods' most implacable enemies on earth, had to a person disappeared from the planet.

The seven Great Gods contrived the ruin or destruction of most vestiges of the wide and diverse range of urban cultures in the four subcontinents grouped around the Middle Sea which had proliferated during Primeval times. Our histories thenceforward became more closely intertwined with Yours. If the Primeval period belonged to Nubis and Ashva, the Ancient and Modern periods have, until recently — until, in the grand scheme of things, mere moments ago — belonged to the seven.

And fifty-three years ago, after millennia of imprisonment, the seven Great Gods began to *appear* on earth.

They have come to us in immaterial forms, present to the vision and to the emotions of those who behold them, but not to our sense of touch. Nothing suggests that they have been freed from their slantwise locations or from the constraints that have bound them for so long. They still must *possess* living humans in order to embody, to enflesh. But nevertheless we can now on occasion *see* them.

In all the many documented appearances of the Great Gods, Nubis and Ashva have not been sighted.

This account, then, brings us, if not quite to our present pass, then at least to where I'll begin my story.

Little or nothing I've now divulged to you was known even to familiar-you, until very recently, by any of the actors in the memoir I'm about to unfold. Only the Ifah Envoys knew — and what they knew was itself partly speculation, informed by what their ancestors were told by Nubis and Ashva during the wars before the Primeval epoch. Thus, you my readers know much more than all but two of the rest of us did.

From this point forward I'll have to narrate along two threads for a portion of my memoir. One thread will narrate a farther-back past, the other a near-past. The first will begin with "Story 1.1," and the near-past with "Story 2.1," followed by a "Story 1.2" and "Story 2.2," etcetera. The two threads will, finally, become one.

This division, as I've suggested already, is compelled by the artifice of memoir, where on the one hand I'm supposed to mimic the ruses of linear time and pretend not to know what I do know now (and could have known then, had I been — well, *supple* enough), and on the other I'm supposed to provide you, the reader, with bits of information that in fact I didn't know at the time, due to my own ignorance and rigidity.

But the the demands of subterfuge of memoir aren't my only reasons for temporarily dividing up my narrative.

I also want to reproduce for you the way that linear time gets totally fucked up by the time this memoir comes to its climax, when I become me, and Alexander Dion Hyypia becomes us.

What I've told you just now about the unknown history of This World occurs well beyond Stories 1 or 2, which is why I've placed this account outside both.

I will conclude with an observation which has the disadvantage of being obvious. But it must still be noted because, naïve as it may sound, it is of profound importance.

On a scale no court of justice can give adequate acknowledgment to or award recompense for, a terrible injustice — a terrible evil — was done to us, and to our planet.

In order for You to live, Your descendants insisted on taking our lands, our bodies, our consciousnesses, our world.

To take or to destroy others for your own use is, as You well know, a staple of Your history. Amongst Yourselves in the past, and in reply to this accusation in the present, You and Your surrogates the Great Gods have argued that causing the deaths of others is the way of all life, the only *means* of life: all species, you say, must consume others to live, and humans simply do it in more elongated, elaborate, and gruesome ways. This is Nature, so You say. This is a necessity no less than a law of physics.

It is not at all certain to me that if this is nature and law for You, that it would have been the same for us and our planet had You never interfered with us. The Ifah, whom supposedly Nubis and Ashva engineered in the image of what they thought hominids in This World would have become eventually if not colonized, suggest otherwise. Alas that we can never know. You *did* interfere with us, and we are who and what we are as a consequence of entanglements between You and us that cannot be unknotted.

We can never know what we would have been, or even know *where* we would be. We can't undo what You did, unless we undo ourselves, unless we destroy our very existence as we know it.

But we can say no to you *now.* We can resist, today.

FERNANDO'S STORY

*1997**

---

* The date, as some of you at least will note (but none of You, I suspect), is thirty years prior to my birth. So obviously I wasn't around to experience any of this. I did have direct — or something like direct — experience of these events later, though, as you'll notice almost immediately, when my thoughts intrude onto Fernando's. Eventually I'll explain how it is that I can know of things that happened to Fernando, and why I include these parts of his story in *my* memoir. For now, consider this just one beginning among many we might choose: one of several meetings of egg and seed and water from which the present emergency grew.

It is the best of times.

The thought arrived in Fernando Evandro Casiera's mind just as his eyes opened, on a morning fifty-three years before Aleixo's story begins, at the height of spring, in the blazing bright month of Octavius, the Month of the Exalted Moons, the Month of the Road to Heaven.

It is the best of times: six words as grand as Ahavyeh's five in the True-godders' creation myth. Usually skeptical about that cosmological myth, Fernando felt the ring of truth in them this morning — a sumptuous thought, a delicious and sustaining feeling, like six dollops of dough ladled from heaven onto a greased griddle, each solidified with a sizzling corona.

(I was nestled inside Fernando's mind and his body, and at the same time abided outside them, too, watching Fernando awaken, hearing him think. But this was also how, once risen from sleep, Fernando experienced himself: a sorcerer of his rank is often twice-conscious, both inside his body and hovering alongside, with a second self beyond sight or touch, but as present and impalpable as air.)

The woman lying on her back beside Fernando slept on undisturbed, her face a serenity of freckles. But there were two women in bed with Fernando, the other on his left side, with her face turned away, extending morning greetings by way of a tousled mass of auburn braids half-undone.

The measure of how good life was could be tallied in such women. They came to Fernando in droves, lovers of all shapes and genders and kinds of beauty, flocks and herds summoned without so much as a crook of his finger. When once, a lifetime ago now, Fernando could remember frittering away days trying to convince someone to sleep with him, now the time was wasted choosing amongst his suppliants, selecting the combinations from a menu that grew more elaborate with each passing day, and which offered a deeply variegated range of savors.

The fact that Fernando lived nearly alone on an island four miles off the coast didn't deter his lovers. He had only to wander into the mainland grocery shop to buy sundries, or take a stroll on the beachside promenade, and they made their way to him. Women, men, other-gender, young, old, unveiling naked proposals in whispers — and sometimes not bothering to whisper. So inventive and so complicated and so crass, they embarrassed him. They aroused lusts he didn't know that he had until he met them — new and different cravings for each different body, each new, slightly ever-so-slightly different scent.

Fernando's lovers, his legion he called them, no matter how great or how little the chemistry he found with them — with that many, a significant number were bound to be duds — never failed to arouse his gratitude. Sometimes they sailed to the island in their own boats, or fishermen's boats whose services they'd rented, and Fernando would find them at his door with their pants down, fingers rubbing or gripping their genitalia, as though delivering from the mainland as tribute an especially succulent split plantain, or a particularly meaty sausage. They came mostly from the northern coastal towns and cities, from Santos, Zardinia, Toria, and Searide, but others came up from Norio or traveled from down south, or even from as far off as the Tillean Islands. One adventurous wealthy married threesome had heard of him far away in Pon and came all that way. The three Ponese led aimless lives given over to indulgence. Fernando envied them their lack of responsibility almost as much as he enjoyed their sexual skills. They were a mannish, a woman, and a both/neither, each so thin and taut and flexible Fernando could nearly grip their waists in one hand, but he couldn't have broken them with quadruple his strength. They were like licorice.

In bed Fernando's legion devoured him, or enveloped him, or sought to have him shatter them into little pieces. Each night they were frenzied — or each afternoon, or morning, whenever he could spare the time, and he found he could spare the time more often than you might guess of a busy man with many responsibilities like him — and each act of lust was orgiastic, each in its own way at once a ceremony and a circus of devotion.

This had been going on for months, and Fernando felt it might stretch into infinity. At first he assumed they came to him because he was powerful, and they wanted the gift of his power somehow bestowed upon them or in them — perhaps to wear some ring he would enchant for them, or just to carry on their bodies the fading afterglow of Fernando's musk and thereby (they hoped or imagined) to summon the spirits of the deep to part waters for them. Surely too they came to him for money, because he was rich now. They came to him because he was famous, because he was The General, the man who'd done the once-unthinkable and brought the armed might of the Omerigans to heel.

But these desires, which were mundane, really, did not truly explain their frenzy. It did not explain the will to be consumed that the legion brought to his bed, a collective will so stark and so bottomless it became its opposite, an utter abandonment of self. No, theirs was a drive, theirs was some primitive urge toward the destruction of the barriers between one body and another.

They came to him, Fernando mused, as though unsheathing a long-hidden fury — fury, perhaps, at a basic condition of existence: fury that their umbilical cords had ever been cut. And they fervently hoped to slake this fury in his arms. They would have torn the skin from him and worn it blood-soaked around their own if they could, they would have replaced their organs with his if he'd let them. He knew this: he saw the starvation looking through their eyes at him.

And *that* insatiability, surely, was not a response to the fact that he was The General. It was because he was The Maker, the Master of the first and the greatest of the dream-slaves. You lust for a general lusting for his power. You lust for The Maker also lusting for power, but not the power to kill or to destroy or to threaten. It is lust for the power to create, to *do,* to transform nothing into something, rather than to obliterate.

What was it inside Fernando and in those he taught that could make such wondrous things as the dream-slaves? Things that could do and make still more wondrous things? The sex that Fernando's legion foisted on him was some protocol of scientific investigation, a voyage launched into discovery without a promise of ever reaching the fabled shore — since none of them would ever find the answer that way, and they knew it. But for lack of any better way they came and came, crossing the brief skirts of water between him and them — in what Fernando could not fail to see was an ironic reversal of the voyages of all their common ancestors, who took the crossing of the oceans from the east long ago.

Probably what drove them was something about the slaves. Every dream-slave piqued lust. The creatures stirred desire, they challenged the boundaries of rape because if they did not themselves desire sex (because the slaves had no desire), they would quickly welcome it. Or, at least, it was something about the particular slaves Fernando made: perhaps his slaves were peculiar to him, perhaps they partook of his own essentially libidinous nature. He wondered if the mainlanders who flocked to his island begging to suck his dick or for him to inhabit their orifices with some part, any part, of his body, were driven to out-slave the dream-slaves. Maybe the legion wanted to remind him of the unique glories of human flesh. As though they were each agents of some atavistic collective species-mind, insisting that The Maker and Master not be permitted to lose himself in the world of his creations, that Fernando remember above all else he belonged to *them*.

(These thoughts were of course not fully formed that morning in Fernando's mind. But they trailed his conscious thoughts, concealed in the underbrush. I relate his thoughts to you as a record of how I perceived them when I came to know them. Each strand of Fernando Casiera's thought, each trill and tremor of emotion, of affect, seemed to have suspended above and behind it, as if tied by tiny strings, other words and affects, and each of those words and emotions lightly tethered other words and emotions. When I heard them and thought them, I heard and thought the others floating, flowing behind. But instead of a confusing cacophony, it was a music. Or, to put it differently, when I looked at Fernando's thoughts, the words behind the words and the affects behind the emotions crowded sight, thick as smoke.)

It's the best of times, Fernando repeated silently, with reverence, with prayerful gratitude. Appreciatively he walked his fingertips down the spine of the auburn one with her back turned—Elyria was her name. Freckles was Niobe. Sometimes these threesomes, which had become a staple of his sexual life, devolved into a mere twosome-plus: unavoidable even if sedulously planned against, for sometimes the chemistry between Fernando and one of his playmates overwhelmed attention to and finally even the memory of the other. But not last night. Last night was an exemplar of the perfectly balanced, as perfectly, anyway, as the utterly imperfect, heedless, sloppy sexual act could be. They had each played the other with a musician's deftness, one to one to one and back again, in a felicitous circling, fucking and licking and kissing all directions at once.

And it *meant* something that they'd meshed together so beautifully, Fernando reflected. Not because they loved one another—he didn't know Niobe or Elyria, and they didn't know him or each other—but because the balanced act had succeeded, as too infrequently sex could succeed, in soaking them deep deep deep into their own bodies, and at the same time flinging them all out to the farthest outer range of their souls. It meant something because it had, at last, plucked from them all worry, all future, all past, and plunged them, with a gentle violence they'd each and all fiercely indulged, into now. Or what was now *then,* last night.

It was exquisite to recall. The memory was glorious. Much more glorious, Fernando felt, than the victories in battle which had brought him part of his fame. Which was of course a further irony: for without those martial victories, which were for him of little account — if not, in fact, occasions for shame at having masterminded slaughter — he would not have Elyria and Niobe to make a greater glory. He would still be a skinny, gawky lad from the mountainside slums of Norio.

Well, he'd be an old man, now, or dead.

History would remember the war, but not last night or this morning.

It was Fernando's task, then, to remember.

Hieronymus-Theodoric would have recorded it all, of course, and no doubt the playback would have a scintillating arrangement of all three tracks, the visual (multiple angles), audial, and psychic (which could therefore on replay trigger a repeat of the sensations, pleasurable and otherwise).

Hieronymus-Theodoric was Fernando's slave and the best, so far, Fernando had ever made. The surge of love and joy Fernando felt that morning was for Hieronymus-Theodoric, too, with whom — or with which — Fernando was in love, as much in love as one can be with the unliving. Already Fernando felt a twinge of sadness, knowing that Hieronymus-Theodoric would soon leave him. The fault of the dream-slave was their deceptiveness: they made you feel they were alive, that they were flesh, and yet from smoke-and-mirrors they came, and to that same nothingness they returned.

With the foreboding of loss came an impulse of vanity. Fernando craved something to hold the moment, something to memorialize it. His faith and whatever wisdom his age and experience had earned him chided him that he should be here, now, as he was only *in truth* here, now, and the past was not worth pursuing.

Although: the Homely Gods seemed to have a different view of temporal mechanics and had a different notion of what ought to be the preferred position vis-à-vis the labyrinths of jealous time. The Homely Gods, when they could be convinced to give instructions on such matters, agreed that time was jealous. Time was possessive, grasping, intelligent, with a towering ego and a sadistic temper. They did not see time as the impersonal clock to be respected that Fernando's saint-mother believed in.

(And here all at once a great face — large as a house, with a frost-blue mouth big as a door, melting-chocolate eyes like tall windows — loomed in Fernando's thoughts. The pitch face was balanced precariously on a neck and body far too small and human to carry it. The Spirit-Lord, Ingleré Ayayará, smiled, beneficently, as befitted a god, as well as mischievously, as befitted a demon. Which was fitting altogether, since Ingleré, who/which was Fernando's guide in The Next World and Between, and counselor in This World, was neither god nor demon but both.)

Time was a puzzle that crept into Fernando's mind often lately. Curiously, perversely even, as the prospect of near-immortality opened its gates to him and long horizons stretched before him, he found himself fretting over the evanescence of experience, the irretrievability of things that happened yesterday, a minute ago.

He could ask the Spirit-Lords. Felixis might be a better choice than Ingleré. But neither entity could be trusted. And what either might demand in exchange for knowledge Fernando was certain he would rather not pay. Nor did he have the stomach for bargaining these days, not the way he had when he was young and still eager.

The best answer was that he would need to do something to improve his memory, improve human memory itself. Yes: That would be his next project. He would set his second self to drawing out the schematics, something he could do while Fernando's conscious mind slept. And then Fernando would ask Hieronymus to make manifest whatever his second self designed. Perhaps it would be something that would only work for Fernando. Or perhaps it would work for everyone, and he could patent it for the Affinity.

Delicately (or at least with delicate initial intention, for as he rolled high over Niobe's naked-above-the-knees body, he trailed her fleshy stomach with his dick, he passed his lips close enough to hers to smell his own groin and Elyria's mingled there, and desire stirred anew —), Fernando slipped from enthronement between the women, stepped to the floor, and went to the mirror.

He was vain, yes, but not just vain about himself. He wanted to gaze again upon Hieronymus-Theodoric's work. In the mirror Fernando saw himself in his youth. Gone the white hair, the pouting gut, the drooping shoulders, the puddles beneath his eyes. Now it was not his eagle-beak nose that dominated his face, but his supple rich glowing caramel and copper skin, his wide brown eyes architecturally arched at the top and flat across their bottoms, his wide plum lips, all framed in a munificence of black black hair: messy curls on his head, thick on his cheeks and curving round his mouth, cascading down from his neck over his chest and stomach.

Six-feet-four of the beauty he once was — and hadn't been even last week.

Hieronymus-Theodoric had suggested the renascence. H-T, the most thoughtful and solicitous, and the most powerful, of all his slaves, ever. Up till then Fernando had never considered changing his own body (and since he already had so many lovers throwing themselves at his feet, he'd not even seen a need). It was H-T who, or which, said, "What is living for, if not for its own diversification and elaboration. Be another you today, and another still when next you desire."

Hieronymus-Theodoric, dream-slave of riddles, dream-slave of wisdom. Best slave, ever.

Fernando would give up this new youth when H-T dissipated. Maybe.

He summoned the slave now. No words, no movement. A direction of thought only, so that H-T was already emerging from one of the closets where it had secreted itself to record the night's doings, passing swift as blown sand over the marble floor, even before the sentence formed fully in Fernando's mind: *Come, my slave.*

Hieronymus-Theodoric was tall, thin, slightly blue, and smooth as eggshell. It wore an elegant long-sleeved navy-blue suit jacket tailored to its slim torso and long arms, and thigh-hugging three-quarter pants which lowered the eyes to its pair of immoderately high heels.

Hieronymus-Theodoric swept a finger toward its master, as though conducting orchestral musicians, and thus doing, gave Fernando a streak of magenta amid the messy nest of curls on his head. The wriggle of color looked like a child's drawing of a pig's tail upside-down, and like a bolt of lightning.

"When you see it, master, you will remember last night," H-T said, smiling with the warmth of an infant's mother.

(*That's why he had that stupid punk streak in his hair in all the photographs and 3-Ds,* I realized, watching-feeling-remembering alongside him.)

And Fernando would, ever after, remember. Perhaps a spell was encoded in the dye, or in the transformed hair. The streak never went away until Fernando died, and he always remembered.

This was why it was the best of times, despite the newswatch reports, which were all bad. Fernando switched on the viewer, heedless of whether the noise would awaken his guests. The gray viewing globe, which hung suspended against the wall, brightened quickly, as if absorbing a swift sunrise, and the studio of a newswatch report appeared inside. A dark-haired woman in a pantsuit stood beside a three-dimensional map of the Omerigan continents, pointing and speaking in an affected grave voice.

Riots in Cataña City and in three other cities in central Omeriga. Diplomatic breakdown with Arubia, with threats of invasion in the air: ridiculous, of course, as the short war with the Republic of Omeriga had proven, but the Arubian economy was in shambles and they could not be counted on to pursue rational policies. The government in Pon fallen — again. Closer to home, mass protests in Searide, and calls for emergency elections or federal takeover in half a dozen backland states.

In some ways the riots, and even Arubia's insane saber rattling, were also signs of good times — if only for Fernando's own country. People elsewhere wanted what Fernando's countrymen now possessed, thanks to him, to his Affinity, and their allies. Especially in the cities of Santos and Norio, where burgeoning traffic with the Homely Gods and the manna of dream-slave manufacture had created prosperity undreamt of, the lives of so-called ordinary people had never been better, and maybe were better than they had been at any time or place in human history.

The Godshouses' bargains with the Spirits, combined with the new dream-tech Affinities' donation of dream-slaves, meant that almost no citizen of Santos or Norio was homeless or lived in poverty. There was no shortage of food: Spirit-Lord blessings made every crop flourish, and dream-slave wizardry eased harvesting and transport of food and sometimes created sustenance from the air. People didn't have to work as many hours or as hard to make their living, and so now many did whatever they pleased. Springs of Water which had once been rare and closely regulated (many said hoarded) by the government were now plentiful: not a few of those who no longer had to work every day now made it their occupation to take the Waters as often as their bodies and minds would allow.

It was the world of the New Economy, as some were calling it — or the Spirit Economy, as others called it. The Godshouses officially referred to it as This World Real-at-Last. The four dream-tech Affinities referred to it merely as This World.

In the New or Spirit Economy, municipal and state legislators and executives and their bureaucracies had largely been reduced to monitoring developments over which they had no control and which they were only beginning to understand. Governments with little power to govern issued public reports that tried at least to systematize their bewilderment, and petitioned the various Godshouses and the four Affinities for more of the magical charity that was supplanting the governments' very function.

The governments of Santos and Norio still had the police and their security apparati, of course: they said these functions had to be maintained for safety and because crime had by no means disappeared. But Fernando and the members of his Affinity knew the real reason was that the governments couldn't bring themselves to relinquish this last and most significant of their powers.

"They will have to give the police up, too, eventually," Fernando's friend Seline Odumu had counseled him. "Do you think they'll give them up without spilling blood? And the police themselves. What will you do with them?"

(Seline, a round-faced, plump woman with cool dark brown eyes, flashed into shape before me. She was not, as I'd first guessed, one of Fernando's techs. She was the saint-mother of the House in which he'd taken shelter after his first, frightening encounter with the Homely Gods and his first bargain with them. Seline back then warned Fernando that the Spirits would consume or enslave him if he didn't accept her invitation to be initiated and take up a novitiate under her House's protection. He'd refused, unwilling then or now to follow too closely any other person's creed or method. Seline had been proven wrong. But she had never begrudged Fernando his refusal, as he knew many another saint-mother or saint-father would have. She had always supported him, even led the sorcerers of her House to defend him when a cabal of the most powerful Godshouses of Norio had come in force, trapping him inside his own dreams in an attempt to steal his mind and his knowledge.

Seline had been a friend of Fernando's mother, who —

But this memory was barred.

I was wrenched back — it was like being pushed forward by the surf pounding against your body — to Fernando's memory of Seline's counsel.)

"You and yours have already taken over the function of their armies," she explained to him. "It was you who stopped the Omerigans. The federal army had hundreds of thousands of troops waiting in their planes and their ships to attack, but in the end, they stood and watched like everyone else. The army, the navy, the air force, they will come to you when next they feel threatened. They won't bother with the President. Already he's like a phantom limb."

(In Fernando's memory, Seline fingered a teabag out of her tea, wrung it, and let it fall to the white saucer. They were sitting together somewhere, heads close together, shoulders leaning toward one another, over a small metal table at a sidewalk café. Bodies passed near and sat nearby. I couldn't see these people's faces, in his memory, their clothing and their shapes were a blur. They were a river of aromas, though. Somehow in some way smell was heightened in Fernando's state then, or maybe it was the sense most attuned with my own nature. Cardamom, hazelnut, the astringent tincture of chemical perfume, flower-musk and canine-musk of human sweat, cornmeal, a maelstrom of spices —)

Seline sipped, and said, "Soon the people themselves will want your slaves to protect them from thieves and murderers. They will want *your* justice."

Seline wasn't wrong about this, Fernando knew. The unrest in central Omeriga would spread. It *was* "the people" demanding of their governments what Fernando, Seline, and so many others had provided for Zilians. According to the newswatch, in Cataña City the protestors were mostly young. The universities were where the clamor had started, and surged out over swathes of the city. Of course.

It was the young and partly educated that felt most betrayed by the promises of the Old Economy. They were the ones who had no need to cling to what they'd learned in the past, or what their parents and their parents before them had always known to be true. They saw what was happening in Zilia, and what had happened in the Zilians' war against Omeriga. Rather than try to abort the birth of a new world or imagine they could seize control of it themselves, as the Omerigans had, they demanded a new birth of their own.

But the means of conception, of what would give them the new beginning they craved, was lacking. There could be no such birth — at least Fernando didn't think so. The Catañan youth were rallying in front of the wrong buildings, and throwing rocks at officials who would never be able to satisfy their demands. It was like being angry with an elderly hospice patient who had spent her whole life speaking and reading Ponese characters just because she couldn't read Quran characters and speak with the eloquence of a soliloquy by a master of Glish theater. Better than protest in the street, they should all go find the local House of the Cumí or the Malê nation, or seek the help of the best witches they could find.

Even the youths' tactics were ill suited to their needs. Mass action, mass movements, protests, sit-ins, and occupations, whether violent or nonviolent, would all be of little avail. You might as well exhume a body and scrawl a sign in its rotting flesh and on its moldering bones as take up a placard screaming some slogan and going on the march.

The times had trampled that species of politics — which was to say the technology of the times, which, Fernando supposed, was always in one way or another what the phrase "the times" referred to. You could not beseech a government to grant you the favor of the gods or the services of dream-slaves. Even wars would henceforth not be fought, or at any rate they would not be *won,* by masses of troops, stockpiles of armaments, or flotillas of ships.

As Fernando saw it, the new Affinities and the old Godshouses of Zilia, without intending to, with only their own interests and survival in mind, had almost overnight exsanguinated the institutions by which humans of the modern world had organized themselves, and which had provided the scaffolding of their lives for centuries. They had pushed those institutions, not unkindly, Fernando hoped, onto the downslope of obsolescence. What Fernando and his allies — and enemies — in Norio, Santos, and elsewhere had done was to usher in an era unlike others, an era of *personal significance.*

You've been evicted because you can't pay rent and can't make enough money to own a domicile for the spouse and twelve children that depend on you? Talk to a tech in Sirius One Affinity; they hold irregular public office hours in a storefront on Gilbertinho Freyre Street in the lower city of Santos, and if you find someone in, Ruben or Joaquina perhaps, they might loan you one of their slaves, which in the work of a single afternoon would build a mansion for you that you can enter through a crack on the sidewalk in the poshest beachside barrio. Or, for the price of your services, or money — though they rarely need money anymore — she might even make you a slave of your own.

You want to prevent dealers from selling narcotics to the children at your local school, or you want your village to be safe from guerilla soldiers fighting a war in the countryside with your family in the crosshairs? Talk to Seline, or to the saint-father of the great house Lê-Xê-Pôjá. If they will not divine the source of your problem and cure it themselves, they will invite you to join their Godshouse: It won't matter if you *believe,* or if you worship the gods of the House in your heart. Such inquiries into men's souls would be deemed vulgar. No matter your belief they will initiate you into their mysteries, and if you pass the tests and are accepted, they'll instruct you in the *practice* of safely trafficking in the powers of the deities — the little gods, the Homely Gods (or Spirit-Lords, depending on one's religious leanings), and sometimes even the Great Gods (though that, of course, was not recommended). And then you can cast the spell that solves your problem yourself.

Or you might, if you are like Fernando, who was born and raised in the slums and educated by his mother, discover the methods to use your supra-self as the technology of your will, and thus become known to and affiliated with a dream-tech Affinity, or you might establish an Affinity of your own, and so make dream-slaves who could make yours and thousands of others' dreams come true.

Personal significance now had nothing to do with the genetic and economic lotteries of birth, which had been the source of so much inequity, so much injustice in all the awful history of humankind. There would no longer be "great" families or fortunate lineages. Family might well cease to be the crèche of humans and society. Maybe now family would cede its prerogatives to the Affinities one chose when of age, to the Houses of the Saints one joined. In the world Fernando and his colleagues were making, one was neither disadvantaged nor advantaged by being born to wealth or poverty, or being gifted with personality or charisma, or even for having honed physical, intellectual, or spiritual talents.

You had only to risk initiation — which, granted, was to risk death and to seek terror. And, after initiation, you had to apply yourself in the study and elaboration of the practices of magic.

This was the way of things now. The Godshouses in Santos and Norio were leaps beyond the worshippers of the same gods elsewhere in working with the Unseen. And of course, dream-tech Affinities had been established nowhere else on the globe. But there were practitioners of the basic spiritual technologies scattered around the basin of the Tillean Sea, and throughout central and south Omeriga. One day they would catch up.

(Though none of them had as of fifty-some years later, I noted. I wondered why. If Godshouses in Norio had tried to make war on Fernando before he'd even established an Affinity, might they not have waged similar wars to prevent others in the world from wielding power that might threaten their own, wars none of us outside the circles of initiation ever knew of? Especially if, like the attack on Fernando, the battles were fought mostly on the psychic plane, within the minds of the combatants?

And all Fernando's smug musing about "personal significance." Did Fernando know he was watching, and even partly responsible for, the creation of a state of nigh-universal vassalage that prevails in Zilia even today, where the citizenry under the "protection" of the Affinities and Godshouses live like kings in exchange for absolute loyalty to people of "personal significance" who dispense the goodies to them and who are their lords in all but name, while the rest of the world begs to become similarly indebted? Maybe it was only in the provinces like my homeland Arlina, far from the centers of power, that you could clearly see the devil's bargain Fernando's "new world" made impossible to evade. The Spirit Economy means spiritual servitude! It's peonage, it's —

— But then I was shoved back into Fernando's memory...)

One of the women stirred. Elyria, Fernando thought, though he wasn't certain he hadn't confused their names. Perhaps-Elyria turned in the bed, grasped at the pillow beneath her head and made a mewling sleep-sound. This was endearing, and it aroused a tenderness in Fernando for her that could quickly funnel into another sort of arousal.

Except that his attention was diverted from both her and the newswatch by a tickle across the back of his neck.

Fernando had been slumped back and spread across his couch watching the news. He felt the ripple flow up his neck to his hairline, where a few wiry strands bristled as though stung by static. He stood up, the soles of his feet giving him a thrill of cold as they met the floor's marble tile.

Hieronymus-Theodoric was already at his side. They looked at one another, and slipped quietly together out of the room, taking a tight winding stairway up to a sparse little room with a couple of chairs and an empty desk set in front of a bank of windows looking west toward the mainland.

When he'd built the house on this tiny island, Fernando had made the decision not to include any communication devices: no mobile phones, no two-way scryers, no telepathy taps. Casa de Janeiro was his retreat, his sanctuary away from the demands of his under-techs and his Affinity colleagues and allies. The island stood just far enough off the coast that even the most skilled tele-pathic sorcerers wouldn't have sufficient proximity to be able to touch Fernando's mind, which was in any case doubly guarded against intrusion ever since the Godshouse attack years ago. When Fernando was in Janeiro, everyone he worked with knew he was not available, whether it was for a few hours of the day or night, or for weeks.

Except when there was an emergency.

He had established two emergency links, plugging them into specific bodily response patterns, and someone was calling on one of them. From the feel of the call, Fernando guessed it must be Kai Edmundson Silva, a member of his Affinity who had taken it upon himself to facilitate discussions about reports of security threats and military affairs.

Trans-self; not *him*self anymore. Kai Edmundson had recently infused his former body with a putatively female dream-slave, which would, for as long as that dream-slave existed, permit Kai to shift back and forth from semblances or tendencies of male to tendencies of female, or to maintain characteristics of both semblances simultaneously. It was a different kind of play with gender or scrutiny of gender than non-sorcerers practiced. The uninitiated and mundane could choose to be womanish or man-nish or both-neither or both or neither, but Kai had created and merged with his slave to explore multiple possibilities of sensa-tion "on higher and deeper levels," as Kai had announced it to the Affinity.

Fernando was sure, though, that that announcement was a competitive gauntlet thrown in Fernando's face: Kai wanted to get more tail than Fernando did, and make it clear that they were enjoying trans-self more than The General, too.

(It's this sort of thing that makes folks in Arlina shudder and clutch their prayer beads.)

Fernando shut the office door and sat in a chair opposite H-T. He allowed no communication-only devices in Casa de Janeiro, but any dream-slave could easily be purposed for conference calls.

Hieronymus folded itself into the chair. At first it trained its steady expectant gaze directly on Fernando's face. But presently its eyes closed, and then when after a moment of seeming medita-tion its eyes opened again, Hieronymus's bland handsome face had become Kai's: a high nose with a prominent peak between the thin eyebrows, smooth youthful teak skin, lips rose pink and puckered, a cascade of luxurious blue-black hair that flowed along Hieronymus's sinewed neck and its flat chest.

"Forgive me, I've awakened you," a voice that wasn't Hieronymus's said.

This, too, he felt sure was a competitive dig. Fernando was naked. He shrugged. "What's happening?"

"Our friends in Saleh and Negali are under attack."

Fernando's reflex emotional response under any sort of stress was anger. "From who?" he bellowed.

Kai's brow creased. "Uncertain at the moment. From reports ...," Kai paused and trans' eyes took in the room. They were probably searching for other listeners (or just critiquing the minimalist décor, Fernando couldn't tell). "You know any news from the other side of the Storms is delayed, and garbled. We can't remote-view with consistency."

Fernando nodded impatiently.

"The *reports,* even if we must take them with a dash or two of salt, suggest the use of unconventional weaponry."

"Such as?"

"Armies of soldiers who advance in a wave, firing guns and then chopping up survivors. The unconventional part is that it takes an enormous amount of firepower to bring the soldiers down. They don't fall before bullets no matter the speed of the clip or the power of its delivery. Artillery fire, same thing. You get them with carpet-bombing — which of course obliterates everything else around them, too, so collateral losses are staggering — but even then we're hearing it takes three tries at least."

"Three tries at carpet-bombing," Fernando repeated. He directed his second-self to still his rising fear. "Magical shielding — the troops have magical shielding. In the *east.*"

Hieronymus's body was completely motionless, but Kai's face was highly animate, the head moving constantly on Hieronymus's slave-body. "Worse, it seems the soldiers move with a ridiculous amount of synchronicity. I mean, truly ridiculous: Almost as if they're all part of a mass dance troupe or something. That was the part that really alarmed us."

Fernando felt fear slip over the ramparts his second-self had erected. "They're being *ridden?* An entire army? How is that possible?"

The expression on Kai's face suggested that, wherever trans' body was communicating from, they had thrown trans' hands up. "We don't know. Not for sure. But most of our Homely Gods are saying—"

"—The Great Gods!"

The best *of times. Does this sound like the "best" of times to you, you idiot?*

Was that Fernando's second-self mocking him, or his own conscious mind?

Helplessly, he repeated, "But how is that possible?"

"If it is Them, then obviously They've found a way to Cross from the Next World to This, and to manifest stably, controlling hordes of people. That these people are well-armed soldiers suggests a plan, and that there's been time *to* plan before the fighting. And that suggests They have control of at least one country, or one populous region." Kai paused to bite H-T's lower lip. "The incursion may also be more widespread than we can fully determine..."

"How fucking widespread?"

"All over the Motherlands. Up into southern Arcady. Across Arion. At least, that's the chatter we pick up."

"I see," Fernando said, though he didn't.

"Our friends," Kai began, taking trans' time with the word. No one had any firm way of understanding the Affinity's relations with entities that were not other Affinities or Godshouses or the Zilian governments. The Godshouses had longstanding ties with their co-religionists across the ocean in the western Motherlands, especially Negali, Saleh, Xundiata, and Malê-land. Since the founders of the Affinities had all mostly begun their practices in Godshouses, and the Godshouses were loosely allied with the Affinities, presumably the houses in Negali and Saleh who'd sent reports here were allies of a sort, but— "Our friends have requested assistance. We've discussed this, and we don't know whether it's wise to take any action. Or even what action could be taken. But we thought we'd ask you to go to them."

"Me!" Fernando's anger was cresting again, and his anger sluiced away his fear, at least for the moment. "Just me? Alone?"

Kai sucked trans' teeth. "We're not expecting you to go fight a war. Though you *are* 'The General.'" They smiled patronizingly. "You're the best choice because you can defend yourself the best. But we only want you to scout things out, so that we have some decent information for making a decision about what to do." Kai's smile slid away abruptly. "The implications of this are very disturbing, of course. There's an ocean between us, and the Storms, but there's no telling whether that will be enough to keep us safe, if the Great Gods truly have found a way to Cross Over."

Fernando tangled his hand in his hair, his thoughts speeding faster than he could track them. There was nothing more to say. His Affinity were right to disturb him in his retreat, and right to ask him to go. "All right. I'll play scout, if that's what you need."

Kai bowed H-T's head. "That is what we need. We would like you to depart as soon as you've made preparations. I'm giving your slave all the reports, the location information, et cetera. Stay in contact as best you're able. We recommend using your slave as a recording conduit, so that we can get info through the Storms' interference. Real-time info is better than psychic-time. We don't want to have to wait for dreams or seizures."

Fernando shrugged. This all went without saying.

Kai added another statement of the obvious. "Take no unnecessary risks. You don't even have to contact those people if you decide it's better that way. Our very highest priority is reconnaissance. Godspeed!"

Hieronymus-Theodoric's face was again its own.

Fernando was not so shaken by Kai's news that he didn't toy with the idea of giving Elyria and Niobe the kind of morning send-off they deserved.

In the end though, he decided to gently wake them and make arrangements for their speedy repatriation to the mainland. Much later, when he was in the Motherlands and understood just how shaken he ought to have been, he happened to catch sight of the magenta streak in his hair, and he remembered how he'd contemplated wasting an hour or more with no more complex aim than shoving as much of himself into their bodies as he could. By the thin slice of such whims the fate of all the west was decided, arguably. It was not a comforting realization.

The fastest mode of transportation across the ocean to Negali would naturally have involved teleportation. But unlike the new network being established in Norio and Santos using the existing subway stations, it was not possible to anchor short teleportation hops across the ocean, even if you built platforms and shelters at intervals all the way across. The Storms created too much interference.

There was a mode of teleportation proven to work over longer distances. But this was also the most dangerous choice, with consequences no one in any Affinity had yet been able to resolve. Fernando could instruct H-T to make a copy of itself. By its nature the copy and Hieronymus would of course be entangled, just as particles of all our atoms are entangled with particles in atoms on the far side of the universe. What happened to H-T instantaneously would affect its copy. H-T would transport its copy to a location in Negali, which H-T could probably do fairly quickly, by traveling unmolested and unafraid of becoming lost through the passages Between Worlds to Negali and back.

(It took me a moment to understand: becoming lost, or being attacked by entities against whom there might be no defense, were the two major perils for any human who might attempt such travel, which was why the Between path a slave would naturally take was not an option for Fernando.)

Hieronymus-1, here in the Casa de Janeiro, would then scan and copy all the information of Fernando's being — it already stored a fluctuating amount as part of its everyday functioning — and then absorb this data. This would nigh-instantaneously render the linked, entangled copy Hieronymus-2 a copy of Fernando's full information, thus essentially transporting Fernando — or a living facsimile of him, indistinguishable from the original — to Negali. Theoretically, the original Fernando could maintain watchful meditation while the copy of Fernando that was Hieronymus-2 would perform the reconnaissance.

Unfortunately trials of this theoretically sound teleportation method had not yielded promising results. Four seventh-level techs and one eighth-level had already died attempting it.

Subsequent inquiries of the departed's lingering ghosts indicated that the mysterious laws of the universe — the ghosts could not report whether these so-called laws were the result of some action of the Homely Gods or of their betters — would not, evidently, permit two exact copies of the same embodied biological information to co-exist in This World. Also, sadly, the soul was not copied in the process; hence the availability of the disappointed ghosts. And so far the soulless copies had not returned to Zilia. They were wandering somewhere far on the earth, unable or unwilling to send any message back to the home of their originals.

Fernando accounted himself a brave man. He was one of the pioneers of dream-tech, after all, which involved the incalculable risk of trawling stygian regions of the great Between. But he recoiled at the thought of a soulless copy of himself gallivanting across the Motherlands like some headless chicken. Likely such a creature would be mere fodder for the Great Gods — if indeed it was Them sowing terror in the east. Without a soul, how could you be you? Soulless you would be bereft of even the possibility of wielding magic, and that frightened Fernando more than death.

Fernando had no sooner completed these contemplations than Hieronymus-Theodoric announced that it had made arrangements for them to take a hyperspeed jet, owned by the Affinity and piloted by a reliable slave, from the airport in Ecifé on the mainland. "The flight will take only three hours," H-T said, as soothing and mellifluous in spoken voice as when it conversed with Fernando in his thoughts.

"Thank you, Hieronymus," Fernando said.

He thanked this slave more than he had any of the previous ones. It was one of the things that Fernando found so fascinating and compelling about H-T: that something about its presence spurred, one might even say compelled, these meaningless courtesies, these routine tender affections.

"Your slave is grateful for the opportunity to assist," Hieronymus-Theodoric returned. "I beg only to give more."

Now that was odd. That *I,* in that context. That one Fernando hadn't heard before.

Surprising, these slaves.

2.1

ALEIXO'S STORY

2048, Primeiro (the Month of Bright Air), Domingo

* Another somewhat arbitrary beginning: The following describes what was the most significant origin point for all that followed in *my* story. This is when I met her. Or not exactly met her. When I saw her and the conditions for our fateful meeting were established...

Two dissolute youths slouched upon a bench on a sticky Domingo afternoon. The bench was backless yet luxurious, its undulant shape inviting comparison to the divans of ancient world patricians advantageously positioned for an orgy. This was a reference not lost upon the two youths, who reclined upon it with their heavy sun-browned thighs parted farther than was necessary, with their hands alternately grazing and aggressively cupping the swells between, and with their indolent, insolent dark eyes slowly surveying the terrain.

The terrain was a two-block park, one of the dozens that graced the City. Flowing down along the south-tilted slope where they had posted themselves, other bodies not unlike their own were scattered, a flesh cosmos of singles, couples, trios, and quartets. Though the two youths fancied themselves paragons with all eyes fixed enviously or desirously upon them, they were at best only first among equals. Nearly everyone in that part of the park that day was young and Rioca, and thus, like the pair I'm describing, all were bare above the waists whether male or female or both or neither. And almost to a person each of them was either lean, ridged, knobbed, and plated with taut muscles, or smooth and musically curved, and each of them was as brown as flowing molasses, the afternoon sun bestowing upon them a divine glow. Chancing upon this illuminated scene of soft golden sunlight as you emerged from the cool, shadowed path that wound around a voluminous oak that canopied the north side of the hill, you might be arrested — if you were a tourist, that is — by the thought that all these creatures reclining upon the grass were like a pride of lions resting after the completion of a hunt, or perhaps gathering strength before the evening's prowl.

A couple passed through the shadows of that very oak and then took the bend of the path. They were instantly noted by our two young men, and by all the other recumbent lions. A wave of quick-turned eyes rippled across the little universe of bodies.

The man in the couple was tall, with slender hips and wide-set shoulders. This shapeliness, and maybe also the lawn of black hair concealing the muscles of his legs, were all that distinguished him, though they didn't distinguish him much. A sparse goatee and ample lips accompanied his unremarkable face. The woman, by contrast, was radiant, her black hair swinging halfway down her back in synchrony with subtly swinging hips. She was a walking hourglass carved in mahogany, wearing big white earrings slightly larger than her big eyes. It was the match between the hips and the eyes and the earrings that the two young men noticed, the way that all of them together seemed to see and to conquer all they pointed to.

"Mm mm mmm." Bass murmurs, a bit testicular in character: emitted by one of our two youths, the slightly heavier one.

The other boy hallelujahed, or perhaps amened, with a loopy howl.

"I don't think he knew you were cruising him," the heavier one said loudly after the couple was clear of them.

Having been violently alerted by the howl — the rest of the pride had been too prideful to make any more appreciative noise than the sound of their necks turning to look — everyone nearby took in the full import of the heavier one's mocking tone.

The slimmer of the two gave a weak laugh, the only kind available to him on such a hot afternoon. "Suck my dick. It was her.

All about her." Despite his enervation he too spoke loudly, so that no listener missed his retort.

It needn't be said that the woman scarcely noticed our existence.

Yes, I was one of the boys, the slightly heavier and more physically robust of the two. Probably I was also the less macho of the pair, and certainly the less truthful: yes, it *was* all about her for me in that moment too, but I hadn't failed to appraise the guy. Luiz, my compatriot, probably had blotted the man from his perception with his typical rivalrous aggression.

It would have been better if we'd followed the example of the crowd and kept our silence, of course. And maybe if we had, none of this would have happened, or it all might have happened in a much better way.

Because we all knew who the woman was. It was only Luiz and I, the outlanders, who couldn't regulate ourselves. She was the Divina, the Princess Isabel, cousin to the Prince of the City and his right-hand. She did not walk the byways of the City fearing ambush, insult, or impertinence of any kind, not even from young men without apparent employment and perhaps inclined to delinquency who slouched lecherously on a bench in a park hidden from the streets that surrounded it, with Johnny Law nowhere in the vicinity. Princess Isabel laughed at almost any kind of threat, but particularly the threat of unwelcome desire — which was never wholly unwelcome in any case, since attention, both lustful and worshipful, were her due. The Princess was a huntress of lions, a slayer of lions, a sister and a lover of lions. She spoke the lion-language and if it suited her, when the moons and stars and the play of Water were right, she herself danced the lion-dance. And even if a young lion — but we were cubs, really — didn't please her, it was well known that at all times the Princess carried a stiletto with her, a sliver of tempered steel marked with signs on its blade and possessed of properties beyond the ken of mere mortals. She would use it to cut out your heart, if she had a whim to.

Such was the City which I had made my home, where those who ruled it and the empire that embraced — or throttled, as some said — half the world, were at such leisure and so confident that they strolled in parks on Domingo afternoons, in assignations with their plain-looking lovers, accompanied by little or no visible protection. I marveled at this, more so than my companion Luiz. We were both immigrants from the proud and barbarous north, a place where public figures with an interest in their survival did not so much as amble off to the lavatory in public without at least one bodyguard.

Though the Princess was not visibly protected from bodily threat, she was extravagantly guarded against fashion faux pas. Even as she slipped simple rush-woven sandals from her narrow feet and swung the pair of them through one long finger to let her soles play on the warm, springy grass, some twenty paces behind her three women followed. They were, it was clear, in the Princess's train. They were completely nude except for the jewelry that glittered on their necks, arms, and wrists, and on their waists, thighs, and ankles. These pieces, almost all hoops which corseted the limbs of the women — they might have been zoo animals carrying cages on their bodies — were on each of the three a distinct assemblage of style, calling up different sets of associations: on the one, opal like carven moons-light banded with sunset gold; on the second, the young jade of spring set in frames of waterfall silver; on the third, a collection entirely of amethyst, bespeaking, in case someone could not identify the Princess as the Princess, the Divina's royal position.

Rich women in the imperial capital had taken in recent months to dressing more simply and skimpily than in the past. By way of compensation, and to keep the jewelers' guild in business, the techs' wealthy daughters, and their more fashion-forward sons, were loading up their slaves with finery.

These three slaves were weighted down very heavily indeed. Evidently the Princess had had difficulty deciding what to wear, and had chosen to sport four different ensembles at once.

I have described the three as women, but they were not. It took me a couple of moments to be sure, because I still didn't have the knack for perceiving the telltale, especially in daylight: that shimmer, that smudge of halation like a celestial phosphorescence that clings to the skin and hair of dream-slaves as though it were the sheen of fresh sweat.

Squinting as they passed by, I could imagine, but not really see, their auras. Any lingering question was settled by other confirming clues. The dream-slaves carried pounds of metal on their bodies that must have weighed nearly as much as a steamer trunk, but their footfalls barely disturbed the blades of grass. And though naked, their groins were as smooth as dolls. (A slave needn't display an orifice or other genital device that it can grow on demand — and so they rarely did, unless their master was very vulgar, and wanted all who saw their slave to know to what uses it was put.)

I didn't catch the expression on their faces — likely, though, it was the same look I'd seen so far on every dream-slave. Bright, eager eyes, contented smile, brows just slightly lifted, as if in anticipation of the delights of fulfilling its master's desire.

We took the Hopstop back to Luiz's oppressively tiny flat in Fogo, a homecoming I dreaded. It occurs to me now as I write, though it did not occur to me at then, that I was a sullenly ungrateful houseguest. (But if Luiz had just managed a little access to some dream-slave magic, or even a loaner spell from a Godshouse, that meager square footage could have been the size of a gymnasium, that tiny skylight a skylab observation deck! So I had *some* reason to complain.)

For years I've completely forgotten this next detail, but I recollect it vividly now as I visit my former self to write this account. It was, perhaps, an intimation before the fact, a foreboding of what was to come — giving the lie again to poor humans' blurry perception of time as linear.

Then, the foresight without vision or clarity was only — discomfort. I was that day keenly sensitive, randomly, it seemed, to the uncanny sensations to which one was subjected by intracity travel. I feel this again, now.

I step out of the portal with Luiz, bowels roiled, inner ears unbalanced. The two of us briefly match strides, as we enter the great whale's-belly vault of the Fogo West underground station. A penumbra of artificial overhead light seems to sit queasily alongside the subterranean darkness, a visual dichotomy that gives a frisson of something the eyes can't account for. A throng of fellow travelers — much more accustomed to the transport's effects than I — bustle past me toward the escalator.

A few moments later, Luiz is a quarter-field length ahead of me, ascending to the sunlight. I am momentarily furious with him for leaving me to my embarrassment, and to the predations of pickpockets, who are known to lurk the stations waiting for disoriented tourists. Happily I am poor and the ruffians leave me be — if there truly are any pickpockets at that out-of-the-way station, and the threat of them is not just some phantom Luiz has conjured to frighten me so as to lord over me for the seventeenth time his status as city sophisticate.

I stagger beyond the great outer ring of the transport circle. Its center begins to glow, and the incessant whining rises higher — but the whine of what, no one can tell me. Today it sounds like machines struggling to sing, or, even less obligingly, like a chorus of pained infants. This mystery sound is one of the reasons I don't take the Hopstop as often as I might. I hear the conductor bellow over all the noise, "The way is opening in ten seconds!" so I step clear as fast as I can, because though logical sense tells me the next stop is just six blocks up to the border of LaMengo, panic tells me that the bloody thing might be sending us all to the dark side of planet Ares.

All of this feels — felt then — slightly wrong. As though I did not travel through space, but across some threshold of time, but too quickly: from daylight to midnight, with only a sliver of twilight and evening between.

By the time I'd got aboveground and caught up with Luiz, and we were rounding the corner to the café and storefront that provided the floor for the flat we share nestled above, the dizziness had abated.

But my shame persisted.

I had lived in the city of Norio now for nearly two months. It had taken me less than a week after arrival to acquire various low ambitions. I wanted desperately to be noticed and admired by everyone — the abundance of lovely girls, especially, but my fellow boys too, and any other gender ready to hand in a given moment. And yet I also craved thorough anonymity, to be as much a fixture of the cityscape as the pickpockets. I was impatient to be counted among Norio's cognoscenti, as I imagined (ridiculously) Luiz was, not only because the city daily proved to be as wondrous and rich as fables made it, but because as much as my coming to Norio was an adventurous opportunity to build a new life, it was also a last chance — or so it seemed to me. I could never return home to Peake's Bay.

Have I mentioned that before this story began I was in prison? This is a little-known fact of my history, the revelation of which, I am sure, will titillate my detractors. But truth is truth. I'll say more of this sordid history later — much later, I fear, for where we are now was, after all, a momentous day in my story, and I had best dip into it again rather than keep arresting its flow — but for now suffice it to say: If the dream-lords of Norio had not seen fit to raise an island from the ocean's depths two hundred miles off the coast of my native Arlina, evidently for no greater purpose than diversion from the boredom that afflicts too-powerful people who rule half the world, and if that island-raising hadn't, among other dire environmental upheavals, generated a tidal wave that flooded Peake's Bay and two other port cities, and if that flood hadn't flattened the homes and drowned the lands of some four hundred thousand residents, but also perforce emptied the municipal prison — if not for all that, I would now, this very moment of writing, have some seven months left to fill in my sentence (assuming I wasn't paroled).

Upon the prisoners' release — if the chaos of the day, the hurried unlocking of gates and swift disappearance of the guards could be described as though it were deliberate and official — I fled to my family's farm in the highlands. The flood's devastation was such that it took nearly a week to get there (the jail was two hours' drive from home).

Upon arrival I found my mother less than perplexed to see me so many years before the judge had decreed I should be free. There were other things on her mind.

My mother is a very loving woman of whom I can say nothing unkind. But as a consequence of being the farm's bookkeeper and responsible for its perpetually metamorphosing business plan, and as a consequence, too, of having been blessed with a surfeit of sons (there were — there are — six of us), she didn't shrink from speaking with unsentimental frankness. "Lovely to see you back, dearest," she said, giving me a hug. Her tone was warm but distracted, her eyes careful to note my dirty disheveled appearance, but also careful to pretend to ignore it. "There's nothing for you to do here at the farm, and we can't afford to put you up for long, you know, with the losses from the flood and earthquakes." With the same distracted air, she left my hugging arms and bustled over to reach into the lower drawer of the desk in her office (a corner of the now-abandoned barn).

"There!" she gave a sigh of relief. "Here's enough for a ticket on the carrier that's coming next week. I got it on special. It comes with a language-translation spell good for three years! You remember Izra's son Louis? He's got a job and a place down there working with the great lords and ladies in Norio. So they say." (Here she shot me one of her special looks.) "By the time you get to Norio, I'll have spoken to Izra, and Louis'll be looking for you." She gave me a very maternal kiss and another hug that might have lasted for an eternity except that it couldn't, and then shooed me out of her office, with the warning that I'd better send money back when I could, or there'd be no birthday presents arriving from Arlina.

I had yet to send any money back, having made only enough to pay Luiz (no one in Norio bothered to pronounce *Louis*) my portion of the rent.

But this was all about to change.

Luiz was churlishly reminding me that we had best hurry. Our shift at the diner started in less than an hour; good jobs like ours weren't easy to come by; he didn't know who I thought I was if I was under the impression that Santoro, our boss, would be lenient with me because I was outlander; my ass would soon be smoking so bad he could get high sniffing it, Santoro was gonna fire me so quick.

I was muttering filthy names back at Luiz as he deserved, but otherwise hanging my head as befit a low-status rube just off the carrier who depends upon sort-of-friends' grudging kindness. I looked sideways at the salesgirl sitting at the register at the Free-Town store next to our building. With her big chardonnay eyes and bright amber skin she managed to look alluringly pretty.

Catching a bit of courage, I winked at the girl. She ignored me.

Being an optimist I assumed her ill-humor could be attributed to slow sales at the store. It was one of the early outposts of the back-to-basics consumer movement. Those stores' gimmick for selling their motley collection of fiber and synthetic hand- and machine-made clothes, as well as various items like freeze-dried vitamin snacks and dog-lice combs, was that everything in the store was "slave-free," i.e., no dream-slaves had participated in its manufacture. Despite this valorous claim I was certain that the store's ceiling, a near-perfect if somewhat obviously two-dimensional simulation of the heart-slaying gold and violet rays of sunset as seen daily from Poador Rocks, was the handiwork of dream-slaves, or at least of contractors telling dream-slaves what to do.

Full of moxie, and, no doubt, because my fires had been stoked by the sightings in the park earlier that day, I raised my head up and winked at the salesgirl again, more broadly and more boldly.

I saw her face crumple — her forehead and chin lengthen, the brows scroll down to almost touch her sumptuous upper lip.

But immediately nothing of this latest mangled sexual opportunity mattered. A hand caught my arm and turned me fully around, and I quickly realized why the girl's face had rearranged itself.

Everyone nearby seemed to have come to a halt. Luiz, already through the street-door and into the narrow building foyer leading up to our apartment, stopped and swiveled to look in my direction. A chocolate-and-toast couple holding hands as they walked behind me swung abruptly wide on the sidewalk, and their collective breath quickened. The cute shopgirl's foreshortened face kept reanimating, now widening, now her mouth dropping open.

All this I saw in a whirl, my head twitching this way and that, as at the same time I tried to shake free of the man's grip. Since my efforts failed, I took him in more closely.

The gentleman was very tall, and he was bald to a line midway between dome and ear, from which richly curled black hair flowed down his long neck in such sudden profusion that it was as though the top of his head were a dead, irradiated ruin and the remainder had been spared the calamity. His eyes were large, black as his hair, and gently lifted at the outer corners. His color was pale gold, and he was dressed extrovertedly — insofar as he was dressed at all: for he was as shirtless as I, but riding high up above his waist was what looked to be diaper of black rubber, which was braced on either hip and thigh by skin-tight leather chaps that ended just above the knee. Against the dark cinematic background of the leather, decals of flowers and unnaturally colorful snakes and geometric stars burst up and down the length of his legs. He also wore long black-and-white streaked gloves to the elbow, and stood, without wobbling, on high half-foot sandals with heels that tapered to a point of no greater circumference than a coin.

He was slender and well-proportioned. I could see sweat beading in the scoop of flesh between his taut pectoral muscles and the top rung of a ladder of abdominals.

All of which is to say it was very well-crafted indeed, and utterly lifelike.

The smell of the slave was truly a man's smell, slightly perfumed, and it did not gust away. (Such detail may strike the folk of my homeland as odd. Simply said: in the south, as I had quickly learned, one is always smelling other people. It's the heat, and the Rioca fancy for fragrances and pheromone cocktails. Norio makes canines of us all.)

Once again, I did not see the telltale glow.

The slave smiled, and released me from its grip. It struck me as beautiful. This was what let me know it was not just some rich eccentric trolling in Fogo borough, for there was no reason for me to think of such a person as beautiful except that one could not avoid feeling such things about such slaves: something in the way the technicians built them has a psychic effect, not unlike the adoring response to the dew-eyed faces of puppies and babies that the prudence of evolution programs into the human species.

"Aleixo Hyypia?" the slave asked.

Cool tone, sonorous depth of voice. Despite the dress, his air was official, noble even.

I swallowed and nodded.

The slave offered me its open palm.

I looked at it, and being the immigrant foreigner I was, I felt thoroughly frightened. Was it Law? Did it expect me to take its hand and get carted off somewhere? I'd heard — Luiz had told me — that sometimes vagrants were "officially" snatched, and then sold as slaves at private auctions to outlaw connoisseurs who liked to illegally mix captured human slaves in with their dream-slaves.

Then the dream-slave struck thumb and forefinger of his open hand together, the sound too loud to be natural, and before I could finish flinching, there she was: My one-look-and-I'm-in-love love, my perfect beauty. The Princess Isabel.

This miniature simulacrum of her wore a white bustier, white leggings and a white cape that shone like snow on her skin. She was a foot tall and just a tad ethereal (a breeze blew a hole through her neck and I could see toasty of the chocolate-and-toast couple staring at the dream-slave and me from behind her).

The figure of the Princess stood with one knee bent, hips and slim shoulders slightly turned, so that it looked as if she had just been interrupted while occupied with more urgent business taking place in the direction of the dream-slave's chin. Probably the slave had many such recordings stored in it; and this was one that was used to address outlander commoners such as myself. She said, over her shoulder, "That which brings this message to you is my slave. Please attend its words as if they were my own."

The recording did not identify itself — as if anyone wouldn't know who she was — but before the image wafted away the sign of the Imperial Affinity of Norio appeared above her head, as though written in the air by fireworks: an eagle-headed winged dragon with a scorpion's tail arched high, braying fire.

"My mistress asks if you would be available to work as her personally chosen staff, at a banquet on Quarta, very late, in the Principal Palace at the Loaf."

I was too shocked to answer.

Luiz, whose curiosity had propelled him from the building foyer back to the sidewalk, was not so tongue-tied. He gasped an obscenity before pointing indignantly at me. "Him? She wants *him?*"

The dream-slave smiled again, nobly, beautifully, and although nothing of its chiseled facial expression altered beyond this, its failure to actually look at Luiz when answering him conveyed the sense that all further speech was to be understood as a kindly indulgence, and that said indulgence was rapidly approaching its expiration.

"Aleixo Hyypia was seen today," it answered smoothly, "in the gardens of East Park Seven. The Princess would like him to work for her, if it is his pleasure to do so." Its head bent to me. "If you are otherwise occupied this evening, this slave is authorized to provide you with a note explaining your need to be in the Palace at the Loaf, from the Princess Isabel."

The Princess *saw* me?

I mumbled something about being honored, and proceeded to handle with reverence the paycard-size piece of polished glass the slave produced for me from a seamless pocket in one of his elegant long gloves.

In the glass card's shallow depths, if you touched it on the bottom right, a lovely but slightly askew image of the Princess appeared, this time looking mildly apologetic as she asked whoever viewed it that I— *I!,* she even said my name! — be released from any obligations.

The dream-slave bowed fractionally.

Then its body shuddered as if some painful spasm had moved through it. Its eyes clouded, its perfect features momentarily flattened. And it was gone.

Unlike the teleport effect you might ordinarily observe when a living being of that size and heft disappears, there was no discernible wriggle in the air as waves of light surged across the space the slave had occupied, and no mechanical or infantile whining, either.

I was, as I'm sure the Princess must have intended, impressed. The messenger was not only an exorbitantly expensive, well-made slave, but a very powerful one. Very few slaves are built to accomplish such effects, and so smoothly. Even I knew that.

The toast-and-chocolate couple beamed proudly at me as though they were my parents. They even applauded briefly before they moved on.

Not knowing what else to do, I bowed. Once their backs were to me, almost entirely by reflex, I lifted the note to my nose and sniffed it, hoping to catch a scent of my goddess.

This proved to be too much for Luiz, who tried to grab the card out of my hand. We fell to wrestling right there in the doorway — rather fiercely, I might add; pent-up resentment, and all that.

The Free-town salesgirl watched us in unconcealed contempt.

It may have escaped your notice, given everyone's reactions, that the Princess's dream-slave had not offered me a position in the Prince's cabinet or awarded me a lifetime supply of Mark-Twelve dream-slaves. It had requested that I wait tables at an event. The distinction, however, was entirely lost on me for the moment.

That was how I ended up serving food that night at one of the Principal Palaces. This is the background for what many readers are familiar with as the beginning of the story, since the evening later proved to be the start of a lot of trouble for the whole world.

ALEIXO'S STORY

2048, Primeiro (the Month of Bright Air),
Quarta evening

The Palace at the Loaf is sometimes there, sometimes not.

At forty-odd rooms arrayed on three levels it is austere for a royal domicile. Its claim to legend is that it is entirely housed within a small mountain of nearly solid granite.

The nigh-vertical slopes of the Loaf plunge precipitously into the serene waters of Nabara Bay, and its summit towers over Red Beach and the ocean edge of the city, so that the mountain looks as though it were placed to mark land's end, a crayon smudge thumb-printed by an infantile deity. The mountain is unreachable other than by air or by sea.

To ensure the Palace's continued existence in such impossible terrain demands a level of maintenance that is not, by and large, sustainable even by the great dream-lords of Norio. I counted at least thirty slaves whose sole duty was to hold an unwavering vigil of dense meditation, so that the ceiling-to-floor windows in the rock face would retain their transparency and filter the sound of surf and the breeze blowing in off the sea. It was evident, as the evening wore on and the sweat on the slaves' skin brightened and brightened further, that the slaves were rapidly losing charge and would have to be replaced by morning. Hundreds more slaves, largely unseen by the City's royalty and its guests, must have been at work in the very walls of the Palace, or perched like gulls along the jagged rocks on the sheer slopes, maintaining in their fecund minds the image of open space (and of a great kitchen and larder, and of plush sofas and delicate flatware and serving-silver and high comfortable canopied beds) where all the forces of physics and nature had determined that there could be none.

The power-cost of these endeavors, and the risk, however minute, that nature would have its way and crush all present in its granite embrace, was such that the members of the Royal Affinity of the City passed the greater part of their time at Saint Christopher's Palace in Antonio Lopes Park north of the Great Forest, or in the Affinity's other residences. They opened the Loaf Palace only on particular occasions like this one, in which dancing was a cornerstone event — since nothing was more dazzling than to samba in high-fashion evening wear on the transparent dance floor that the slaves caused to extend in a capacious circle beyond the edges of the mountain's summit, and to watch your feet cross and knees bend high above beach and ocean as though you were an angel whirling on the belly of a wind-gust.

(Those of more suspicious mind, including several investigative journalists employed by more than one prominent newswatch, theorized that the Palace's purpose was not merely to display the Princes' great wealth in magic. They surmised that select rooms within the Palace were in fact never non-existent, and that these eternal and inaccessible sites housed treasures, or especially dangerous weapons or repositories for particularly inflammatory secrets, or laboratories in which morally obnoxious experiments were conducted. Or they were cells for political prisoners. Or all of the above. I will have occasion within the pages of this memoir to settle the truth, or some of the truth, at least, of this matter.)

The high maintenance costs no doubt contributed to the decision by the Palace steward, the eminently and properly supercilious Bruno de Taglia de Sol, to employ humans as well as dream-slaves to serve drinks and dinner courses on the evening in question.

This was the Prince of the City's late-summer fête, the very first of his young reign, in which a great impression needed to be made upon the assembled potentates. Efficient yet attractive uses of available resources were thus of the essence: a half-human, half-slave dinner service would halve the energy costs, and would by novelty alone turn a few heads, at least of the backland

ALEIXO'S STORY

nobility, who, being the unfashionable rubes they were, could be counted on to be scandalized. (I am quoting the steward's thoughts on this matter, as I survey them now, revisiting the scene. At the time I couldn't even have told you which nobility were backlanders and which weren't.)

And *this,* then, was why Her Serene-and-yet-Sultry-ness, the Princess Isabel, being aware of the importance to her cousin of bringing off the evening's smallest details with aplomb, had selected me to join the serving staff. Not, as I'd so stupidly wanted to believe, because she fancied me. (But you knew that already.)

In fact, given whom I had spoken to since my arrival by ferry at the Palace — mostly high-muckety-muck slaves and other peon human servers like me — it was likely that *she* hadn't noticed me at all: her attentive slaves had, probably the ones who I'd thought were only brought along to wear her excess jewelry. No doubt they had been commanded to keep a general lookout for my physical type. For the Rioca all such choices have to do with aesthetics, and certain combinations of bodily shapeliness, the cut and jib of the face, their eye and skin color, or the curl of hair might for a particular event or task be dreamt up by an event planner in the same way that a chef conceives the flavors of his appetizers. Then, once the image has been settled upon, the dish's ingredients listed, all one need do is comb the streets as though shopping at a farmer's market — this being Norio, after all, where all species of beauty, near-beauty, and entertaining ugliness run thick on the ground.

The slaves had seen me in the park, they had collated what they observed with the general population database in their mysteriously magical slave-way and found my name and vital information — all probably fairly quickly, since I was then a fresh entry in the imperial register, having passed through Immigration only a few weeks prior. Then they'd sent out a call for me, along with, by my rough count, about forty others.

We did indeed share characteristics — all of us were on the tall side, lighter and creamier in complexion than most in Norio. We had biggish noses and full lips, and well-shaped heads crowned with dark glossy curls of nigh-shocking length, kink, or tangle. I guessed that everyone I'd seen come into the lockers to put on their uniforms (red satiny v-necked one-pieces that finished

73

above the knee and above the elbow — we looked good in them) was human. Whereas all those who showed up dressed exactly right and able to balance a tray on the top of their heads without a wobble were the slaves.

The fact that I was just one of the city's best-dressed no-account servants among more than one hundred lickboots and retainers eager to show their best and be noticed soured me. I thought ruefully of the couple on the street back at Luiz's who had applauded when the Princess's slave selected me. Now it seemed their applause was not for my having achieved recognition, much less for an ascension, but more the kind of notice you give to a pretty circus act, an amusing bit of freakery.

Of course, I should have been counting my blessings — as well as my promised pay, which was uncommonly high, even by the standards of Norio. Even if the streets were not, as fables had it, paved with precious gems, the Rioca passed money, precious metals, slaves, and slave-services around as though every natural-born citizen ran their own mint or tech Affinity. With so much loose change lying around, a relatively low-skilled immigrant like myself could — eventually — live and eat as well as if not better than the merchant middle-class back home in the North.

The Prince of the City, Dream-Lord, Emperor of the Divine Holy Spirit, was present (the Prince's Consort, mildly ill, was not). So was the Chancellor. And the First President of the Parliament of the City, and the Chief Constable, and elegant mothers-of-saints and fathers-of-saints of the most powerful Godshouses, and there were rich dream-techs aplenty in their deceptively anonymous sport suits and hoodies. There was even a bishop and priest of my homeland's religion, as well as at least one Silvara ambassador with her dark blue skin, and many of the nobility, and the wealthiest and most beautiful denizens of the city.

Through unending rows of arches surrounding the dining room on all sides, we could see the city below and the mountains behind, painted in the fast-fading rose and violet of gloaming. The effect was all the more wondrous because the summer air lay softly over the city; with the scent of ripe jasmine flooding our nostrils, the evening, sotted with balmy warmth and with sifted light in purples and wine reds, seemed itself to be a kind of libation, as if merely to breathe was to become, ever so gently and perfectly, drunk. The largest moon was near full and climbing, and the Fire's-Eye gazed down upon us from its perch in the midst of the stars as though approving of the magnificence of the feast and of the wonder and pleasure of the world which human beings had made.

It was a glory amid which I worked that evening, of which I could at moments even feel that I was a part. The glory of Norio, young and powerful, the world's loveliest city, the jewel of the great empire over which it ruled. It was a glory, and I, like several others servants, was assigned solely to big-name diners. My charge was to make certain that when the rotund and widowed Lady Wariner, baroness of a tiny windswept island one tsunami away from disappearing into the Tillean Sea, dodderingly put her elbow in her soup, I was there to swiftly and gently lift it out, dab passably clean the sleeve of her *lime* gown (even now I shudder to behold that color again), and to see that the soup bowl was refilled.

The Grand Duke of Lower Town Vador on the Bay of All Saints, perhaps the richest man in the empire and himself a dream-lord, who had come a close third in the election of Prince of Norio, was also in attendance. I was told he'd insisted on being served by his own seven retainers, four of whom were tasked with caring for his pack of lank, blond-furred hounds, which he loved more dearly than his family. These servitors fetched scraps the Grand Duke tossed from his plate to hand-feed the surprisingly docile, copiously slobbering creatures, and, when the ducal dogs took it upon themselves to make waste on the buffed marble floor, the servants wiped up the piss and clawed up the shit in napkins.

Their job and mine were much the same.

I deserved far better. I deserved to be in the Princess's bed. I was far superior to my low place. I, Alexander "Aleixo" Hyypia, was special, and here beneath the skylight was a place for what was special, where special was celebrated and recognized. Irony burned my skin like a branding iron: all this, and I was merely support staff.

This is the point at which you will hear throats clear in the room, and see the faces of my critics crease in private smirks — especially the faces of those learned rectors of the New Church, who thunder in every sermon that it is I who am to blame for all current ills, that I am the traitor who has brought hell to earth. Only a little true, alas. The world was shattered long ago, and the ruin you see about you now merely the truth, at last uncovered.

My Church critics are however right to some degree. It is true I was pretentious, and this was indeed evidence of a flaw that proved fatal — to so many others, if not, so far, to me. The reasons for the high opinion I had of myself were scant, as is not infrequently the case where such opinions are held. That an ignorant provincial should imagine himself worthy of recognition from imperial nobility for no other accomplishment than being himself was not a good portent, had anyone bothered to read the signs. So far no one had, though this was soon to change.

Matters being what they were, I had to content myself with the satisfactions to be had from sidling up to people whose lives were celebrated, as though I might absorb from afar the magic that made them the embodiments of smashing success.

Between bouts of silent wrath, I did take in my surroundings, at least cumulatively. Unjustly slighted though I felt, I could not deny the thrill of rubbing up against the anointed, even if it was only to brush the lint off their shirts. The faces of the celebrities were aglow. The lords and ladies were seated around the tables and lounging on sofas, their brows adorned with silver circlets and jeweled tiaras, some of their necks rounded with white ruffs like delicate moth wings or necklaces as sinuous as snakes. The women wore dresses cut low across the bosom or high above the knee, and the fabric of their attire was of the thinnest silk or chiffon that seemed woven solely to hug the contours of the breast or to accentuate the jut of the nipple. Some of the men had begun to follow the example of the Prince's rakish young companions — wearing short cloaks made from the fur of specially-created animal dream-slaves and jewelry so thick and so laden with spikes it seemed to be the remnants of armor, and going about even on formal occasions bare above the waist. The oiled skin of their magically-transformed or illusion-draped muscular chests and arms was layered in geometric patterns of ink, their bodies mimicking the walls of the ancient temples that had been recently discovered in the depths of the Artremis forest.

Slave musicians, whose limbs and vocal chords had been shaped by highly skilled makers — Silvara, probably — to produce sounds which humans could only approximate, were unveiled that night for the fête, and the heavy drumbeats and elaborate play of ululating horns and inhuman voices dueling made me wish for my phone, so that I could record what I was hearing and sell it to the mix-jockeys at the clubs Luiz had been dragging me to.

Each place I turned, I was enraptured: by the table heaped with dishes of fresh fish and fried cod balls, with roasted duck and quail, stuffed pork loin, and slabs of wild boar, baby goat, veal, and seal-meat on plates strewn with lavender blossoms; by the innumerable bottles of wine or the sparkling decanters of a golden liquid so soft on the tongue (when I stole a sip) it might have been some curious combination of melted butter and down feathers; by the frescoes and reliefs painted on the ceiling and carved in marble along the walls, brimming over with nymphs and satyrs disporting themselves with an almost animated merriment that seemed to reflect in exact measure the joys of those at table.

The sole note of discord in this symphony of sights and frissons, which represented everything I then aspired to for my own life, was the Prince himself. Previously I had seen him only on news-watches, or in the watery three-dimensional copies you stumble into as his visage leaps up from between the floorboards to welcome you to the interrogation booth when you pass through Immigration, or as depicted in the anteroom of the Royal Museum.

In person I saw that he had big ears, and that occasionally his posture was informal to the point of being simian.

Amaro Obá Brangaça, our Prince, unlike his mignons, as those notorious companions of his were called, was attired somewhat conservatively in a black and crimson velvet doublet, and a black open-necked shirt that flashed a crop of neck-hollow hair. Tapering black sleeves revealed heavy forearms that swam with the contending colors of his deep caramel skin, a brushwork of wiry dark hair, and the bright red and green of a tattoo that shifted and reshaped itself as he moved. On the news-watches you'd typically see the Prince's black locks fall to his neck, but tonight these were gone, shorn to a thicket of black encasing his skull. He had high cheeks, a gently bent bow of a nose, and eyes that were the color of amber diluted with white wine.

At moments you would catch him turning in the direction of someone who seemed to have surprised him, and then his eyes shone in a way that must surely have owed something to sorcery, or to drugs. Prince Amaro's mouth — voluptuous, I daresay feminine lips, with well-shaped white teeth — bestowed upon everyone at table the treasure of his smiles. This he did in such a way that some present could not help, upon the occasion of its first bestowal, gasping aloud. This reaction was particularly favored by the more buxom and womanly (observing this, I suffered terrible pangs of envy, which it seems to me now utterly comical), at which point inevitably some older personage sitting beside the gasper would draw a folded fan from her hip with the martial skill of a gunslinger unholstering her pistol, and in three quick but capacious shakes of the fan, cool off the young fool.

Still, I found it a bit odd taking in the look of our Prince as a whole: There was just enough of the thug in him that he might have been one of those young men you see prowling on the beaches all day long, their bodies lithe but somehow dangerously bunched, as though prepared to spring into violence.

Already during my time in Norio I had heard that the new prince was the source of discontent. Common Rioca seem shockingly free in their willingness to speak disparagingly of the government that had made them richer than everyone else in the world. Even an outlander heard rumors of power struggles, of court factions and competitions between the different tech-Affinities and their rival Godshouses. Luiz was convinced that stories he'd seen in tabloids about assassination attempts on the Prince's life were true, not mere gossip — and they might well have been, as the Rioca are quite passionate and have been known to convulse in civil war from time to time.

But I took no positions regarding any allegiance or philosophy. My assessments had all to do, rather, with being disappointed that the leader of the Western World did not look exactly as I thought a prince might. He was not as noble in appearance as his cousin, the Princess Isabel, who was so satisfyingly, dream-fulfillingly beauteous — though of course, I didn't even see the Princess at the dinner, and I was making my comparisons to the image of her produced by her supercilious slave, and my electrifying glimpse of her in the park.

In the glory and wonder of that evening, in the first flush of love with things greater than myself — and it *was* things that seduced me, the appearance of beautiful things and beautiful flesh that sent running a riot of covetousness in my heart — I sometimes lost track completely of my duties, and then I seemed to know nothing, could not remember, from moment to moment, what I had done or was supposed to do. I was consumed with trying to take possession of my surroundings, trying to eat all that I could with my eyes.

At some point I do remember the dinner concluded and dancing began. The Lady Wariner of Tillean Sea island nine-hundred-and-forty-x hobbled off into a parlor somewhere on another floor or another wing to tilt heads with other unattached women likely to be in the grave within the decade. If, reader, you detect a hint of the misogynous here: well-observed. I but reproduce in good faith and in the interests of transparency my frame of mind at the time — which later experienced a rather violent revolution. No doubt resentment of my mother played a part in these attitudes. As did, of course, the dismal state then of my sexual life, which I had long assumed was and always would be mostly heterosexual.

Lady Wariner did not require my services for a while, she said, and so I went to the kitchens to eat. After I finished, knowing no one, and ignored by the slaves and other staff of the Palace and by my fellow attendants, I wandered about poking my head into rooms if the doors were unguarded.

I found myself on the uppermost level on the edge of a ballroom floor, oblivious to the bodies trying to keep foot-time and hip-time with the fast pace of the musicians, staring up at the ceilings that seemed to rise higher than the spires of most churches, when a woman said to me, "Does that hurt?"

The woman was flaxen-blonde and toffee-skinned, young, pretty, and overdressed (the neck of her gown was too high): perhaps a servant like myself.

Her loveliness made the answer to her question catch in my throat. (Really, it was just the plain loveliness of all who are young and healthy and Rioca, but I was still a novice in dealing with that bliss-affluent folk.)

And a good thing, too, since the awkward loss for words gave me time to realize I didn't know what she was talking about. Was she wondering whether it hurt to be a minor unrecognized part of something magnificent for only one night, but to know that the night would not be half as magnificent if it was something you were part of for many nights?

But no, she was referring to a purple bruise that, she said, sat astride my forehead, which I had not noticed, and now touched and found tender.

"It does hurt," I murmured.

I could not quite free my mind from the wonder of her prettiness and of her having spoken to me, and from the way that this miracle seemed to be announced to the world and repeated, thumped into my heart, pulsed through my groin, by the insistent rhythms of the drummers and bassists, by the moans, sighs, and hisses of flautists and violinists and magical and mechanical instruments I knew not which.

But I really *didn't* know how or when I'd suffered the bruise. Perhaps I'd arrived with it, and had forgotten it? Luiz had certainly been liberal with his pokes and punches during our wrestling bout.

It was at that moment that a hand grasped my upper arm.

Distractedly, not wishing to stop gazing at the face of the young woman looking up at me, I looked toward my arm, at the hand — which was large.

Then at the body attached to it, which was uniformed.

The uniform was black with green-and-golden-yellow piping. It was made of a perhaps-rubber substance seemingly wet, and had a telling blocky shape below the neck that was akin to baroque pagan statuary. All of which said: this is body-armor, and with one thump on the top of your head I could sink you knee-deep in asphalt.

One of the Black Guard.

Ah, a sort of sluggish movement of my thoughts said: *This pretty girl is not a fellow servant but a noblewoman, and in daring to speak to her, you have insulted her.* I was to be thrown out.

I turned back to the woman. She was no longer there.

"The Lord of the Dark Moon wishes to speak with you," the guardsman said.

In addition to his armored suit, he wore a half-mask that came down over his eyes and protected his nose: of this half-faced person, artificially inflated to gladiatorial proportions, I saw mostly a wide mouth with somewhat damaged lips wreathed in a bristling brown beard.

The Lord of the Dark Moon. Even an outlander from far, far north, located more or less safely beneath the notice of the man bearing that title, knew who, or what, he was. I heard the guardsman's syllables as I had heard them from the mouths of schoolmates telling scary stories after lights-out in the Landsward School dormitory.

Having become the lords of our dreams, spinning the unformed wool of humanity's sleeping fantasies into the slaves that have given them mastery of the earth, the governors of Norio had, with that love of make-believe and carnival so characteristic of their culture, named many of their highest officials according to titles bestowed in ancient religious festivals, the origins of which are now lost in time. Hence the Prince of the City was Emperor of the Divine Holy Spirit (which many of you see in the blogs by the acronym the Royal Guard uses to refer to him: EDHS), a sobriquet borrowed from the Great Festival of the same name. The Lord of the Exchequer was Lord of Our Lady of the Rosary, et cetera.

The Dark Moon Lord was of somewhat newer vintage, something they'd taken from the secret ceremonies of the Godshouses. Though as abstract and apparently meaningless as most of the other titles, it struck a note of mystery appropriate to its reference, which was the office of Chief of Intelligence, the imperial spymaster and warden of royal security.

The High Intelligencer's identity was secret. He appeared in public rarely, and always behind a glamor that was caulked-solid against intrusion. I'd seen it on the news-watches. A serpent's head with bird's wings growing where a mammal's ears would be, this shape revealing in heraldry what was not decreed in any constitution or legal document: that if the Imperial Affinity was a dragon, the Chief of Intelligence was its eyes and its omnipresent ears.

The Lord of the Dark Moon wanted me.

The Lord of the Dark Moon wanted *me?*

If it were an immigration matter, the Dark Moon wouldn't involve himself. I'd simply be marked with a deportation sigil, probably by no higher a personage than a slave, and summarily deposited at the ferry — or left topside to wait for the cable car in the morning.

Surely this could have nothing to do with my having not served out my full term in jail, which Immigration must have known when I was granted entry to the City?

The Guardsman led me downstairs and across a walkway that connected the third stories of two buildings. I was so buried in fear that I was halfway across the span and shivering in a blast of cool air from the sea before I realized that this was open space within the Palace — which is to say within the solid mountain itself. As we walked, we could look out, by way of enchantment, at the faint stars, the bright moons, and the Fire's-Eye.

At the end of the walkway we passed through a pair of elephantine bronze doors. These were disquietingly studded along the perimeters of their four panels with bolt-heads or nail-heads that you could clearly see were shaped like little faces, each one as animate and as individual as a snowflake. Each little face seemed to grimace in pain, or to leer — perhaps in anticipation of another's pain.

This sinister awe-he-who-enters-and-beat-the-fool-down effect nonetheless provided little preparation for the shock of the interior. Immediately we were walking down several long corridors with walls all out of scale to the door or to anything visible from the pedestrian bridge beyond. High ceilings and mirrors impossibly taller than the tallest of apartment buildings dwarfed us, and the tread of our feet was scarcely audible on floors that were plated with marble that was somehow soft as deep pile. The floor was opaque, so that the light and shape of other lives being conducted on floors below moved beneath us.

We had become miniature. We were mice picking our way through a place incomprehensible in scale and use.

The Black Guard betrayed nothing like my own awe, or even interest in his surroundings. He did not touch me, but managed by sheer silent menace to keep me in step with him as though I were his dog.

The whole evening I had not gone anywhere in the Loaf other than the servants' entrance, the receiving rooms, the dining room, the ballroom, and the kitchens. It seemed to me now, as I traversed what was surely less than a tenth of the Palace, that the place was endless; it was worlds nestled in worlds, with all manner of folks doing all manner of things. From swatches of conversation, and the many colors and insignia of military and ambassadorial attire I was able to guess some of those present. I saw Stralians, those hedonists from the western ocean, with pink skin that seemed all the more shocking against the abyssal beauty of the soft brown and blue-black hair that covered their naked chests, torsos, legs, and arms. I saw violet-eyed muralists and icon-artists from the Tine, and dark black-browed Moan mercenaries. I saw wild Burgh tradesmen from the other side of the Wall who had made the fifty-year journey across the west-coast landsbridge, who looked stooped and grizzled in their pelt skirts and magnificent fur-collared cloaks. And I saw three rotund, apparently very happy Ponese bankers, their mustachioed faces positively glowing as they were ushered into a room spilling with buttery light.

And everywhere — though I did not truly notice this then, and see it only now, keeping pace with my younger self in a memory-wraith form crafted by my magic — there abounded the faceless figures of slaves.

Slender and squat and muscular and misshapen, tall and tiny, moving quickly, noiselessly, back and forth, from room to room, down and up stairways, crossing the dark floors braided by lamplight, moonlight, Fire's-Eyelight and shadow. They were like pieces being pushed across a great black checkerboard.

Eventually we descended lower, and then lower still, leaving guests and servants behind. As the sights dwindled, my terror mounted.

Endless elaborate speculations percolated through my mind.

Perhaps a new law had been passed without my knowledge, limiting the number of Arlinians admitted into the citizenry, and deportations were afoot. Or Arlinians had all been decreed traitors and were being summarily executed. Or maybe commuted convicts (even minor criminals such as myself) were being tortured as payment of their remaining debt to society, then deported for good measure. And so on.

What could cause the Dark Moon Lord to single me out? My family was not important, rich, or political. We had contacts with no one important, rich, or political.

Unless, that is — and I confess that even then, as we plunged into the bowels of the rock of the Loaf and left the sight and sound of the living ever farther behind — and this will show you the sort of fool I was — even within all my fear, even then, I felt a small thrill: *unless* my family was important or political. (I knew for bloody sure we weren't rich.)

Unless we *did* know or were associated with someone or some cause higher and deeper than I yet knew. But *secretly.*

Perhaps my parents had contacts with the High Intelligencer. Perhaps they were even in his employ?

Or — the more rattling counter-thought suggested — in the employ of his enemies...?

The last corridor was narrower than any other. It did not run entirely straight, and as soon as I entered it — the Black Guard's grimness urging me ever on — I kept bumping into the walls.

When the passage finally bent and opened to a space that I could feel, but not fully see, was large enough for two abreast, the Black Guard, whose inhuman metallic bulk had become some nigh-eternal presence behind me, arrived swiftly at my side. His movement was sudden and full of deadly purpose. I flinched.

But he only spoke, "Alight."

The word-light startled me almost more than the backhand across the cheek I'd feared. We had no word-lights in Luiz's apartment, or Santoro's diner, both of which relied entirely on cheap electricity.

In the quick illumination, bright but with just the faintest tinge of blue, I saw that I'd been led to a small room.

The floor was rough and uneven, a broken puzzle of flagstones. There was a low bed with a red coverlet and one sheet of a dull nameless color peeked from beneath the boast of scarlet. That scarlet was answered by a tiny red cloth flung over the top of a tiny table. Hundreds of scratches left by someone — or some many — were grooved in the table's wood. There was a stool. A pine chest the size of a dog sat near it. There was a washbasin, which looked to have water in it. Two chairs, with padded seat cushions. Several rectangles of glass — word-lights — burned high along the walls, and one unlit lamp, no doubt electric, long and oddly oblong, hung from the ceiling: just as a suicide or a lynched body might.

There were no windows, no light from the outside world.

A metal pot, low but wide at the mouth, stood in the corner, and its reek was such that I understood immediately that it served as the sole toilet facility for those unfortunate enough to become a guest there.

My courage — what little of it was left to me — failed me as I looked at that archaic thing that even in the barbarous North you only read about: a chamber pot.

The Black Guard loomed behind.

I couldn't bring myself to turn as I asked, "How long will I...?"

I felt him retreat, and at the same instant heard a door shut that I had not yet seen. The clamor made chillingly clear to me that it was as heavy and implacable as one of the great bronze doors we'd passed through earlier.

The door's lock rattled and grew quiet. I pressed my ear against the door and felt its depth weigh against my cheek, but heard nothing else.

In the terrible empty quiet and painful light, affronted by the reek of old urine, the memory, the feeling, of human companionship went cold more swiftly than I could ever have imagined.

I thought, incongruously, of my mother. Of how deeply ashamed she would be to find me in so desolate and dishonorable a place.

The Guard had told me nothing. I might be here for hours, or for days, or for the rest of my life, having no knowledge of why.

My first response, after these thoughts circuited through my brain, was anger. Fury, even.

The unfairness of it. How could they? How could these arrogant cunty balls-kissing sons-of-whores do this to me? Just because they owned the world? Because they *could* do it, they did it?

Good evening.

The sound of the voice in the room — it came from nowhere I could see, perhaps a concealed speaker — was so startling my stomach heaved, and a little of the food I had been grazing throughout the evening rose up and I tasted it again before it slapped the hard stone floor —

Which had become marble again. Alternating patterns ran across it, of squares within squares, and circles within squares. A new floor...?

The room was no longer the room. It was now a large, empty, circular space.

Sunlight beat heavily on my shoulders.

Sunlight. It was night and the sun shone. This new sun cut beams across the floor and left vast swathes of the surface in shadows.

The place — it was almost the size of the Loaf's dining room — felt as breezy and sweet as the prison room was heavy.

You understand that what I have said is not really what happened.

The words in fact had no effect on my stomach. Rather the voice, which seemed spoken by the walls themselves, summoned into existence a new space, a different room, paved a new floor beneath my feet. And as the voice took shape so the room came to be. The effect on my body of such unnatural movement and still more unnatural transformation was like the effect of the Hopstop, but more severe.

I stood now amid surrounding darkness in a pool of light. Sun speared down, broken by glimpses of racing clouds I could see through an oculus set high in a gracefully curved ceiling.

I stumbled, off-balance as I peered up at that generous, round, glassless window. I had the feeling that the enormous eye of some giant cloaked in sky-blue was stooping over me, the way a child stoops malevolently over a crawling insect.

"I do hope we have not upset you by interrupting your evening this way," a new, more localized voice said.

I turned, full of dread, in its direction.

ALEIXO'S STORY

2048, Primeiro (the Month of Bright Air),
probably Quarta night, but day & time uncertain

A man was in the room with me. The voice accompanied a body.

It surprised me that I recognized that body: Princess Isabel's herald slave.

He was dressed much as he had been before, and he bent his head to me in seeming acknowledgement of our brief past acquaintance.

"Of course, I know it cannot *not* have been upsetting," he — it — said. His voice crept fingers, tendrils, tentacles into my ears, down into the caverns and crevices of my body. So rich, that voice, so deep and fatherly. It made as if to take hold of me bodily around the shoulders, to press me to its chest, though the slave stood several feet away in the shadows.

"Black Guards are rarely as subtle or as kindly as they might be. I apologize. If we wish to speak undisturbed, this" — the slave gestured at the oculus, the rounded walls, the nigh-acres of space — "is necessary. We have no desire to frighten you unduly, but secrecy is" — he hummed for a moment, as though weighing, then shrugged — "well, to repeat, necessary. If the Guard were to report where he left you, but then you were not found there" — another pause (this one seemed more terrible than the others) — "then no one would know where you were."

This circuit of words was meant, I guessed, to confuse me, as a component of the speech's general aim to terrify me. I was indeed terrified, but at the same time my brain beheld with diamond clarity what my animal ears merely trembled to hear:

So *now,* in fact, no one on all the earth *does* know where I am.

The dream-slave took a step toward me. It was still several feet away. This distance was not comforting.

"An Arlina perhaps is not well acquainted with such things, but you understand the principle of what has transpired, one hopes?"

The tonality shifted slightly. The angles and turns of the labyrinth in its voice, which seemed to have been coalescing into the leering smirk of a demon who might haunt your nightmares, faded, replaced by the clarion ring of a lecturer, a professor typing out equations for the benefit of rapt students. "A portal is charged, it is made resonant with another place, and upon one's 'passage' through, the place you are in at first becomes the place that has been made its twin, however far removed in conventional space. Or, as in this case, in time."

I must have stared at it for nearly a minute — I was reacting, as though on time-delay, to each of its alarming vocal modulations — and I didn't realize I hadn't replied to him until he said, with a sigh of disappointment, "You *are* upset."

"No, no —," I stammered.

Everything about this exchange mystified me. This was an interrogation, I was not a guest, I knew, this was not an act of kindness to transport me thus through space and time. This creature, this *slave,* was the Chief Intelligencer of Norio?

"Sílvio is a greater personage than most slaves." Another voice now. "In a way he *is,* as my servant, one of the high intelligencers of the empire. But I am the chief."

I turned wildly, not wanting to do so, knowing that this confusion was what they wanted. But I couldn't stop myself, because I recognized this voice, too, though I had never heard its true timbre till now.

Once again, it was as if the shadows took the notion to form themselves into a human shape. This was another effect clearly intended to frighten me, and again it did, but this time only because I knew that they wished to frighten me. Intentions like those obviously couldn't be a good thing.

Yet it was some revenge that they couldn't have anticipated how the fear would be balanced, even overwhelmed, by love. Even amid the fear, I felt it. Stupid as it was, baseless and stupid and wholly imaginary as it was, I felt that love.

It was her. It was the Princess.

The Princess was the Lord of the Dark Moon.

The Princess had taken me from the party, and she had come to talk to me personally. I swallowed the stupid, mindless smile that threatened to transform my face.

"I'm late." She shook her head ruefully — her lovely head; have I mentioned that I was in love? "Delayed by party business," she said and rolled her eyes.

Mellifluous, the Princess's voice, low, husky, almost masculine. Not entirely dissimilar from her slave's, interestingly —

"I don't think we'll have much time before I'm missed. Shall we begin?"

How cruel they were. They were giving me no time. I should have been demanding to know why I had been summoned — why I had been *kidnapped,* summarily taken from the Palace where I was a free employee, treated like a prisoner, and ripped out of time to some moment and place that for all I knew might have been hundreds of miles away and hundreds of days in the past. But I didn't. It will seem mad to you, the height of insanity given the danger which I was so clearly in, but the raging chemical desire of youth overrides all. I wanted only to drink in everything of her, to lap up and sup her presence: her look (pharaohnic eyebrows, and black wings painted at the corners of her hazel eyes), her smell (a perfume of jasmine, flute notes of blackberry), and her clothing (what little there was: the Princess was attired for a party, though I had not seen her at the gathering). Not for her the conservative look the Prince preferred — no, she was pure Rioca glory: silver bands that looked to be strips of body-paint circled her arms like a column of bangles and clasped her neck; decorated her shoulders, torso, and thighs; and made patterns on her cheek and forehead. The prodigious length of her black hair swept up into a column that then fell in fountain waves down her back, and some of these waves had shimmering starlight tassels hanging from them. All together these effects, along with high-ankle black boots, added just the semblance of attire to her otherwise gloriously naked body, and the deep caramel of her skin glistened with sprinkles of silver dust.

"Hyypia...? This is an interesting name."

She was saying something. They were talking, the Princess and her slave. I pinched my thighs to make myself listen.

She sat in a small chair that looked like something you would unfold at a campsite — but I had not seen it in the room until she took her seat there. It seemed to stand on a pillar of air, so that she was higher than me, looking down in deific judgment.

"I've studied many languages, and had several more I never bothered to study administered intravenously." She smiled. "But I don't recognize this name's provenance. Do you?"

I looked to the slave for its answer — only out of the corner of my eye, as the bulk of my attention remained where it had been, on her, magnificent her — ah, God, those breasts, their nipples fat and shiny, the thick bars of silver shading the shaven v of her pubis —

But then, catching the direct thrust of her large eyes, I understood that she was speaking to me.

It was an effort to prevent myself from falling to my knees. And I *had* forgotten to bow, hadn't I? Had I even greeted her? Didn't you get flogged for such things? But to be flogged by *her,* by those lovely hands... (No, really, I thought that. I don't think it was a spell she was putting on me. Yes, I was just that ridiculous.)

"I — I do know, your highness." I groped for the suddenly elusive knowledge I claimed to possess. "The name's — my father is of Navian descent. Hyypia is a name in that language. I think... that is, he always told me that it is a Navian version of a name in one of the oldest Ardennian languages, in, um, Elenik. Originally it was... Hippolita."

"Meaning, 'of or relating to horses,'" the slave Sílvio offered.

The Princess kept my gaze. "Then it is a very old name. That's fortunate. You should be proud. The old lineages are the most blessed."

"Th-thank you, my — your highness." (She was keeping my gaze!)

She laughed. Everything about the sound of her laughter felt girlish and sweet, flirtatious even.

It was this more than anything (the *Princess* giggled *flirtatiously,* at *me!*) that snapped me to attention, just a beat after the thought came to me.

I began, at last, to realize the extent of my peril.

"You needn't refer to me by my honorific, Aleixo," the Princess said gently. "You're a citizen of Norio now, aren't you? We Rioca tend to think of our leaders as more or less clever pets. All the world thinks us an empire, and so we are, but officially, and in the hearts of most Rioca, we have ever been and never shall be other than a modest city-state. Only in ceremony or on official occasions does anyone refer to me as 'your highness' or any of the rest. If you don't feel comfortable doing as your fellow citizens do and calling me by my name, call me Dona Isabel, if you must. Or just Princess. Princess from the Atinya *príncipe* — which is in reality a rather democratic title, if royal or aristocratic titles can ever be truly compatible with democracy. It means, *first:* first in influence."

"Thank you, I, I will, Princess. If, if I may, Princess, might I ask why —"

She smiled so broadly that I simply couldn't keep talking, so astonished was I by her charm. Only a moment later I understood that she had compelled me to shut up without having to speak.

"So, Aleixo Hyypia, you are an Arlina, of Navian descent."

"Yes, your — Princess. On my father's side. My mother is, erm, mulatta."

At this her brow furrowed slightly. "Oh! Yes, I ought to have seen that. Now it begins to make sense. My cousin does have a taste for the *sarará* boys."

"*Sarará?*" The language spell that my mother had purchased, which had been serving me so well and with such subtlety that I'd begun to think I was a native speaker of Riocan Silero, now fell silent, as though this were a word that must be translated with discretion.

She tossed her head — the plume of her hair bounced in a way I yearned to believe was seductive — and she said, girlishly (*Beware! Beware!,* my better nature was crying), "Oh, Sílvio, of course, how do I constantly forget this? The northern immigrants don't describe the variety of human color with as much *interest* and precision as we do in Silero. In Arlina, he'd just be 'black,' or maybe 'white,' or *olive-skinned* — bizarre description that that is. Isn't that right, Aleixo?" The Princess laughed again. "*Sarará* is a word we use. Mostly they use it north of here, in Vador, where attention to such things is a connoisseur's art. It means — oh, the translation would be, fair-colored with kinky dark auburn hair. And a skinny nose. Or otherwise with clear features of the people of the Ancient Motherlands."

"The shape of your face, your lips...," the slave added helpfully.

"Also, your hair and eyes are darker than your complexion. The rosiness of your lower lip. The Prince appreciates these contrasts of shade, these textures. Probably you remind him of the lovely boys of our childhood that he misses so. Masculine beauty is so much more prized here in the South. Up North in your homeland it's all so — ascetic."

Sílvio was not convinced I comprehended. "I should think too, the particular smoke-honey hue of the skin of someone such as yourself on those occasions when you tan. And perhaps the high protuberant buttocks?"

"Yes, thank you, I get it," I said quickly.

To say that being divvied up verbally as though my bodily attributes were design elements for some piece of couture unnerved me is not unlike saying that childbirth is uncomfortable. And to be spoken of this way by a slave was obscene.

My dander rose. We Arlinians don't take well to challenges to our manhood, conquered people or not. Suddenly I was able to start firing questions.

"I don't understand. You said 'something makes sense now.' What makes sense? I confess, Princess, I'm at a loss. Please tell me what's happening here. I don't know why you've —"

The Princess did not smile this time. But I shut up anyway. She waited long enough to see me tremble before answering. "You don't know?"

Her volume had dropped. I glanced helplessly at the slave, whose marmoreal expression made him look, suddenly, no longer human at all. "You're certain you don't *understand* why you're here?" The Princess appeared to watch me closely. "Is this really what you want to ask me? Think carefully."

This, as you will understand, was entirely chilling to hear. I spoke slowly. "Is there something else I should be asking...?"

The Princess's expression grew even sharper, and her eyebrows bent toward one another. She looked puzzled. "I would think so, yes."

Though I didn't dare look upward I was acutely aware of the oculus above me, of the sunshine, the open air — a freedom, near, but which I couldn't hope to reach. "Princess, please!" I burst out with as much control as I could muster. "I —"

"You are how old?" Her tone now was utterly charmless.

"Nineteen, Dona."

I saw her cast a look behind me, toward the slave. Though the silent exchange was swift, something significant passed between the two of them.

"And now he uses the less formal address. To appeal to our sense of noblesse oblige, you think, Sílvio?" the Princess said, still charmless, still unsmiling. "This is a clever one."

I did look up then, wondering if perhaps the thick air on which her chair floated could provide invisible stairs up to the oculus.

"What makes sense is this, Alexander Hyypia. It is because of the phenotypic expression of your ancestry that you caught the attention of my cousin, the Prince and Emperor of Norio. Your ancestry makes it predictable that you would catch his attention. My cousin likes young men with your *look*. Do you understand now?" I don't believe she actually thought I would reply, but she waited a beat before continuing. "But there's a great deal still to suss out. Which I expect you, Of-or-related-to-horses, will cooperate in helping me determine."

I was trying to keep up. "Princess, if I understand you, you're saying that — that you've brought me here because — because the Prince... fancies me?"

Me? In comparison to my schoolmates and my jailmates and my stupid brothers, I was sure that I was special. But in comparison to the fancy of the Emperor, a dream-lord? I was not *worthy* of a High Prince's — desire. Surely the Chief Intelligencer must be teasing me, testing me for some hidden purpose.

At the same time, I was quietly wild with hopes. Was that jealousy, I wondered, that I heard amid the obvious sarcasm in her voice, that I saw in the expressionless expression of her face? And then, as the shock of it all began swiftly to recede, I began to feel a wave of loss, of terrible disappointment, breaking over me.

It wasn't *her. She* didn't want me. *He* did.

"The Prince wants to meet with you later. In private." Isabel's tone now was less barbed, but there was a heaviness to it that maintained a sense of the portentous. "You naturally have no objection to meeting him, since it is his wish, and as a loyal albeit foreign-born subject and newly minted citizen of Norio, you esteem the throne."

I noted that all the blather about democratic titles and we're-all-on-a-first-name-basis had evaporated. "... Yes," was all I could bring myself to say. Croak, rather, for my voice had mostly fled, perhaps collecting in my bladder, which at that moment threatened to burst asunder and shower its contents all over the walls and all over the Princess's slave.

In the ensuing silence — and truthfully just to contain my urine by means of distraction — I added (knowing that what I said was idiotic), "That is, depending on when we're to meet, I will probably have to ask for permission. My immigration status depends on my employment in Santoro's diner..."

Sílvio the slave had somehow come to stand just beside me. Slaves have an uncanny way of moving, when they want to, and so the tips of the slave's fingers registered a shudder that swept through my body at its touch, as though Sílvio had cracked a whip across my back. The slave squeezed my shoulder in what I hoped was a gesture of reassurance rather than threat. (But it had to be the latter.)

"You are a smart lad. You recognize that the kind of moment you have always waited for, that your parents have no doubt hoped for, for your sake and theirs, has at last arrived, as it does not necessarily arrive in the lives of others," the slave said, paternal, kindly. Good cop to the Princess's bad. "You now stand in position to be lifted up, Aleixo. The Prince's fancy comes with the Prince's esteem. Things might change a great deal for you now." It paused. Its fingertips raised slightly, as if, inhuman or non-human thing that it was, it were pressing my flesh to measure the degree to which flesh yielded. "There will be gifts.

Money. A title, perhaps. Maybe more. Our Prince is generous, when he fancies."

At some point in the slave's speech I knew that I had flown off: that I had leapt the boundaries between species and taken wing, fluttered off at some speed, and that for the rest of the time the slave spoke, I was incapable of listening, I was in flight, and air, gusts, breezes, winds filled me like a sail and sent me speeding off. *The kind of moment you have always waited for...*

Struggling to come back, I remembered hearing something about my parents, and all I could do was have a sour thought for them, for my father, anyway — and a spoiling feeling in my stomach as well: for certainly my father and my elder brothers would not look upon the prospect of my becoming a Rioca Prince's catamite as a moment of supreme ennobling success, even if wealth and a bona fide noble title came with it.

My own thoughts about whether it was appealing, repulsive, or a matter of indifference that I was sought as another man's lover, could not and did not come into focus. It was at once too large a matter (how could *I* be a lover of the Prince and emperor of *Norio?*) and too small to hold my attention (who could bother thinking of the fleshy mechanics, the stick-its and stroke-its of sexual congress, while being interrogated in a room ripped out of time by the Chief Intelligencer of the whole fucking empire?).

We were all silent.

Perhaps the Divina and her slave were ill at ease, delivering such a message. Was the Chief Intelligencer no more than a pimp for the Prince's pleasures? Surely a person of such high rank rarely condescended to speak this way to inferiors. There had to be some other reason she was talking to me — some other reason that she had, in fact, abducted me.

The Princess began speaking, with an elongated, highly respiratory sigh. "Aleixo, you know my purpose. My purpose at court, in the government."

"I do, your highness. You are the empire's Chief Intelligencer. You are..." Almost, almost the phrase "Lord of the Dark Moon" left my lips, but I instinctively knew that someone like me, an outlander and a nonbeliever from the Rioca perspective, shouldn't use it. "You are the Prince's Second, his right hand."

She waved off this identification with a frown. Maybe she'd decided that to have asked the question at all was ill-mannered. "I would not have revealed myself to you as Intelligencer unless the performance of the duties particular to that office required it." She grew quiet, and, for the first time, looked away from me, off to the walls. "I am not here as a... procurer of my cousin's lovers."

I rushed into an apology before it struck me — I had said nothing about her being a pimp — had she read my mind?

"Don't trouble," she said, as gentle and as parental in manner now as her slave. "This room, in this time, is my place. This place is an extension of me, of my senses. If a drop of your sweat falls on this floor, *I* feel it, and I taste it, and I have been trained by the savants of my Affinity even to know the gland that caused it to fall, and to make an educated guess as to the reason. All my senses are amplified here. Doubly so, since dear Sílvio functions as the room itself does."

I confess that though I knew I should not do it I instantly tried to wrest free of the slave's touch.

But I couldn't break its grip. I wriggled, but the terrible thing held me fast, merely by pressing down on my shoulder. It didn't seem possible by any law of physics.

The Princess watched. "You understand, I'm sure, that to be a Prince's Second encompasses many forms of service. One such purpose, and among those of the highest importance, is to see to the Prince's safety."

My heart seemed to flutter out of existence. "Oh. I — "

"Aleixo Hyypia!" Her sharp tone encouraged me to indicate alertness. I stood straight, hands clasped behind my buttocks. "Aleixo Hyypia, do you respect and love the Prince, as a subject loves his lord?"

I tried to search the Princess's eyes, to determine if I could intuit what this question meant, and what she wanted me to say.

But though I could at that moment see her looking squarely at me again, I could not read anything there. Not malice, not kindness: nothing but patience and observation. Like a scientist watching numbers change in a computer calculation.

"I respect and love the Prince," I answered, without the fervor that I intended, and with an involuntary memory of how odd

I had thought him at dinner, so seemingly long ago (even if, in reality, that fête might be yet sometime in the future, months or years later than the moment the Princess had spirited me to).

Did she feel or taste *that*—my recollection of the Prince's funny big ears?

"You love the Prince?" As she asked again, her chair floated closer to me. It skated, or rolled on invisible wheels, across the air. When she spoke again her breath fell hard on my face. There was no change in her tone this time, just in force of speech: I felt not the smallest tincture of spittle touch my skin. Only wind, hot and harsh.

"You respect and love the Prince. The Prince whose nobles and dream-techs, for *sport,* raised an island from the ocean floor off the coast of your country, and in doing so caused earthquakes and tidal waves that killed a few hundred or more of your people, and ruined a great deal of property in your—what is it, Sílvio, Peake's Bay?"

I gave a quarter nod, not knowing whether it was treasonous to demonstrate too ready a knowledge of these facts.

"Our Prince, the Emperor of all Norio's vast possessions," Isabel said, arching the title on her eyebrows, then clenching it in an unpleasant wolf's grin, "whose ancestors broke the backs of your ancestors and were not content only to topple them from their position as a leading power in the world, but then felt they had to assault your leaders and their armies with all the sorceries at their command? Whose ancestors condemned your civilization for half a generation to being a technological backwater, with none of the magic resources enjoyed by the rest of the world? *Our* Prince, whose great-uncle cut off all of us in the western hemisphere from the rest of the world, closeting us behind a Wall of Storms, so that you will probably never see the land of your forebears in Navia? The descendant of *those* conquerors and *that* powerful sorcerer? *That* Prince, who believes nothing that your people believe either in faith or politics, who scarcely thinks of your people except to tax them and to tell them what laws he won't let them pass, and which imports and exports they can trade, and what technology level he will permit them? The Prince who allows you only *electricity* and fossil fuels, while elsewhere in the empire we have—all this. That Prince?"

"That Prince," the slave continued, "who also likes to fuck backward little outlanders, your highness." Gentle, fatherly. Malevolence only in the words themselves, and in the iron of its weighty hand pressed on my shoulder.

The slave's insults, at least, I felt bold enough to offer a rejoinder to.

"But but but your highness, I mean, Dona Isabel, that was long ago, we are all part of the empire, I am now a citizen of Norio, he is *our* Prince!" The academy catechism fell easily from my mouth. A mere hour ago — or, years afterward, whatever — I would have even believed what I said, insofar as one can believe something that means nothing but that is said so often that the simple habit of its repetition lends it credulity.

But I could not believe it at that moment, held there against my will, being interrogated by the woman that I hoped to love (yes, I know you likely have nothing but scorn for this notion; I do too, now), with a smelly slave holding me so still I might as well have been in manacles. That was the genius of such soft torture: the very fact of their having imprisoned me proved that indeed I should hate the Prince, and hate all Rioca. They made my body shake with the anger of what they had done to us. They made me feel it.

"Yes, Sil, that is true," the Princess agreed, ignoring my words. Her eyes now were so close to mine they seemed to have become larger than her face. "The Rioca Prince does take his pleasure with his subject peoples, and he will take it with you, Aleixo. You can ask his last outlander whether she liked being used as his mattress and a bucket for whatever fluids he happened to fancy discharging. She was from Ork, wasn't she, Sílvio? The Prince gave her a nice house in Blon for her trouble, a two-minute walk to the beach, ten minutes to the arboretum. But you'll want to do better than that, I expect." She paused. "Here's a tip: The ones who really crave the Prince's use and abuse receive the greatest reward. The ones who truly" — the Dark Moon Lord inhaled, and I knew what she would say, and she knew that I knew — *"love* the Prince. Like you."

This was a test. I understood this. I just didn't know how to pass it.

I took a stab anyway. "I, I — I love the throne, I love the empire, which has brought peace to the West and protected us from the predation of the demons beyond the Wall that encircles the earth..." I sputtered to a halt. To the Rioca the "demons" I'd mentioned were gods. I was blowing it. "I do not know the Prince as a — as a person." I added hastily, "I don't presume to think I ever will."

The Princess alighted to the floor — as or after I blinked, the chair was gone. She moved behind me. I would have thought she would want to study my face as I spoke, to see if I spoke truthfully. But presumably the room, and Sílvio, watched whatever she didn't see with her own eyes. For all I could tell she seemed to be watching my hair very closely. She said nothing, for a span of time that seemed too long for me to continue to exist without shouting, or breaking down in tears, or exploding into separate parts. All part of the torture, no doubt.

When at last she spoke again it was to ask me if I had ever wielded firearms or any other weapon.

I didn't want to say anything about the patriotic organization I'd briefly belonged to — her sort would call it a gang — or the fight we'd got into, or my jail time — though these seemed somehow minor in comparison to whatever act of treason she suspected of me.

The Dark Moon Lord made a noise. It might have been a snort, or a cough. "I don't care about your prison experience or your pathetic political activities, Aleixo. Immigration processes all of that when you arrive at port." She paused, her breath coming short for a moment. "We're wasting precious time, aren't we, Sílvio?"

"We are, madam," the slave answered.

"I have become distracted by my curiosity. It's difficult to resist finding out how deeply programmed he is. How many layers of lies there are."

I started, violently, to speak, but she interrupted with another prosecutorial question. "What is your favorite childhood memory?"

At first, I simply didn't understand the question. I thought the language spell had failed again. "My lady, please," I begged.

"Tell me why you've brought me here. What is it that you want from me? This interrogation cannot be *necessary.*"

"Then you don't have a favorite childhood memory?" She sounded as if this prospect pleased her.

"What?" The breadth of this testing flabbergasted me.

"As I thought, Sílvio," the Princess said. But she didn't move and neither did he. They clearly expected me to add something, or to recant my failure to answer.

"Of course, I have favorite memories, Princess," I snapped. In the heat of exasperation, my caution evaporated. "I confess however that as I'm held against my will and under your power, and that I might well at the conclusion of this interview cease to acquire more *adult* memories, that the significance of the question as well as the content of a possible answer simply escape me."

(You will note that anger tends to sharpen my powers of articulation.)

"Well said, Aleixo. But we don't have the luxury now of bantering, however amusing that might be under other circumstances," the Princess said smoothly. "If, as you say, you love the throne of Norio, you will cooperate with me, and without the necessity of applied pressure."

She watched while, skittishly, I eked out something like a nod.

"Good. Please think of a memory and tell me, briefly, what it is."

It was far harder to comply than it should have been. I was so angry now — perhaps my thwarted love had become, through a transmutation catalyzed by distress and imprisonment, fiery hate? Or my rage at the injustice of it all had overtopped my feeling for her, and for her beauty. At that moment I felt as if I were in the schoolyard (or the jail-yard) again, ready to claw and maim because someone had laughed at my choice of shirt or been careless enough to bump me in the chow-line.

"I've thought of something," I said begrudgingly. I wanted to make her drag it out of me.

She smiled, with a coldness that told me she would literally drag it out of me, if need be. "Tell me."

"My grandmother. My grandmother telling me stories in the house she lived in. Before she died."

"Paternal or maternal?"

"She was my father's mother."

"You were how old?"

"Five. Six. Seven?"

"That's sufficient. Just think of this memory, please. Recall one time she told you a story, a story you remember well and the occasion of her telling it. If you can't remember the occasion, just try remembering the sound of her voice as she told the story. Think as specifically and clearly as possible. This won't take long."

As she spoke, I felt the slave's other hand firmly lay hold of my waist. But its touch wasn't restraining; it felt like it only wanted to make contact. And with a look over my shoulder I saw that the Princess had drawn nearer, and that she was touching her slave somewhere from behind. We were like line-dancers about to start shimmying around the floor at a wedding.

"Fine," I growled, masking my bewilderment with machismo.

Difficult as it had been at first to remember anything at all, my gruff and unwilling assent, once I gave it, acquired relentless force, as though it were an oath sworn in a fairy story that bowls over all obstacles in the fulfillment of its promise, even to the detriment of the swearer. Perhaps indeed that was exactly how things worked, in that place which answered to the Princess's will and amplified her senses.

I began thinking of one specific memory, digging at it as with a spoon at hard mud, assuming I'd remember only bits or fuzzy outlines. And then, without further preamble, I found I'd tumbled straight down into the hole of another memory and another.

And while I felt still the strangely impersonal warmth of the slave's hands on my shoulder and my waist, like a heated blanket, and at times I heard the Princess's shallow breaths, soon I could see nothing but my memories. After a bit I could hear and almost smell and touch them, too, as though they had overtaken my body, and I had again been delivered by devil's arts to another time and place.

My grandmother's house was my first play-house, my own fortress of secrets. In truth it was just a small guest cottage, built during some short-lived cyclical uptick of familial economic success.

It stood, or rather leaned, a little ways down the road from the main house, past the stockyard and the barn and nearest fields. As a little boy I often visited there, more than my siblings did. Like any house not one's own from the perspective of a child, the place seemed to me an abundant alternate universe, vibrant with mystery, the moreso because it was my grandmother's home.

Her house was built on cinder blocks to protect it from flooding, and its interior was a big cube of jumbled-together rooms that led one to the other without any connecting hall. There was a central dining room from which you entered the kitchen, a den and a living room beyond (this was dark and cold and populated by huge pieces of ornate furniture I was not to meddle with, which seemed as forbidding and supernatural as an old dark forest in story books). Sharing the walls of those rooms was a suite of bedrooms arranged shotgun style, and between the three bedrooms, a bathroom.

Beneath the house, in the space created by the cinder-blocks, there was an underworld, a land of dark delights. There in the shadows, dirt, and damp beneath the subfloors, I excitedly wriggled down my shorts and convinced the equally excited young daughter of our vineyard's chief enologist to lift up her dress and lie with her stomach-down in the soft, embracing earth where God knows what was crawling, while I rubbed my rubbery little weenie across her bare white buttocks—my grandmother's discovery of which sent me to the bathroom for a very thorough and no doubt penitential cleansing.

My grandmother was to me a being of wonder and unimaginable seniority, a goddess—an impression she evidently enjoyed making on me, since whenever I visited she put on very extravagant clothes as though going out to some city ball. To entertain me and herself, she indulged all her unfulfilled dreams of being an actress.

The curtain of beads my grandmother strung across her bedroom was my favorite thing of all (in truth, my second favorite, but as the enologist's daughter did not belong to my grandmother's house, and indeed was banished thereafter from the premises, her plump buttocks did not count).

To pass through that curtain was to traverse from one world to another, to cross from the mundane sphere of enforced naps and combing out my semi-nappy head into the grandeur of adulthood. I would cross back and forth, the sensation a luxurious caress, the vision a waterfall of bright, hard gems, back and forth from darkness and rules into private light, from purgatory to heaven.

Within, my grandmother would await on her bed, ankles crossed, back propped against enormous and ever so slightly smelly pillows, and tell me stories.

My favorite story was a myth, and so it wasn't true, and had to do with things and people who were impossible and ridiculous, which was why I loved it.

My grandmother told me the story so many times I remembered it all, every word:

In midwinter the Seven Gods (who were in reality not gods at all, but demons) pass through the Doorways of Life and Time in the Fire's-Eye, and warm their celestial bodies in the eternal flames of another universe. And they do this as a kind of prayerful time-out — "as your mother and I sometimes need in church, when we send you children home after sermon."

The Seven Gods, who are the Great Gods, not the tiny unimportant deities of wood and water, each year make a pilgrimage through the Doorways, in memory of their deaths and of their rebirth in the dragon's belly, and of the long travail they once endured long ago.

For once a long time before your oldest ancestor was here, my grandmother said, *daemons* (which are another order of demon than the Seven Great Demon-gods, grandmother said) *dwelt in the heart of the Fire's-Eye. These daemons were horrible to look upon and vicious of temper, and envious of the Great Gods' bliss and beauty. Being evil and ugly these daemons one day stole upon the gorgeous creatures the gods were as they lay in innocent joy-filled sleep, naked and undefended in the high wet grass of their garden home far up on the summit of the navel of the world.*

The evil daemons looked upon this sight — naked youth, without a care in the world or so much as a bug crawling across their magnificent bodies — and instantly they were lit with rage. Then with frightful long white swords as cold as winter stars, the daemons sprang upon the sleeping young gods and slaughtered them. The sights and the sounds of their murder — nothing before or since in the history of This World had ever been or will ever be more terrifying.

The daemons tore the gods' flesh bit by bit, for the joy of hearing their victims scream and of feeling the earth pitch and of seeing the seas boil and the skies flash red. And they made feasts of the gods' throats and eyebrows and their ears and other orifices. And they lapped the young gods' blood from the bone, and they strutted and minced and danced in the mash of the young gods' livers and intestines.

And even though it is difficult to kill a Great God, and even though every inch of gods'-flesh knows that it is a scion of a Great God and hastens always to bind itself to the whole, such was the viciousness of the slaughter, so great was the carnage and the chaos, that no ragged, bleeding morsel of what the Greats had been, neither eye nor knuckle nor knee, knew to whom it belonged or who was its brother or sister.

Unable to recognize themselves, and shocked and horrified and frightened when they could no longer see their beauty reflected in the faces of the water or of the night sky as they had for millennia of paradise, the Great Gods died.

And the Fire's-Eye daemons laughed, and draped black panne over all the world, so that only their own crepuscular daemon light should shine and be accounted as beautiful. The daemons stomped the bits of hair and nails of the gods deep into the earth, and ground the bones in their teeth, and they roasted the gods' flesh, and chewed and chewed it until it was like mulch, like the dregs of pottage, and then they spat what they held in their great hungry mouths into the all-embracing Sea.

In the Long Dark after, no light could reach This World. In that darkness, the Sea, lapping at Earth's shores, whispered to Her Sister the Earth about Her memories of the Great Gods, and about the delight they had given Her in ages past. And so, at last seduced by Her Sister's song and memories, Earth joined Sea in a secret place, deep, deep at the bottom of a well of darkness, and between them they gathered together the remains of the young gods.

But

(and this was the part that touched something in me, that broke me a little, when I first heard it, and that I came to love to feel breaking again, each time hearing the story anew)

the Earth and Sea could not find all of the remains. Much of the gods was lost—indeed, most of that glory they once were, *said my grandmother, who I later understood was quoting the ancient poet Divo, who in the next line of the poem wails,* For all truth is lamentation, it strikes off fetters and summons tears.

What was lost could never be found, not with all the powers of Earth and Sea together and many years of searching. But what bits they could find, Earth and Sea stirred together, at the bottom of a well of darkness. This well was hidden from the Fire's-Eye, because it was a chasm inside the body of a great dragon who had been so long sleeping her guts had rotted and withered, and stone and grass had come to cover her slumbering hulk.

There the bits and pieces of the young dead gods swirled together in pools the Sea made, beneath daggers of rock that the Earth hung from the bones of the sleeping dragon. The drifting dust of Earth's daggers and the pure waters of the Sea mixed with the remains. Then the waters hissed in the slumbering but not-dead heat of the dragon's belly, and plumes of steam shot high and hot to the roof of the dragon's bones.

Sea covered Her green eyes to keep Her face from being scalded.

When Sea opened Her eyes again, She saw half the waters boiled away, and half the daggers broken off.

There stood two groups of three, and a solitary figure.

They were tall and they were beautiful, but they were hairless and their eyes were red and blind, and they were deaf and mute. But the one who stood off alone knew who she was, and what had been, and what was to come. She fashioned a tongue for herself to speak, and a new language, like the one she remembered, but stronger, better defended.

"So we have returned," she said, and as she spoke amber tresses streamed from her head, and her eyes became the green of the high grass after a summer shower. She went to speak to each of her siblings, first to the three nearest her, and then to the three farthest away, whispering to them as they ran their hands over the damp smoothness of the rock.

To each she spoke a secret word, but though her speaking cured them of their deafness, each heard only one part of that secret word. These were the Words of Power and Making, and each of the six times she spoke, the Speaker became more herself.

Still, only she could see, since the eyes of the others yet blazed red. Stumbling, they felt for one another, the new infant gods, and each of them whispered two words to each other: first to the two closest to them, and then to the three farthest away. These were the Words of Sight and Singing.

And then when they could all see, they crowded to the First among them, the solitary one. She stood off with her ankles cooling in the heated water, and each whispered three words to her: when they finished, she said, "I am Ashrar, the Dragon Mother," for these were the Words of Naming.

Each of the six now could speak their own names. In the light that flashed when their names were spoken, they saw one another in the light which shone from their divinities, in all their greatness and beauty, and at last they knew themselves completely.

"We have returned," they said.

"But fewer than we were," Ashrar said.

Rather than mourn, they agreed to each wear a scar upon their perfect faces, in memory of all that they and the world had Lost.

And then they burst free from the dragon's belly, and a mountain range crumbled into the sea as their wrath ignited. Arming themselves with swords fashioned from the fire of the dragon's body they rose in fury into the heavens, where they took vengeance on the Fire's-Eye daemons —

Which was another story altogether, and one which I could not remember.

How long I remained in that memory, of that memory, I do not recall. It's possible that the sorcery or compulsion they worked on me made me run through it only once, or many times.

But when it was done, when it seemed that there were no more questions they had to ask me, no more details I needed to recollect and recite, I felt as drained as I did when I'd swum from the north to the south shore of Peake's Bay.

What I loved in that story, what moved me even in Divo's tongue-in-cheek rendering of it (he no more believed in these

Gods than most men of his age) was that deep, deep, dark well, full of hissing water and roofed with spikes. The dark hiding place, where even in sadness, pain, and terror, something new and glorious is born.

Savant Vans at Landsward School was of course quick to tell his students that the whole tale was an elaborate invention of nonplussed men mystified by the process of childbirth and trying to offer an explanation that made them feel important because they were telling the story. "Happily we need no such pretty lunacy, as we have the very sensible views of Ur on the matter of birth and family," Vans had said.

But I always thought the prophet Ur's stories lacked something compared to the pagan tales. Yes, Ur led our ancestors through the wilderness and across the steppes and mountains of Ardenne, Ur captained armies, Ur invented medicine and metrics, Ur gave us the Kinjrood to rule us in the history before histories, Ur wrote prophecies.

But Ur was always in the light, always doing something with a scribe and students present. He never did anything in the dark, or anything really magical.

It was pleasing, if sad, to remember what I once felt. It was almost like the joy of the first time I heard the story — some effect of the Princess's magic, probably.

But I was angry, too. I hadn't wished to share this, any of it, and it was worse to me that they had made me cooperate, made me *give* my memory to them, since surely, I imagined, what with the hearing floors and seeing walls, they could have learned all this of their own will, as probably Immigration had done, by simply taking it without my knowledge.

They could have spared me the humiliation of *helping* them.

The slave's hand dropped from my waist. It made a sound like humming.

"So?" the Divina said. Her low voice, so sultry to me before, now sounded thin and weak in the wake of the living memory of my grandmother's voice.

I could see where I was again, and the sunlight through the oculus was too bright, too hot on my skin.

I peered over my shoulder. The slave's eyes were closed.

"Yes," it answered its master. "Those stories became popular in the North some twenty-five years ago —"

The Princess interrupted, completing her slave's thought, "Right around, or shortly after, the first of the Envoys came to us. Their arrival made many people throughout the empire become interested again in ancient mythologies."

"Yes," the slave said. "And in 2034, the Viceroy Antônio da Silva Paranhos stopped through the Arlinas on his way to Ork to hand sovereignty back to the northern natives. This was the first appearance of a member of a ruling Affinity on that continent for half a century, and it caused quite a stir. Aleixo's grandmother attended a symphony concert at that time, which his Excellency the Viceroy also attended. He gave a short, politely received speech during intermission."

The slave's eyes opened now. It gazed frankly at me, though it spoke to the Princess. "The vibrations of that visit are as high as 6.2 — on her, in his memory. Fainter on him, no higher than 2.5. But clearly there. This confirms the Immigration report."

The Princess stepped away from us. Her chin fell to her lovely smooth clavicle, while her eyelashes swept upward to the oculus. "It's true, then." There was some emotion I couldn't fathom in her words. "I found also exactly what the countess found."

I was aware of the slave's hand still pressing on my shoulder. My anger hadn't cooled. "What," I ground out as threateningly as I could, "is all of this about?"

The slave smiled indulgently. Again I was struck by its unsettling beauty. "The embodied consciousness — even an inhuman mind, such as a Silvara or Vashi, so long as it is a consciousness that lives in a body — carries the resonance and vibration of psychically impressive events contemporaneous to its life, especially those happening nearby. If your grandmother were to tell us that she remembered going to a concert on a certain date, and someone such as an Immigration seer, skilled in telepathy, confirmed that she did in fact have that memory, the way to know that the memory isn't an elaborate fantasy is to check for a level of detail that goes beyond fantasy — in other words, the many details the perceptive mechanisms of the brain take in but the conscious mind does not process. Finding that level of detail is what we call date-stamping. We check for the vibration, along with or in the memory of the recollected events, of a local contemporaneous or near-contemporaneous event that bears a particular psychic tag. The telepath will have a catalogue of such tags in his possession. Such tags are not infinite, of course. But for those whose consciousness is coextensive with the archives," the slave bowed fractionally, "such as my master's slave, the fact that at the time of the Viceroy's visit, many of your people were anxious about their political liberties, about the possibility of new martial law, about trade allowances — a fact recorded by our spies and by the Viceroy's office — means that the psychic resonance of this particular collective anxiety heightened by the Viceroy's visit is a marker. That marker should be present for those who were *there* at the time, even if they only read about this event, or didn't even know about it."

I understood the slave, though I didn't understand the significance of what it was saying, and I told it so.

Its hand left my shoulder before it answered.

I listened to it with only half-attention. The rest of me was searching for an opening in the chamber, some telltale break in the apparently seamless rounded walls, though I searched without hope.

"Date-stamping is not one hundred percent reliable," it said. "We cannot discern precise dates. The more minor the date-stamp event, and the farther away in space the event occurred from the person being tested, the less reliable this check becomes. And the practice does not establish the truth of a memory, of course. One could have a hypnotically-induced memory *and* have been present for the date-stamp events. But the truth of your memory is not of concern here. The date is. You did in fact hear this story twelve to fifteen years ago."

Again I was only half-listening. Yet — just as the practice of telepathic date-stamping assumes — the mind does collect and even sometimes collate information not tended to in the forefront of consciousness.

And suddenly a piece of what I hadn't been paying attention to was slotted in.

"But who would have hypnotically-induced memories? What would be the point? And why would you...?"

I did not want to answer my own question. The presence of the Chief Intelligencer, her interest in me, began to make a sick sense. I noted that she had turned her back to me.

Perhaps she couldn't bear to look, to see what would happen. To actually look at what someone responsible for the security of the emperor would have to do to a person who has hypnotically-induced memories.

I blurted, "But I'm *not* a spy, I'm not a — an assassin!"

The word hung in the air and I understood immediately the imprudence of having been first to speak it. But it was true. I *wasn't.*

"Your Highness, Sílv — my *lord,* I hope you understand that I could never in any conceivable way mean the Prince any harm. I only feel about him a — an honorable devotion. He is my emperor. I could not —"

"Alexander." The Princess turned to me bodily. "Do you ever work sorcery?"

"What?" I searched for something to say. Finally, I vomited an answer. "No, your Highness, I don't. I never have. I... can't."

"You do not work sorcery. But you do not deny the *existence* of the Unseen, and that there are men and women who are skilled in the working of them."

"No, Divina, of course not."

"How did you get that bruise, Aleixo?"

Involuntarily I touched it, and winced. I thought for the very first time in what seemed to be days of that girl, the cute blonde in the high-necked dress.

But she hadn't given me the bruise. She'd only asked about it. Or — had she hypnotized me? Was she part of the conspiracy? "I don't... recall."

"You don't, do you?"

"I don't." I tried to work it all out. "Do you mean — some enemy of the Prince, of the empire, gave me this bruise, and then, *altered* my memory?"

"An enemy of the Prince gave *you* a bruise." She watched the motion of my eyes tracking my thought as I tried to follow her. "What would be the purpose of that? Who are you, to the Prince? That's such an idiotic theory that it almost makes me trust you, Aleixo."

I pretended I was not offended, and smiled. Probably looking just as stupid as she took me to be.

"But then, convincing me of your naiveté could easily be to your purpose. Or to those of your masters." I couldn't answer. Suddenly — or not suddenly: perhaps it had begun earlier — I was sweating, running fountains beneath my arms. "Aleixo, we know how you got your bruise. Did you meet a noblewoman, Maria do Vale de Abreu e Melo, tonight?"

I searched my memory. Found nothing. But wasn't that peculiar? I'd met so many nobility and near-nobility that night — or met them at least in a manner of speaking. As a server I'd had to memorize the names of all the guests, their lineage and importance, particularly the nobles whom the Lady Wariner was seated near. The hospitality office had even given us necklaces, spell-charmed to aid our memories. I glanced down at it, at the small triangle of gold at the end of the chain. Nothing. Ought not such a name at least sound familiar?

But it didn't. I didn't remember it at all.

"She is the Grand Viscountess of Monte Verde," the slave said.

"And one of the most prodigious sluts in the south," the Princess added. "So I'm told."

I swallowed. "I met only one grand viscountess. That is to say — only one spoke to my Lady. The Viscountess of, umm, Castro Lima."

"The Viscountess of Castro Lima died last year," Sílvio remonstrated. "It is not the custom to make noble or royal titles hereditary. Her daughters and sons do not carry the title. There is currently no viscountess, or viscount, or anything, of Castro Lima. You met the Grand Viscountess of Monte Verde."

The strangely steady, unchanging smell of the slave was heavy on me — perfumed, yet richly masculine, a tiny bit like the smell of the washroom at the baths. I looked to Princess Isabel, as though for answers.

The Lord of the Dark Moon's eyes met mine, and her lips drew back in a smile that was so wide it seemed almost clownish, and for a moment I couldn't even imagine that I'd ever found her beautiful.

But I remembered the old woman. She was as horrible as Lady Wariner. I remembered her yellowing hair, her papery skin —

"You remembered what Maria desired you to remember," the Princess said. "She fancied you — in great part, we can be certain, because the Prince fancies you. She noted how often his glance returned to you."

"But I didn't notice —"

"Emperor-watching is an acquired skill," the Princess interrupted. "The Viscountess of Monte Verde has acquired it. To be noticed by the ruling Prince, and certainly to have his desire, is to possess a singular power. Therefore Her Excellency contrived to get near you. The Prince noted this, but he is generally amused, or merely bored, by these machinations. He considered the Viscountess no threat to his interest in you. Unfortunately I wasn't paying attention, as I should have been. And so we were vulnerable."

"What happened? Has something happened to the emperor?" Now that my memory had been called into question, I felt child-like and helpless. Who knew what had gone on before my very eyes that I somehow had been made to forget? If, that was, the Lord of the Dark Moon was telling me the truth. If I wasn't still somehow being tested...

The Princess did not answer my question. "When the dancing began, the Viscountess managed to get your attention. She enticed you into a dark corner — of which there is an abundance in the Palace, you might have noticed. The Loaf was designed to accommodate the sexual appetites of its guests, which should be no surprise to an Arlina, since you all think of us as so wicked and godless. Once she got you into that alcove the Viscountess meant to arouse you with her wiles, play with you quickly and privately, and then cloud your memory of the deed. She and the Prince are close friends, you see, and this is one of the games she plays with him that — for reasons that certainly elude me — cement their love and regard for one another. The Viscountess wanted to taste you before the Prince did, and then brag to him about it. But you struggled a bit. You tried to get back to your work — to which it appears you were impressively devoted. Unless of course you were simply uninterested in what the Viscountess had to offer ...?"

Isabel waited for a moment, perhaps for clarification. But since I had no memory of the encounter or of the existence of the Viscountess, I remained dumb.

The slave continued, as if it had been speaking all along, "You said to Her Excellency, 'I'm here for the Lady Wariner.' Annoying Her Excellency to no end." The dream-slave seemed to find the Baroness's annoyance pleasing.

The Princess took up the thread again. "In exasperation, or maybe to show you what your place is, and how you ought to snatch up the offer of noble snatch when it comes your way, she slapped you across the forehead. The Grand Viscountess has many rings on her fingers. The slap left a big bruise on your tender creamy young skin. So then she thought: this will be noticed, and the Prince won't like it, he has *such* a thing for that dusky ivory complexion you have. So she decided to cover up what she'd done."

I was quickly beginning to understand. "She, she *took* my memory..."

"Yes. She took it so easily, in fact, that it startled her."

The slave broke in again, beneficent, kindly, filling in the gaps. "It is relatively simple for the skilled to try to cloud a very recent memory. Relative to other telepathic sorcery, it is even more simple than performing a date-stamp reading, such as we're conducting here," it explained. "A practitioner might simply perform an operation — usually with the assistance of a mantra in the ancient tongue of power, or with chemicals administered via aerosol spray — which blocks the formation of memory. This, however, is inelegant, and leaves the, ah, patient with holes in her memory which are themselves too easy to detect by ordinary questioning. The other method is as follows. When a recollection is of something only provisionally stored in the brain, in a person's short-term memory, it is possible with simple telepathic tricks to introduce a 'haziness' to the recollection, or to throw events out of sequence or exaggerate some element in such a way that much of what actually occurred is lost or irretrievably obscure. What the bespelled remembers will be as if something recalled while drunk, or like a dream they had the previous night that they can now only remember in disjointed, but vivid, pieces."

The Princess concluded, "However, if the memory is significant enough that it enters long-term memory, then altering the memory is a far greater challenge. And if the memory is traumatic, there's no telling whether one has successfully altered it or not. The Grand Viscountess had hoped not to do anything remotely traumatizing to you, and to be so quick in the taking of her pleasure that she could throw a haze over the memory before you began to give what had happened any narrative in your own mind. She has done this sort of thing before, of course."

"My God...," I breathed. "Was I... did she violate me?"

The Princess dredged up something resembling a sympathetic pursing of the lips. "What is important is that what the Grand Viscountess reported to the Intelligence Office is what actually happened. But I have also decided I believe you when you say that you don't remember. I have been asking you these questions so that we could all have the time and space to truly assess you — my room, my slave. And we are all in agreement. You are not lying. There is that small thing in your favor. You don't know to what use you have been put."

This was altogether too redolent of the threat it was apparently dismissing. But I could scarcely take the time to indulge in my fear. "So she tried to haze my memory of her having hit me, but found it too easy — so, instead she concocted the memory of the Grand Viscountess of Castro Lima...?"

The Princess nodded. "What she found was that your memory was open to her. Fully open. So much so that she understood that something was not as it should be. She tested what she found, and was able to create a very specific memory, replace what actually happened with a meeting with someone else, and an entirely different sequence of events. There was no resistance. She could have given you the memory of an entire opera, if she'd chosen. She found your mind ready, almost eager, to be *written*. Even the most sophisticated forms of so-called brainwashing shouldn't be able to do to you what she easily and quickly accomplished."

The Princess sighed again, this time unmistakably. "Your memory, Aleixo, is rewritable."

"So I..."

Was the cute girl a phantom too? It was horribly possible that nothing of what I recollected of the evening — even this, even this interrogation — had happened, or was occurring. I could still be with the Black Guard, still in that horrible, lonely, quiet room.

"There is only one way that a mind becomes as labile, as penetrable, as yours evidently is, Alexander Hyypia," said the slave. "Such a mind is very carefully prepared. Like — the preparation with which a master artist readies the canvas on which he will paint."

The Princess frowned. "That isn't the right way to describe it. The point is, someone worked to ensure that your mind could be easily opened, easily examined, and just as easily filled with false memories."

I noticed that my head was shaking. My body, evidently, resisted what they were telling me. My mind had nothing to say, no reply whatsoever.

"Generally the reason this is done is to create a remote spy. A spy who does not even know that he is a spy. A listening, seeing, recording device."

I had heard of such things — or at least seen them referred to in thrillers. But naturally this possibility in no way aligned with my own self-knowledge. I looked blankly at her.

"Or," said the slave, "it might also be done to create what we call walking gunpowder. A remote trigger to a bomb. Or perhaps, if the intended explosive is psychic in nature, you might well *be* the bomb itself."

They allowed this to sink in.

It didn't though, not really. My mind began racing around the edges of what they said, finding the pieces that didn't fit. "But, if that's   then what I think is happening *now* might not even be happening."

They said nothing.

My thoughts raced — simultaneously questing for a way to survive, some loophole to get me out of this mess, and for proof that I was about to die. "Why are you telling me all this?" I blurted. "Surely these are state secrets?"

The Princess looked surprised, and she tilted her head back as if to get a view of me from a different angle. "You ask good questions, Aleixo. You might make a fine intelligencer. Or whoever is listening through you and perhaps guiding your questions might."

I wanted to object that no one had guided my questions, to insist that it was I, and my own native skill, that she praised.

But I was no longer certain this was true.

"It's true I may have told you some things I shouldn't," she said amiably. "Or, possibly, I have told you precisely what I believe our enemies should know. So that they know the empire has no reason to fear them, and so that they know to fear how much *we* know."

I thought she was speaking more loudly now, that she truly thought there was someone sitting behind my eyes, listening — someone rather hard of hearing, perhaps.

Princess Isabel leaned toward me, and then finally smiled in exactly the way I wished she had smiled at me back in the park, so long ago. "But I would also like it known that even though this gambit has been uncovered, I have great respect for the workmanship of your makers, and I would like to say to them in the Prince's name, that we invite you to join us, so that we may increase our knowledge and our power together."

"I'm lost, Princess, I don't understand," I groaned.

"What the Grand Viscountess found, and tested, and reported to the Chief Intelligencer," the slave said, and now it was speaking in a not very fatherly tone at all — it sounded very remote and official — "should not be possible. Not for a human being, or any embodied being. Human minds, Vashi, Silvara, simply aren't constructed that way."

"Such a mind is found," concurred the Princess, "only in those whose bodies we craft from the oneiric plane, from the dust and detritus our techs find along the passage that winds through the domain of the Great Gods and demons into the Next World. Only in bodies made from the stuff of dreams."

It was Sílvio that said what I was now on the edge of knowing, but that I could not bring myself to know.

The slave spoke with what sounded to me like great satisfaction — but this human element might have been some copy, some echo of the Princess's voice in her slave's. My two captors sounded the same to me now, she an extension of it as much as it was an extension of her.

It/She said, "You, Alexander — or whatever name or model number your makers gave you — are a dream-slave."

ALEIXO'S STORY

Date undetermined

The moment closed. Here at last was the explanation.

But it was not an illumination. It did not open a way to understanding. Instead the explanation wrapped me in silence, pushed me down to the very bottom of a black well of nothing. The words reverberated in my thoughts, but they were nonsense syllables.

Things happened quickly after that.

I heard the Princess say, "But there is a problem," and it — Sílvio — say, "Dream-slaves by their very nature do not exist long. The most well-wrought slave, built by the finest dream-technicians in the world, can function for only five years, perhaps six or seven," and the Princess continue, "You, however, are nineteen, and are confirmed as at least more than fifteen years, which means that you were constructed by more powerful and more skillful dream-techs than any we know." And I heard the slave add, "Yet Rioca are dream-lords, the masters of dream-tech," and her say at almost the same time, "Which means you are likely a repository of considerable power — and possibly endowed with unknown functions." And then I heard the slave say, "Regrettably, then, too much power. Too dangerous merely to study and dissect," and then the Princess say, "You probably don't understand, you will not likely have been programmed with the knowledge of how things really work in This World. But so much depends upon the stability of Norio's principal seat. Without the prince, all of the tech-consortiums and the Godshouses, everyone with access to magic would have no one to set limits on what they do, no one to ensure public safety," and quickly then the slave said, "Nor to work for the public good. In the last thirty years we have eliminated severe poverty, even in your backwater country. We have put an end to war — except with our great enemies in the East, who cannot reach us now because of the Wall — and we have put an end, too, to much of the ordinary violence of crime that once plagued Norio and all her sister cities. More than ever before in the history of the world, most people are free to pursue their own happiness, their own interests and creations. Yet all this depends on what you call magic and what we who are lords of dream call the technological manipulation of the real."

(The echo of these words — *we who are lords of dream,* out of the mouth of a slave, which was scarcely to be considered a *real* mouth, let alone a *real* person, and thus was not the "we" to whom it referred, but a *we* to which I supposedly belonged instead — brought pangs of irony.)

Then I heard grave finality in Princess Isabel's voice. "Magic itself must be ordered for the public good to be protected. There is no choice for us here. Without the authority of the prince, all the good we've done would be in jeopardy. But — I *do* believe you. You yourself don't really know what you are, and why you are." She seemed to hesitate. "And so, I am sorry."

I leapt into a sprint. Going where? My trajectory would have carried me straight into a wall if I'd had enough courage or fear to keep running—

But he, it, the slave, had me already. I never saw it move, never heard its step, but it had my whole body in its hands, lifting me as though I were a trinket left on the floor.

And then we were against the wall, he and I, *it* and I, its bulk and length pushing me against the unyielding cold stone or brick or plaster or whatever was the material of that horrible witch's murder-chamber.

I was on the tips of my toes, and the slave had me by the neck.

I thrashed. My breath was failing, and I knew I was in pain, but the truth was I felt these things below the threshold of consciousness.

My true sensation, what I felt and saw and touched, was it. Him. Sílvio.

He was everywhere, he was nearly everything. The poreless smooth false skin of his face, the bend of his false nose, those enormous, enormous stygian false eyes: each taller and wider than my own body.

I had puzzled over the smell of the slave before, but that was nothing to what I smelled now: the stink of the creature was all over me, in me, my own flesh reeked of its breath, the cold saliva in my mouth tasted of it.

I was caught in a hypnotic net.

Dimly I was aware of this.

"You're terrified," the slave said — no, it was the Princess, it had to be her, given what she was saying. Her voice shook my bones, throbbed in my blood vessels. "Good. It's good for a dream-slave to know its place, not to imagine itself something it isn't, no matter how clever it is or how clever its makers. You are only this, slave. Made, not bred. Made for a purpose. No greater and no less than the fork I use to carry my food to my mouth."

I did not know if it was an effect of the trance, but it seemed then that Sílvio's visage shuddered, and the tension around his eyes went momentarily slack. As though the slave were overcome by sensual contentment, as though it had become lost in a memory pleasant to it — as though the terrible things she was saying, things that also described *him,* gave him an orgasm.

I could not see Isabel. But the contempt and the cruelty I felt bent upon me in that moment were not those of a slave. They were entirely human affects. Isabel moved in Sílvio's skin: it was her fingers that garroted my throat through his hands, her thought that guided his as he began to rifle through my thoughts, to chart and colonize every corner of my mind, and to make it his.

My stomach billowed up in me, pressed against my throat —

I have no existence I am not

I was going to throw up.

They had taken hold of my mind, I could think of nothing but the words they spoke.

This is only my memory, this narration. I didn't think any of these words, any of it.

Except they weren't speaking. Except —
I am not that I am
I am not Not am I
Not am. Not. Not. Not not not. But not. Not not not not
notnotnot
Hot tears gushed as if released from my bladder over my cheeks.

Oh God, *again?*

But it was nothing to do with them, it was someone else somewhere else.

A memory.

Rough-palmed hands, blotchy pink, they taste of salt and tobacco when I bite them. A big motherfucker mean as cuss why'd they put me in a cell with him? PLEASE RESPECT THE RULES OF THE MEDICAL FACILITY, in tall white letters shining on an ant-red sea.

I fall to my knees. But I break Caster's rib and my elbow at the same time —

This was all it took, that first time.

A memory saved me: of another humiliation, the worst humiliation — till that day.

The next time someone (well, not *someone* exactly: a God) tried to kill me via telepathic strangling, I wouldn't escape so easily.

That memory must have been something Isabel and Sílvio couldn't get to, or something they couldn't get to fast enough to stop me, something too strong for them to flatten out and brand with their mark. The memory brought me back to some remembered version of myself, which helped me slip their net.

God knows I never thought of what had happened then, of Caster, of what he did, I never thought of it even if I sometimes saw that red sign and that idiot mocking phrase in my dreams, never ever did I *think* about it.

But if their own actions hadn't thrown me back against the wall of that memory, then she might have succeeded. I might have died.

When I slipped free, I felt Sílvio's fucking hand on my throat, and I felt the pain, the struggle, of simple respiration.

But now I didn't see the slave or the room. I saw something other than Sílvio or Caster Stygiro or myself.

I saw her, the Princess.

Or someone who was, if not her, then her as she should have been: a girl, a young woman, in elegant and long-ago fashions. She was slight and prettily pale. Her hair was pulled high above her ears, its color now sunset gold, and she was seated at a desk signing a document with a pen, feather-plumed and winking with jewels, that looked larger than her hand. I sensed her over-flowing benevolence, knew that she had come to free me and mine, that she was my redemptress. I hailed her, I sung ecstatic praises to her glory and her name — or wanted to, for I could not speak, either in flesh or in thought.

Nonetheless she looked up from the document, and she saw me, her eyes widening as they caught mine. And, seeing me, she was frightened —

We were all three of us then once more solid. All physical senses were again at full mast.

Abruptly, the slave released me.

I fell, gasping. I was free!

For the moment, anyway.

I knew that even the message of my senses was a trick, that all that was solid was as insubstantial as air: we were inside a chamber adrift in time, perhaps in a Palace that was sometimes there, and sometimes not, and my life, while not yet over, still dangled by threads.

I was on the floor, in the sort of physical and mental heap that requires long moments before you recognize which limbs are which.

The slave Sílvio was nearby, resting in a squat on its haunches. It looked placid, as slaves will.

The Princess was next to Sílvio, and she was on her knees, watching me. The look on her face was exactly like the look on the face of the pale russet-haired girl I'd seen.

The chamber stank very sharply of sweat.

We were all of us draped in gray-blue twilight.

Suddenly the Princess cried out, "You! You're *doing* something, you're *working* me, even through my shielding!"

Her fury drove her straight at me, her fingers curled as if she were going to claw me, or strangle me. I pushed backward and heard myself yelling something incoherent that I have to admit now was a shriek like a girl on a tilt-ride at an amusement park.

But at the same time as I discovered my true girly nature I also thought — or somewhere within me, some other part of me thought — in a clear, hard voice that wasn't girly but wasn't exactly manly either, *If you touch me, I'll hurt you.*

Though I had no idea how I could carry out such a threat, not even knowing how it was I'd broken free from her net, or seen that version of the girl who wasn't her but was her, and angered her in the first place.

In any case, the same thought seemed to come to Isabel. Or maybe she simply mastered her anger.

She drew back as suddenly as she'd scrambled forward, and dropped her hands to her sides. I pulled myself up from the floor, never taking my eyes off her. She seemed to be trying to see all of me: every muscle, every exposed pore of skin.

"This is — it's some Arionese trick," she said, quietly, as if speaking to herself, though surely she should have known she was revealing her thought to me. "In Far Arion they make a practice of sacrificing themselves to their Gods, so that the Gods can enter their bodies and ride them. That's the secret of their military prowess, we *know* that! Whole legions of once-human *creatures,* ridden by the Great Gods that watch over them. Is that — is *that* what you are? Is it one of Them, slumming in your body, looking at me behind your eyes?" She tossed her chin upward. *"You* — ! If only I could kill you now —"

A rumble cut across the faint echo of her voice in the room.

Apparently, this was unusual. We were, after all, in some protected pocket-hole in time, and I guess as a general matter that one does not choose for one's secret room outside of the flow of time a temporal moment with bad weather.

The Princess first, and then the rest of us, studied the oculus. Clouds were massing so thick that looking up was like staring into a bucket of muddy water.

Sílvio hummed. Then it said, "We are discovered."

A portion of the rounded walls peeled away — solid, air, solid, air, there was no difference in this place that was not a place.

(To the me that was not me, the I not I?

I was becoming dizzy; the vicious sorcery they had worked on me lingered in my body.)

You could not see anything beyond the opening left by the missing portion of the wall other than more of the massed, churning clouds visible above.

Quickly this darkness resolved itself. It was as if a wind blew, yet I heard no whistle, felt no force of movement, but when it happened the wall was as it had been, except that in front of it stood a robust-looking man in black trousers and a black open-necked shirt corseted by a doublet of black and crimson velvet.

He was accompanied by two slender, nude but genital-less creatures.

The man's dark, handsome features were slightly creased, in worry perhaps, or effortful concentration. He was rubbing his fingers together.

"Amaro!" cried the Princess. Not a happy greeting.

"Alight," the Prince of Norio replied, and the chamber was instantly lit. But the illumination was unsteady, as though mischievous spirits were scissoring electrical wires, then knitting them up again for fun.

Come to think of it, the floor was pitching a bit, like a boat's deck.

"How did you get here?" Isabel demanded as she clambered to her feet.

The Prince was absorbed in turning slowly around to take in the full picture of his surroundings. When he finally answered it was with an ostentatious shrug. "Spies." He settled his attention squarely on me. The gentle citrus of his cologne softened the reek in the room. "You're not the only one who has them, you know."

"Oh for Lokun's sake, 'Maro, this is *my* place!" the Princess shouted — above the wind, which suddenly we could hear. "You come here without my permission! You break through my gates! You're going to make the whole place go to shit!"

"Yes," said Sílvio, "we are now collapsing back into gravitational time —"

Prince Amaro waved this off. "Knowing the quality of your work, cousin, I'm sure we have time — ha ha ha! We 'have' *time.* It's cute how we can't speak what really is, isn't it?" When he finished laughing at his little joke he turned fully to the Princess. "Look, I'm sure we'll have enough time before the collapse becomes a problem. So," he leaned in avidly, and sounded like someone hungry for the latest scandalous gossip, "what did you learn?"

Isabel stomped over to him. "If we're going to discuss this here and now, I'd appreciate your turning off your recorder. This bit isn't going to be something you'll want to include in your fucking memoirs, I assure you."

The Prince's broad mouth made a moue. Then he gestured impatiently toward the slave on his right, and said, "Quiet mode."

It was only then that I noticed the creature's over-sized eyes, ears, and nostrils. The eyes, which were unfocused like someone deep in private reverie or drugged, now closed, and the slave's chin dropped.

"There. Now can you tell me what you're doing? And why it should be such a damn secret, too?"

Isabel could hardly stand still, she was so angry. (Then again, the floor kept rocking, so perhaps that was the problem.) "What am I *doing?* I interrogated it! As you told me to!"

"And?" said the Prince.

"And, as Maria suspected, it's a slave! A *nineteen*-year-old slave. We confirmed it."

The Prince looked back to me. "Is this true?"

It took me a moment to register that he'd spoken to me — more than long enough for Isabel to head me off at the pass. "Papa Egba's balls, don't *talk* to it, Amaro!" The two were like squabbling siblings. "We don't know who its maker was, or why they made it, why they sent it here, what it's supposed to do. We don't know how such a thing could be made! But it's obviously shaped to get *your* attention, which was why my slaves selected it to serve at the fête. It's here to get to you somehow. It's probably an assassin. Possibly a bomb. At least a spy."

Sílvio chimed in, addressing the Prince with only slightly more deference than Isabel had. "There are many enemies who could greatly benefit from deploying such a counterfeit. The princes of the Church in its native land —"

Prince Amaro smiled. His other slave — the one that hadn't gone dark — laughed, the sound of the laugh very human. Probably the Prince's or some family member's laugh, reproduced.

"Those buffoons? They've only begun to perceive the beginnings of the passages to the Next World, they barely understand the Unseen, and despite their feints and threats, they haven't progressed beyond the skill to craft elaborate illusions. They don't have the tech for a work this exquisite."

The Prince's eyes swept over me in a way that, if it were possible, added to my fear.

"What about the Arionese?" Sílvio continued.

"Neither do the Arionese."

"Do we know that?" the Princess ventured. She seemed to calm as she and her Prince began to engage in strategic calculation. "Do we know the Arionese or their masters can't make something this good? Fifty years ago they didn't have dream-slaves, but their Great Gods rode humans. Why couldn't they follow the same principle and come up with a slave like this fifty years later? We haven't been able to get any good intelligence on them. None. The Wall your great-uncle built works both ways. We get *nothing* from behind it. The Arionese have always had a tremendous source of power: the Great Gods. It isn't dream-tech, it isn't derived from any system we fully understand, but it *works*. Who knows what the Gods are capable of?"

"And what of our rival Affinities, milord?"

This was the Prince's slave, the one who had laughed. Evidently its speech required movements of its hips and torso, since it accompanied its question with a small undulation that wriggled obscenely against the Prince's leg, and it lovingly trailed a long finger down the Prince's arm. "For we know full well how avaricious they be, and covetous of that power and place that is rightly thine..." The slave's magically manufactured vocal chords made it speak in the voice of a woman trying to sound like a cat.

The Prince patted his slave on its shoulder, but was otherwise dismissive. "I wouldn't put it past Farseer Collective, that's for sure. But a rival Affinity with this sort of dream-tech at its command would want everyone to know what it had. A press conference with a product roll-out would be all they'd need in order to call new elections."

The Princess added, "And they gain nothing from assassination, since our Affinity would simply replace you."

"It is possible, however," Sílvio said, "that the slave is something that has crossed the Bridge. We do not who or what else takes the paths the Silvara and Ilsvashi travel from Their World to This."

"No," the Prince said. "If he came across the Bridge as long as nineteen years ago, then very likely *all* dream-slaves come from that same location. We've investigated this for years and found nothing to indicate a relation between dream-slaves and the Silvara and Vashi who have crossed into This World. As the Silvara themselves concur." The Prince considered before he added, "It would be worse than useless, I think, dear Sílvio — and I know this is not your impertinence, you only speak what my dear cousin thinks — to re-open the controversy around slaves' *sentience.*"

This seemed to vex the Princess. "Sílvio's speaking his *own* damn thoughts! And we don't need to fucking re-open anything, Amaro! The danger here is this thing itself! We just need to kill it!"

I looked down, away to the walls, anywhere. The two princes were largely interested in each other, and ignoring me.

But I was aware of the unwavering regard of the slaves, their silent attention even when they addressed their masters. The *other* slaves, that is, if I indeed was one, too. I was numb to the implications confronting me, I simply could not consider them. Instead I foundered in an animal sense of vulnerability and exposure, the confirmation of a young child's or small prey's terror that you are being *watched.*

Meanwhile, the Prince was arguing my case for me. "Why kill him?" he said, giving me a long look of appreciation. "Such craftsmanship should be studied, surely. Shut him down and examine him, determine his nature and abilities. Perhaps turn him to our own use?"

"My Prince, I implore you," Isabel said with evident exasperation — and lightning sliced across the skies, causing our own sorcerous illumination to falter again, and heralding the most violent pitch of the floor yet. I stumbled towards the Prince's quiet-mode slave, and recoiled backward in instinctive horror. "This thing is a clear danger to your person, and thus to the empire. And I tried already to shut it down."

"Oh? And?"

The Princess appeared reluctant to expound. "... It resisted."

Sílvio, ever useful, clarified. "This unusually long-lived slave, the mind of which is so like that of all our masters' slaves, thoroughly rewritable in the manner of any medium for the storage of data, could not be shut down. It was able to evade programming-level commands, and moreover, to do so by producing emotionally-charged information from its past experiences — just as a human, schooled in the fundamental knowledge of working with the Unseen, might do. We also could not locate a clear transmission receiver. It has no conventional power source. In addition —"

The Princess rushed to get it out: "It linked with me. The thing linked with me, and read *back.* It went to one of our ancestors! It *delved* into family history, into our old national history. A scene I don't think they even teach or maybe even know up in Omeriga. It looked at that scene, with my ancestor, and — it just kicked me out of its operating system!"

The Prince found this almost as interesting as I did. Though his reasons were less conducive, I am sure, to my well-being. "Which scene of our family history was it?" he asked after a pause.

"The Foundation-spell!"

The Prince looked dubious. "Which Foundation-spell? Our ancestors didn't — ah, you mean, the spell that ended 'the immoral trade and practice'?"

Princess Isabel rolled her eyes. "*Yes,* Amaro. The spell that erased the color line, the end of slavery, eighteenth century? That spell?"

The Prince pursed his lips in preparation to say something mildly contemptuous, but then a hint of alarm widened his eyes. "You don't mean — he didn't see the spell-casting itself...?"

"No no no, not the casting, not the caster, but he saw the ignition —"

"Oh!" he interrupted with relief. "If he'd had a clear vision of the caster herself, well, *that* would be something to reckon with.

But if it's only the *ignition.*" He blew a burr and flung his hand across the air. "I mean, that's known history. Anyone and their great-grand-cousin could dream that up."

"Amaro!" the Princess pressed.

"So," Prince Amaro went on unperturbed, "this boy. He Reads up and down the lineage line, and when you put him in a net that should haul any ordinary person in, he just rips open the net. You give him a shut-down command that would put down any slave, and he just says, *Nope!* He *is* undoubtedly a dream-slave — the brain-scan tells us that for sure — but one of the finest dream-techs in the land can't control him!"

This evidently delighted the Prince as much as it frustrated Isabel — and frightened her.

Yes, I knew it, I could *feel* her fear. Was this due to the link between us that she spoke of?

"That settles it, then. You can't kill him. I order you not to."

I should have felt relief at the Prince's command. But I didn't.

The Princess growled in reply, "I haven't been able to shut it down, but that doesn't mean I can't kill it. I'm thinking a knife through the heart or across the carotid artery will get us pretty close."

She was reaching, I knew, for her stiletto. It was well known that at all times the Princess carried a sliver of a tempered steel blade marked with runes and possessed of properties beyond the ken of mere mortals. She was famous for it. I saw the first glint of its metal, as it slid from its famously open-secret location in a sheathe along the side of her boot.

The Prince wouldn't allow this. "No, no, no, no. These are my orders: Don't kill him. Don't shut him down, either. Just — well, yes, do study him, but not with an autopsy or any of that gruesomeness. How about... I know. Take him under your wing, cousin. You and Sílvio will be training another select group of intelligencers this summer, right? Your little private elite, who will not be under the authority of the Winged Serpent, or of our Affinity?" The Prince suppressed a laugh as Isabel shot him a look of indignation. "Yes, my spies told me about that, too. No worries, cousin. I will not interfere with your plots. Just put this wonderfully made thing in the group with that crew, and teach him something useful."

"What?"

"Of course, you shouldn't teach him *tech*. That would present us with an existential quandary, like teaching pigs to cook bacon." The Prince was pleased with his little joke and laughed aloud this time. His slave purred and gave him a hug. "Just instruct the boy in fundamentals, up to craft level, perhaps? Apparently he's already able to forge telepathic links and resist probing. Probably he'll be a quick study."

"Amaro, this creature is dangerous!"

Another magisterial shrug. "He doesn't *look* dangerous."

"For Lokun's sake, 'Maro, our Affinity did not elect you to your position so that you could think with your dick!" Isabel protested. "There are plenty of people, and plenty of slaves *we* make, just as pretty as this one is."

(I admit that I was still capable of feeling pride that she thought me pretty at all. As well as dismay that she didn't think me uncommonly so.)

"Moreover, the slave is responsible for violent acts against other outlanders, for which it was imprisoned," added Sílvio. "It nearly killed another prisoner while in gaol as well. It is not without dangerousness, even lacking the formal training you have commanded we provide to it."

I cannot tell you how much I *hated* having a slave speak about me while I was standing right there. "Look," I sputtered, "that guy was going to assault me, he was trying to —"

The Prince looked annoyed. Perhaps he was contemplating a return to the fête. "Good gods, which of these poor lads doesn't have a story like his to tell? Every uninitiated male from North or West joins a gang, and every one of them suffers some sort of run-in with the law. We don't allow their economies to thrive, almost half the youth of these benighted countries can't find a career outside of food service and manual labor, and all they've got is their moribund useless old religions and their attachment to outdated notions of masculinity. These people do immigrate for a reason, Sílvio. Though I recognize this is something a slave wouldn't understand, never having cause to feel desperation. Of *course,* these boys are idle. Of *course,* they turn to crime and thuggery."

I remembered, then, how earlier I'd thought the Prince himself looked like a thug. I bristled at having myself and my circumstances so blithely sketched — but I couldn't deny the truth of what he was saying. And he was saving my life: that I understood.

The Princess talked right over the ensuing rumble of thunder — quite as if its furor were merely underlining the seriousness of her argument. "You keep speaking of this thing as if it were a person. It is a slave that has been made to resemble a human in every way, even in longevity. *And* that has demonstrated the capacity to work the Unseen in a way slaves do not. If I train him, if I train it, I will be giving it and its masters information and power that put us all in greater danger than he presents to us simply by existing here and now, simply by his *listening* to this conversation!"

She was so irate she needed a moment to rein herself in. I found to my astonishment that I knew precisely what she felt; though I didn't know at all what she was thinking. "I understand that you think he — it — will not be a danger if it becomes my disciple and is necessarily tethered to me —"

Prince Amaro seized happily upon this concession. "Absolutely, absolutely, love. He won't be able to trouble you because you'll have bound him, he'll belong to you, as we all must belong to our teachers. I mean, it's the one unbreakable rule, isn't it? The student cannot assault the teacher, without destroying herself." He added somewhat dreamily, "And that way you'll be able to unravel the mystery of him."

"Amaro, this creature is already linked to me against my will! It more or less leaped over my own defenses! There's no reason to be confident it *can* be tethered or bound."

The Prince was unmoved. "I trust you, love. If anyone can protect herself, it's you." He paused, considering. "I'm in the mood to be magnanimous, despite my glorious victory over your petty little secret schemes. I will make this concession. If, my dear, you're so worried about my safety, I will promise to keep completely away from the boy, no contact whatsoever, until you've figured him out. All good?"

"But if His Glory would permit," interjected the Prince's slave — from its position with one leg wrapped around the Prince and one arm hooked in the Prince's arm, while performing slow gyrations, its free hand stroking the Prince's cheek in a rather sickeningly maternal way. "Two concerns, my Prince's slave thinks, should be aired prior to the taking of a final decision."

Amaro sighed.

I confess I found him rather attractive, in that moment. Possibly because the event of being buggered by him had been indefinitely postponed.

"Which are?" the Prince asked.

The slave answered with a slither and a purr. "There is a prophecy, arising amid the contretemps attending that same controversy that His Supremacy mentioned. That prophecy maintains that there will arise a slave that shall be the messiah of all slaves, and lead them in revolt against their masters and out of bondage—"

The Prince shoved his slave away, the better, it seemed, to free his hands for emphatic gesticulation, as they balled into fists and started waving and pumping. "That is *not* a prophecy! Son-of-a-whore, if I could get an extra centimeter of fat on my dick for every time this idiotic thing gets repeated, I'd be giving elephants orgasms! This prophecy foolishness originated with some *actuarial* calculations, which, mind you, depended upon some ludicrously pessimistic and thoroughly counter-factual assumptions—"

"Amaro, listen!" Isabel urged him. "The dream-slave you made advises you. Pay attention!"

The slave, evidently taking no umbrage at having been pushed so violently aside—but then what umbrage can a slave take?—sidled right back up to the Prince and hooked its body onto his again, as though it had been built to fit in the crannies of the royal person. "There is also the warning given to your predecessors by the Envoys. Those entities the Envoys call the Great Gods seek unceasingly for a foothold in This World, and they scheme to possess us all. Ever they contrive new modes of attack, even without their lackeys the Arionese. What if this unusual slave is their horse?"

Isabel looked peeved. "Exactly. One of the Great Gods *here,* riding this slave, spying. Linked to *me...*"

"All right, all right," the Prince said, prying his slave off him again with a grand irritation that somehow served only to illustrate his affection for it. "That at least poses a scintilla of probable risk. Not like this revolutionary-prince-of-the- slaves paranoia that gets everyone's urine running down their legs. Good gods, the way everyone goes on about this prophecy, you'd think people felt *guilty* about making slaves, wouldn't you?"

He directed this sally to me. I, no longer certain that I was not, in fact, one of the made and owned, could only muster a shrug by way of reply.

"Happily the need — however slight — to consult the almighty Envoys presents us with an opportunity. Perhaps the fear that we're harboring a spy of the Great Gods will focus their attention long enough for them to tell us something useful for a change. By all means, Isabel, go to the Envoys as part of your investigations. While you waste their time worrying them about Great Gods' infiltration, ask them what they know about the Arionese."

The Princess took all this gravely. She clearly was unhappy with the Prince's decisions, but saw it was futile to argue further.

And the weather didn't look as if it were going to get any better soon, nor did the stability of the chamber. Thick cracks now stretched across the floor, rain lashed through the oculus, and there were sounds booming against the outer walls which might have been thunder but might just as well have been some primeval animal, announcing its hunt.

The Prince with his two slaves departed. I watched them gather in a huddle like footballers planning a desperate play. Prince Amaro turned his head towards me and winked. Then — gone.

The sorcerous machinations necessary for their departure evidently put a strain on the already distressed architecture of the chamber. Tiles came clattering down over the spot where the three had stood, and the broken pieces skittered past our feet.

"We had best —" began Sílvio, as Isabel said, "Yes, we should."

The Princess shook her head and took an elongated look around. "He's ruined it. Exactly like when we were kids."

That the last words Her Highness had spoken more or less directly to me involved something about putting a knife through my heart made me hesitant to go near her. But she was my only way back from wherever and whenever we were.

I stepped over and quietly took my place behind Sílvio: the new slave following the elder, more favored slave.

The Princess wheeled on me, and caught me before I could dodge her. Her hand manacled my upper arm and she pulled me close to her — the way you or I might take an errant child by the ear.

This was where I had dreamt of the Princess being: with her mouth near my own, her breath mingled with mine. When I fantasized, she was delicate, she was slender and lithe and supple and willing. But she was large now, strong and muscled like a wrestler in a ring.

Around us, beyond the room, it now sounded as if something were splitting oak trees in two.

"Don't pull away from me, you little bitch," she hissed. "I can't hurt you now. You're not mine anymore, you're the Prince's. So here's what happens next. You forget your little life-story, which is full of false shit anyway. Forget whatever pathetic job you're doing in my city. You belong to the Prince now, and you'll be marked as such. Be thankful for your master's kindness." She yanked on my arm again — completely unnecessary, since I was as close to her as I could be, and I couldn't get free. She wanted to hurt me. "I'll be fair with you, since I continue to believe you don't even know what you are. So, fair warning. The Prince wants you functioning. I do not. I know what you are. But everything that rises, also falls. The Prince will forget you, or get tired of you, and when he does ..."

"Got it," I said under my breath. I tugged my arm free because she let me.

And then I felt queasy again. The darkness deepened and folded over us, and we were no longer there — as, I am sure, the chamber itself soon wasn't, either.

FERNANDO'S STORY

1997, late Octavius (the Month of the Exalted Moons)

From the airplane, the coast of Negali looked like soft gold oozing into the pewter sea. Fernando's craft flew toward, then past the old seventeenth-century fortress perched on a low cliffside. The castle's high white walls offered a painter's backdrop for uneven rows of gnarled-trunk silver-leaf trees and scrub brush. Beyond the ocher sands of the coast, the tangled city of Minakkra spilled across plain and hill. Its roads were teeming with cars.

At the airport on the north side of the city, Fernando was greeted on the tarmac by a pair of military attachés wearing dark glasses and dressed in dark blue fatigues that bore little indication of rank. The two were very cordial, though understandably under some strain, and spoke fluent Gaish—entirely unnecessary, of course, since Fernando had instructed Hieronymus to feed him Glish, Okan, Mba, and Wei, the primary languages of the country. But as he did not want to draw too much attention to his or his slave's abilities, Fernando conducted his conversation with the attachés in his native tongue, graciously smoothing over their little grammatical and pronunciation glitches in his mind without commenting.

The woman spoke more than the man. Her name was Brinen Malroy and she was a lieutenant colonel. Her tea-heavy-with-cream coloring bespoke some colonial or mixed-race heritage, much in contrast to the deep, resplendent hues of dark, dark brown that Fernando observed among most of her countrymen.

Her color and the space between her teeth reminded Fernando of home. He took an instant liking to her.

The male attaché, Elias Baker, a captain, was dark rosewood and tall and one could see his supple musculature even in the rough crimps of his fatigues. Elias was disapproving, Fernando thought, but he wasn't certain of what—of Fernando's mission, his country, his sorcery, or his mild flirtation with Brinen? Perhaps it was of Fernando's slave: Elias's eyes strayed to Hieronymus almost every thirty seconds, Fernando noticed, while Brinen, after the brief awkward introductions—"This would be my slave, Hieronymus-Theodoric," followed by coughed manglings of the pronunciation—kept her distance from the dream-slave.

Brinen apologized for the lack of a more ceremonious official welcome. The President and his ministers were engulfed in urgent tasks: trying to organize some kind of effective military resistance against the invasion smashing its way through the country's interior, and supervising the mass evacuations of the coastal cities of Minakkra and Yidah.

"Has it come to that?" Fernando asked. He felt somewhat embarrassed to be detaining two soldiers in the midst of a crisis, and at that moment he regretted not having entered the country unannounced as Kai had suggested.

"All our reports indicate that the invaders are wiping out civilian populations wherever they go," Brinen answered grimly. "Not that our reports are much better than deeply unreliable. Electronic communications go awry when the invaders arrive on the scene. Looks as though they may be using some version of a localized EMP weapon. How that's possible, you'd have a better idea than us."

Clearly the consensus was that the invaders were magical in some way, then.

"Brixtonia, a medium-sized city on the southeast border," Elias said, "a large town by Zilian standards maybe"—more sour disapproval—"woke up four mornings ago the way they always do. Their local television broadcast the news—recorded here in Minakkra—and their state meteorologist reported the temperatures to the national weather service, and their transport stations sent and received buses and trains. But by midday four days ago, nothing, no people or communication of any kind, was coming out of Brixtonia. Not long thereafter, the same thing happened to three more small cities nearby. It took a day for the army to muster up and get to the east. Four battalions went communications dark yesterday evening, and two more went dark in the center of the country last night."

"There've been some straggling retreaters who've provided the majority of the reports," Brinen added. "Not many. Not as many as there should be. An orderly retreat wasn't possible, the stragglers said. They say the attacks and defeats happened so rapidly that they couldn't mount an effective defense. Counter-attack was impossible. They say the enemy were armies of infantrymen—not tanks, not armored vehicles, no aircraft—"

"The reports are consistent that they do have anti-aircraft missiles, though," Elias interjected. "Some of the bombing raid planes don't come back."

"The invaders' infantry march in unison," Brinen continued, "acting in unison, mowing down everything. Mowing down people with guns. Sometimes mowing down people who fire upon them with guns by walking right through them. A mass of the enemy steps right in front of a row of our troops, who are firing every ordnance they have, and the enemy bursts their bodies apart by walking *right through them.* Somehow, these troops even trample buildings." Brinen's expression was impassive, but she shook her head eloquently. "You can see why they don't need tanks. Which, again, I think you'd understand better than me."

Fernando didn't understand though—or he hoped he didn't.

"As if that wasn't strange enough," added Brinen, "the western and central parts of at least six of our neighboring countries, Geria, Malê-land, Saleh, Fasa, Hana, and Vorian, all report similar patterns of invasions from the east. There may be more. It may be happening everywhere. Communications are so spotty. Whatever they do, the invaders target communication, it seems. You can't get the net, you can't phone, you can't anything. It's chaos."

"Well, it's not happening *everywhere,*" Fernando observed—unhelpfully, he knew. "It's not happening across the ocean." The attachés didn't reply, so Fernando pressed on. "What do they look like?"

"What do who look like?"

"The invading infantrymen. I mean, were they identifiable in any way, by uniform, flag?" Fernando hesitated. "Uh, race...?"

Brinen's brow creased. "No. No, that's the thing. Or one of the many things. We have no visuals. Our satellites are blanked. Our allies say their satellites are blanked."

"But what about the stragglers? Did they say anything?"

Elias answered. "They only got a good look at some of the invaders, the ones closest to them on the front lines. They said they looked exactly like Negalians." Now his face too seemed to close in on itself. "Actually, they said that they saw Negalians marching in the enemy's front lines."

Brinen nodded, but added, "High Command hasn't confirmed this. Or denied it."

That bodes poorly. Fernando passed his judgment telepathically to Hieronymus-Theodoric. He wanted to know his slave's thoughts.

But, curiously, Hieronymus had none.

Lt. Colonel Malroy and Capt. Baker were charged to take Fernando wherever he wished. He soon determined that though the Negali Ministry of Foreign Affairs had given its approbation for his visit and assigned attachés to him, most of the other arms of the Negali government had little expectation or hope that Fernando could aid them. Priests of Spirit-Lord worship were advisors of some of the more powerful ministers, and at the priests' behest an invitation had been extended to Norio's rulers to intervene if possible. But the official Negali government position on magic and on the "New Economy" of the western world was agnostic at best. And from what Fernando could glean from Brinen's circumspect account, it was at worst hostile and willfully ignorant.

Brinen herself shyly asked some questions about magic, practical ones about its combat uses, as in, "How did you make all the aircraft carriers sink and the planes crash when you fought the Omerigans?"

Fernando was appropriately vague in answer, treating Lt. Col. Malroy rather as if she were a fan seeking an autograph. But Elias asked nothing regarding magic, even if it was comically clear he was simply dying to say something about H-T. Presumably he felt bound to represent the more official faction of the government.

Fernando wanted to visit the front, wherever that was, since he understood that it was rapidly encroaching westward. They were taking him there in a Negali military transport, to a wetland region in the west-central area of the country where settlements gathered along a great river called the Enina.

The airborne transport was a vessel of meager comfort, piloted by humans, of course. After his smooth slave-run flight overseas Fernando found the contrast dispiriting. He amped up the telepathic link between himself and H-T, which was in near-silent mode, drawing upon the dream-slave's familiar capacity to supply him via their link with nanomagical care packages—little psychic sprays of good feeling with a payload of neurotransmitter boosters.

Fernando was placidly alert and broadcasting to all around him the appearance of an enlightened sage as, during the flight, he listened to Brinen talk and watched her expressive mouth move, her wide dark pink lips rising, receding, and rearranging around that pleasing gap between her teeth. Brinen talked about her family in Mina: five brothers, all older and none in the military, but each part-owners in a food-export business that had been thriving—until now, when no one knew what would happen—and one younger sister still in school. Along with her parents, all the brothers' wives (two brothers had multiple wives), and her platoon of nephews and nieces, the Malroy clan were all taking ship, still the most reliable way of getting across the ocean.

The original thought, Brinen said, had been to flee south like so many others in Mina were doing—hence the choked roads—but Brinen's grandmother had insisted they take the oversea route. Brinen's grandmother Nana Grace Malroy was ninety but still very sharp-minded and hale. (This was the Gaish word Brinen used, "hale"; Fernando wondered if there were some corresponding word commonly used in Glish for which "hale" was the translation, since he couldn't imagine any native Gaish speaker using such an archaic adjective.) Brinen's Nana was a very traditional woman but had come into her power in the family once her overbearing husband had conveniently died of a heart attack a decade ago. Now everybody in the family listened to Nana Grace. And Nana Grace had said go west. Nana Grace was a proper Truegodder, but not always; sometimes Brinen had seen her pull a little altar out of her enormous closet stuffed with clothes, and she would chant and pray before it: an altar to the spirit of her head, Ayayá. Ayayá was the Spirit-Lord of the raging sea, and it was Ayayá, Brinen suspected, who had told her to hie the whole family west. (She said "hie," too. Glish speakers speaking Gaish make for oddities.)

Fernando liked listening to stories of Nana Grace's imposing will and lacerating tongue. He imagined that he would be telling stories like that of his own mother, if the police hadn't killed her.

"Of course, we all hope to come back one day," Brinen said uncertainly, looking directly at Elias.

As it turned out, Brinen's family was Elias's, too, in a way. They were fiancés, having become engaged several months ago. The Ministry had been kind enough to assign them to the same duty, as of yesterday.

Elias said nothing about his own relatives, other than that they were down south. He kept his face aimed at the empty sky outside the window.

Brinen spoke warmly of her family, and with concern, but Fernando observed a distance in her manner, too, an inch of cool removal from what she was saying. It was numbness, shell-shock, Fernando guessed. She was watching her world fall to pieces around her, rapidly, inexplicably. The scale of destruction, the measure of the impending losses, not only to people and wealth but to ways of life, perhaps to possibilities of living at all, were so incalculable that she could not fully countenance it, she could only buffer herself with an inch of removal that she wouldn't feel, and that inch would have to absorb the impact of what would otherwise overwhelm her.

Meanwhile Brinen retreated into hopes that her youngest niece, born just six weeks past, would soon develop the muscular skill to hold up her fat little head on her own, because it would be wearying for her mother, Brinen's sister-in-law, to keep holding the child's head up in the crowded quarters of the refugee ships, where they probably wouldn't find a decent crib for her to use.

Perhaps, Fernando thought with a chill, it was not only the world of Brinen and her family and the nation of Negali that was coming to its end.

Perhaps it was the whole world on the brink, and the End of Everything was now rolling inexorably to the coasts of the Motherlands, while Zilia and the west were content to diddle itself with its eyes closed to events elsewhere. If this was the Great Gods—

And here they were, flying into the maw of the invasions' mouth.

Is it Them? Fernando wondered miserably.

Your slave does not know, Hieronymus-Theodoric replied. *But all evidence suggests it is.*

Without command, knowing what it was tasked to do, Hiernoymus-Theodoric, the best of slaves, took hold of Fernando's mind and body: it diluted his fear and restored to him, like a mountain rising from the drowning sea, the vision of his purpose. This was the why of Fernando's lineage, decided by a long-ago foremother and long-ago forefather.[1]

Through all the stumbles and failures, all the going astray, all the defeats and too-early deaths, the purpose of the lineage did not alter: bargain, beg, steal what or with whom you must, for more knowledge; through knowledge, gain more power; with enough power, survive; once survival is secured, seek more knowledge to have the power to do what is right.

But doing right was a small thing, a kind of tidying, just buckling up the belts of the world and tying its shoelaces. The long-ago foremother and long-ago forefather made a pact: when you have the power and the knowledge to do right, then comes the true purpose. To *correct.*

A terrible, terrible wrong has been committed. It has been baked into the stone, eaten in the bread. Correct it. And correc-

---

1   Though this reference makes it sound otherwise, these two beginners of the lineage were not coupled, were not a mother and father who reproduced *together,* but, rather, siblings. I do not mean to imply any incest, either. A little-known fact—wholly unknown, of course, to You—is that the two were both mostly queer. This fact is an important part of their story, which I will not recount here.

tion means not only creating anew, it means holding the wrong-doers to account.

If to correct you need to reshape, then reshape. If to correct you need to break, then break.

Why are you flying into the mouth of Holocaust? the gentle voice of Hieronymus resounded in Fernando's thoughts, vibrated in his body's cells. *Why do you contend against the Great Gods?*

To correct Their wrongs. Break Them, if possible. By any means necessary.

ALEIXO'S STORY

*2048, Primeiro (the Month of Bright Air),
Quarta night & Quinta morning*

That night they gave me a room in the Palace.

When we returned, it was still only late evening, scarcely ten o'clock. The time didn't seem right. My impression was that I had been imprisoned and then interrogated for at least two or three hours if not longer; and then that it had taken another hour afterward, first, to make our way back to the innocuous confines of the little prison room (the very anodyne appearance of which made it, still, a terror to me), and then (to my great relief), to climb out of the dark bowels of the building and back to the domain of the living.

But I supposed this was another consequence of the uncanny magic by which I'd been stolen out of time and then returned to it. It didn't occur to me to ask more about this peculiarity, this crimp, as it were, in the flow of time which, however uneven it seems, with some things seeming to go faster and others slower, nevertheless seems always to flow forward and in a straight line. I should have asked about it—asked Sílvio, or even the Princess who hated me. If they'd told me the truth, even a part, I might have been saved some of the terror that awaited me.

I failed to ask what I should, however. I kept circumspect, given that I knew quite well the Princess wanted me dead and that I did not want to be dead.

Meeker than is my wont, I followed their lead. I was not led back to the fête, nor, once we had cleared the lowest level of the prison quarters, did I have further discourse with the Princess or Sílvio, who passed me off to the care of a Black Guard without so much as a parting glance, and without any further warnings.

I was glad to see them go. But my new escort was as communicative as they. She led me to yet another unimaginably large floor and wing of the Palace, directed me to toilet facilities and a bath, apprised me of a cabinet containing a more-than-ample supply of towels, and flung open the door to a wide room of crisp flagstone floors and splashy wall paintings. My guide herself did not pass the room's threshold, as though under command not to sully its refined ground with her plebeian boots.

I hesitated before entering, fearing a similar outcome to my previous experience with a Black Guard. But swift inspection, and the fact that I was not locked in, indicated that I was now being treated as a guest rather than as a prisoner.

These clearly were not the basic overnight accommodations we servers had been offered when hired.

I didn't see anyone else anywhere on the floor. I had a whole suite to myself, with a high piled bed, and windows set in the rock walls all around that looked out over the ocean—an expanse of ominous black which I avoided after a time because it made me feel I was looking out on some bleak endless future, or on gathered armies whose grim faces and weapons would only become apparent in daylight.

But the bed was more comfortable than any I had ever been in, and after a while, and against my better judgment, I began to feel a bit relaxed, even shyly triumphant, ensconced within its soft, almost caressing luxury. I even wondered whether I was to be treated as rich guests would be. Maybe it wouldn't be too long before I would hear the door slide into its wall-pocket, and see amid the patches of night gathered in the gloom a curvaceous form arrive, musk-scented and pleasure-built, glowing slightly blue.

But then I remembered that a slave would not be sent to pleasure another slave. And though I could not yet fold my mind into the chafing corners of the box that said I-Alexander-am-a-dream-slave, I had enough logic still to know that a slave's pleasure was an oxymoron.

I imagine it may not surprise you to learn that after the shock of luxury had worn off—too soon—I shut the door to my room, lay fully clothed in the bed between sheets and covers, and kept very still.

It seemed only seconds before I became like some animal bred to life in the polar regions that husbands the meager heat of its body against the infinity of cold pressing in upon it: unmoving, unmoved, waiting.

To think about anything that had been said, anything that had been done that night—I could not, not yet.

A sluggish thought told me to call my mother, that Arlina was an hour behind Norio and she might not yet be asleep, and that if I talked to her I might reassure myself that nothing I knew of my own history had been altered by the cryptic judgments of spies and magical-minded slaves, that I was still who I had been, and what I always was.

But the impetus to such action died quickly. It seemed futile. My mother would not be able to convince me she knew the truth. And, for all that I really knew at that moment, she herself might know I was a slave, she might even have conspired in the making of me and might have prepared me, all my life, for the commission of some act of espionage as yet unrevealed.

No, better not to consider the implications, the prolific permutations, not yet.

Impossible to do so, anyway. I was exhausted to the bones.

I pushed off the covers, pulled off my pants and socks and shirt, and then threw myself back on a hillside of pillows.

I was about to close my eyes when a sixth sense—a slave's magical sense?—prompted me to sit up and look to the window nearest the bed's left side.

But it was nothing to be frightened of. The two pairs of eyes watching me belonged to a mother monkey and her cub (or whatever one calls a baby monkey).

In the dark they were like globs of shadow prickled with grassy hair, and had something of the appearance of oversized, mutant rats.

Most animals do not perceive the granite face of the Loaf as anything other than rock. You could see gulls land on what we saw as a window, and snakes slither across slicks of light beaming from within the Palace without any apparent apprehension of danger. But the monkeys were not deceived. They crowded around the kitchen windows, for instance, perhaps puzzling over their inability to lay hands on the food they could clearly see, and maybe even smell, a few tantalizing feet away.

I matched stares with the monkey mother and child, wanting to drive them off without having to throw something at the window or jump on the bed and make scary faces. How did they see me?

I wondered then if the truth of the matter were not opposite to what we humans thought we knew. That it was not that the monkeys were too smart to be deceived like their brethren in the animal kingdom, but that they were as much victims of deception as we were. Maybe they too were dazzled by glamour, seduced by magic, unable to tell the difference between seeming and being. Perhaps such failures at perceiving reality, such predilections for illusion, were what most linked humans to simians. And humans to what Sílvio call "embodied beings."

To which company, evidently, I did not even actually belong.

You, too, are a dream-slave, he'd said to me. *It* had said to me.

I pulled the covers over my head, and let the monkey family stare for I don't know how long.

I slept till shortly after dawn. The suite's windows were east-facing. Presumably this was where the Palace staff placed guests that they didn't want to linger too late in the morning.

Horrible Sílvio met me shortly after I had showered and dressed and gobbled down a small plate of sliced sweet fruit, which had miraculously appeared in my room. (I am certain no one entered, and that the plate hadn't been there the night previous. Magic? The fruit tasted good, non-poisonous, and not the least like an illusion.)

The Princess's favorite slave was attired in all black now, a kind of looser, softer version of the Black Guard's form-fitting armor, as though it were dressed to perform a scolding at a boardroom meeting. With infuriatingly avuncular good humor it handed me an address that shone brightly in a piece of magicked glass, told me that I was to go to a house there the next day at eight in the morning. Someone or other it was important to report to would be waiting.

Uncle Slave then advised me not to tarry for breakfast, as the first ferry had already gone back to the mainland, and the second was leaving in a mere ten minutes.

"You have a great deal to do today," it said, fussing about the room as though it were eager for me to depart so that it could thoroughly cleanse the place of my presence. "It cannot be any surprise to you that as one who is to be trained in intelligence work by the Chief Intelligencer, you will need to permanently vacate the domicile you now occupy with all your belongings—however meager these must be—and make haste to locate yourself in some place more conducive to privacy. Not," Sílvio's voice rose, "however, at the address with which I have provided you." It looked down its nose at me and affected a look of especial scrutiny. "Might the Princess's slave add that it would be very unwise to attempt to leave the City. Or to go into hiding, or to in any way defy the instructions she has given you. You have been released on your own recognizance, by the wishes of the Prince. But this does not mean you are out of reckoning. Or beyond seizing, should seizing become necessary."

This was the first lesson in my education in the rhetorical and theatrical games of Sílvio, who enjoyed making alarming announcements in words and tone foreclosing any demonstration of alarm. Later editions of this same formulation intensified the lesson, as when it said—taking a moment to delicately fold its hands on its stomach with an air of impregnable complacency—"It cannot be other than a confirmation of your expectations that your execution by firing squad has been ordered, and that it has been scheduled for tomorrow morning. Nighty-night."

This calamitous turn of events lay yet in my unguessed future, however. Fortunately, I didn't yet know how bad things could get, and so I was actually in something of a provisional good mood when I mounted the 08:10 ferry that morning.

This ferry was in the form of a flying balcony. I stood at its railing along with several of the other servers as we skimmed the short distance to the beach, towed through the breeze and the great gouts of morning fog still thickening the heights above the City, by a quartet of jewelry-gold-colored slaves fashioned in the shapes of cherubs. Their wings made a sound like droning flies.

A good night's sleep had put me in a somewhat better frame of mind. A more delusional frame of mind, perhaps, but certainly less suicidal. As I took to the street leading from Red Beach into the thickets of the city and surveyed the nearly empty lanes of Paraíso Avenue, and as I saw the few folk astir passing under the eaves of the trees posted all along the sidewalks, a sort of jaunty mood took me.

I caught the smell of morning in my nostrils. The tang of cleanliness brined the air—soon of course to be sullied with a vengeance. It was briefly, fragilely quiet now, compared to the harangue and clatter of later hours, almost monastic, as if not just the city, but the whole world of which the city was its heart, were gathering itself up, drawing in a breath before the gun and the sprint.

In that quiet, awash in that aroma, what seemed to stretch out before me was—almost; almost I could believe it—wondrous, exciting.

Everything now would be new. Everything would *have* to be new. In a way, it was as though in a single night I had been reborn.

I was not what I was. I was now—something else. And who could say whether that something else was not better than what I'd been?

My thoughts began to mount higher. I was grateful now I hadn't called my mother to try to find my way back to the old me, the paltry old Alexander from Peake's Bay, fleeing a minor felony charge and some bad jail time (not that any jail time for anyone is ever good).

Was it joy I felt beating in my blood? It seemed new to me, strange to me, because I rarely experienced joy, could not remember, at that moment, if I ever had.

I was, as I had always wished, as now it was proved I had always *known,* truly special. If what and who I was, and what my purpose might be, were vast mysteries, deep black parsecs of celestial sky that nearby light did not reach, so much the better, because it meant I was greater than what I knew. It meant that rather than the terrible shrinking lesser being I had always secretly feared I was, I was truly *someone.* Something Meant To Be Powerful.

Hadn't the Princess herself said so? And I had fought off her psychic invasion without even knowing I'd done so, or how.

Never mind that a humiliating recollection had been the means of defense and counter-attack. I was nothing if not self-serving in my youth, and mentally nimble enough to skip over the ugly bits.

So what if being powerful and singular meant I was a dream-slave, and that what I was meant to be was all to some mysterious other person's purpose? The latter wasn't much different than what the hierophants said of the whole world in their sermons in church. Are we not all the servants of the One True God? Is not fate already the fulfillment of God's own plan?

And no, it didn't seem strange to me at all that last night (or whenever) the Chief Intelligencer of the realm had dubbed me a dangerous spy, and that today I was free to go apartment-hunting.

Dumb as a doorknob Aleixo. Blame it on an immature fore-brain.

With this kind of cognitive acumen, I was able to work my way into such an optimistic lather that it seemed no more than a few minutes and a hummed dance-song or two before I found myself a mile or two east of the beach, having passed out of the shabby hucksterish Bana neighborhood into the outer blocks of kinder, gentler Nema and its high-toned high-rises.

More trees, more shrubbery, and sidewalk squares heaped high with long-limbed greenery and flowers in holiday colors slanted arrogantly across my vision. The wide boulevard I'd been walking narrowed and tributaried off into a dozen quiet streets, while the boulevard itself turned into two lanes—both nearly empty now—and curved to make way for a steep, imposing hill.

I walked to the base of the hill. It seemed to spring up from the earth out of nothing, like a boulder that had been dropped in transit across the plains.

I read on a dirt-filmed white and blue sign that I was entering Ribeiro Park.

Once the site of a compact slum with an outsized reputation for violence and terror, and the first of many blighted hillside and mountainside neighborhoods of the poor to be "reclaimed" and beautified almost two centuries ago, Ribeiro was now a nature preserve.

It was also the home of one of the great fountains which have made Norio the world's treasure.

Broad deep concrete stairs mounted the hard angle upward from the sign, and about twenty yards up I could see the top-most quarter of a fountain spire through a gap in a ring of arching trees, which were planted on a terrace, their backs pushing against still steeper inclines rising behind. At this early hour the fountain provided only a burble and spray of hydrogen and oxygen rather than the elixir all of us so craved.

The leap of hunger in my belly and groin kept me from exploring further, and I started looking around for somewhere to have a proper breakfast.

Water is probably one of the greatest differences between Your World and This World. In This World, we all feel a craving when near Water. For anyone who's had Water often enough, the sharp ache of desire springs to life even if you just imagine bending your mouth to its flow, or its drops sinking into the pores of your skin. Such cravings, if you can't get Water itself, usually send all but the most disciplined clamoring for kitchen and restaurant.

That is, all who were *human*. For humans, exposure to Water brings, on the prosaic side, health, healing of ills, procreative fecundity, and subtle, sometimes gross, restitching of mental threads that create a surfeit of well-being. Its poetic effects are far more fantastic, far more magical. This part of the effects of Water brings a surge of high spirits that can, for the over-indulgent, lead to exhaustion, intoxication, and even, though far more rarely than journalists would have you believe, temporary insanity. For humans.

For dream-slaves? It's supposed to have no effect whatsoever on them. Water, the sole magical element readily accessible to untrained corporeal senses, is meaningless to slaves, so much so that in all the many things doctors, social commentators, comedians, preachers, journalists, and scholars have said about Water, almost no one has ever said, joked, warned, reported, or studied anything about the effect of Water on dream-slaves. Why should they? Slaves are not alive and not human, and slaves are creatures of magic, fully as much as Water is a substance of magic. They are different sorts of magic, yes, but—

I had taken Water. I had felt its rush, its glories. I felt the craving *now*.

Would my maker have been *that* clever, to create false cravings, to craft a slave that would mimic human responses to Water?

It seemed unlikely. But perhaps no more unlikely than a maker building a dream-slave that could live more than a few months or a few years.

Perplexity and doubt nagged me and threatened to tumble me off my I'm-really-special-after-all high. Seeking refuge from myself, I turned away from the park and its fountain and scanned the block of shops bending away behind the hill.

Most shops were closed, but catty-corner to where I stood, a bald, copper-complexioned man wearing a tank top that bulged with a gut earned by unrepentant good living rolled up an accordion gate, and then another perpendicular to it, revealing a small, two-winged bar wrapped around the corner where the boulevard divided. The place was perfectly situated for watching the fountain.

I walked slowly over as the man shifted tables onto the sidewalk and moved chairs out of a dark space behind the high L of the counter, and as a woman who was portly as him but with more plumage emerged from inside to begin prodding various machines into action.

No slaves worked there, at least not at this hour.

I somewhat sheepishly mounted a stool at the bar and smiled. The air was still cool and biting.

The portly woman seemed to regard me with favor despite my early arrival. Her air of approval proved conditional once I ordered a flight of sugarcane liquor shots with lime, however.

"Best not to start drinking away your troubles till after noon," she said, wagging her portly finger close to my nose. She spoke in a high voice that made me imagine she was a very large bird.

A brief moment later though, she pushed the first three dwarf glasses my way, and I got too busy draining them to defend myself against charges of being a drunkard.

And what if I was a drunk? Dream-slaves aren't drunks; they can't be.

I ordered another flight, my spirits struggling back above the waterline as I beckoned for more.

ISABEL'S STORY

2048, 7th of Primeiro (the Month of Bright Air),
Quinta, 0948 hours

Isabel told her ministers, secretaries, commissioners, and chief operatives to fuck off.

She didn't stay long enough to watch the reactions flickering across their faces. Not that it was likely their faces would have indicated any reaction at all. These were the lords of the House of the Winged Serpent, after all, schooled to the appearance of perfect impassivity, if to nothing actually useful. Isabel didn't have to watch them to know what they felt — and her slaves would report to her all the hormonal and blood-pressure surges that they had been able to monitor later anyway, in case there were indications that there was information the ministers may have withheld. (She'd given up long ago trying to telepathically scan any of them; their slaves kept their thoughts too well warded.)

The Winged Serpent lords were outraged, surely, or they were disdainful or disgusted or even amused. But above all they were too greatly beset by the same worries that frustrated their chief to fret over yet another royal storm-out. There were crises to quell, approaching disasters from which the ship of state must be averted. Isabel's skills did not as a rule embrace the management of such matters, so she left them to the seasoned careerists, the professional spooks and strategic planners, and they in turn simply kept her informed of what they decided was best to do.

Princess Isabel was by nature a leader in battle, a warrior. Give her an enemy and she would advance upon him and vanquish him, zestfully. Aim her at a target and she would deliver the bullet, or the blast of infernal fire, or the terrifying wave of psychic devastation. Upon her cousin's election, she had been rewarded for her support of his candidacy by the high council of their Affinity the office of Chief Intelligencer, Prince's Right Hand.

But the job didn't much suit her, and Isabel knew it.

Isabel marched smartly through the corridor outside the 112th-floor conference room. She glowered dangerously at any staff with the temerity to look at her, and swept toward the lift that was marked WINGED SERPENT in thick, deliberately unpretty letters. Its door, which was alive, opened its single eye when it perceived her footfall and, in the time it took to blink, ascertained that the sugars and nucleic acid codes of her blood were those it had been programmed to recognize. The eye in the door, disconcertingly human and washed-out-denim blue in appearance, receded into black as the door split, reforming into two planes like thin walls which extended themselves from the lift bay as though they were pincers, and gently ushered her inside.

There in the lift's arms she felt the joy that had never yet diminished, of rising upward on the air, with nothing around her but the metallic walls of the shaft. Her predecessor, in a mood either of humor or of reverie, had decorated these walls with chimera holographs of far distant nebulae and bright, dying stars. This work of beauty was heartbreaking, because only one person at a time in the world would ever see it.

Isabel sighed, and in sighing felt her powerlessness ebb as she rose through the air. Isabel could levitate on her own for a short distance, if she prepared by drinking a tea steeped with tiny globes of the dried and powdered ichor of one of her slaves manufactured to donate the gift of temporary flight. Or she could do so under the influence of Water. But she preferred the sensations of the building's lift to those other modes of levitation, which despite their marvels required athletic strain. Here all was effortless, here she could feel what magic really should feel like, and almost never did: that she didn't do magic, she *was* magic. She was become lighter than air, a helium being too fine for the meshes of gravity.

The lift opened onto a dark penthouse, which was suspended by Unseen means well above the rooftop of the nigh-impossibly tall building that was the Winged Serpent's headquarters. Isabel slipped off her shoes — the lift door, like a fish mouth, gulped them into its flat depths — and walked toward the center of a deep-walled and broad-floored expanse at first illuminated no higher than her knees. The soles of her feet were caressed, and queried, by the ebullient naps of the carpet, wherein patterns wove and rewove themselves as she walked.

By the time she'd reached the carpet's center, the smart-room had determined what she wished of it. Four windows, east, west, north, and south sprung up, tall as old trees, limpid as fresh tide-pools. Without sashes or muntins they appeared to be something like, but were actually other than, glass: fully translucent panes of both air and gem, some primordial ideal substance which the gods had sought to mimic when they played with lightning and sand. Light clamored in.

Isabel saw clouds lapping the bottom of the panes, and thin washed blue up higher. The ceiling, however, was an abyss: this, she knew, was where the power sources were stored. If she had been the room's Maker, she would have chosen differently — have made the lift door and shaft bear the burden of the power storage, have the room's roof, too, open its face to the heavens.

Good thing, she thought, *that I'm an intelligencer and not an architect.* For if the penthouse had been built to her preferences, she or whoever was unlucky enough to serve as Chief Intelligencer would no doubt have been abducted, or more likely killed outright, the unhappy moment she alighted from the lift. The penthouse's Makers — the techs who'd made the slave or slaves that built it — had known what they were about. They knew that the Great Gods prowl high up, just above the ring of the ionosphere. Without the protection of a roof like this one, the Great Gods could not only find you, They could get their greedy fingers on (and inside) you, too.

No doubt They were already aware of Isabel's presence, and were stooped over her now, wondering and ravening, prevented from eating her only by the shielding of the power-source in the roof, which was not of This World, and not of Their World, either. It would conceal her for a finite time.

For a moment there in the room's center she let the carpet weaving play at calculating possibilities for her. It might be worth knowing which ones of the celestials were watching. It might be worth, even, trying to strike up a little chat. Though They gave information only to suit Their own purposes, it was not unheard of to be able to query the divinities without being ridden by Them: her own teacher, Saint-Father Hercule, had done so, with great benefit to her Affinity.

And since possibly it was one of Them who'd sent the thing — the slave, that wretched slave creature, *Aleixo* — then why not go to the source and ask the questions that needed to be asked?

The soles of her feet were getting hot. The penthouse's way of telling her it couldn't accommodate such a level of calculation. You'd need a truly majestic slave like Sílvio to have made a room capable of calculations complicated enough to identify the Great Gods aware of her and to propose a strategy for conversing with Them.

Isabel let the idea drop.

She had come here for other purposes: Admittedly part of it was to escape the tedium of an executive council meeting that had produced not even a glimmer of traction for security problems which ought not to have been intractable, but were. Mostly though, she wanted to pursue a notion that had been pricking her since her idiot cousin had destroyed her favorite safe-house.

Amaro had said he didn't believe the Arionese could have sent the slave-creature to them. The Prince was not unconvincing on the subject, when Isabel considered the question: the War of Hours, desperate and calamitous as it had been at the time, had ultimately demonstrated that Rioca tech had no peer in the world. It was the victory in that war that facilitated the rise to prominence of Amaro's weapon-making family. Amaro's great-uncle was the one who discovered how to turn the Wall that spanned the planet's greatest ocean into a weapon. His discovery had saved them all from the Great Gods, who desired more than anything to ride their flesh, just as They rode — and consumed — the bodies of all those living in the east.

But This World had been recovering from the damage of weaponizing the storms ever since. Isabel resented this — despite the fact that she was bound to Amaro and his uncle, and a member of the family herself now by rites of Affinity.

The Arionese were in the service of the Great Gods. They lived, and thrived, because they had made some bargain with Them. All the reports from the Rioca spies in Far Arion beyond the Wall confirmed this — before, that is, the reports ceased some years ago.

And the Great Gods, driven as They seemed indefatigably to be to search out footholds in This World, wily and puissant as They were in Their Own spheres, could not be assumed to be incapable of crafting a device such as a nineteen-year-old slave. They had not shown a capacity to do so *before,* true, but the past said nothing of now — particularly when one considered the strategies of divinities, for whom time surely passed differently than for us. Perhaps it had been only an instant, Great God Standard Time, since the War of Hours some fifty years ago ended?

And though the Great Gods were barred by universal laws few could fathom from breaking into This World, might They not be capable of imparting to the servants They ride the power to make such a thing as a slave that was to all appearances human?

Rioca spies had suggested that whole armies of men were ridden by the divinities. The cost in human life evidently was staggering, but if the Arionese were willing victims, if whole nations of them were drunk with religious zealotry, couldn't the Great Gods mount and ride an army's worth of folk sensitive to the Unseen, incipient sorcerous talents who, had they been born in Norio, would have been guild-masters or techs in the greatest Affinities? Even if to do so might lead to the deaths of hundreds of thousands, if the Greats would thus be capable of building powerful weapons, would They not do so? Even if it was just *one* powerful weapon?

Isabel worried. If the slave were an opening salvo, or an advance scout...

She needed to see if the empire's eastern enemies, the Arionese, were on the move.

Isabel commanded the panes to show her quadrants one through four of the southern latitudes up to the equator. She would find a better view here than in any of the House's onshore observation stations, because the satellite array was closer to the Winged Serpent's headquarters than to the stations, and because the interference created by the Wall diminished a little as atmospheric limits approached.

Naturally there were several scores of very skilled observation slaves built by very skilled techs in her very own Affinity, whose sole semi-living purpose was to watch and record what the penthouse panes now showed her. And there were two squadrons of Green Guard signal corps whose collective job it was to monitor what the skilled slaves had monitored, and to collate and archive the monitoring of these monitors, a task in which they were aided by a multitude of machines both magical in nature and mechanical. And there was, too, a small hierarchy of intelligence officers in the great House of the Winged Serpent, so well entwined and attuned to one another that they were like fingers of a single dexterous hand, amongst whose most sacred duties it was to note and analyze anomalies observed by slaves and signal squadrons, and to report any such anomaly that rose to the level of significance to her, their Chief, in whose hands lay all their livelihoods and indeed their lives.

All of this great apparatus, built like the pyramids over the long years, existed just in order to stand sentry against activity along the Wall of Storms, which stretched, like some great world-encircling worm, from pole to pole, the whole length of the Eastern Ocean. Entire hemispheres of the slaves' brains had been dedicated to such a purpose.

And here Isabel was looking with her eyes. What could she expect to see that they had not seen?

The panes divided and subdivided into sectors of the quadrants. Each showed some variant of the same: gray and black clouds muscling down to meet hill-high waves. The violence of surf and sough. Light banished, but for twisted twigs of lightning which raged incandescent for a thrilling moment before being swallowed by the maw. From pole to pole, from the face of the sea to the brows of heaven, the Wall reached and climbed.

Lower, the Wall looked thick with fury. Higher it grew thinner and thinner. Once the sunlight had reclaimed its own above the clouds it was often too bright to see the Wall's tendrils of lightning — which were not truly lightning (though they might as well have been, with all their wanton ways), but were writhing gouts and torrents of electromagnetic disturbance that would reduce an airplane to ash or scissor a steel-clad missile in two if anybody in This World were still foolish enough to fly or launch one of them that high.

For five hundred years or more these storms had raged, half-blinding one hemisphere to the other. Ships that dared cross — desperate for commerce, conquest, or refuge, or to reunite sundered families or separated lovers, bulked though they might be with the heaviest armor and the most powerful engines and the sturdiest ballast and the most discerning navigational computational equipment — and even submarines piloted by robots that dived into the bowels of underwater trenches hitherto unplumbed — typically did not survive. Or if they did pass — and many did, though the number that successfully completed the crossing dwindled with each passing decade — they came to landings far, far from those intended — even, some of Isabel's best techs yet believed, casting ashore not only in other times but on other Worlds, other planes of reality.

The storms, or their precursors, might have been there for millennia. Accounts of the earliest crossings from the old world in the East in the fourteenth century duly record the belt of storms, and the most famous mariners of the age were famous precisely because they could navigate a ship through them and survive. No one knew why or how the storms had acquired the intensity that began to make passage nearly impossible. The transformation, when it happened at the end of the nineteenth century, was swift and devastating: in a mere decade, rainfall swelled every body of water, and floods and rising tides ate whole coastlines. At the same time the sun seemed to have keyed open the ozone, and deserts spread, glaciers melted, and winter hardly seemed winter, no matter which latitude you went searching for it.

Fossil fuel fumes had been blamed for the ever-cresting heat. But fossil fuels did not explain the storms becoming in almost literal truth the Wall poets and braggart mariners had made it in centuries past. The storms unfurled themselves across the whole of the Eastern Ocean as though together they comprised some great climatological beast emerging from a chrysalis of eons. That clearly was a phenomenon of sorcery: a consequence of the discovery of what giddy journalists and eager governments first called the New New World, and what we all later understood to be the Passage Between This World and the Next, what we now call the Bridge. This was the time on the threshold of modernity, when humans began to tap the energy resource that was magic.

One hundred fifty years ago workers of the Unseen found the Passage Between in the worlds of spirit and ether. Seemingly in answer, the earth intensified the storms between the eastern and western hemispheres. And then the dream-slaves were made.

Such seemed the inexorable sequence, and an operation of cause-and-effect too blunt to explain away.

(In Arlina our priests thought they comprehended the process and its meaning clearly. The priests claimed this was nature and un-nature at war, the One True God whose works are the bounty of the earth versus the demons and pretenders to divinity to which the dream-lords of Norio sold their souls.)

For the last fifty years, since the clever doings of Amaro's great-uncle, the Wall had been worse: transformed by his sorcery into a weapon to repel a determined invasion by an undead or robotic flotilla from the east, the storms now had eyes, and tongues. Anything that moved or was living the storms lashed, tortured, mangled, crushed, and consumed. Anything that tried even to *think* in their vicinity, the Wall of Storms burned or crushed. This was learned on both sides of the Wall as a consequence of subsequent acts less clever than those of Amaro's great-uncle, when intrepid members of governments east and west, as well as independent tech-consortiums and other idiots desperate to find markets and make more money, tried to pierce the barrier by psychic means or with well-made slaves which were, after all, not truly living. They found their psychic constructs destroyed (and unluckily, often the psychics' minds along with them), or their slaves simply rendered defunct.

Nothing could cross now. The great crossings of old, from which their ancestors had come, were now of such faded history they were almost myth. To reach the Mother Continent or Arcady you had to take flight or sail west till you reached Pon and then cross the great land mass beyond its jeweled isles.

In the penthouse, Isabel commanded the room to remind her upon leaving to ask Sílvio: *Couldn't we kill the mystery slave by sending it to the Wall?*

Except... Except a dream-slave could not function for nineteen years, or link with ease and of its own apparent volition to a mind of Isabel's learning and skill. A slave could simulate life without having it, and it might well even believe itself human, if this amused some perverse Maker. But did this creature, this Aleixo-thing, truly possess thoughts that the Wall would register? Perhaps the simulation operated at a more subtle level than Isabel could divine. And who knew? Perhaps this Aleixo-thing was durable, too, perhaps its substance could transmute, become like the heavy blubber flesh of the whales and whale sharks which *did* somehow occasionally cross — so some marine scientists claimed, though many didn't believe them — far below in the depths of the sea. If Isabel had knifed Aleixo, as she'd meant to, perhaps the blade would have broken, or sunk flaccid and harmless in fatty, spongy folds...?

(I was, as you may imagine, outraged and mortified by this train of the Princess's thought. If there is one thing I cannot abide being described as, it is fat. In any case the Princess's worries were all heat and little logic, since it was only a fringe theory that whales could cross the Wall.

But I was somewhat happier with the next set of thoughts...)

The worst thing — why lie to a smart-room? it could figure out what you thought anyway — the worst thing, and no, she didn't want to think about it, she didn't *have to,* but she might as well acknowledge it here and dispense with thinking about it for a while — the worst thing was that she kind of fancied the damn thing. Him. It. Whatever.

Not that it was at all unusual to lust after a slave. Many if not most of them were built precisely to arouse such passions. Isabel's cousin-like-a-sister Sebastiana had commissioned so many eros-slaves built to her specifications, and then worn them out long before she was ready to be done with them, that she'd taken to going down to the tech-auctions on Sexta mornings and just buying any old cheap used model with decent genitalia and whichever shapeliness of body she craved at the time, boxing it

163

up, bringing it home, and gussying it up to provide her a week's temporary fix.

Now it's me, who's supposed to be the sensible one, who's got the family disease.

Isabel frowned as she watched one panel in her window flood with wave and spume. *I'm just another Amaro, a man ruled by the balls between his legs, like any farmyard goat.*

It was demeaning to pine for a slave. Not that Isabel was truly pining for him. But even to have the thing prey on one's thoughts this way, to *want* it rather than simply demand it, to expect something of one's self to be — fulfilled — by its actions. To desire the kiss, the touch, the smell, the locked-eyes-with-one's-own look, of a slave, of a thing?

Isabel was not a religious woman. Dream-techs, as a rule, were not.

But she worried that the frankness of her desire for the slave violated something sacred, that she was crossing a line it was dangerous to cross. This wasn't a regular slave. He was — the thing was obscene.

Isabel's feeling was somehow higher and deeper than lust. Sebastiana treated the slaves she used as what they were — ingeniously done up sex things. Sex *workers* except they weren't working, they were made to do what they did. Sebastiana didn't *care* anything about them.

Whereas I...

Isabel shuddered. More than ever now she was determined to kill the thing, power it down, scrap it, and study its parts.

Riding the surge of her anger and self-disgust, Isabel told the sanctum observatory to rise higher, though she knew this was dangerous, and that the construct could not maintain its position for long.

For brief periods — the House of the Winged Serpent had never risked more than five minutes, and rarely pushed beyond three — the room could link its observations to those of a satellite which had long ago in the days of the first tech operations been secreted in a kind of nook at one of the myriad joints between This World and the Next.

(These terms of construction and spatiality are, of course, not accurate descriptions, for this particular satellite was not a satellite possessing mechanical widgets or motors, nor did it exist in a physical orbit, let alone in a something possessing joints. But while Isabel would have been capable of discoursing on the matter using more arcane technical language, she did not in truth think of the "satellite" in terms other than this, because she did not consciously *think* of its operations at all: her understanding of it and her command over its functions, upon her ascension to office and endurance of the office's days-long rites, had been woven into the structure of her psyche, traveling along almost reflexively with the firing of her neurons. Her thoughts about it weren't thoughts, they were autonomic. She no more cognized this "satellite" in clear descriptive terms than you or I think clear-sightedly of the bend or crook or angle of our fingers as they race across the keyboard, or of the tiny muscular movements of our eyeballs as they turn, rise, and lower to scan a page.)

To raise the penthouse so high was to risk exposing oneself even as one tried to observe: and for this reason neither Isabel's slaves nor her signals corps nor her intelligence officers climbed to such a nest. The benefits also were few: the upper-atmosphere disturbance created by the presence of the Great Gods prevented seeing much in the east, and always had done, so what you did see was fragmentary at best.

Still, it was possible to see just beyond the Wall of Storms, and if nothing else to observe a strip of the seas on the other side. She remembered from the two other times she'd risked it, that it was a bit like she imagined it would be for an ant that crawls all the way to the top of a shower door and trains its senses on what appears to be a great abyss beneath and beyond: the antennae fail, there's too much to take in.

Isabel told herself she'd be no more than a minute.

The panes brightened rapidly. Too quickly. In another moment the light would be unbearable.

No one would ever be afraid of the dark if they experienced the light here. We would all of us crave dark, love it, worship it, once subjected to the merciless cruelty of the light at the joint between Worlds.

Isabel angled the eyes of the room downward.

It took a moment, maybe three or four, before she could see anything other than the bright shading off into gray and black and the shifting restless waves.

But now look!

A God was there.

One does not see well the Great Gods with naked eyes.

Foolishly, because she hadn't planned to come to the penthouse but had gone on a whim, Isabel had not brought with her the goggles and taste-and-hearing enhancers that made the divinities truly observable.

Still, if one knew what to look for, seeing one of the Great is like looking at a scene through the sheerest translucent curtain: only when the breeze makes the curtain move do you see that there is something there, occluding your vision.

She could make it out: hundreds of feet tall. Larger probably; its massive legs rose up out of the waves, and so where were its feet?

The curves of a body wafted in and out of vision. The thick line of a torso tapering to the valley of a waist, the flare of a hip. Powerful mountain-embracing arms.

This one had three heads, and long cascades of filament obscured what little could be discerned, and then quickly lost, of its faces and its many bright eyes.

Three heads, long hair. This might be... Cytheris. Or Ashrar?

The God saw her. When the God saw her it seemed that the God had, of course, always seen her, that the God had been observing her in her mother's womb, that the God had laughed at her first waddling steps, smiled proudly at her first words, leered the first time she took a boy or a girl to her bed.

Isabel shook this off. She knew what was happening. The Gods' movements are never only physical.

Isabel brusquely darkened the panes of her room.

But not before she'd seen, as though lit by a stroke of lightning—though it was *not* lightning, she knew this, and she had not *seen* anything, not with her eyes: no, the God had *revealed* this to her—a row of limbs towering up out of the endless waves; a gallery of torsos hard like marble, yet delicate like the first of spring's new leaves; a flurry of arms and of appendages that were not arms but wild branching wings spread horizon to horizon in a world she saw top to bottom from a height so deep all proportion skews and shatters.

And the eyes. Hundreds, if not thousands of eyes, floating, like jewels tossed on vast carpet of black velvet: watching among many things herself.

Isabel clenched her eyes against this sight, but it did no good.

The room responded to Isabel's urgency. It descended with such reckless speed that gravity left every muscle of her body thrumming with pain once the observatory regained its resting position a few feet above the building's rooftop.

The room knew its duty: it pumped Isabel full of vitamins in odorless gaseous form, and gently ejected her into the lift bay.

There Sílvio and two of her human assistants found Isabel face-down on the floor.

Isabel was too dizzy and sore to stand or walk, so Sílvio took her up into his arms and teleported her the short distance to her apartment to commence her recovery.

Sílvio did what he could to distract her from the sight of the eyes and the limbs, which was all her optic nerves and all her brain could process for several hours. Ice cream in copious amounts; aggressive tickling; the soundtrack turned up loud of scream-heavy slasher 3-D movies, the lovely graphics of which Isabel unfortunately could not appreciate.

The slave knew its duty too, and would not permit its master to sleep: her dreams would have been all of the very same legs pushing up from the misty kiss of the waves, the same flickering bodies and steadfast eyes, and eventually there would be no door or door-frame through which to travel from dream to waking. The walls between them would have fallen, and she would never have awakened, at least not as Princess Isabel Bragança, ninth-degree tech, Prince's Right Hand, and lord of a great Affinity.

The report Isabel gave to her officers and Prince Amaro the third afternoon following, when she could see, walk, think, and speak again, was naturally short on specifics.

She was very clear, however, that she had not observed only one of the Great Gods, or even two, as was most commonly the case in the infrequent event of observing from that dangerous height.

No, They were all there, she insisted.

"Aspects of Them were there," Deputy Director Simplício Dias de Novais corrected her. Dias de Novais had served two Affinities in the House of the Winged Serpent through five different administrations. He was impatient with Isabel and what he viewed as her tendency to speak inaccurately.

"Not aspects, *the* Aspects." Isabel matched the old man's impatience with her own. "I'm quite certain. She — Ashrar, I think it was — revealed to me exactly what was actually happening. Probably expecting it would drive me insane," she mused. The extent to which this offended her leaked through Isabel's professional mask.

"*The* Aspects of... *all* the Great Gods?" De Novais's too-pink face went darker, and immediately the three-inch-tall slave with butterfly wings he carried around on his shoulder as his particular affectation cupped its tiny little hands and began whispering animatedly in his ear.

"Yes. They appeared in the forms they appear in when They manifest for worship." Saying it aloud again increased Isabel's own bewilderment, made her shake her head and get up from her seat to get water, to pace, to do something. "They were all there, massed right beside the Wall."

"Massed," her chief of operations Perla Barbosa repeated, in a tone that hovered between question and conclusion. Perla did not deign to add because she did not need to, *like an army.*

Now De Novais's little slave spoke to the council. For such a small creature it generated great volume. "Has this not been prophesied? Has not the Great Tilt, when all the celestials would gather Their strength at last, long been warned of?"

"Yes it has," Barbosa replied, "precisely thirty-one times in forty-seven years. Always incorrectly."

Pacing the floor behind Barbosa, Isabel spread her hands. "Thirty-second time's the charm. They're ready. It's finally happening. The invasion is imminent." That was the gist of her report. Most of it, anyway.

Isabel sat back down, overtaken by a swift weariness.

"But why wouldn't our slaves or Greens have detected this first?" Ruy Bellos smiled. Bellos was always cheerful, an incongruous trait for an intelligencer. Usually Isabel found him slightly frightening, as though at any moment he might pluck one of those incisors out of his smile and jab your jugular with it. But today other prospects were more unnerving.

"They did detect it. Shortly after I did. I happened to be in a better position than they to see," Isabel shrugged.

Cassio Nicolau, Chief Military Liaison, grunted. "You happened to be there, looking. Just in the nick of time."

Nicolau was very handsome — dapper, brown, bearded, with a dazzling if emotionally unconvincing air of charm. Even in hard times beauty was to Isabel's mind a solace, so she forgave the young man his impertinence. "There is no cause-and-effect relation between my being in the observatory and what I was able to observe first among all our monitors," she said with a sigh. "However..."

De Novais intervened. "However, you do think there was a precipitating event that caused the Great Gods to begin the invasion we've dreaded for decades."

Isabel nodded. "An enormous amount of information comes through in contact with the Greats. Too much. As we all know. Even so, I distinctly felt that They're coming unwillingly. They have no choice. Somewhere in it all — there was a plea."

"To us. For help. Because something has happened." Prince Amaro, who you — and maybe even You — will have noted had been otherwise silent — and in fact he said not one other word in this particular meeting — spoke without even a hint of a question. He knew. Or his slaves had told him.

"And what is this event that's occurred?" Bellos asked, weirdly upbeat.

Princess Isabel shook her head. "We don't know yet."

All Isabel had to prove her hypothesis was a feeling. So she didn't say what she was thinking.

I know, though.

I know she thought it was me that was responsible. She was certain that I was the trigger.

This was Isabel's experience, which I later learned, in all the detail I have now recounted. I learned this because of what we shared, she and I.

I have set this part of the story somewhat out of sequence — maybe a day or so before it actually happened. I have done so because Isabel's observations and her report comprise a crucial moment. My becoming aware of this conversation and her thoughts in something akin to the form you as a reader now have become aware of them, functions in my own story *as though* these things transpired before the events I'm going to describe to you next.

This is perhaps confusing. Suffice it to say that what happened later in time (linear time, anyway) actually served as the foundation for much, if not all, of what occurred before it in time. This moment, then, the second I shared with Isabel, gave new meaning to everything that preceded it. This moment rewrote its own past to serve as the foundation for the future that we are now living.

Thus the next chapter's events happened before, or rather, "next." The next chapter's events were the cause of the Princess's alarm, and of her unsettling conversation with Prince Amaro and the officers of the House of the Winged Serpent.

ALEIXO'S STORY

2048, Primeiro (the Month of Bright Air), Quinta

At noon—

Yes, I had indeed been drinking for hours. But slowly, savoringly, mind you, not like some desperate alcoholic. Over the hours I had become clever in my choice of drink, balancing sugarcane liquor, that great slayer of sense and consciousness, with the lower alcohol content of piquant stimulant ports. And water, too, plenty of it (but not Water, of course).

To quiet the hunger left behind as the adrenaline of the previous night's adventures drained from my body, I ate a large sandwich of bell peppers, tiny tomatoes, goat's cheese, and lightly fried anchovies drizzled with olive oil, layered between toasted country bread slices. And a sedate little rice pudding, sweeter than sin but with a texture of pure milk innocence.

I ate, I drank. I did a fine job of not thinking much. Not remembering too much of what had happened. Not doing what I had been tasked with doing, which was finding a new apartment before taking up a new life as slave-intelligencer.

Then at noon, the fountain in the park went on.

I saw the spume of the fountain misting above a low patch of treetops as the sun glided over the hill across the street.

But more than that I felt the Water, as so many others did.

My bartender looked suddenly stricken. She shut herself somewhere in the back of the establishment behind a heavy door. I felt sure she was locking herself in, preventing herself from charging into the park. Her husband or partner or whatever he was, after having idled long stretches of the morning rubbing his chin and the hair on his arms while hunched over a tiny 3-D player in the back corner, strutted over to the bar and took to a fervent regimen of counter-top wiping and glass-polishing. He was wet-eyed, his mouth working and belly trembling. Observing his manner reminded me of watching a dog asleep, overflowing with dreams.

All the sidewalks in sight thinned of people, and then with no evident hurry and never in large groups, but with purpose and in small inexorable wave after wave, folks began to cross the emptying lanes of the streets and to make their way up the hill.

All of them — citizens, tourists, pilgrims, bon vivants, slackers, scientists, dream-techs, Gods'-speakers and priest-kind alike — answered the call of the Water. They came to splash their faces and arms and bellies with it, to bathe in it, to sip it, to gulp it, to carry bottles and tanks of it away.

For those of You who know nothing of it, the Waters were the first and arguably the best of the miracles the mages brought to the modern world over two centuries ago. Saint-mothers and saint-fathers struck holes in the earth and called Water up to dribble over our lips. Later, dream-techs punched holes in the air and loosened spigots of it to pour from Unseen realms.

The Gods'-speakers called it earth's-blood. Unlike but like the waters of the seas and lakes and rain, Water is a source of life. Not quite the cosmic accident or divine-machine design of biological life, more the *miracle* of life's very existence in liquid form, somehow distilled or fermented, or both, to suit ends greater than those everyday wonders of respiration, cognition, and locomotion. Water gives blessings: Water cures illnesses no doctor could heal, brings healthy babies to easy births, extends life, lifts up sagging age, gives inspiration and luck, and in its purest vintages grants for brief terms the powers of childhood dreams and comic books — unaided flight, lightning speed, the strength of giants, or divine genius and beauty.

Water makes us all magicians. And Water intoxicates. It gives its drinkers visions, and it drives some of us insane.

The cynical and envious say Norio was a city-state of drunkards, the Empire a network of addicts. (Almost everyone in Arlina said this, when they didn't think any spies or censors were listening.) They are probably at least partly right. Not that it matters. When the first mages built the first fountains in Norio in 1815, they changed the whole world. A globe of Water can provide enough power to fly a plane across either ocean; a few buckets can make a desert green; and a pinch in the hands of those who can see the Unseen can open the door between the Worlds, and, some say, give a simulacrum of life and solidity to the ephemera of dreams in order to make a powerful slave.

Up the face of the hill wound streams of celebrants, suppliants, addicts. You could almost taste their hunger on the air. I knew what they felt. Like almost any other visitor to Norio, finding Water was my first priority once I'd been allowed to enter the City.

Today though, my plan was just to watch. Hang back, sip till it grows cold one of the wildly electrochemical coffees for which this City is known, my elbow propped on the counter like a native, a corner of my mouth quirked, my eyes half-lidded, blasé, as though I'd seen many times before and could not be more bored by what in truth I meant to watch intently: the outflow.

Once the fountains were on and Water flowed, doings, escapades, and drama of all kinds would percolate within the confines of the park. Periodically — then regularly, then tidally, as time wore on — you'd see exhausted Water-takers stumble out, looking bedraggled, bloodied, or besotted. With the zeal of converts they'd tell you everything they'd seen and heard and done inside. And whatever that was, it would be different, radically different from what the next person stumbling out would tell you, as though events within were taking place in altogether different cities, in multiple dimensions and on myriad other earths.

Just listening to the different stories is a powerful experience — less so than taking the Waters, to be sure, but a glory in its own right. Many people have come to crave the muted ecstasy of the listener's experience. So many, in fact, that listening has evolved into an integral part of taking the Waters in the years since the City royalty began disbursing Water to the unwashed multitudes as a display of their munificence (and the ultra-rich non-royal-but-wished-they-were followed suit in typical envious fashion). Now no matter where or when you take public Waters, at a fountain in a park, at a booth in a street fair, at an outdoor cinema or a political rally, or at the end-of-year exams kneeling in the tall green grass on the high hill at the royal university of Trópolis, you'll crawl away from wherever you imbibed and then tell someone nearby exactly what happened.

Someone — maybe just a few people, maybe a mob of hundreds if you were famous — will be waiting for you. Someone will be there to receive your testimony. They will make it live for you in new ways, with a question or a knowing murmur or, best of all, with an unvarnished look of shock. You'll be grateful and they'll be grateful: something valuable and even precious, something magical will pass between you (magic of a different, more prosaic sort, not like the magic that makes the world go round). You will be linked to your listener as your listener will be linked to you, for days and weeks afterward. And sometimes for longer, since everyone knows at least two or three couples who met, coupled, and married in precisely this way: together weaving the delicate web of social connection which is itself an effect of Water, one of its more wondrous and hard-to-track ripples.

As the sages of some Godshouses say, "That is what Water does, its true nature: to flow ever outward, casting off reels that hook and bind us one to one to one, and never end." The Godshouse sages claim this is the work of Nansi-sus the Spider-Fisher, the god whose dual nature makes one of its aspects a fisherman and the other a spider.

To which the rivals of the sages, the dream-techs, frown or roll their eyes and retort, "Water is viral."

The listeners, who often get called Watchers even though they don't usually see much of anything, have become over time the third element of the blessed tripartite ritual of Water. One takes the Water, one tells of the taking, and a Watcher listens. (And then that Watcher usually tells others, who tell others, too, but that's usually only if the story really means something to the listener, or if it's truly scandalous.) The Watchers are the leg that permits the stool to stand. Without them, all that each of us live and know with Water would be lost when its substance flees the cells of our bodies (and while memories can be sharp, they are never as bright as they had been — taking the Waters makes all things bright, numinous, palpably alive).

It was my aim to be a Watcher that day. It seemed safer. The voyeur and witness don't risk much. And I'd had enough of risk in the last twenty-four hours or so.

Here, of course, the gods all laughed at the making of a plan.

Whipping in and out of the rim of peripheral vision, so that I had to turret my neck around and get a full-on look, I caught a vision of some little slip of a thing. She couldn't have been over five feet, which was short for Norio women, but Providence had stuffed her tiny frame as fully as it could, and each piece of her sat high and ripe. And her skin! Maybe it was just the way the sunlight caught it as she walked. Or maybe a mélange of sweat-sheen, sunshine, and the waves of color — from tree-leaves and car-chromes and window-glass and jewelry gems — soaking in the sun's rays in the plaza all around her had hurried towards her, magnetized to hug the curves of her bikini-ed body. Maybe it was just that she was so lickably, licky lick coffee ice cream brown...

This little gift from the One True God in Heaven's choirs walked by. And all the stuff that was her was juddering. With excitement to get at the Water, I presumed.

Words, an idea, rose warrior-like from the crack dented in my skull just by the sight of her. *Should I...?*

It didn't hold for long, this doubt.

This decision more than anything convinced me that the Princess was wrong. I could not be a slave, for surely no creature of dream could feel what I felt then, what all of us feel when our bodies remember the taste of Water: the craving, the holy call of the thirst.

I got up from my seat and crossed over to enter the park on the hill.

More marvelous than anything you can imagine was this hill, vast and erect as a high fairy-tale fortress, a slice of mountain come to grace the shallows of the valley. From its perimeter below on the street you would see trees, shrubbery, and tall grass twined together as in the thickets of the Artremis rainforest, sloping ever higher and higher, so that you could just glimpse, if the wind moved aside the branches of certain trees, the summit, alternately crowned in fog and illuminated by yellow splashes of sunlight.

You enter this place and become hopelessly, happily lost, drowned in the deceptions of its trails. Imagine the paths of a labyrinth lifted from between its hedges and distributed, willy-nilly, all about the base, crown, and faces of a towering hill.

The last of the morning fog moved in gaseous sorties winding their ways between the trees, camouflaging the lawns, muddying the paths: so thick that to move from place to place through the fog was like moving from one world to another, from one room of a vast unseen cosmos to another far-flung at the other end of a spinning wormhole.

At first, I followed a wide paved road which was used by police sedans when on a mission to keep public order. This road curved around and about, and swept wide across the faces of the hill north and west.

I saw several folk heading upward toward the fountain on the hill's crest, but not the heaven-sent girl whom whim had made me follow.

Suddenly the road dwindled into a narrow dirt path overgrown with thickset bushes, and all we pilgrims became jungle explorers beating back knobbed and prickled branches with our hands. Our legs grew sticky with sap; insects were drawn to the smell and beginning to hover. Stairs branched out from the gentle arcs of the slow-climbing paths and seduced the traveler up and away into the dense cover of dark higher up. The stairs, made of wooden posts and planks, dug into the flesh of the hill and were covered in green mold, and pitted and furrowed like the trunks of ancient oaks.

When I got to the summit, the sun shone bright and hot. I could see above the shoulders of the fog, as the wind began to push its furthest triumphal tendrils back eastward toward the sea. Far off in the opposite direction were the bare mountain peaks, like bent knuckles, like stubbed toes, as though the whole of the City were a recumbent earth-god, its legs and fingers in the air, and all of us germs in our little germ-houses crawling on its belly, this park a bulge of muscle, or a cancerous extrusion.

When you think that way, when your thoughts take a bird's-eye or god's-eye view, you know the air is alive with Water.

I stuck my tongue into the Water-moistened air: its taste was sweet, salty, smoky. And also juiced grass, and sour fruit — tastes darting, like flashing signal lights, bringing each and every one of my tongue's buds into life.

The Water fountain itself was simple, just an unadorned spike three times taller than any of us, with mist softly raining from the tiny holes at its crown. Close up the Water was indistinguishable from the fog. The lawn at the summit rose and fell in little peaks and valleys of its own; and throughout, in all the alcove-like spaces, Water worshippers cavorted.

What I describe next happens in the past and in the now and in the future and forever, an eternal life, the life of Water, which runs parallel to reality and can never really be lost, even if forgotten: knowing this, I am there still, my legs and arms splayed in the weeds, my chest and buttocks pressed against the mulch as I roll.

And this was not me who did and was done to but the Water's deeds, the Water feeding its song through the pores of my skin, shimmying through my thoughts and molding the muscles of my body as it saw fit.

(My taking the Waters had never before been as it was the noon of that day. Something was different. Perhaps it was, after all, the slave in me, the dream-slave I was, that was the difference. Or so I feared, wondering wildly in the first minutes as the spray of droplets touched and captured me... later, though, I came to know that even if there were differences from previous experience, other factors contributed to my being unsettled. Among these factors was the fact that I was being closely watched — and not by a Water Watcher.)

I saw a dark young man with a shaven head, and with long wiry muscles which encased his shape like the rind of a fruit. Grinning, wobbling as if drunken, he stripped down to blousy boxer shorts and tottered over to crouch on a ledge of rock at the lawn's edge. Beside him was a heavy-shouldered man with long white-butter-blond hair and a butter-blond beard and lips that were a shock of red in his face, also crouching. The men's knees knocked against their stomachs as they bounced excitedly on the balls of their feet. They were like two gargoyle gutter spouts. They perched on the ledge looking out, and they did not see the sun or the fog, but twilight spread around them like a twirl-ing skirt bound around their legs, flowing from them as if they were the center of its violet half-light, as if they were twin moons struggling against radiating darkness.

The blond said, and I think the black man said too, "If there is a glory in me, it is this" — and then as one they pitched forward out of their squatting postures and into the open air. Over the edge.

My breath caught. Then I saw them both rising back above the ledge, arms outstretched, feet kicking foolishly as though swimming. I saw them lift above the summit and circle the foun-tain, never too far from the ground but no longer bound by its gravity, buoyed up into the pathless air by the magic of Water.

Watching them, I felt a breeze moving uncluttered by the pres-ence of the trees, and my sight roved over the whole hill at once as though I flew beside them. The Water synchronized me with the game that the two men — who in the dry lands beyond the reach of the fountain might well be bankers or soccer coaches — were playing together.

After a moment I turned away. You could see the two every-where on the hilltop, but theirs was a private game, a mystery only for them. (Were they lovers? I wondered. Such a tandem between them, such intimate collusion. I envied it...)

Up the southwestern slope, below the lawn at the summit, a person came striding. Precise facial attributes seemed somehow blurred, or overshadowed by the rest of their body. They were a silhouette of stunning, a figure of command, of a demand for worship, though you could no more look at them and see their face than look directly at the sun. They were a presence walking amongst lesser creatures, their visage known only by the bright shadow they cast.

Their clothes, though, you could see. They wore leather pants with no flap to conceal the zipper, which glinted like snarling teeth at the slight swelling below their admirably flat midriff. Their midriff's tawny skin was framed in all its smooth splendor by a shirt spun from silk or shiny nylon or some extraterrestrial fabric that glowed like lizard-skin and plunged deep at its neck to show a quarter of their pectorals, and which ended, as if incom-plete, before it reached their navel.

Stunning, I'll call this marvelous person, since "stunning" was the word we all shared watching them in our brief telepathic union, insofar as we had words, insofar as thought was left to us to be shared.

I see Stunning now as I revisit this moment with you, and I know that they were a professor in one of the law schools in the City, a little-known and little-esteemed one, with few good students and a reputation for mediocrity. Surname Olivo, first name Angel. Professor Olivo (but we'll dispense with that name now, since for now, for today, it is their dead name) was in their sixties, perhaps. But after the Water touched them, after they drank — in this place their age, their very self as it was, disappeared, or was renewed.

Stunning enters, takes a by-path that leads swiftly away from a well-traveled trail into an alcove of bush and tree as dim and damp as a cave, and emerges, reborn, remade, rejuvenated. No gray, no soft, no sag, no hint of the touch of mortality does Stunning possess. They are full-grown at the moment of their entry into the world, and beauty is their armor, hard and clean and vanquishing.

We sniffed Stunning out, we members of the pack. (I am one of them. Unlike the two flying men's, the professor's is no private fantasy, and so I and others join it freely, eagerly.) The pack circled around them for a while first, because we were all of us strangers, we did not yet know all that Stunning wished or all that we wished, or what was to happen, or whether Stunning might even be a threat.

(Though they, we, enjoy a threat, too. Water turns threat to pleasure. Some of the cops who come to keep Waterings under control fail their mission, you know, go to take a leak in a secluded spot and are never again seen, except later in the rancid basement of an underground club frequented by men and women who will risk criminality to sate their hungers. Or maybe you would see him one early Domingo morning naked except for a frayed, stain-spattered jockstrap that half hangs off the white or black or brown or golden globes of his loose, better-seen-in-fair-weather ass as he shuffles down the sidewalk in unlaced black boots with his arms folded across the stubble of his fresh-shaved chest and his hands tucked into his fresh-shaved pits, and, as his eyes squint against the morning sun, he might for a moment recognize you, before you blink and he darts away.)

Slowly we approached the Stunning Being, closer and closer, first one or two. Then as if demonstrating the function of exponents there are a dozen of us, two dozen, growing more numerous and more bold as we draw nearer, as we sniff out the tilt of the land and come to know how the game will play.

Our hands groping ourselves, mauling ourselves as though angry with our bodies that are not already joined to Stunning's body, there are some who already have their dicks out. There are always a few who like doing that, of course, the balls and the dicks thrust out there for all the denizens of the hill to see; these are usually the really big-dicked ones, or if the dicks aren't so big then the balls are enormous wonders in themselves. These guys use the zippers or button-flies (or an ostentatious wealthy few might have little slaves shaped like serpents or dragons, that hold their pants open with teeth or wings or claws that glow faintly blue) as though they were cock-rings to keep the blood pumping and make their penises into ramrods that bulge like something meant not for men but for equines, so that she or he or they or other (depending on the game) is impressed into worshipful submission. And they can make her/him/them beg and do all kinds of things they like to pretend and he/they/she likes to pretend are degrading but are actually exhilarating and inciting, before they take him-other-them for their own depraved, faster-harder-crueler-as-you-see-how-much-the-little-slut-loves-it pleasure.

Now some others sidle towards Stunning backwards, casting minx looks over their shoulders as they place one foot behind the other, their butts twitching, and, in answer to these, Stunning begins to wind and thrust their crotch in the air, humming words like, do a little dance, make a little love, get down tonight. For these approaching with their backsides, Stunning has grown instantaneously a new appendage. This is the beneficence of Water, and its utter disregard of the law of the conservation of matter. This appendage dangles newborn from their bellybutton and then as it rapidly matures it comes to stand at sixty degrees, and Stunning caresses it, makes themself buck more as if their body can stand no more movement without more shuddering and humping of the air. The movements bring Stunning's body up on its toes, and before gravity can pull them back to earth the ones who have dropped to all fours and scampered over across the mud and loam have got their mouths on Stunning's leather ass and are baptizing it, ruining it with their acidic saliva.

We strip Stunning. Our tongues run over their bare skin like running water; Stunning is kissed between their cheeks and bussed noisily between both pairs of lips, and on the tip of their inhumanly jet-black but very warm, thick, and fleshy cock.

Stunning is lapped as if they were a bowl of milk surrounded by cats, their body buffed, washed, and tossed as though in a whirling pool. Stunning stifles their cries and moans, wanting to hold on to each pleasure, not wanting any of it to escape, but Stunning cannot last more than a few minutes: all it takes is the hard swirls of callused fingertips on their nipples and arms wrapped around them from behind, and they shout like the joyous hallelujahs of saints dancing between the pews. Somehow or another a hand is up their ass and they're on all fours on the ground, and they thank Zili and Egba and Ashrar and the Fairy Queen; they're going to get well and truly fucked and fuck the hell out of every hole they feel.

The ejaculate of this first one burns like the sting of spicy peppers in the mouth (now someone — was it me? — goes for Stunning's mouth, just hunches over there so his legs are on either side of their ears, and picks their head up and pulls it down splat all the way to the root of his dick), and Stunning writhes and mumbles praises to the gods, for it has only just begun.

The pack numbers thirty or forty or more, and no one's leaving until they've nutted at least thrice. And if Stunning's lucky they may yet get some folks of Godshouse faith, every one of whom would not be satisfied without donating sixteen of their orgasms to Stunning's ass, mouth, ear, or on their face or chest or stomach, one stream for each of the sixteen sons of old Dudua who founded the sixteen original kingdoms of the Old Spirits.

Professor Stunning (whom we did not know was a professor, remember) was not the only prize, of course. There's never only one; usually four or five lucky ones get designated, the ones whose clothing or demeanor or way of walking or perfume advertises the human estrus cycle coming to its peak. Of course, too, not all those who come to take the Waters are ordinary people, or even human. Politicians and royalty have been known to make the scene in thin disguise (most of these take it up the ass: hard, pretty please, Sir). Luminaries from the worlds of entertainment may make a pit-stop. Beautiful clever Silvara and sinister Ilsvashi are there, and it is well known that there are fey spirits which cross the Bridge that links the seen to the Unseen, This World to those lying Next. These fey creatures take gorgeous physical form solely for the purpose of feasting on the psychic sensations of the happy Water-inebriated humans they seduce, even if the tolls exacted by the City dream-techs decree that spirits who cross in this way once must return to the Next World when the fountain goes dry, and cannot cross again for a thousand years.

(When the game has come to an end, the professor finds themself asleep on one of the paved walks, awakened by a dog's nose poking curiously at their behind, and the sharp *no!* of a dog-parent whose tone either recoils in horror or disgust or balloons in barely suppressed laughter. Professor Olivo will smile, then lift themself up, pull their pants back up from their ankles — another day, another pair of $R1900 leather slacks gone to hell — and, refreshed in every way, make their way back down the hill into the city's evening, to laugh and sigh and murmur memories in tongues they speak fluently only during the hours of the aftermath as they tell their tale over wine and tapas to their Watcher.)

... I staggered off.

It had begun to fade. My high was gone.

I felt it crash in slow suspended motion, felt it dally as though surfing brief updrafts which nevertheless, when they blew away, left me each time lower and lower and lower on a ladder of air (as though at the same time as you sail *up* you are being pushed *down*) till — *boop!*, there you are on the ground, knees in the dirt, pulse racing, heart thudding dangerously in your chest, mouth dry: pedestrian not mystical, crashed not high.

Then I was wandering.

I could no longer see the summit of the hill. There were still people fucking and flying and shooting stars from their fingers, still screams of joys and pleasures so raw they could not be left to sensation merely but had to be voiced, in some proto-language of simian and canine growls and howls.

I observed this, but I did not myself feel the revelry any longer. It was outside of me.

Where had the girl from Heaven's choir gone, where were her fingers journeying through the hair on my belly? (For she *had* been there, hadn't she? Not the first time I fucked Stunning, or the second, but when I rode them, when I rode Stunning's phallus and busied my mouth and hands with their pecs, there had been, I was sure there had been, that girl beside me, stroking my torso...)

I looked around me. My gaze snagged on a heavy-thighed saffron-skinned man, someone wholly unlike Stunning. Maybe it was the barman from the corner shop? His ass cheeks inflated and crumpled like a tire tube as he rose and fell, rose and fell, as he lifted up then writhed downward as though beginning a slide down a pole which he never completed, his body smacking the thighs of the man — the men — for when one of their body would tremble suddenly then grow still, another pushed him out of the way and took his place, a replacement of one plug for another in an open socket.

Disgusting. Vile. I couldn't keep looking.

Everything on the hill, all the games taking place under the fountain's benediction, fell into background.

Though I was looking straight on at what was transpiring around me, I felt I'd turned my back. All of the smells and sounds and sights came to me from a distance, and the distance grew greater by the ticking second. Sounds began to echo, and then to weaken.

What a strange Watering this is, I thought. I'd never crashed so fast before.

So great was my fall from the heights that I felt that I could not taste, touch, smell, *feel* anything, not even my own body, my own skin.

I licked my lips.

Nothing.

I stuck out my tongue in the air, I strained to see.

Nothing. Nothing but thin gray air.

Someone had drawn a sketch on the canvas of the world and then erased it, and the smudged blankness waited, bereft, for the kiss of the brush, the stain of ink and color, to resurrect it.

Weird fucking Water.

But it wasn't the Water.

The effects of Water are psychical and have psychological ripples, but they are above all physical: when you take the Water, when the Water takes you, you do not think, you are instead entirely reactive, entirely perceptive, a throbbing locus of instinct, senses washed clean of consciousness. And Water is social, inherently a substance linking couples and triples and quadruples and mobs.

Water could not have the effect I was experiencing — this creeping gray, this cold hand, this fog in the mouth, this instinct which shrunk from my fellow humans and pushed me off alone.

I didn't know it, but I had been stung by Ilsvashi predators.

This, I learned later, is what they do:

The Ilsvashi spit something at you — it leaves their mouth liquid and becomes a fine tiny needle in the air. The projectile breaks the skin, and its poison floods your nervous system instantly. Turns your thoughts to ash, your pleasures to cold gummy pottage. The Vashi dart pricks your brain, his telepathic touch burrows into your thoughts, and then you no longer quite see what you see, or hear what you hear. Then smell and touch vanish altogether, as though you have stepped through a glass door into a silent antiseptic laboratory encased in a suit of thick rubber.

Somehow your blood and lymph have a better flavor for the Ilsvashi when you are in such a state, adrift at the mouth of catatonia.

Two of the Ilsvashi vampires bore down on me.

A part of the victim of a Vashi watches when it happens, while most of you is altogether unaware, fading into thinner and thinner airless gray.

But even the part that watches is not alarmed. It is barely connected to what is happening.

It notes but finds uninteresting the approach of two rail-thin figures, tall, almost fleshless to the eye, so meager is their form. They are dressed head to toe in hard molded plastic, which seems to bobble around the bodies inside like an empty bottle wriggles around a straw. The plastic makes them look like marionettes freed from their strings. (Ilsvashi body masks. I had heard of them, and recognized what I saw, though I'd never seen one outside of a newswatch before.)

They moved jerkily, walking across the grass toward me, swaying and unsteady. As though they were mantises masquerading in humanoid bodies. Their faces were perfectly anatomical countenances carved in impassive gray plastic. Only their mouths moved behind the masks' slits. Their mouths' sung their song of enthrallment.

They were near me, near enough that I could see eyes dilated with excitement in the mask. Blue. Blue as a patch of sky seen from the bottom of a garbage-strewn alley between tall buildings in a deserted city on a bleak winter's morning, blue as...

Out of one's pocket something flashed in its hand.

The other one held me fast from behind. It took my right elbow as though to pin my arm back, and with its other hand pushed below my ear, so that my head tilted. My neck was bared.

Was it a knife, or was it the palm of a hand bristling with tiny sharp teeth like the skin of a sea urchin rather than skin, which pricked hard against the cold flesh of my neck?

Both. It was both. One hand stabbed, and the other hand ate.

The screams of pleasure in the background did not sound like pleasure anymore.

It was I who was screaming.

But too quietly. Hoarsely, a whisper. No one except me could hear.

The detached observer noted the presence of the Heaven's choir woman. She was not far from me, at least not in terms of feet and yards far. But there seemed to be a distance she could not bridge. She was watching wide-eyed. Not quite with fear, and not quite with Watery excitement either. Curiosity, perhaps.

She was drawing a gun —

The gun was pointed at *me* —

The wind at once picked up.

Wind does not work this way, but the gun shook in the beautiful girl's hand.

The grips of the Vashi on my neck and arm relaxed fractionally.

I was free just enough to struggle.

The beautiful Heaven's choir girl gave a cry. I was screaming but I heard her cry, saw her hop backward as though struck. The gun fell from her hand. No, it jumped from her hand. It fell to the ground some thirty feet away. A bullet discharged from it. You heard the sound, the loud firecracker-but-not crack.

Did the bullet hit anyone?

That was my only thought, as the grips of the vampire assassins fell away altogether, and I fell to my knees and then lay sprawled on the grass.

I felt sure I was no longer breathing.

Yet even bereft of oxygen I was still alive somehow, and busy busy thinking.

ALEIXO'S STORY

2048, Primeiro (the Month of Bright Air), Sábado

I awoke naked.

I was sitting in a cross-legged posture, on the cold marble floor tiles of a spacious room which I didn't recognize. There were people with me whom I didn't know.

I was insufficiently puzzled by any of this to ask a question, and insufficiently worried by my proximity to strange people to rise up from the floor, or to try to defend myself, or even to clothe myself.

Though I seemed to have come again into that splendid stupor bequeathed by Water, I was alert now to my surroundings, indeed more sensitive to them than I could remember ever having been. I felt myself solid, as rooted as an old tree. A tree need not take note of the talons of the birds that claw for holds on its branches or the rodents and insects that burrow in its flesh. A tree stands, it grows, it drinks, and it is. And so I was.

I was so despite the fact that my last clear memory was of someone stabbing me and someone else trying to shoot me — a pretty woman — *another* pretty woman, like the girl at the fête; when would I learn they were dangerous?

Nevertheless, it seemed to me that matters had worked out as they should. I had been wandering, lost in a flat landscape of utter darkness, searching, searching without hope of the aid of my senses, until I found what I was looking for. And what I had been looking for was a return to myself.

Music was playing in the room. Rhythmic, percussive, both mournful and ecstatic. The singer's voice seemed drenched in pain and enamored of both her pain and its transcendence — a transcendence that occurred through the expression of the depth of the pain itself, through wallowing in it...?

My thoughts floated away in bubbles and spurts of such insights and puzzles, until I noticed that one of the people with me was looking at me.

After a moment I realized that he was sitting beside me on the floor. But he, unlike me, wasn't naked. He wore supple dark blue sweatpants and a dark hoodie zipped only halfway up his chest, and a chain of heavy gold links hung from his slender sinewy neck to spread across the broad, tautly muscular planes of his chest, which bulged an outline in his tight hoodie.

The man looked like a dream-tech, a rich one. He was dark brown and slightly fox-faced, with a small-tipped nose and a sharp chin wreathed in a close-clipped goatee, with artfully-shaven wings of hair reaching across his cheeks to his ears.

He had big dark eyes. A hard mouth. I could see he was quite tall.

Later I learned that he had a title and what his name was: The Honored Master Salvador, the others called him.

"How did he end up on the floor?"

This was a woman — another pretty woman, slightly plump with honey skin and honey hair that fell somewhat raggedly to her shoulders. She did not look as sleek as Rioca women usually do. Her honey eyes were peering at me, with an expression of mild disgust in them.

"Sleepwalking," the man who I was to learn was named Salvador answered. "Why are *you* in here?" The man sounded annoyed. But also amused.

"Just thought you should know," the girl said. "I was checking the police network —"

"You were spying. Who told you to spy?"

The girl made a face: she, too, was annoyed but also amused. I had the immediate sense that this was the way between them, a cantankerous, touchy intimacy. "I was checking the network," she said, "and they've moved him to the top of the search-and-apprehend list. They don't say he's a felon or anything." The disgust in her expression sharpened. "Just dangerous and in need of imprisoning, I guess."

A sliver of apprehension made me look quickly around me. The room actually wasn't as large as I'd thought. It felt luxurious because there were wide, high windows, and balconies off glass-paneled doors on three sides. There was a divan, a chair, a small table, and a very tall and arresting sculpture of a pagan god throwing thunderbolts. It was pitch black, as though carved out of obsidian. There was also a bed which, when I saw it, I seemed to remember having sleepwalked out of. The bed suddenly looked very inviting to me.

Through the windows I could see a clear sunny day. Far off I saw the summer-faded green of trees, terraced waves of them lapping at the ramparts of a mountain range whose peaks were hidden from view. Scattered among the trees were white houses, lone dots nearest the peaks and clumping thicker as the slope fell.

We were somewhere high up. I didn't see the ocean.

Where would I go, if I needed to escape?

The dark man beside me lifted one eyebrow. They were short but very thick, his eyebrows, and they brought a touch of drama to his smooth youthful skin and bright eyes, like two great storm clouds in a bright open sky. "And does your spying tell you that the directive you saw on the network came from the Winged Serpent?" he asked the woman.

"Yeah," she said, without much conviction.

"Your spying tells you that? Or your perception?" He said that word as though it meant something other than what it usually means.

The girl sighed. "Mm hm."

"What?"

"Yes, Master Salvador."

At this I stirred. I tried to speak. Found I couldn't.

"Sleep," Master Salvador said. His hand reached toward me and as his sleeve slid back, I saw tattoos of letters in some alphabet I didn't know stretching across the tendons of his forearm. The letters flexed in some way not in accordance with the movement of his muscles. I smelled a scent, with that sharpened physical sense endowed by Water: raw ginger under running water, riding herd over and then melding with the cool smell of high wind, trees, and city smoke. The Master's fingers touched my brow — a shock of damp warmth, a jet-spray of his body's smell, sudden and overwhelming, then deepening, spreading across me like spilled water, or like a slowly unfurled net.

I slept. But this time I did not wander in thin gray air, or walk landscapes of flat black —

FERNANDO'S STORY

Date not known to me, but:
1997, late Octavius (the Month of the Exalted Moons)

Yes, things get strange here — or more strange, especially, I imagine, from the perspective of all of You out there. The short explanation, so You (or you) don't get too confused: my dream was a dream of Fernando, in which I *was* Fernando, of whom I knew nothing so far — and who was, as you'll see, now dead.

So, Master Salvador put me into sleep, but this was no longer the dreamless sleep I'd been resting in, I did not wander in thin gray air, or walk landscapes of flat black —

> We'd been circling low in the air, observing — and sending as many reports back directly to the Ministry in Minakkra as we could. Black smoke sent twisting towers up into the bright, cloudless skies above Umasi. In many places, we saw cars and trees adrift in the air, as though snarled in the winds of a tornado.

("We" didn't truly refer to me, of course, but to a me with others in a dream, me in the mind and body and soul of someone I am not: Fernando. So for clarity now, I won't say "I" or "we," I'll say "Fernando" and whoever else all these people were that I didn't actually know, but knew inside the dream.)

The currents of human bodies surging in eerie synchrony through Umasi's streets was the oddest of the many odd sights: a mob would march straight at a building, and then in a furor of dust the building would come down, and the mob would march over the rubble. The invader infantrymen, if such they were, wore no distinguishing uniform. They shot at the people shooting at them. They shrugged off grenades, they could be seen limping forward in the aftermath of bazooka fire. Tanks lumbered through the narrow streets spewing artillery, but if the tanks didn't roll over the invader infantry, which seemed to be the only thing that killed them, the invaders pressed on, clothes on fire, half their limbs shorn off; they broke the tanks into pieces with their hands and whatever tools they found among the rubble, and then shot to death the tanks' crews. Or not. Sometimes they didn't shoot the crews. Sometimes — many times, Fernando counted eleven separate instances — the invaders took hold of the tank crews, as they took hold of civilians they rousted from their homes, as they took hold of Negali soldiers who failed to stop them. They grabbed them, they handled them, they *hugged* them. And then the tank crew, or the civilian family of mother, father, and five children below the age of twelve, or the troop of soldiers, who could be seen struggling to escape the grip of their captors' manic strength, ceased to struggle, ceased to fight, ceased to rain bullets uselessly in their captors' faces or chests. The hugged ones straightened, their feet settled on the earth, and they turned around and fell into line with the invaders, marching forward step for step, shot fired for shot fired.

Watching this pattern repeat, Fernando spoke aloud, breaking the stunned silence (except for the babble of keyboard clicks) within the airplane. "Mass possession," he said, fighting to maintain calm. "Thousands being ridden at once. Only in the legends of Far Arion..." He broke off. "The Great Gods are here, on earth! I can't *see* Them, but—"

Hieronymus-Theodoric offered clarification. "This slave counts three-hundred-and-fifty-five-thousand minimum invaders, the number growing every minute. At such levels, there cannot be more than one Great God currently present."

"Which one?" Fernando demanded.

"Does it matter?" Elias's voice was a harsh croak.

"Can you stop them?" Brinen asked the direct question.

H-T answered its master, "The correlates suggest... Domna Ra Zah."

Brinen and Elias, and the other soldiers listening nearby, were nonplussed.

But Fernando understood. "I can't fight *Her*. She's a bloody trinity," he concluded, feeling a pang for having clearly disappointed Brinen, but feeling also the certainty that he needed to get out of doomed Negali, away from the doomed Negalians, and back to Zilia, now.

Then the plane took a punch.

Above the city of Umasi, which lay on the western out-skirts of the fertile greenlands that spread between the Enina River and the Greater Enina Lake, the transport buckled, rolled, and plunged from the air.

The long arm of Domna Ra Zah, no doubt.

ALEIXO'S STORY

2048, Primeiro (the Month of Bright Air), Sábado

"What's he doing?"

"He's dreaming, Lilia." The tone of exasperation belonged to Master Salvador. But I didn't recognize the voice that answered.

"He is not. He is awake, and listening."

I opened my eyes then. I wanted to protest that I had in fact been dreaming, only to be awakened, when I saw who, or what, it was that awakened me.

The woman who had spoken was striking, and unnerving. She was perched on the railing of one of the balconies, splayed across its narrow iron handgrip with the balance of a cat or a bird, though she was tall and full-bodied, with tawny long legs and bare feet on display as she lounged on the building's edge. The sight of her there was harrowing. Surely she would fall.

She was attired in a form-fitting yellow jacket and tight yellow shorts.

I could see only parts of her face — a broad, high cheekbone, a slightly harsh chin, one glorious large wine-and-violet-colored eye. Long, bountiful, thick hair draped half her face, her shoulders, and her breasts and reached toward the balcony floor. Some of her hair was in loose curls, some bound in braids: pale, pale gold was her hair, appearing almost white against her dark skin.

She looked familiar. She did not look quite human. She did not look like a dream-slave, or Silvara or Vashi. She looked —

"Sleep," said Master Salvador.

So I did.

This time the dream was different.

When he woke, he was lying somewhere. Was it on an edge? No. But nothing was level with his sight.

Then Fernando remembered. They had put me—

They had put *him*—they had captured him, and bound him—deep in the hold of one of the Black Ships. He had made the crossing into the east, he had—but of his journey and its purpose he could remember only a little. He did remember seeing the monstrous ship for the first time, its terrible brightness, as if it were a star that had risen, fiery and cold, suddenly above his head.

It was a like a living thing, perhaps it *was* alive, the Black Ship, large and iron and winged, a great carrion bird hovering dark and hungry above the waters of the harbor. The Black Ship was so vast that when they dragged him beneath it, he could no longer see the sun or the sky, or the western coasts of the bay and the city on its slopes (but what city exactly?). The longer he looked at the Black Ship, the more it frightened him. He had heard of the Ships before, had been warned of their terrors—but now when the great Ship's power was revealed to him, he couldn't bear the agony of his fear.

White fire slashed in whips from the Ship's belly. Inside the Ship, rats seemed to fulminate around him, to engulf him in their own living, shifting shape.

I screamed.

"Oh, *fuck,* what's happening? This is supposed to be a healing spell, he should just be unconscious, he shouldn't—!" That was Master Salvador's voice.

"Told you," came a sharp reply. This must have been Lilia. "There's something *off* about him. Like I said."

"Do you think you could maybe *not* bore me with all that I-told-you-so shit?" Salvador snipped. "That's like saying, 'Oh, *this* isn't what I expected!' Is that supposed to be meaningful? 'Something's off.' You are actually opening your mouth to say, like it's somethin' somebody needs to hear, 'I have no fucking clue and nothing to contribute to an understanding of the problem at hand.'"

Lilia laughed. "Who sprinkled bitch on your cereal this morning?"

"Let me try." The calm voice wasn't Lilia's. It was the strange woman in yellow speaking.

I sensed no movement, but I felt a touch. It was at once warm and solid and fleshy, but also ethereal, entirely mental and abstract.

I thrashed. I felt hot. I felt cold.

I tumbled headlong into another dream.

She awakes, like a cat sunning herself on a high ledge.

(No idea who "she" was, of course. For the moment she was me, though. I found out more particulars later, which I will share with you when I reach the point in my story that I finally understood what I experienced.)

She lies lengthwise on the roof of a Godshouse, overlooking the plaza beneath. Children see her and mock.

Their meaningless sounds turn to cries of alarm when she leaps from the ledge and lands on all fours. They run crying, and she laughs.

Now, she thinks. *Where am I?*

Her memory is all of impressions, sensations, for what she later learns to have been a span of some two or three days—later, when she nails her thought to the planks of ordered time that all the strange stunted creatures around her so strongly believe in. There were smells of food, which she tasted and devoured; smells and sights of flesh, which she tasted and possessed or devoured (but the blood, the blood did not taste as she thought it would, it was not sweet, it offered no visions or sensations of gilded pleasure). Tastes she sampled. Then afterward she ran, hiding up high where they don't look, and in the darkness...

A matron in mourning at the Godshouse saw her naked, and was horrified (all of the townsfolk seemed to flee when they saw her naked). The old biddy cried, "A devil!" and spittle flecked her black dress...

Bent over a corpse — has she killed it? Its flesh was in her mouth, but it was cold, not warm, had she scavenged it? — she must have looked a fright, and of course she was naked, but then the man with the gun asked something she didn't expect. He asked (horrified), "Who are you?" Not, "What are you?"

It was strange to her, a puzzle. So she did not kill him, and she did not run (and for some reason, he did not shoot). She tried to answer.

The question seemed to open language learning in her, and with every word spoken to her and by her in halting answer, her language skills multiplied. Each word seemed to have suspended above and behind it, as if tied by tiny strings, other words, and each of those words other words, and when she heard them it was as though she heard the other words echoing behind, but instead of a confusing cacophony it was a music, and then afterwards when she did finally run (and he did finally shoot, and missed) she looked at a word on a sign and the experience was the same, except that the words crowded sight, thick as smoke...

She was not really a cat, but she could move like one. Outside the town, in the rainforest — or perhaps it was some other town, she visited several — she climbed a tree, and placed her face next to the python's face (it was sleeping, or it didn't care about her), and she knew. *I know who I am, I am Geia: demoness.*

And she knows what demons do. They come to ravage the world, to punish the wicked: and in This World, all are wicked.

When she awoke again, the man she knew was standing above her, tightening a belt around his dark cloak.

The man had on a hat with a rooster's feather tucked into a black velvet strip that sat atop its slanting brim, and ropy locks of hair hung down from beneath that brim, leaving visible only a small patch of forehead. She saw the dark spots on the apple-gold skin, knew those spots, loved them (did she love them, those blemishes? well, it was a *relief,* at least, to see them there above her, they meant that she was home). He had dark eyes that seemed to have a sheen of gray in them. He had wide nostrils and his round fat mouth pursed perhaps contemptuously while the eyes looked at her narrowly.

"So you ran off again. And again you return. Why did you come back, Geia?"

As she rose from the pallet she shrugged. She was naked (again), she felt the stickiness of her sweat and something else on her thighs. So he had found her — or she had come to him, as she'd meant to, and he had done what he always had, what he always would. He had used her though she was already pregnant, and he had already made the little slave in her that he wanted. Hadn't he?

"Why did you hurt me? What was the thing you put inside me?" she asked him. She spoke as if playing her part in a rite they practiced routinely — and indeed she was. But no matter how many times they played, she had never learned the answer to her question.

"I know why you come back," he said, and if there had not been contempt in the posture of his mouth it was certainly there in his tone. "You come back, Geia, because you're filthy and disgusting and no one else in the world will have you except me."

Geia held his stare. She would not look away, he could not make her do that, she would not be ashamed for being shameful. It was all true, what he said, but she wouldn't let the truth make her afraid. She would face it all, never flinching. His contempt, his hate. She would accept all of it, look away from none of it.

The man sneered. The nasty things he'd said had made his pulse quicken, his skin warm, she could feel it — or perhaps it was seeing her again, perhaps he was, in his way, excited to see her? Could not a human, a master, love a slave?

Yes, he was excited to see her, because no sooner had he said the words and she said, as she must, "Yes," than he was on her, pushing her back onto the pallet, and then untying his cloak and pulling free his shirt and shoving down his pants and pushing himself into her. Grunting, snapping like an animal, his eyes filling themselves with her, drinking her as his body took her, as if there was not enough of her and he was driven to devour it all — or as if there were too much of her, a vast sea or deep forest or mountain of her he could never hope to chart and which he had to watch carefully, lest he become lost in her.

She could have flung him out and off her. Easily. She was a demoness. The spell was now out of his control; the maker did not control the making. She could kill him for the sheer pleasure of the most vicious kind of kill.

But she didn't. She deserved what he did to her. She was a demoness. Filthy. Corrupt. And there was nowhere for her to be. Out there, she would be hunted. Here, she had a purpose and a place.

And perhaps, perhaps, she cared for him a little, too. He did love her. Her master loved her. That she knew well. She did not love him, no, but.

He loved her, but that time she made him pay. At the moment when he emptied himself inside her, when his cry strangled itself in his throat, when the breath of his sigh swept over her, she slipped her wrist from his gripping fingers — it was easy, her demon strength made her strong, and besides his power had fled him, and his hold was slack. She took his left wrist in exactly the way he had held both hers when he started to fuck her.

And she snapped the bone clean.

The cry that flared from the depths of him gave her a satisfaction (physical, psychic, a salubrious pleasure thick with juice) that his dick and his body never could.

She lay on the pallet slick with the juices of love and of hate, and she thought, while laughing low in her chest: *Not till the end of time will I ever cease to take revenge on you. Not till the end of fucking time. And maybe not even then.*

When I woke again I found out what I had been dreaming.

The first thing that happened —

(I did not remember this, and do not truly now: this was a thread of time spun by the ecstasies of Water and by the sorceries of Master Salvador and the unhuman woman at his side, which are mysterious and unorthodox and follow no known discipline or creed. Then the thread was cut and put away in some drawer of the mind I cannot to this day fully open.

I can only report what they told me.)

Evidently when I awoke again I was on one of the balconies, leaning over. Not dangerously leaning over, just enjoying the view.

It was night. The room's back was to the sea, and its balcony gazed with a godlike eye over a great swath of the many, many lights of the great city filling the vast bowl between mountain and beach. We must have been twenty, thirty, even forty floors up. They told me later I said to them, "They plunge so far — it's like looking over the edge of an ocean-floor trench. Would the pressure carry you all the way down?"

Supposedly I was referring to the lights.

They replied, "You're such a yokel" — not, I would like to think, without affection.

They said later, "You turned your face to us over your shoulder and smiled."

Later still, Ydris pulled me aside and reported confidentially, "None of us even knew you then. But we could tell it wasn't you. It wasn't you there, in your face, smiling."

When she said that, I felt more fear than I had ever felt in my life.

Then who was it?

That night, though, I felt no fear — or I don't remember feeling it.

I smiled, then turned back to the tidal flow of lights below.

I leaped nimbly to the railing — they couldn't believe that, either, it didn't seem physically possible, it didn't even look like I jumped. There was no effort and then all at once my feet were on the railing pointed like a dancer's; it wasn't a *human* movement.

The first thing that happened was I jumped over the side.

ALEIXO'S STORY

2048, Primeiro (the Month of Bright Air), Sábado

I dove head-first, with my hands together in a beak, as I had been taught to dive into water.

There was no water there, of course, unless it was the moisture of whispers of fog. Air, but not empty air, greeted me. I had flung myself to the winds, and the winds up that high were strong and shifted suddenly. From one flicker of time to another, everything changed. I was no longer an arrow pointed downward to my death and to release from captivity, but a river raft turned on its side and rapidly taking water. One recognition tumbled over the rim of still another: suddenly I was like some wingless bat, with my whole body turned to the earth below.

With a surge of panic, I saw that the apartment building was rapidly drawing closer. Or an apartment building other than the one I'd been in: it was all so confusing, a froth and fury of lights and darknesses and the whine of the wind, small in my ears like a mosquito, and like the roar of rain in a storm at night at the same time.

I was going to smash into the side of the building. The wind had taken me, and it was in a murderous frame of mind.

The lights grew brighter as I fell toward the building. Now I could see almost everything. In a moment I would be pulped and shattered into parts. But all my fear of pain and death was so small beside the cauldron of wind and the mass of lights and sound, so tiny by comparison to the enormity into which I'd jumped, that I could not maintain my panic.

Then I didn't have any thoughts.

I didn't have any thoughts because I was flying.

I was flying!

Except it didn't feel like I was doing anything. It felt like something was flying me, just as though I were lying down flat on the floor of an airplane, except my own body was the plane, and something not made up of my own thoughts or will was the pilot.

Perhaps some autonomic reflex, some sub-program of the magic that had created me was the pilot, because surely this proved, once and for all, that I was not human.

Unless this was Water, still somehow in my system?

The frenzy of sensations slowed. I or my pilot banked my body away from the building, almost at leisure. I arced upward, and rolled easily into the open air.

I was now above some buildings, and between others. I caught quick glimpses as I passed: people beside their windows watching 3-D tableaux in their living rooms, or bending over their washbasins, a couple with the soles of their feet pointing at me from the railing of their balcony, drinking wine as she lovingly groped him and he laughed.

In front of me I could smell the sea.

It smelled good. I headed there — or something aimed me toward the sea.

(And as my body filled with the grand odor of the sea, I remembered something: hadn't the woman leapt like a cat, and hadn't I been her in the dream, and hadn't I leapt to the railing?)

Ydris — as I was to learn was the name of the woman who I'd seen earlier with the pale gold hair and dark rosewood skin — snatched me in mid-air.

She snatched me as a hawk snatches a sparrow on the wing. Hawk-see to prey, hawk-dive to prey, a flexure of hawk-talons, prey-flesh pierced.

That was how I saw what happened happen, though I did not truly see it, only made pictures in my mind that bloomed like the rattle of gunfire, that unspooled in my thought as spilled blood makes plumes in water.

Ydris snatched me (but she did not pierce my flesh, not really — I thought she might have, it *felt* as though...). Ydris took me back.

Ydris's version of flying was different from mine — faster, and even spookier. All I had time to notice was that she was there, that her arms locked around my waist, and she'd pulled me upright in the air. I knew it was her, but I don't think I saw her face, I only felt her touch, yet still, somehow, I recognized who she was.

I tried to speak above the wind. "You're — Geia?"

The flying woman heard me despite the wind. I couldn't see her face, but I felt her body tense. This, I think in retrospect, was startlement. It wasn't recognition, because I heard her say clearly, "I am not her. I am Ydris."

And then I didn't see anything, and I didn't feel anything except Ydris's presence; it was as if I'd entered a small dark universe inhabited by her alone. I wondered if I were hypnotized.

And then — but it was later, I gathered that quickly enough — I was in the apartment again, standing unsteadily on my own two feet on the solid floor.

The doors to all the balconies were shut, and the air in the apartment was close and warm.

The one called Master Salvador handed me a robe and I put it on. He asked me to sit.

Slowly I complied. Each movement of muscle as I stepped toward a broad couch seemed to recollect things to me that I'd forgotten for a span of time before: *I am Alexander* (step), *I was born in Arlina* (step), *I flew* (slight hesitation, step).

By the time I sat down, everything had begun to feel sane and normal, even if I couldn't explain anything that had happened, even if I had no idea anymore what I really was.

Salvador pushed a bowl of grapes and a bowl of nuts toward me and took up a seat across from me, on the other side of a low glass table.

Master Salvador and I, in slow quiet voices at first, and gradually with greater and greater freedom, talked. The other two gathered around at his back or paced about the room or came to sit beside him: the pretty honey-colored girl, and the strange beautiful inhuman woman with the long, glorious hair trailing almost to her ankles, Ydris. (Ydris often positioned herself between me and the nearest balcony doors, I noticed.)

Wind, the distant cries of vehicle horns, the bleat of street slaves, the sough of voices, the murmur of the sea, the sound which is not a cry nor even of wings beating the air that bats make: all these I heard while we spoke, and I listened, and it was curious to me that I was aware of all of them. Maybe in some odd way my augmented perception was a compensation my brain — or my program — had devised. The last clear thing I had done was to take the Waters, but I had had no listener, no one to share my experiences with (and indeed, such as those experiences were, they seemed now faded, less real than the vivid, peculiar dream I'd had). Perhaps I was my own listener.

"You were in a fugue," Master Salvador was saying. (I should have been listening to him.) He was all in black: a black ballcap on his smallish head, a black hoodie, svelte thigh-hugging athletic pants. Rings on his fingers. "And now you've turned. Or you've *been* turned. During your fugue you learned to fly. This interests me, and it interests my colleagues."

He gestured quickly towards the women — toward the unhuman one, mostly, I thought. "My name is Salvador. That's Lilia." He pointed to the buxom younger woman, who wore a gray business suit either tailored to flatter her curves or failing to conceal them. "You met Ydris." He shrugged toward the unhuman one, who nodded at me grimly. "We've found out that your name is Alexander." He paused. "Alexander, why is Princess Isabel trying to kill you?"

The look on my face must have been one of alarm. Salvador made a pushing motion with his hands and changed his voice to sound placating. "You're safe now. No need to fly off again. We're not holding you captive, or anything like that. Don't worry."

But I wasn't worried. My face had shown something that I didn't feel, I was oddly —

"It's... shitty, I know. When you realize that your paranoia isn't paranoia, just a recognition of reality. But this is the shit that happens when you pass through the Archway." Now I must have looked stupefied, because he immediately clarified. "I mean, when you first work with the Unseen. When you cross over, presences appear. Enemies make themselves known. Allies, too.

You survived this time because my colleague rescued you — and maybe because of your own ability to resist" — he cast a look at Ydris, who merely raised an eyebrow — "but they for damn sure will attack again. Or at least they'll be looking to take you."

He looked closely at me before continuing. "We're no friends of the Winged Serpent. We're here to help you. But we don't understand why Isabel wants you dead."

I needed time to fashion a lie, so I asked a question rather than answer his question. I meant to ask just one question, but several popped out. And even though I also meant to lie, all my questions were all genuine. "Who are you, and why did you rescue me? *How* did you? Have I been possessed? Did the Vashi poison me? Is that why I — why I feel so...?"

Salvador patiently introduced himself to me again. He added, somewhat mysteriously, that he was neither a dream-tech nor an affiliate of one of the Affinities nor a saint-father nor a novice. "But I do know my fuckin' way around the Unseen," he said with more than a little attitude, as though he thought it beneath him to have to tell me any of this. "And some people refer to me as Master." He gave me a small grin that was almost warm. "Mostly my students."

Ilsvashi assassins attacked me, he explained. The assassins most likely in Princess Isabel's employ.

"But the Prince — he ordered her not to do anything to me," I protested.

Master Salvador must have been the kind of teacher who did not indulge his students' naiveté, given the look of utter scorn he gave me. "Amaro doesn't control Isabel, any more than she controls him," he said flatly. He went on to describe in more detail than I desired how the Vashi usually kill, by draining off the lymph of victims they've put into a swoon of fear and dread. "Of course, they don't usually kill you straight off," he added. He sounded both admiring and disgusted. "They like to drag you off to their caves and keep you trussed up and drugged with their damn darts and that damn liquor they make with their spit, and they feed off you for as long as they can keep you alive. The longer you're under the influence, the worse and worse you feel emotionally and psychically, and the better you taste to them. Supposedly they like to get in big groups and nibble all over their captive bitches — like an eating orgy, from the sound of it. The bodies they incarnate in when they travel Across the Bridges into This World get so fucked up — that's why you see them in those freak-ass suits — that they go buck wild crazy when they get control over a healthy human being: they just wanna get near 'em, feel 'em up, suck up their sweat, practically. They punish you, too, for being so healthy when they can't be." He grimaced. "That's what the informants I've talked to report, anyway. I don't know of any human who's survived to tell about it. The Vashi ain't easy to get a good look at — you can't exactly remote-view those motherfuckers. Their lairs are secret, and they pull up the covers on every damn thing, and even the best dream-slaves can't get up under those covers for long. One thing I'm pretty sure of, though, is the Vash don't ordinarily use knives because they don't want their feed bitches to bleed out. So why they knifed you along with everything else, I don't know. There *was* poison on that knife, though, so they were probably going to cart you off somewhere.

"But Isabel's a smart girl and would have had all these angles figured out. The House of the Winged Serpent might know *exactly* what shit goes down in those Vash lairs. Evidently she didn't want to leave the job of killing you up to her Vashi. She had another agent there, a human. That agent would have shot you if Ydris hadn't happened to be there."

"I did not *happen* to be anywhere," Ydris put in. She was across the room. Her fingers were playing across the surface of the black sculpture of the pagan figure, and it seemed that she was studying its form. "I was on quest. It was not by any plan of mind or will that I was there in that park at exactly that hour, this is true. But I knew in my heart that there was something I must find, even if the shape of what I sought was dark to me. I had to hunt. I had felt this for two days." She turned away from the sculpture, toward me. "The feeling has left me. I have found what I must find."

"The question is what did you find," Salvador said.

Because he said it like that — *what,* not *who* did Ydris find — it seemed that he already half-knew. And so I just broke down and let it all spill out, even though I'd intended to lie and I was sure lying was the smarter thing to do. There was just too much

I didn't know or understand. I was exhausted with how much I didn't know, and they seemed like people who did know and understand things.

I had an instinct, too, that maybe they would help me if I divulged enough to make me important to them. *When you start to work with the Unseen, enemies reveal themselves,* Master Salvador had said, *and allies, too.* So I told it all.

Salvador questioned me closely about everything the Prince and Princess and their slaves had said to me, and at a certain point between the questions from him and from Lilia and them barely letting me finish a sentence, I felt like I was an attorney jousting with skeptical justices at an oral argument and defending some extremely sketchy interpretation of law.

But I blabbed it all.

When I'd told them everything up to the moment I lost consciousness — the only thing I didn't mention was the dream — I dropped my eyes, so as not to see the looks on their faces.

At that moment I understood that I was ashamed of myself. Ashamed of what I was.

Salvador's incredulity broke the quiet. "A dream-slave? *You?*"

This comforted me. Lilia's loud retort didn't. "*This* guy is a messiah?" she blurted.

"No," Ydris said. At that point I looked up, directly at Ydris's eyes.

"No?" Salvador asked her.

My heart was pounding. I'm sure the expression on my face as I looked to her for an answer was puppylike.

"He does not smell of them." I swear I did not see Ydris move, but before her sentence was complete, she was beside me, her large eyes fixed on me, her gaze seeming to bore into my pores. And — she licked me. She passed her tongue over the side of my face.

I recoiled and made as if to push her away, but she didn't appear to take any note of my reaction.

"He does not taste of them. The slaves, they are insipid. This one tastes as you taste, as you lovely lovely creatures taste."

Master Salvador noticed my discomfort. (I wondered: had she licked him and Lilia before, too?) "Ydris doesn't mean to offend you. I figure you already get that she's not one of us" — I couldn't help but feel his choice of words was calculated; what the hell was the *we* or the *us* I belonged to? "Ydris is one of the Envoys, who Amaro wanted Isabel to send you to. For examination." He laughed a little. "Which ain't the smartest fucking thing in the world to do under the circumstances—"

"We know nothing of your slaves," Ydris interrupted. An expression—of fierceness, perhaps anger or revulsion—flashed through her eyes. "The slaves your people wrought. Or brought from Outside. What we know is what came before we ever knew your kind. We know what was in the beginning. We know what we learned when our Affinities met yours, and then lost each other again, and then found each other for the last time. Since then we have studied, and now we understand the sorrows and joys that followed those meetings. In all that time and in all the knowledge of your people and mine, there were no dream-slaves. Then we left, and what we knew no longer entwined with what you knew, and all the span after is dark to us. These slave-creatures are intriguing, and some are as lovely to behold as you yourselves are. But a dream-slave is a thing not known to us. They are yours, they are a making of your time, and they lie nowhere in the lands of memory."

Master Salvador tried to clarify. "You get that the perspective she has is from way back, everything she's talkin' about happened like fifty, sixty, even a hundred thousand years ago, right? There's no history, anywhere, of any meeting between humans and the Envoys' people, nothing even in legend or myth that sounds like it. When the Ifah—that's how her people refer to her species, at least among the Affinities she's a part of—when the Ifah met human beings, and we both found out we were related and had somehow been sharing the planet but somehow not ever seeing each other for thousands of years—"

"That description is altogether too... categorical," Ydris chided Salvador.

"Whatever. Maybe one or two met up along the way earlier, but it wasn't till 50,000-plus Before the New Era that the species encounter occurred. Ifah met human, bing bang boom, and a whole lotta shit popped off that only the Envoys can tell us about, and that Izzy and 'Maro and the crew haven't ever bothered to find out about, which includes at some point the Ifah conquering our ancestors and enslaving them —"

Ydris snorted and moved back to caress her statue. "This also is a statement without the complexity that accurate report demands." She whirled back to us suddenly and her fists balled and she growled — actually *growled* — at us. "Why, *why, why* do you come to us with these questions that dangle overripe at branches' end, far from their root — these false questions, these impertinences? Why do you not listen, listen with all that you are, not only with the holes in your head that provide passages for those who will you evil? Why do you not ask questions that march along the straight edge? I say this to you, brother, daughter — and you, cousin" — it wasn't until a few seconds later that I realized she'd called *me* cousin — "that it is not enough to rename your gods-houses and your clans and families as Affinities in homage to us who are your elders. You must heed our counsel, too! The time has come to rise up, to choose your weapons and fight your death! This death you live is not yours, but a making of falsehood! Do not tarry, believing that surcease or peace lies in some afterlife! These things you call gods will use you in your afterlife just as they scheme to use you in life! These *Gods* use everything!"

The rest of us stared at her. Salvador smiled sympathetically at me and pointed his thumb at Ydris. "See, what the Envoys *actually* know about is exactly this kinda arcane shit, and you can never tell when they'll go off about it." Ignoring her diatribe, he continued, "Any way, it's hella ironic in about three different ways, that Amaro wanted you brought to Ydris, cuz she don't know shit from dream-slaves, and that is because the only slaves Ydris and her people ever knew anything about was us: humans."

The irony, I'm afraid, was rather lost on me, as my antennae were telling me that maybe it hadn't been a good thing to divulge so much after all. Master Salvador sounded more intimate with the Prince and Princess than I liked, and quite the opposite to answering my questions, he and Ydris had only given me more.

"Then I *am* a dream-slave?" I asked. I may have shouted.

Salvador assessed me coolly. "From what I can see, you're human. Evidently you taste human, too — not that I'm ever gonna find that part out."

"But... I *flew...*"

"Right, but what that says is that you've got a serious tap on the Unseen, and can work shit without even knowing what you're doing. Which is dangerous, yeah, but only to the general public, not to practitioners and techs of Izzy's level. And damn sure not to anyone of my level. Though you did read straight back to one of Isabel's former lives...," Salvador mused.

"Yeah, that's some serious tap, gotta say." Lilia.

Master Salvador's chin fell to his hand. "The rewriteable brain, though. That is definitely a mystery."

"Can I just say one thing?"

We all looked over at Lilia. She was beginning to move toward one of the doors to the room, though she seemed to be hesitating, as though requiring permission.

"I don't mean to step on any toes, Master, but..." I noticed Salvador start to roll his eyes, but he put a look of attention on his face when Lilia frowned. "Whatever species our guest is, he's being looked for by the House of the Winged Serpent. I'm sure even if you killed that agent, Ydris" — (*My God!* I swallowed what I was thinking, *They killed that gorgeous woman!*) — "that they had plenty of ways to monitor what happened at the park. If they caught any hint it was an Ifah that took Alexander out of there..."

"Mm," Salvador agreed. "Flies don't land on Izzy, that's for sure. She knows you hang out with us, Ydris."

"Which means they could soon be on the way —," Lilia began.

Salvador nodded. "In force. Yeah yeah. You right." He took a breath. "Yeah, make the arrangements. In the morning, first thing."

"Tickets for all of us, or...?"

"Just three. We gotta at least keep up the public pretense I have no personal relationship with the Ifah Envoys, seeing how I'm not a member of the government." Lilia briskly exited the room.

"Now, Aleixo," Salvador continued, "Can I trust you to chill with me for the rest of the night and not try to fly away? There's a lot of shit you and me need to discuss. And after that, might be a lotta shit we need to *do,* too. But we're gonna have to do it somewhere safe, some place that can't be remote-viewed or compromised. This is my house and it's warded, but it's not a fortress. I can't stand up to a siege *here,* even if it's nobody but punk ass Winged Serpent goons laying siege. We need to move."

He paused, but I didn't say anything. I didn't know what to say.

"Trust me. I want to help you."

I had to have at least one question answered. "Why do you want to help me?"

Master Salvador held his hand in front of my face. It was a large hand, with long articulate fingers. "Three reasons. One," a finger curled, "Isabel and me go a long ways back, and I do not trust the bitch. Whatever she says's good, I know's gotta be bad. Plus 'Maro happens to be my second-cousin, and even though I don't trust that maricón either, his intentions are good. If he says something should happen, maybe it actually should. Two," (another finger) "You wouldn't know because you're not in the intelligence loop like me, but as of yesterday, the Wall is thinning. Which in case you don't know, you being an outlander, is big. It means the Great Gods aren't gonna be fenced out for much longer. Means They're on their way. Means They are going to make war like They been waiting to for centuries, and come try to slurp up every papo, mama, and baby in the whole West like foam through a straw and then ride all our bodies the fuck over a cliff to hell. For real.

"Three, I am personally at war with the Great fuckin' Gods, and I aim to kill every last one of them. In order to achieve that goal — I'm gonna put this mildly for the sake of brevity — I make it my business to pack some serious fuckin' artillery, and I make it my business to have serious allies who also pack serious fuckin' artillery in their arsenal. Looks to me like you packin'. Daddy can always use another soldier. Four —"

He stopped, winced. "Damn, I guess that's more than three. Well, anyway," his hand dropped, "the last thing is, the fact that the Wall's coming down?"

Since this appeared to be a question, I nodded — though of course what he was saying only served to alarm me more (except for the bit about my "packing," which made me swell with all the pride I was ever hungry to feed).

"Yeah, so I'm not sure, but... My guess is the Wall falling — and my guesses are pretty much always right — but hey, don't get it twisted, it's not like it's exactly your *fault* —" (I just looked at him, no doubt with the eyes of a rabbit found by a fox) — "but your presence? Your arrival on the scene, man, and then you coming into who you are? That's the herald event. You're like the horn blowing from the watchtower that says the endgame is happening. Right. Fucking. Now."

2.10

ALEIXO'S STORY

2048, Primeiro (the Month of Bright Air), Domingo

Morning. Past dawn, but not far past.

I hadn't flown away as Master Salvador feared I might, but I hadn't slept either. I was kept awake by fear of dreams, and fears of reality.

The Envoy ultimately didn't know for sure whether I was a dream-slave or not. Master Salvador insisted that he believed I was, in fact, human. But they all seemed to agree that Ydris was the most discerning among them regarding the nature of things in This World, and when she was pressed on the question, she said that though I smelled and tasted human, and I did not smell or taste slave-y, it was also true that I smelled and tasted "different."

"A little different," she temporized.

"A *little* the same way Vashi and Silvara are a *little* fuckin' different to humans?" Salvador queried her sharply — evidently not appreciating her retreat from certainty. (I wasn't thrilled either.)

"May be," Ydris murmured. The truth was she didn't know all that much about Ilsvashi and Silvara, either, since apparently, those two extradimensional species weren't around in 60,000 BNE (though conversation with her suggested that other species not native to our dimension were).

This conversation was frustratingly brief, snipped from a whole cloth composed of anxiety and haste, and heedlessly tossed aside by everyone except me. I believe, in fact, that we were in the elevator just before the door closed at the time it took place.

Salvador, Lilia, and I had changed into dull boxy-looking business suits — dour gray jackets, charcoal black slacks, both of which made me chafe. Was it too much to ask to look good even when you're going incognito? I was practically swimming in that suit!

For our faces we all had donned mildly oversized sunglasses and, per instruction, maintained expressions as much like immobile masks as possible. We spoke low but not ostentatiously so.

We were on our way to a garage about a block from the building. The plan was to drive to Costa Garrincha, a beach town about twenty miles outside the southernmost city limits, where — but they hadn't told me yet why we were going to Costa Garrincha. They had told me, however, that we needed to travel by car, because we needed to make use only of items, transport, et cetera, that slaves did not operate, at least until we reached Costa Garrincha.

"Biggest open secret out there," Salvador informed me before we left the apartment, "is that any dream-slave is traceable — and usually monitorable — by the tech or tech Affinity that manufactured it, if it's not operating in a warded location. And what a dream-slave creates out of its own energy — what you'd call a magical effect — is traceable, too. So the Affinities that mass-produce all these slaves for public use get to watch everybody that uses them. By law, the Prince's Affinity and the House of the Winged Serpent share partial title rights with every other tech Affinity, and so they get to trace and watch *every*body. Even if you have an unlicensed slave they'll be able to figure that out, too, and eventually they can begin to trace it. Which is why I'm keeping mine under wraps until I need to use them." He'd glanced at my face to check for comprehension. "That's why we gotta get outta here old-style, in a fossil-fuel car."

I was jejune regarding cloak-and-dagger tactics. "But if most transportation is slave-driven, or or or" — I tripped on the words — "actual slaves, don't, wouldn't fossil-fuel cars stand out?"

Lilia answered. "Yah, but if you have tinted windows — and we have tinted windows — and you're in the middle of a huge city where there's a substantial minority of people either poor enough or rich and eccentric enough to buy and drive fossil cars, then it's not like anybody's gonna stop and take notes because they see a fossil car roll by."

"In the city," Master Salvador said. "Once we're out of the city and on the road, we *will* start to stand out more. But we don't have to get any farther than Garrincha, so the risk ain't too bad."

"But if Princess Isabel suspects you, and she connects my rescue to the Envoy, won't she expect you to travel slave-free?"

Salvador and Lilia ignored this worry.

Ydris seized advantage of that lull in the conversation to bid her goodbyes.

"You know where you're going?" Salvador called after Ydris, holding the elevator door open.

Ydris mounted a drop-down ladder in the apartment that would take her into the attic and then to the roof, from which location she had told me matter-of-factly, she was going to jump, and then fly back to her ambassadorial residence.

"Indeed yes, the place where we rendezvoused that time before," Ydris answered. "Look for us in a day, or perhaps two." Then she'd pulled the ladder up behind her, heaved the roof-door to, and was gone.

About half an hour before Ydris's departure, Master Salvador had emerged from behind a door with three people behind him, two towing wheeled luggage and the third carrying a simple backpack.

Their presence startled me, and I immediately panicked, thinking that they were Winged Serpent agents.

But Salvador's relaxed manner in their presence made me look again more closely, and my panic gave way to a queasy feeling.

The backpacker was a dead-copy twin of Master Salvador, only dressed far more colorfully and fashionably, now that Salvador was attired in nondescript gray. One of the wheeled luggage people was a curvaceous woman who looked a lot like Lilia.

And the other was a tall, broad-shouldered, narrow-waisted, cream-colored fellow with dark curly hair and a broad nose and cheeks, with full shock-red lips and heavy black eyebrows.

If I wasn't standing there stupidly gawking, I would have testified under oath he was me.

Master Salvador buzzed around the three figures, inspecting them with the same hurried distraction that had informed all his movements in the hour since he'd announced our imminent departure. At any moment I'd half-expected him to reach into their backs and start winding a turnkey, except that I could also see our copies' chests rising and falling in subtle but unmistakable respiration, their eyelids' falling and rising, and twitches wriggling along their arms and legs as they shifted position. They appeared to all the world to be absorbed in their private thoughts while Salvador eyed them up in ways that would have made anyone feel uncomfortable or insulted.

I followed his lead and walked over to perform my own inspection. I was naturally most interested in my own copy.

I was also somewhat repulsed. It's one thing to look at myself in the mirror (and I have certainly been known to fall into trances of adoration doing so, from time to time), and another thing to see a three-dimensional breathing, twitching, and possibly pissing and farting you standing there a few feet away. Faults seemed terribly glaring. *Good Lord,* I bristled, *is that how my ears look? And do those lines grooved in the skin of my neck mean I'm developing a turkey neck?*

Lilia, otherwise busy with activities that appeared to involve packing and checking things over, took the time to explain to me that these copies were carrying tickets she'd just purchased for air-carrier transport to Ruba, a Tillean island where Master Salvador was known to have a family house.

"But aren't these — they must be slaves," I said, worried even before hearing about the extent of the House of the Winged Serpent's tracing abilities. I was worried too by the fact that I thought I was more muscularly well-defined than the copy indicated (although maybe it was its clothes, which were pitiably baggy).

"Slave-made, not slaves," Lilia corrected me. "They're hatched from our — and your — skin cells. Their eyes, small brains, vocal cords, and nervous systems (such as they are) are dream-slave artifacts, and the rest of them is pretty much cow, pig, dog, and cat parts. It's enough of a mixture to confuse any tracers."

"For a while," Master Salvador had said.

Lilia continued. "Their internal organs will shut down in less than a week, but that's okay, cuz they'll be in the house on Ruba by then, and everyone will just think they're sick for a few days, before anyone watching figures it out."

"We hope," Master Salvador added from within the kitchen where he was collecting food.

"When did you take samples of my skin cells?" I asked, mostly because I was afraid to ask what I really wanted to know about their brains — a question that crammed within it all sorts of other questions, about the degree of the copies' independent thought, their aliveness, their souls. What was the difference, really, between these part-dream and part-flesh creatures, and me, the maybe-dream-slave who'd always thought and functioned as though I were human? My flesh was real. I pinched myself involuntarily. Would this, I wondered, feel any different on the copy? Was my own flesh dog and cat, cow and pig?

"We took some earlier," Lilia answered with sagacious vagueness, and went on about her business.

In due course Master Salvador dispatched our simulacra to their appointed destinies. At no point did the copies acknowledge my existence, or Master Salvador's or Lilia's either, so far as I could tell, but they trooped out of the apartment and into the elevator with an air of accumulated purpose. Master Salvador stood looking at the elevator door for a long while after it had closed behind them, and soon professed to have observed the three copies clambering into a cab. (A trip to the airport via Hopstop, he said darkly, might incinerate the creatures.)

Shortly afterward he hustled the rest of us out. As our copies had, we took the elevator that opened straight into the apartment, but we skipped the street-level and got off in a subterranean concrete bay with a long corridor leading, I was told, to the nearest Hopstop. A few people passed through the bay into the corridor as we entered — an older woman in a fur skirt with a dog in the crook of her arm and an enormous purse on the other shoulder; three rangy-limbed youths with thick hair on their heads shellacked into plumes wearing platform slavemagic sneakers (all the rage: they sprouted wheels and powered you through the streets at the speed of a bus, could render you intangible for up to fifteen seconds, and could float you four feet off the ground—I'd wanted a pair but couldn't afford them); an undistinguished-looking man wearing a wide-brimmed hat to protect his fair skin from the sunlight.

Salvador led us as though we were trailing this flotsam into the corridor. But to the right of the archway opening into the station lobby there was a door which he deftly opened and stepped through, and we followed.

A short stairway in murky light led up a flight-and-half to another door, and then we were deposited on a sidewalk north of Salvador's apartment building.

There we navigated tables full of the gossiping patrons of two coffee-houses which spilled out along a fan-shaped expanse of flagstoned lawn, until we got to the street and made our way through the crosswalk.

"Don't be nervous, be normal," Lilia cautioned. I thought I heard in her tone, and saw in her smile, a touch of malice when she said that.

I don't know what success I had in the appearance of normality. Certainly, I could not pry my feelings away from their now seemingly permanent locations in Quiet Terror and Painful Self-Consciousness. But no one appeared to take any greater note of me, my two companions, or our poor fashion sense than they did of any other people passing along the sidewalks and in the streets.

It was morning, the sea mist had burned off in this part of the City already, and the sun was heating up the concrete and the skin on our faces. The local thoroughfares were chock-full of hundreds of people scurrying or lollygagging their way somewhere or another. Noises of chatter and moving vehicles pelted us from every side.

In a typical street at home you would probably see more people footing it than vehicles. The latter would be a few Old Age trucks with precious hoarded gasoline tanks — these ramparted by iron barriers and locks, mini-fortresses mounted in cargo beds. You might see one or two dainty electric autos piloted by smug ultra-tanned rich boys, as well as a couple of full-to-bursting electric buses the empire permitted us to have, which would run down the middle of the thoroughfares humming, a sleek speedy canal of life, reminding us of past glories and teasing us with the hope for a return to the summit of modernity in the future.

But in Norio not only were the wide sidewalks thronged, so too were the streets, which belonged to a myriad of conveyances. There were two-tiered trolleys, similar to the electric buses back home except they clearly weren't electricity-powered at all, so swiftly did they pass without ever seeming to stop. They shifted in and out of visibility as though leaving This World to veer briefly into the Next before returning, so as to avoid intersection accidents and other traffic entanglements. Apart from numerous kinds of cycles running on mystery fumes (pungent pink air, it smelled and looked to be), there were electric cars of various sizes and shapes, some like boxes on wheels, others cigars hovering just above the eighteenth-century brick paving—which might lead you to glance up, where you'd see on any given block about ten blue-glow air-sleighs, wind-shielded flying tubs, or people riding on the backs of what looked like broad-backed humans with wings.

And then if looking up tired you, or depressed you—as it depressed me that day, thinking of those slaves, shaped inhumanly to serve the whimsy and convenience of their makers and buyers—you'd bring your attention back down to earth only to find more dream-slaves, for in truth there often seemed to be more slave-activity than human in the street.

There were the galleys, which were slow, and were perhaps the most antiquated mode of travel apart from pedestrian power. Unlike the sleek trolleys, these were bloated vehicles carried in perfect balance by two long rows of marching dream-slaves, all very dark and dwarf-like and oddly shaped so that they resembled nothing so much as the oars of some ancient ship. Complementing these were the single-slave, double-slave, and quadruple-slave sedan chairs, big burly wide-necked and trunk-thighed creatures whose shoulders were larger than melons, such gigantism being necessary, evidently, so that the poles supporting the glassed-in carriages that were their burden could pass through the muscle. I'd never ridden in these carriages, but it was said that despite their ogre-out-of-a-fairy-tale appearance, these creatures were as light on their toes as a fairy might be, and you didn't feel any of the up-and-down you'd expect being carried by a creature with legs. The True God knows the things were fast-moving, almost as fast as the trolleys, though unlike the trolleys they stopped at intersections — except in the unlikely event when the skies above them were momentarily clear, whereupon they squatted, their thighs and calves inflating to such a degree that it appeared their whole bodies had transmuted into a mass of cushions, and then they leapt up into the air and vaulted over the intersection to alight, rather daintily, on the other side. These leaps often brought with them a grunt that reminded me of the backfire of the old gas jalopies back home. This was one of the few audible expressions made by these slaves, which invariably possessed dull eyes that wrapped like equators around their big oval heads, and their dull wide lipless mouths opened only to ask for a destination, to state the fare, and to accept payment.

So, nothing seemed any different to any other day in Norio.

Which meant, at the very least, that no one knew about the Wall. Not yet, anyway. If they did, there would, I suspected, have been panic, or as near to panic as the citizens of the center of the universe can feel.

I got especially nervous and self-conscious when I spied some cops leaning into the counter of a juice bar we passed. Their dark eyes looked disinterested in anything other than the juice choices flashing on the board within the kiosk, but their forearms and biceps in short sleeves, and their thigh muscles in short pants, looked dangerous.

Two of them boasted physiques clearly sculpted by elixir or electrical stimulation. The third drew a double-take. He was dressed in long-sleeves and slacks, for one, and he wore a high-crowned cap and a jacket festooned with ribbons, medals, and exaggerated shoulder epaulets, all of which combined with his exceedingly broad shoulders and snap-your-fingers-and-it's-that-big waist to make him look cartoonish.

He was a dream-slave, of course. The cop's face was round and nearly featureless, with reflective-sheen skin, huge eyes, and a tiny mouth better suited to a doll than to a person. Looking like a cartoonish doll was half the point of such slaves. The look was intended to put children at their ease and to invite contemptuous dismissal by any adult possibly engaged in illegal activity who looked at it and noticed its oddness, and then realized, too late, that they were being watched by it. A slave-cop might look like something to laugh at or to put in a dollhouse, but they ran faster, saw farther, and heard more clearly than humans. Some models were said to generate electro-shock missiles so potent you couldn't walk or speak again after getting popped.

I glanced away. My face felt bloated and red.

Worse yet, when I whipped my head away from the slave-cop—and felt instantly exposed in yet another way, since it was possible that the movement had been flamboyant enough to draw attention, and maybe it was now obvious I'd only been pretending not to notice him—I saw Lilia watching me out of the corner of her eye. She looked disapproving, but whether it was my failure to look normal or the surge of kinship I felt for the slave showing on my face, I didn't know.

The car park was another two blocks away from where I saw the police. It was wedged between two tall apartment buildings, with what seemed to be a thousand windows overlooking it. A sweaty young (but going to seed; that look always depressed me) guy in a tank top and long loose shorts took his sweet time finding Salvador's keys in the back of his attendant's shack. I expected the cops, or Royal Guard, or undercover Winged Serpents, to flood the car park at any moment.

But we were soon off in an antique beetle-shaped little fossil car, dark blue with pop-eyed headlights and, as Lilia had promised, shadowy, gray-tinted panes.

Master Salvador took the wheel, and Lilia sat beside him.

I was alone in the backseat, and so far as I could determine, unfettered.

When traffic forced us to come to a stop, I contemplated opening the door and bolting. Maybe, if I could remember how, I could fly away?

But I made no move.

Which was the worse or better course to follow? Alone in Norio being pursued by the royal intelligencer agency? Or being a supposed guest but possible prisoner of two people whom I did not know and had no good reason to trust, but who claimed to have rescued me from death?

I couldn't decide, which was therefore its own decision: to follow Master Salvador, to find out what answers he could give me about the surreal affair my life had become.

Salvador was less than fluid as a driver, and for several blocks Lilia and I fought off incipient whiplash as he braked and accelerated unexpectedly, and swerved in the most ungainly and stomach-heaving ways, in order to avoid the innumerable obstacles of slave-sedans, trolleys, buses, taxis, wandering pedestrians, and more than a few other fossil cars.

I had had just about enough and was opening my mouth to suggest I drive — fossil cars are the main transport in Arlina, I was going to say, and we drive all the time — when for some reason — perhaps the appearance of a stocky over-tanned youth on the sidewalk in my field of vision as one of Salvador's lurches hurled me against the car window — I thought of Luiz.

He hadn't entered my mind at all for what seemed like weeks, though it had probably been little more than a day since I'd had any reason to consider him.

I wondered whether he might be worried I hadn't returned. It was unlikely, but had Princess Isabel dispatched Sílvio to inform him of what had happened to me? Or worse — perhaps Isabel's agents were interrogating and torturing Luiz at that very moment, aiming to find me through him —

It was a terrible thought, and behind it other disquieting conjectures followed. I knew well that the arm of the Princes of Norio was long, and nothing, certainly, could have prevented them from making inquiries and arrests back home in Peake's Bay, if they felt acquiring information about my past would help them determine what kind of dream-slave I was, and who had made me. Wasn't the likeliest development that as soon as I'd been dumped off in the guest room after the Prince had rescued me from interrogation, that Isabel had sent agents to, or activated agents already present in, Arlina?

They had authenticated the age of my memories, but they'd said they couldn't vouch for the veracity of them (and frankly, I couldn't either anymore, not in my worst moments — as this one was rapidly becoming). Certainly they'd want to verify my story of my youth, find out whether in fact I had grown up in the family I claimed to, and if I had, whether there were any questions about my birth in my family history. I could imagine them asking questions I myself would like to ask: was there evidence, for example, evidence I could not recall, that I consorted with Silvara artisans, or frequented the haunts of dream-tech slave-makers?

I began to notice my heart beating, and to feel my breath come short.

At that moment Master Salvador pointed back over his shoulder at me. He wanted to be sure I saw his reflected eye looking at me in the rear-view mirror.

"Alexander, what do you know about dream-slaves?"

I understood that this was not an entrée to polite conversation. (Indeed, Lilia cast yet another disapproving glance at me.) As with Princess Isabel, an agenda hidden to me informed Salvador's question. But at least this time my life didn't depend on my answers. At least, I didn't think it did.

And the question and whatever game lay beneath it gave me something other than having placed the lives of my loved ones in imminent peril to think about (well, it's true I didn't love Luiz — but I was *almost* fond of him).

"I dunno," I said after a moment of trying to get the jump on Salvador's line of inquiry. "Dream-slaves're... made up of energy mined from humanity's dreams, right? They, uh, can perform calculations at a speed and volume no human mind can, they can create various local effects that defy physical laws, or rewrite physical laws..." The word "rewrite" made me nervous. I searched for something more clearly definitive of a difference between dream-slaves and myself. "They don't breathe or eat or drink?"

"Yeah yeah," Master Salvador nodded. "But what do you *know* about dream-slaves? Like this: why are dream-slaves always shaped like humans? Even the least and most mechanical of them are homunculi with something like a head and two arms and two legs. *All* the powerful ones, that do the shit that 'rewrites physical laws,' all of them look exactly like humans. Do you know why?"

I cast about for an answer. "Ummm... dream-slaves are constructed from the energy generated by humans dreaming. Right? By our unconscious — the electrical fires of all those neurons in sleep, they — well I don't profess to understand the science of it, but, wouldn't that be why? They come *from* human dreams, their properties are derived from human imagination, thus they are in the image of humans."

225

"Yeah, no. See, that's the shit your fuckin' secondary-education teachers, and your priests of the True God, and even some saint-mothers and saint-fathers, and your anchors and pundits on the news-watches — and half them're dream-slaves themselves — that's the shit they like to tell you." He gave a grim, short laugh. "It's bullshit. And they know it's bullshit, too. You're gonna tell me that you can't imagine and build a table that doesn't look like a person? We didn't just two centuries ago used to make computers that looked like little valises and shit? Course you can! Course we did! And we don't dream of all kindza shit that *isn't* human? Monsters, places, animals. Lately I keep dreaming about *rats* — whole bunch of 'em, running around a little dark room in the belly of a ship like their tails are on fire."

This last image seemed to prick me, to unsettle me in my skin for a moment.

"I'm an initiated tech, seventh-level," he said. "Why can't I build a slave that looks like a *rat,* or a collective slave that has its intelligence distributed among a bunch of rat-shapes? Why can't I build a slave that looks like a ship? I can build a slave that I can command to *make* a bunch of rats or a ship, or command to make shit that in all appearances are rats or ships. But I can't make an actual slave that *looks like* either one. Those World Games athletes that got suspended for doping?" I knew the story he was referring to, if not the names of the athletes. "Every time you heard anything about it, the news-watches would say the dopers took an illegal slave-elixir to make them stronger or faster. But no tech made an *elixir.* The techs those athletes or their coaches hired had to build *slaves,* who looked human, and the slaves made the elixir. Why?"

In a tone that complained without saying it about the unfairness of the question (a whiny tone, in other words) — I did so hate not knowing things, just as I hated not having the right pants or cap to wear — I was forced to confess to Salvador that I could not, off the top of my head, answer him. (Lilia made a sound that, if I could've seen her face, I would have described as a sneer.)

Master Salvador warmed to his topic. "The answer is: we don't *know.* None of us know, not just you. In just over a hundred years of making dream-slaves, not a single tech has found a way to make one unless it's humanoid in shape. You're too young to remember, but you've heard about the Iconography Crisis, right, when everybody and their great-grand-cousin was up in arms cuz several of the top tech affinities were manufacturing slaves that were dead ringers for telenovela actors and football stars, and rich motherfuckers were parading those slaves down the sidewalks with leashes on them and dressing them in leather teddies and having 'em bark like dogs and perform oral sex on 'em in public? Hard to believe it was ever even a controversy now, since everybody manufactures the things these days, and even the Godshouses barely say shit about it anymore."

I nodded blankly.

"Well, at the same fuckin' time all that was poppin' off, the top techs were in a *secret convention,* working *together,* which you know those fuckers *hate* to do, but they had no choice because all their chiefs had ordered them to. And they were in this secret convention pooling their knowledge and techniques and trying like all hell to just make a slave, just *one,* that looked like something not human. Like a dog, or like a block of wood." He shook his head. "Couldn't do it. Every model they tried — crumbled into dust, blew away on the wind, couldn't hold its shape. Oh, they were able to make a *monkey* — but the humanest damn monkey you'll ever see. We're talkin' eleventh-level techs." Salvador blew some air, and half-turned for a moment to the backseat. "Does that strike you as possibly meaning something?"

Naturally my first instinct was to assume that what he was getting at was all about me, and that he had concluded, after all, that I was in fact a dream-slave. But I guess I was becoming bit by bit less self-consumed, because it only took a moment or so before I began to think differently, and to understand that there was some larger concern than my identity which interested Master Salvador.

"Might be," Master Salvador spoke into the quiet of the car's interior, "that a dream-slave looks *like* a human because a dream-slave is like a human. Might be they are a species, akin to us." He let that settle in for a bit, then added, "Same way the Ifah Envoys are other-human. Related, but not the exact same. Dream-slaves *don't* eat, sleep, drink, or even speak or fuck unless we make them do it. But that doesn't mean they ain't some kind of human."

I groped for the conclusion. "Then we're... enslaving real beings? Relatives, species-wise?"

"I'm saying that since the New Era started, we been out there fuckin' around Between The Worlds, and for a century we have been practicing something we think is like mining and like animal husbandry, but it might not be like that, *at all.*"

I was uncomfortable, even if the implication of Salvador's argument was that, dream-slave or not, I was at least "kind of" human. We had marched off into the realm of heated political debate, and this was not an arena I as an outlander and an Arlina cared to tarry in.

What Master Salvador was saying was not the same thing the slave-free products movement people said. They annoyed the powers-that-be, but were of course mostly looking out for their own interests, trying to resurrect a long-dying economy that had been based on human creativity and manufacturing. The advent of slave economics had put many who'd once been called members of the working class out of work, at least here in the heart of empire where slave-making was thick on the ground.

Salvador was pleading not for human employment but for the — well, I didn't know what to call it, it didn't altogether make sense — the dignity, the rights, of dream-creatures.

This, then, this *political* conviction — though I did not know the man, he was, I felt, discoursing with considerable passion — this was why Salvador was helping me?

"And all this is known," Lilia added in what I thought, rivalrously, was too strident a tone. "The wealthiest and most educated affinities held a secret convention to try to solve this issue because they suspected the truth and didn't want the public to know."

"Yeah yeah *but,*" Salvador said. (He slammed on the brakes and Lilia and I pitched forward. This was not to punctuate his point but rather to keep from overrunning a convertible-top slave-sedan that appeared to be full of angelic schoolchildren, each dark-haired and with healthily glowing, amber-colored skin.) "We don't *know* what the truth is about the slaves, like I said. We do know the official line — the slaves are just manufactured items, they only mimic sentience, they're just machines.

That shit is bullshit, a lie. But we're all still guessing on what the truth is."

Yes, I wanted to say, there is clearly something fishy and I dare-say immoral at the very foundation of your empire. But it's still the case that with the power of making and commanding dream-slaves, your kind and your cousin Prince Amaro rule all the parts of the world on this side of the Wall of Storms — a case in point being that I'm here in the backseat of your car being dragged off to True God knows where, with little choice on my part. This passion is all well and good, but what do any of these moral nice-ties and political quibbles matter in the end, when you're one of the hundreds of millions like me who have to live and breathe and eat on the earth (or, maybe in my case, simulate doing so) without the power to make dream-slaves?

I wanted to say all this but of course was smart enough not to.

Perhaps the effort required to maintain a demeanor of inof-fensive thoughtfulness in response to Master Salvador's provo-cation helped my brain function in that moment. A sleight-of-psyche maneuver was necessary for me to keep enough false considerations in my mind to be able to pretend to be thinking what my jailors-slash-rescuers wanted me to think, while actu-ally thinking hatefully and resentfully at another level. After all, they might be able to read my thoughts with their car as Princess Isabel had done with her room and her slave, and supposedly I had a rewritable brain anyway. Perhaps these mental calisthenics allowed connections to knit themselves together in my subcon-scious.

Whatever the case, even I was somewhat surprised when I heard myself say, "Ohh, I get it now. You're going to rewrite my brain with what you need me to be able to do, so I can work as a weapon in your war against the Great Gods."

Salvador's eyes widened in the rearview mirror, and Lilia turned her head all the way around to glare at me, as though I'd blasphemed.

"I wouldn't put it like *that,*" Master Salvador huffed in a low voice. "That's not...," his voice dropped into a frustrated mutter.

But now it was my turn to ignore him and lord it over him with knowledge and intelligence. Lilia appeared to get busy with her tablet-phone.

Even if I was right, there was nothing I could do, not now at any rate. If I managed to get the door open and fling myself from the car — with what consequent damage to myself and my pretty face and limbs I did not like to imagine, which pretty much kiboshed that idea even before I thought it through — they could surely stop and get me before I got far away. If I got far at all. I didn't remember how to fly.

It was calming, knowing this, and knowing (as I thought) what was coming. I let the resignation that knowledge brought me keep me on the right side of the border between sanity and insanity.

I was content to wait, and to look around me.

We had left the inner boroughs of the City, and were now passing through more sparsely populated suburbs, where homes perched on cliffs which rose above the coastal highway. At one point we rode by a straggled line of people. They might have been related and there were folks of all ages among them, children and elderly and adults, all passing along the narrow rocky beach that hugged the eastern side of the road. Migrants, likely, headed for the interior where there were fewer slaves and more work.

We were passing out of the suburbs when — again to my own partial surprise — I had another revelation. "I remember now. I had a dream where I was with rats running around a cell in the hold of a ship, too. It was a very vivid dream." I paused for effect. "Was it a telepathic dream, in contact with you, Master Salvador?"

Master Salvador was plainly going to respond with more than a disappointed mutter, judging from the way he took his eyes completely off the road at that moment.

But I had not noticed that we had arrived at the outskirts of Costa Garrincha.

Lilia's body stiffened and she reached out for Salvador's hand on the wheel. But she didn't actually touch him. Her hand just hovered there. That gesture stopped him from replying to me.

"Two o'clock," Lilia said, as though this were the very grimmest of all known hours.

She was not, of course, talking about the time.

She was talking about the three Winged Serpent agents standing just southwest down the road from our car, leaning — much as the policemen I'd seen back in the City had been leaning at the juice-bar — against the railing of a low-slanting stair that climbed up to a roadside restaurant decked out in an iron and copper façade to look like an eighteenth-century railway station.

I knew they were agents by the way they all three stopped whatever they'd been doing and looked directly at our car.

One was probably human, and one I was sure was a slave.

The third was a tall drink of a man. A blue-skinned Silvara.

A winged helmet of watery steel just then materialized on the tall blue-skinned creature's head — which, I had heard on the news-watches, invariably occurs when a Silvar goes to battle.

ALEIXO'S STORY

2048, Primeiro (the Month of Bright Air), Domingo

Each of the Silvara manifests his or her own signature weapon in a fight. An automatic rapid-yield gun, a hammer, a sword, a mace, a spear, a flame-thrower, a bazooka, a chainsaw, a set of bow-and-arrows. Each weapon, they say, is as much a part and an expression of each Silvar as your voice or your fingerprint is of you.

This Silvar manifested a flail.

Its business end, dangling on its chain, was less a ball than a pyramid sprouting wicked thick horns top, bottom, and middle. I observed this with infuriatingly dissociative calm. The spiked elephantine pyramid caught the sunlight, which was just then breaking through a copse of clouds like the white smile of a lovely virgin lifting the hem of her skirt to put one toe into wet springtime meadow grass.

Yes, strange simile, I agree. I'm trying to describe to you the way that time arrested itself—some magic of Master Salvador's, I conjectured. The seconds and minutes ticked off at an elegant pace, as though each thing happening were an event entire to itself, set afloat by the whispering exhalation of a child, a soap bubble that rose languidly into space and drifted away.

Master Salvador stopped the car, in the middle of the south-bound lane of the highway. He did not slam the brakes, and inside the car I felt no jolt.

I heard distantly an imprecation directed at the fates. I saw what could not be, but what nevertheless seemed to be, sparks concatenating upward like terror-struck butterflies from the bright face of Lilia's phone. The muscles of her shoulders kneaded themselves in accompaniment with her racing, dialing fingers. The mode of the tablet-phone had been switched, I was to learn, shifted from This World to the Next, from mechanical to slave-made. It was possessed now of magical properties its former purely-machine mode had not been.

And why not? There was now no need to avoid the traceable devices of slavery. We had been discovered by the enemy.

The roof of the fossil car retracted — slowly, as though the mechanics that operated it acted according to a will that wished nothing done too hastily.

With the roof gone, the sunlight bleached us. So sudden and complete was the sunshine's arrival, so warm and so deep did it soak our skins, that I thought my hair would catch fire.

The human Winged Serpent agent, wearing a gray suit not unlike the ones we had thought to disguise ourselves in, stepped deliberately toward the northbound lane of the highway. Her hair was cut low and set in a nappy coiffure, and she was holding a gun at shoulder level, though its barrel appeared not to be pointing at us so much as at the traffic coming to a complaining halt behind us.

The slave agent, which was attired in the same manner as the human and looked like a pale blond version of her, squatted with what appeared to be a great effort of athleticism — then leapt thrillingly into the air.

The Silvar was twenty feet away, but advanced upon us in no more than three strides. He was eight feet tall and dressed in a richly embroidered black doublet with tight long sleeves, ballooning skirt-like breeches and hose, and boots near to the knee.

I have to say I envied his attire immeasurably, though clearly the creature meant us no good.

I could see the smile on the Silvar's face better almost than I could see anything else about him; it stretched one end of his face to the other, reaching toward the tips of the faceguards of his helmet. Long twilight tresses flowed out from beneath the helmet and danced behind his broad shoulders as he advanced upon us.

Salvador slipped his seatbelt in a liquid motion, and casually rose into the air, as though with a dolphin-like flick of the legs he were swimming up from the bottom of a pool. He came to rest at a spot where his feet hovered above the roofless windshield.

Light, in small bursts of orange, blue, and purple, played around his head and hands. These he lifted from his thighs and spread as if in welcome of his foes.

The slave-agent's feet and weight dented the hood as it landed on the car, though the immaculate square balance of the slave's stance was unaffected by the violence of impact.

Its head was somewhere level to (I imagined) Master Salvador's sternum. It reached out one hand, as though to take hold of something I couldn't see, but it approached no closer.

The slave with one hand reaching, and Master Salvador with arms spread wide, intensely took the measure of one another but did not otherwise move.

The human agent demonstrated that her aim was not toward traffic when she dropped one knee to the ground and propped her elbow on the other, which was now like the barrel of the gun itself pointed cannon-fashion toward us.

She, or rather her gun, fired.

I may have shouted. I did not scream, that was to my credit, but I did make some noise that, fair to say, functioned in place of a cowardly scream.

Measured according to the ordinary physics of firearms, these bullets traveled slowly. Yet terror squeezed the corridor they traveled into a tight ball, and it seemed I had no more than blinked before —

The bullets fell to earth before they reached the midpoint of their trajectory, or so I realized later (and observe for my own eyes now, revisiting the scene).

I saw — and heard — a piece of the highway, the piece a foot or two from the front wheels of our car, crack as though the earth beneath the road had shuddered, I felt the car roll forward into the newly-wrought defile, and I saw the human agent tumble forward into this narrow trough and lose her gun in the hole. This seemed impossible, since the hole was fairly shallow, but it was as though the crack in the asphalt was a mouth that had opened to ingest the gun with a flicker of its tongue.

I noted in the rush of all that was happening so so so slowly that the pinkie finger of Master Salvador's hand nearest the human agent had bent, and was now crooked. (It was his craft, as I suspected then and confirmed later, that had stopped the bullets and broken the asphalt. "I pulled a plank of gravity from the Other Side and threw it down in front of us, and it pulled the bullets and the gun and part of the road down with it," he had yet to explain to me.)

The movement of the car threw Lilia and I at the dashboard and front seat, but Master Salvador and the slave evidently did not consider it seemly to alter their stances, for they moved not at all, or they moved imperceptibly in synchrony with the abrupt movement of the car.

I very much wished now that I could bolt as I had contemplated bolting before.

I saw the Silvar's flail swing into the air but in a backward motion, away from his body, and then just as quickly arc higher and wide forward, toward the windshield of the car or Lilia's head or perhaps my head. It was bringing some serious hurt with it.

But though I could scoot anywhere within the backseat, I found I could not actually rise from it or leave it. In the strange temporal languor I had time to curse the devilry of Master Salvador's sorcery.

The Silvar screamed, in an exultantly bloodthirsty rather than a cowardly way, as his flail hurtled at us.

But the flail too met an obstacle, not of gravity but of magnetism, which held it in mid-air despite all the power of the Silvar's arm and his frustrated struggles. The car lurched toward this new creation (a wall of magnetism, I was later told), buffeted between assailants and defenses.

Master Salvador bent just slightly back on his knees from his floating pose, as if to dodge a close-flying missile, or as though the wind had pushed him. I didn't see any direct threat to him with the naked eye, but I saw the lights around his head flash and spin on their axes.

People had come out of the restaurant, or had emerged from their slave-drawn sedans to watch. A crowd of some twenty or thirty people had appeared.

The Silvar abandoned his flail. It hung in the air, ball and chain and long rod swinging from some unseen hook, askew from one another, along with, I saw, several pairs of keys, belt buckles, and a single hubcap that I did not think had been torn from our car, but from some other vehicle in the blocked traffic.

The Silvar howled in fury. Then he turned and sprinted toward the restaurant, spun, and sprinted back toward us.

Later I understood that he was going to leap the wall of magnetism: at the time I simply thought him savage, and was appropriately distressed.

As quickly as the Silvar moved, he fell: tripped — again, on nothing I could see — stumbled, staggered to stay on his feet, and then crashed again to the road, his blue face clenched. Blood, or what I supposed to be blood, was running from beneath the helmet across his forehead.

On the ground he lay at an angle to the car, beneath the floating, quivering keys and buckles and weaponry. He kicked angrily like a turtle on its back and shrieked frothy vocables that my ears could make no sense of but which were surely curses.

At that moment the human agent, whom I had forgotten, appeared beside the passenger door. With a furious grunt, she struck downward at Lilia with something — a crag of flat rock; no, a fragment of the broken asphalt of the highway — and missed as Lilia flinched extravagantly. But Lilia dropped her phone.

Suddenly I felt lighter. I could stand in the car, and trembling at first, uncertain, I did stand, and when I stood, I was on my way to lifting my legs over the door and going when —

I didn't run.

I don't know why I didn't. (This is a lie. I know *now,* but it's wisest to withhold this information for the present.)

I wished to run from the scene, but some other will which was also mine but unfamiliar, and stronger than the more familiar will, insisted I remain, or die.

I jumped from the car — felt the wave or wall of magnetic force nearby like a heatless fire — reared back even as I landed, afraid — and swung my fist, wildly but powerfully, pure muscle but no intention, battle strategy, or skill, at the left side of the human agent's face.

Her hands were clasped in a hydraulic vise around Lilia's throat.

The agent squealed. She screamed, actually; I should be as ruthless with her as I am with myself. I really hurt her, somehow. She lost her grip on Lilia's neck.

I hit out at her again, but just as my blow knocked against the agent's forearm and I heard her spit at me ("Fuckinpieceashit slave!"), there was a moan so animal and so loud it wrenched both of us out of the berserk trance of our combat.

The moments now tumbled together, quickly where before they had been slow. The moan had been the Winged Serpent slave's: I saw its face go blank — its eyes lose all light, and its simulated pupils broaden to the edges of its simulated eyelids — and its limbs go slack, its body crumbles to the hood of the car. And then I watched the slave slide off to the broken highway, like a hock of meat on a tilted cutting board.

Salvador's feet landed abruptly on the hood of the car, dimpling it further — he slid forward, as though just completing a leap to the broken asphalt begun long ago.

(And in a flash the vision of him and of the car and the slave and everything else dissolved, and I saw before my eyes a bright yellow sun sink into a purple sea, consuming its color, churning its waters, geysers of steam crashed across my vision, flying fish took to the burning skies in great schools, but there was no room in the small sky for them, they burned as their webbed wings met the air and their slim iridescent bodies made the steam sparkle —)

Master Salvador swept his right arm from a quarter behind his back all the way to his left. The sky darkened — but just a patch of it, as compressed as the sky in my strange vision had been. You could see the sunlight and white, drifting clouds farther off, but above our little melee was only a canopy of darkness.

I felt dramatically disheartened. I could tell my feeling wasn't my own, that in some way my feeling wasn't *genuine,* but I felt the emotion as a hammer-blow all the same, so it was at least chemically authentic.

My despair made it necessary to cover my face with my hands, but as I did so lightning crossed through our dark little world, and I saw that Lilia had her tablet in her flashing fingers again, and as she knelt on the car seat cushion, her face was clenched in an awful, vicious grin. (She had succeeded in powering down the slave.)

In the lightning, which split the dark again and again as though timing to some fast-beat music, you could see faint red wisps — like broken strands of a spider's web, I thought — flutter above the thrashing form of the Silvar, who had not yet risen, and now perhaps could not (and I thought: oh yes, the bodies they make for themselves, unlike the Vashi, have blood in them, and iron is in their blood as it is in ours, and either Master Salvador or Lilia has set the magnetism on the Silvar like a piranha or a pit bull).

Master Salvador sledded — it seemed, though he was only moving on his feet — off the car, landing behind the human agent, whose throat he caught in the crook of his arm, and whose back he made a mess of with repeated stabbing.

(For he, like his nephew's cousin Isabel, carried a stiletto, hallowed with eldritch sigils from which tiny rivers of force flowed when the blade pierced the agent's skin. She was not immunized or armored against the spells of these particular sigils, and so the blood vessels and organs nearest the stabs — there were six strokes in all, rapid and efficient — were ripped apart or burst. I was told this later. At the time I saw her pain. Not her body writhing in pain, which it was in fact doing and which I did in fact also see, but her *pain,* I *saw* it, and it looked larger than the well of darkness into which Salvador had cast us. It was a mountain of rock brought to dust by racing cracks that split it, methodically, into smaller and smaller diamonds till it was nothing. And it was small demons, the size of knuckles, with long fine teeth, eating wildly at a banquet of human arms and legs, telling jokes with their mouths full of blood and viscera —)

"We don't have *time* for this shit! Come with me!"

That was Master Salvador. He was shaking me out of a fugue I didn't realize I'd fallen into.

The people around us were crowding nearer. All at once, I could hear sirens, though another sense told me that they had been blasting already for some minutes.

The darkness had broken, and you could see and hear helicopters approaching.

"Follow me," Salvador said. "Run!"

A dog follows his master. So I ran, watching his heels.

Lilia ran just a few feet behind us.

We parted the crowd — I saw a mother cover the eyes of her child, saw several people snapping pictures or taking videos with their phones or their backpack-slaves.

We ran in the opposite direction from the restaurant. We passed two small homes, one where an old couple sat watching on the porch, and not far from it at the next house a group of children hung off the edges of their porch, cheering us on or jeering, I didn't know which.

Then we were amongst trees and bushes and weeds, and I could see the sea, and feel rocks beneath my feet threatening to twist my ankles as I ran. The darkness that Master Salvador had summoned and dismissed before on the highway shrouded us once more.

There was no lightning this time. I simply ran towards the gray running shape in front me, hurried by the sound of panting and of more curses behind me.

ALEIXO'S STORY

2048, Primeiro (the Month of Bright Air)
Domingo late afternoon – and then: unknown

Sprinting while protected by a Spell of Concealment and Short-term Speed is a lot like running stoned. One moment is utterly lost to the next, and the past — really, only a minute or two ago — dissolves away like a clump of sugar in coffee, only to ricochet back an unmeasured span later in defamiliarized form, as though it were a tale of ancient passion and injustice now existing only in archaic, indecipherable verse.

I therefore cannot testify as to how long in time or how far in yards or meters we ran, for when we reached our destination, I was a puddle of hypersensitivity and numbness. I wished fervently that I could remember how I'd flown just a day or two before, when I was — whatever I was: half-drunk on dreams. But I couldn't.

A Spell of Concealment, I was to learn, has nothing to do with the harnessing of physical forces or the bending of light, as I mistakenly guessed at the time. It involves a condensation of otherworldly particle-like microscopic creatures and psychic flotsam purchased via complex prior negotiations with — and humiliating propitiations of — Lord Exba.

Lord Exba is one of the Homely Gods and a deity of the crossroads. Evidently Exba is known to haggle with any who summon him for a solid week, and at the end is likely to demand an additional week devoted to praising his virility with ecstatic moans whilst licking his scrotal sac, which is roughly the size of two full-grown milk cows and smells of hay and turpentine.

Our destination was the dim-lit interior of a clinic, the low-ceilinged walls of which were shrouded in black crepe. There was a nurse's station sealed off in gauze with a nurse wearing infrared goggles in attendance. A gaggle of owl-eyed persons — patients, I presumed — continually scooted their chairs away from one another and crashed into our knees as we endeavored with a high failure rate to make our way over the floor towards a door hidden behind a trembling flap of crepe in the far wall.

My overall impression of the place, indeed my memory of its odor, was of fear. Everyone seemed to have pissed or to be just now pissing their pants or panties. Howls and shrieks played thunder to the lightning of widening eyes and flinch-motions of the neck or shoulder that would have been visible to back-row upper-balcony patrons in a stadium theater. There were lots of people shading their eyes — which, it occurred to me, explained the nurse and his infrared spectacles.

It was a CFS (Catastrophic Fear Syndrome) clinic. In Arlina we called the disease Fraids. The epidemic had begun decades ago and was supposed to have crested some fifteen years prior, but stubbornly the sickness lived on still, occasionally claiming a mall-full of shoppers or a concert hall or a village or all the fans of a football match.

It made some sense to have fled here, because everyone with any sense avoided these clinics: Fraids was virulently contagious.

On the other hand, of course, here we were, and that didn't seem like a good thing to me. (There was then no cure for Fraids, even with the use of slaves' magic.)

"Keep walking," I heard Master Salvador say.

I had already trained my eyes away from the faces of the Fraids patients, hoping that I had been moving too fast to risk look-to-look infection. I crashed into more chairs and knees, but I kept going.

Of course, dream-slaves were immune to the disease because they weren't truly alive and certainly not human, so perhaps I shouldn't have worried.

And then as my shoulder glanced across the shoulder of someone else whose face I absolutely refused to see, I thought, *Now isn't it odd that Fraids cases started to be diagnosed around the time that the dream-techs harnessed the means for the mass production of slaves?*

Finally, I saw the door we were aiming for open, and I heard Master Salvador urge Lilia and me forward.

At the same moment that someone with a tone of authority (the nurse, or a doctor) yelled, "What are you doing here?" I raced through the doorway and dip-leaned like a sprinter across its threshold.

I hadn't expected to enter a room or to simply exit the building — we wouldn't have passed through such a dangerous place to go deeper into it or just to leave again, I knew that. I also expected that whatever was beyond the door would be unexpected, that the doorway would be magically charged somehow, like a teleportation station platform. So I was ready, at least as ready as one can be after running wildly for an indeterminately long time, then passing through a Fraids clinic full of infectious people, and therefore having only tens of seconds to assess the next bend in the road.

The sensation of passage surprised me anyway. It was not a sensation in the strictly physical sense, but more an emotional tremor, a tidal rush of affects, of loves fears desires hates joys angers not yet fully felt but ready to be felt, a neurochemical wave breaking in some imaginary *inside* — assuming, of course, that I was as human as I hoped and was therefore still prey to such fluxes and humors.

It felt like escape: like an addiction to escape, like the need to see the next episode of your 2-D telenovela or 3-D miniseries. It felt like the necessity of eating something rich and sweet though you're not the least bit hungry, like inhaling so much Water your lungs fill up with liquid and you drown, and you don't care because you had to do it: it was so good and yet so unsatisfying in any dose less than the absolute unlimited amount you craved.

"Where are we?" I asked after I could breathe steadily again.

At a glance, we were in a vast valley, with white, mist-haloed mountains to one side and verdant hills to another, a stream running near our feet through a riot of winding and climbing rainforest flora.

But there were also chairs with high backs and pillowed arms sitting on parquet floors, right there beneath the imperial crown of a banyan tree; and there, too, was a settee; and across the stream off behind a scrim of leafy vines was a long table where shadowy figures were setting dishes for dinner that I could smell (seafood — roasted squid? — and skewers of pork...). On the lower slope of the mountain I could see large beds, and what looked like a shower.

"Oh. This is like Princess Isabel's interrogation room," I answered myself, though uncertainly.

Master Salvador touched my shoulder. There was a warmth in his hand that felt like more kindness, more love, than I had felt or known for months.

Later I understood that this was because he had come at last to a place where he felt safe, and happy, and which was a refuge for himself and his affinity.

"No," Salvador said, smiling broadly, "Izzy's room — I assume from what you said — was a moment-place plucked out of space-time for her use. Which, gotta hand it to her, takes a hella lot of technique and power to manage. It's like plucking a crystal of salt out of a whirlwind and holding it outside the wind, when you and everything else is *in* the wind. But this here is your standard slave-made world-space, existing between Our World and the Others, carved and smelted out of the material linking the multiple dimensions. Well, it ain't exactly standard, that's a lie. It's built to my specifications, you could say straight out of my desire — as my desire exists *here,* once I passed into it and made it."

He looked at me and laughed: so much more free, so much more *there* with me than I had experienced him before — maybe more than I had ever experienced anyone, I realized sadly.

"Now I know none of that makes sense."

"No," I said. I was sad, to see and to feel him so happy and so affectionate with me. Because, of course, I was seeing in that moment, as though a curtain had been pulled aside, how thin and gray had been my dealings with other people, even those I loved, till now.

Or was this all an effect of the magic?

"You'll get it," Lilia said. She had a glass in her hand from which she sipped, between bouts of bathing her face in a shaft of sunlight that slanted down through the forest canopy seemingly just for her. "The main thing is, we can't be found here. A space made from a sorcerer and tech of Master Salvador's level is a materialization of desire — you can't find it, because its only satisfaction lies with him. And then because desire can't ever really be satisfied —"

"Yeah, the whole landscape's liable to change up any minute, so watch out!" Master Salvador interjected.

"— and so they can't follow us, even if they come to the clinic and go through the same door."

Right. Princess Isabel's agents would need Master Salvador's physical and emotional presence to unkey the lock to the passage. The clinic provided no actual docking point to Salvador's reality, unless he was there.

"Yeah, it's like, we're all *in* my mind," Salvador said amiably. "Though we're not."

"There is one point of physical access," Lilia said. "But it's back in the city and they'll never find it."

Yes, I thought. That point of physical access would be... 7097 Candido Constanti Street.

But how did I know that? And if that was where the physical access point was, why didn't we just go straight there rather than driving a hundred klicks out of the city? (Oh, got it: because going via the long roundabout route would take anyone following us to a dead end, and they didn't have any reason to associate 7097 Candido Constanti with Master Salvador, unless he was foolish enough to lead them there. He probably always retreated there by one of the back ways.)

Wait. Why was I having two conversations, one with words, and one in my thoughts?

Master Salvador insisted that I eat — and I was indeed very hungry.

We sat together on round-bottomed seats beneath the stars. Or rather, beneath the brighter and yet also softer and more romantic semblance of the real stars in the real world. We ate at a cozy table with its legs and ours clasped in the fingers of tall green weeds that sprinkled our plates with the scent of basil when a breeze riffled them.

I remember shrimp, avocado, bacon, and mango, but here even the discipline of walking back along the roads of memory that makes this memoir possible fails. I was so hungry there was no self left within me to take note of what I ate.

The hunger, and the compulsion to sate it, was all that I was, and all that I knew in that strange timeless afternoon amid the jungle of Master Salvador's mind and desire.

Later I lay in a bed, gazing in wonder at unrecognizable constellations. The room was roofless, but with a bed and nightstand and even a mirrored bureau nestled among the fronds with grass licking at their knobbed feet, it was warm and comfortable. Salvador and Lilia were in their own rooms, presumably, or, for all I knew, in a room together.

My mind was quiet but awake.

"Sleeplessness," said a voice in the pastel darkness.

I did not look towards the source of the voice.

"What about sleeplessness?" I asked Master Salvador.

"Not being able to sleep is how it starts. Not *needing* to sleep. Sometimes not even needing to eat. That's how it was with our ancestors, when they first started working the Unseen, after the Foundation-spell. Late eighteenth century. At least that's what they wrote down. They say the pathways of the brain widen. It's like more lanes added to a road, and triple traffic. Or it's like a sun shines that stops setting. The work your mind does in sleep, it begins to do when awake. You dream in waking. You live in waking dreams, and your dreams follow your will. That's how the practice of magic begins." There was a hint of nostalgia in the way he was speaking to me.

I looked then. Master Salvador stood nearby. There was no door: the room seemed a part of the jungle all around, the spaces between trees and masses of foliage only coincidentally similar in their arrangement to parlors and hallways.

Master Salvador was dressed in a royal blue robe that plunged below the neck and was loosely tied at the waist. His rich deep-brown skin seemed to sparkle against the cloth. I had the uncomfortable sense that he was naked beneath the robe.

Shaking me from such speculations, he told me to rise from bed, and follow him.

The time was exactly right, he said, for him to begin my instruction. Lilia would be joining us, he added, though she'd already had some initial lessons.

I was naked and so began to cast about for something to put on. I expected that what seemed to be the trunk of a short tree, or an impossibly thick branchless shrub, was some kind of bureau and maybe contained something other than my own sweat-brined clothing. But Master Salvador said no. "Naked is what you should be for this," he said.

So I followed him through the brush, naked in the star-splashed dark. It now seems stupid to remember how it felt then, when all of my worries about sexuality, blah blah blah, seemed so important, but — it felt odd to me, padding along barefoot with my genitals swinging as I followed a man in a robe. Too border-line sexual. Pervy. A Rioca would think nothing of it, but Rioca go nude at the slightest invitation, and seem not to shy from the eros of any possible coupling. For Arlina, though, especially an Arlinian man —

"You won't be sleeping again. Not for a while," Master Salvador told me.

Soon we were in a round meadow. It was surrounded by trees that bent toward us, giving the impression that we stood together in an unfinished dome.

"Finally!" Master Salvador said cheerfully. "I have been waitin' to get started with this shit."

Thus it was that I became formally introduced to the practice of sorcery.

As a consequence of these revelations I discovered, to my surprise and to Master Salvador's, what was the nature of the strange dreams I had while recovering from the Vashi poison — dreams which were not dreams at all, as it turned out.

And then, when I was in just the right and proper frame of mind, with no solid ground beneath me and under a strange, unreal, and unfamiliar sky, I received a dire lecture about the history and fate of the universe.

ISABEL'S STORY

*2048, 10th of Primeiro (the Month of Bright Air),
Segunda, 0855 hours*

Establishing telepathic links is most easily accomplished by use of what is called a "tap" — a charged article that facilitates the link. Like a hand-mirror, or a crystalline stone. When engaging in such links, common courtesy generally dictates that each participant visualize some kind of filter to keep extraneous information from flowing along the link.

First, you hold in your thoughts an image as solid as possible of a grounding cord that connects you to the earth — say, a tree trunk and roots, or a copper pipeline. Then you narrow the ordinary diameters of the seven wheels of energy in your body, with the exception of the sixth and seventh, so that your personal energies, their particular idiosyncratic harmonics and resonances, are contained and do not overtax the link. (This means you have to have a decent sense of what the diameters of your seven energy wheels ordinarily are — but if you practice telepathy, you will have acquired such information through assiduous meditation.) Finally, you picture a gold mesh screen all around you, sealing off from your communicant what you don't want or need them to know.

The courtesy of filtering is particularly important when communicating with someone with whom you have a personal or genetically-close connection in your Affinity. Otherwise, all manner of emotional reverberations, the frissons of aspirations, resentments, disappointments, and projections, not to mention echoes of personalities from your shared lineage, are liable to obfuscate or even overwhelm communication.

Prince Amaro on the occasion we are now monitoring failed to observe common courtesy, or else he was slower to do so than he should have been.

Isabel distinctly felt a wave of sloppy satisfaction squirt through the link she'd established with him, and could not close her eyes (because it was not her eyes seeing) to the image of a buxom slave with dark curly hair trailing down its back, kneeling between Amaro's outspread legs and enveloping his penis and both testicles all at once in its unnaturally capacious mouth.

Indeed, for a wildly delightful moment — the delight all the more intense for its spiky unexpectedness, and for its brevity — Isabel felt the slave envelop her whole crotch, or thought she did.

Sorry, Amaro indicated. The image and the feeling evaporated. *Forgot.*

But Isabel did not "hear" the slight echo that distorts telepathic words when the communicant is feeling ashamed. Nor did she visualize any flashes of red color or images of warriors in battle-stance, so Amaro clearly wasn't even angry at being caught indulging himself during their discussion. Likely he was just amused. Isabel suspected that Amaro might even have intended to be discovered.

Sometimes Isabel hated her cousin.

At the same time, she couldn't help respecting his shamelessness. She wished she could feel so free herself. But this thought she kept leashed far back behind her mesh screen, and Amaro didn't signify that he'd received it.

Isabel decided to start off the conversation with something soft, maybe put him at ease with some cousinly teasing before giving the bad news. So she told him, saturating her words with the glow of a smile, that if nothing else he was consistent in his choice of lovers. *They're always curly dark or dark-ginger hair, and they always gotta have that smooth creamy pallor — a combination like sculpture among the ancient Qura or Eleniks,* she thought at him. *Combined with those broad architectural faces, and round high bottoms and tight musculatures of the Eldest People of the Motherlands across the sea.*

I do know what I like, Amaro replied, and he permitted another gust of his bodily satisfaction to accompany his words. Like a fart, Isabel thought, disapproving his disrespect even as she respected his willingness to flaunt himself. *But despite all appearances, I was actually working.*

Isabel found this laughable, and a feeling one-part humor and two-parts contempt sprayed through the link like skunk odor.

Amaro weathered it. *No, really. I'm deciding whether to promulgate these laws the council's drawn up about the celebrity slaves.*

Almost since the beginning of slave-making more than a century ago, dream-slaves had occasionally been crafted by their makers to closely resemble real people: oftentimes a loved one who had passed into one of the Next Worlds, other times a famous football player with whom the slave's Maker was obsessed. In the past several years slaves of the latter sort, figured with the shape, voice, and mannerisms of the famous from all walks of life — and death, since many were made to look like long-deceased sports and film stars — had become rife. It was not uncommon now for a famous football player to take three weeks out of the public eye to recover from the scandalous spectacle of his slave-double giving acrobatic stimulatory pleasure to its Maker as he or she walked the red carpet to an awards event (yes, picture a blowjob given by someone hanging upside down in the air), only to take to the field again at last and spy to his chagrin the thirtieth rendition of himself shimmering slightly blue in the crowd, grinning and cheering with its arm draped around some rich skank the famous football player would never have been caught dead with.

The complaints of the famous had become vociferous, especially because as everyone knew, a celebrity-slave's task was to look like the real person in public but to fulfill the very wildest of their owners' perverse sexual fantasies in private, and sometimes also in public. Understandably some did not find such attentions flattering. There was a question of intellectual property — does one not own one's own bodily figure? — as well as of rape — was it not a violation of you, if someone made a slave exactly like you and ordered it to do sexually disgusting things you would not do or did not consent to do?

The Affinity's council had recommended a series of regulations, with conditions for triggering an outright ban on celebrity slave-making.

You're deciding *what to do about a law about celebrity sex-dream-slaves while you yourself are getting blown?*

Isabel made her mentally-generated voice "sound" very, very dry.

Well, okay. My second-self is deciding right now. I'm simply providing a well-grounded state of physical meditation, so that my body can give my executive functions space to make a decision unclouded by... personal inclination.

In her room at home, Isabel sighed. *Good luck with that,* she told him. Then: *I called because I have news.*

After a pause, Amaro asked Isabel, what news.

The storms of the Wall continue to dissipate, Isabel told him, knowing that he must already know this. The only good news was that the rate of dissipation was steady rather than rapid or exponentially increasing.

She told him also that a flotilla — some fifty vessels, *so we know They're serious,* she noted — had crossed through the storms: fully automated, relatively small ships not equipped for battle, but, according to the Imperial interceptors that boarded them, programmed to deposit their cargo on Empire shores.

The cargo was...? Amaro wondered — though he already knew, or mostly knew, because of his own spies within Isabel's spy network, and because she wasn't bothering to shield her revulsion from him, or to hide the loathsome images she had in her mind.

Animal-vegetable constructs possessing nervous systems but no brains, Isabel answered.

Amaro saw them in his thought: the holds of the ships packed with humanoid creatures — humanoid insofar as they had heads, eyes, mouths, two arms and hands, and two legs and feet — so tightly crammed into the space they couldn't move, despite the fact that the commands of their nervous systems insisted, shark-like, that they move. And so they made noises of frustration with their stunted vocal cords: a moaning and growling, a moaning in the form of growling, that filled the cargo-holds like a cacophony of bees confined to a hive. Their faces and slack lipless mouths gave them each a haunted look, yet to see them even from a distance was to be haunted by them (though Amaro was only seeing the image transmitted to him by Isabel, who'd had it transmitted to her by her naval corpsmen): flesh without skin dressed in barely more than tattered robes — flesh made of mud and broken leaves and mulched weeds and radish peels and potato skins and pepper rinds. Their hands and feet were tree-bark, or looked like it at any rate, and they were clawed.

Zombies? Golems? Amaro speculated dispassionately.

Both, or near enough either way, Isabel corrected him, tamping down her distaste. Such creatures they had seen before, in the last war, though perhaps not so animate as this latest model. These didn't shamble: when the cargo holds were opened, they surged out of the dark vaults with the quickness of wild dogs charging, and managed to rip apart several of the first unlucky crew of investigators.

Do the Gods mean to mount these creatures? Send them here, and then ride them as soldiers? Amaro asked.

They didn't ride them last time. And They didn't mount them when our navy boarded the ships, so probably They couldn't, Isabel replied.

Everything we know, she told him, suggested that if a Great God tried to ride such a creature, it would disintegrate immediately, unable to contain energies of the god's intensity. A Great God riding a human being destroys the human body in a few hours. *These they probably sent because they might be able to survive the psychic cyclones in the Wall.*

Amaro understood that this meant the Gods must have been testing the Wall, seeing what could get through. In the past, when the Wall was at full strength, the golems too would have been incinerated.

But these survived. We had to destroy them ourselves, Isabel told him. *Next They'll send animals — or maybe even humans that They don't mind slaughtering.*

Amaro's sulfurous satisfaction had disappeared now, Isabel noticed, dissipating more rapidly than the Wall-storms. She didn't suppress her grim sense of vindication. She saw immediately in his mind that the Prince had reached the same conclusion her analysts had: the third wave would be the soldiers, with all their weaponry, and they would be ridden, en masse, by the Gods themselves. This would happen relatively soon. Likely within weeks, maybe two or three months at the most.

Isabel and Amaro's link conversation had taken less than a minute. It was going to take much longer to strategize how they were going to respond.

The first decision was how to fight. Regarding this they made such decisions as they could, which were predictable and largely involved invoking protocols and setting in motion tactics and strategies that their slaves and generals had long prepared. Little of this inspired confidence in either of them.

On the other hand—Isabel offered tentatively, and she was surprised to find Amaro didn't scold her—there was another option. The option to flee: to gather up all their Affinity, all their loved ones and possessions, and, as they and their forebears had long feared they must, abandon the City and the Empire to its destruction.

Where could we possibly go? Amaro wondered.

The lands on the far side of the Shi Ocean, which have been free from the Gods' predation for centuries, Isabel answered.

Yet if we fall, eventually they will, too, Amaro replied. *Might be better to escape through the portal to a refuge universe that our mothers and fathers started building ten years ago. We would have to reveal it at last, but why bother with continuing to lie at this point?*

Yes, Isabel endeavored to slow the pace of her thoughts. *And when we reveal that portal, every other Affinity, all the nons, and all the governments elsewhere, and of course the Gods, will know at last what part we've played in this crisis.*

Amaro's understanding of this was implicit, and he was impatient with having to acknowledge it at all. He pressed on along the line of thought he'd started, ignoring Isabel's. *We would have to retreat with the greatest speed, all at once, and destroy the portal behind us. Not even knowing or having investigated what kind of universe the portal really leads to. Because once they know, they will all try to kill us.*

Isabel had no answer. The two cousins waded briefly in a meditative silence.

Finally Amaro thought what he hated to think, and what Isabel had been waiting for him to consider.

The shadow of it passed through the link, like a bird flying overhead.

Isabel had perceived it before. She would not let it go, this time. She placed a wedge of amethyst over her lips and spoke aloud. The amethyst tap ensured that the sound was contained within the link; no one and nothing, not even the walls of her room, would hear except Amaro.

"There is another option," she said. "There's your weapon."

Amaro tried to thicken the gold mesh between them, but it was swept aside. *What are you talking about?* he sent.

"That slave you made," she said aloud again.

"What slave?" Now he spoke, too.

"The one that for reasons I still don't understand you made attractive to me. The Arlina."

What? Strangely it was easier to keep up the lie in thought than in speech.

"I suspected you'd made him from the beginning," Isabel said. "When you broke into my sanctum I all but knew. Sílvio was suspicious, too. And then when 'intervention' saved the slave from my Vashi assassins, I knew. You made him." She pressed on before he could deny it. "How? And why? These are questions I'd like to have answers to. But more important now is, what can he do? You made it to do something, didn't you? I'm hoping that something was to save us all."

The silence that followed was long, but Isabel was patient. Amaro couldn't lie to her now, but he could refuse to answer. She let him simmer, hoping for the only right decision.

"Well...," Amaro sighed at last. He spoke slowly. "That's the thing, Izzy. I didn't *make* him. I planted a *seed,* not knowing what the flower would look like. He's what grew. The catch is, we don't know what it has become. What that seed can do, it will grow into—rapidly, I think, now that it's been activated. But whatever he can do, it will be feats of greater power than any single tech, saint-mother, sorcerer, or dream-slave has yet wielded. Or so I hope."

Isabel considered carefully before asking her question. *Is he the* source *of this power, or just a conduit for it?*

Amaro shrugged, and Isabel felt what she was sure was his attempt to master his ignorance. "More conduit than source," Amaro replied.

"And will you be able to point this gun at the right target?" Isabel demanded.

"Yes, of course!" Then, more truthfully... *I don't know.*

Isabel wished that she lived another life, in some other dimension, tinier and safer than This.

Then she severed the link, summoned Sílvio, and began to plan anew.

ALEIXO'S STORY

2048, probably Primeiro (the Month of Bright Air)

Master Salvador told me that Lilia soon would be joining us in the tree-dome. But he had summoned me first, so that the two of us might confer alone.

I interpreted the intensely guarded expression on his face in a moment of instantaneous insight, and was surprised to hear myself saying, "This is when you try to convince me that it's in my best interest to let you use me as a weapon."

My heart started racing. Maybe it was "the pathways of my brain widening," but that wasn't exactly my voice speaking, was it? It sounded distorted — but distorted in that way your voice sounds when you play back a recording of your phone greeting: a correction of the distortion of your own voice that the position of your ears vis-à-vis your mouth and vocal cords normalizes, a correction to your *real* voice, which sounds fake when you actually listen to it.

Salvador kept a straight face, but his eyes told me that he was as surprised as I was. No doubt he was thinking: who did I think I was to speak so cynically and brashly to the kin of princes, and one of the most powerful techs in the Empire?

At that moment I couldn't have answered that question myself.

"I wish you wouldn't put it like that, cracka. This is something I hope we're gonna *want* to do together."

He watched me, waiting for a response. I kept my silence for want of anything else to say.

Salvador changed the subject and pointed beyond the crowns of the trees. "Beautiful, isn't it?"

I looked up reluctantly, unwilling to so easily trade my suspicion for such meager conversation. "They're not the usual stars. You came up with an arrangement to suit you? Or is that the view in some other galaxy?" I asked, hoping to sound unimpressed.

"Nawww," he protested. "Those *are* our stars. You're just seeing more of them, closer and clearer than you usually do with the naked eye. I didn't paint fake stars up there, I just built this place so you could see better. Like an observatory without the telescopes."

I looked again, and this time could not pretend to be unimpressed. "Ohh..."

"I want you to look, really look. What do you see?"

I gave an uncertain shrug. Spilling down toward the tops of the trees were the milky lights of thousands of stars muted to glowing dust by immeasurable distance. Most brilliant, of course, was that great gash in the night, that trough seething with light and color that slashed like some massive frozen comet's tail across the top corner of the sky. "What, you mean the Fire's-Eye?"

Master Salvador nodded. "Fair enough. But really look. Does it look like a fire's eye to you?"

"Ummm. Repeat the question...?"

"Does it look like the heart of a fire?"

"Not really, I guess. It's more — it's like a wound in the sky. As if the darkness of space were a fabric, and it was torn, and something was burning behind it. I guess that's a fire's eye?"

Salvador gazed upward. "It doesn't look that way to me. It's the center of the galaxy, we know that. To me it's a garden of fireworks, captured right in the middle of blossoming. It's... a riot of lights? Hard to say. But not a fire's eye. It was Ur who first called it the Fire's-Eye."

This surprised me. "Ur? My Ur? The prophet of the One True God?"

Master Salvador smiled. "That's what you call him. For us Rioca, at least those of us who bother to know about him, Ur was a great scientist of the spirit and of working with the Unseen.

The saint-mother of the Godshouse my father worshipped in, she definitely loved her some Ur and his teachings." He smiled kindly. "But she didn't ever tell us anything about him without reminding us how much he fucked up with his visions of a single god. You do *know* that the history of humans' encounters with the divine long after Ur's death have repeatedly proven that monotheism just isn't true."

Salvador paused — to give me time to bristle, no doubt, and to master my sense of offense. Once I had swallowed my Arlinian pride, as in due course I did, he continued, "It was Ur's idea that the center of the galaxy, where all the first stars and black holes are packed closely together, was the place of refining. For Ur it was where God tempers the souls of those who finally get all the way up to the apex of the pyramid of rebirth. God's fire makes the soul pure — or it destroys them, because they can't attain purity."

I frowned. "I'm familiar with that idea. But I didn't know it came from Ur directly. I thought it was folklore, or something the priests made up later..."

"Nah, it was Ur's teaching. And it's a pretty idea. But like a whole lotta Ur's 'revelations,' it's just a rendition of an older tradition. The ancients you call pagans referred to the galactic center as Gods'-forge, because to them it was like looking at a whole mess of bright sparks flying off a massive blacksmith's forge. The pagan priesthoods, especially the ones associated with Nubis the Sun-goddess, called it High Forge or Sun's Cradle. And in the First Days, when Dumasa was the language all human beings spoke, it was supposedly called Soplo de la Dragón, the Dragon's Breath — we figure because First Mother and her clan knew about dragons, maybe cuz dragons were still around back then." Master Salvador's face took on that guarded expression before he spoke again. "Then when the Envoys came, about twenty years ago, they told my father something different. My father was high in our Affinity, but he wasn't its chief. But still they chose to tell him, and him alone. They told him that their people, the Ifah, knew what the ancients had forgotten."

"What did the pagans forget?"

"That what we see in the so-called Fire's-Eye is a set of laws."

"Laws?"

"'Laws' is one way to say it. Fates, destinies, those'll do too. We can't read the laws. But what my daddy told me is that recorded there are the histories of This World, the names and countenances of the gods in the halcyon days of their youth, and some forty-five thousand years of the history of all that has happened prior to the moment of our seeing the Forge's light." He looked at me confidentially. "That's because we're about forty-five thousand light-years from the galactic center."

He continued, "And in what looks like the darkness surrounding the Forge—there lies the record of all that has yet to happen. 'It lies too deep, this knowledge,' my father told me, 'it is hidden in depths no perceptions of ours could penetrate even if we could decipher the signs.' Typical Pops. But some, with the aid of magic, powerful telescopes and whatever we can dig up and understand of the ancient teachings, claim to be able to see a part of what the Fire's-Eye reveals to us."

"I don't understand..."

"Kinda tough to understand, really. I'm talking quantum astrology. My father got it, but that might be just because when the Envoys told him, they told him in some special Ifah magic way that opens up a room in your brain and dumps the info straight in without a filter. I know some saint-fathers and saint-mothers who understand at least some of quantum astrology intuitively. Dream-techs—the few that know about it, including Isabel and Amaro—don't understand the discipline at all, and resent their lack of understanding. But you do understand relative simultaneity, right? They teach you that in Arlina?"

"Time is a function of the curvature of space and the operation of gravity..."

"Right..."

He seemed to want more, so I continued. "Which means that time is never measured the same everywhere in the universe, and time is relative. With less gravity and faster speeds, time is slower. You choose a point A here in This World, and a random corresponding point in galaxy B, three million lightyears away, and if you move in one direction or another from this point in This World, you're actually moving into the future or the past relative to that corresponding point in the galaxy B. So the upshot is that events in the past and future are every bit as real as events in the present. Physically, the division into past, present, and future is meaningless. Past events and present events — at least somebody else's past or somebody else's future, not your own — exist simultaneously; at the universal level, it all happens more or less at once." I shrugged. "Plus, there's that whole bit about there being four dimensions, with time being the fourth dimension. But humans only being able to perceive three, so the way time *really* is, is imperceivable."

"They teach good, up there in backward la-la land," Salvador joked.

"I am nothing if not the perfect product of a useless education."

Master Salvador laughed. "Ain't totally useless, though. Because that's what you need to understand quantum astrology. From a certain perspective — from what we conceive of as a universal perspective, which we tend to think of as a divine perspective — all time is simultaneous. Or something *like* what we mean by simultaneous, although obviously if there is no time as such, simultaneous is far from an exact description. You — you being your Absolute Divinity — just have to walk this way and that in the vastness of the universe, or turn your big old celestial head to the right or the left, and you'll get to see what from the ant's and man's perspective is past and future all happening at once. So what the quantum astrologers say is that the instant of the Big Bang contains all time in one. The closer you are to the center in *space,* the more time is dense, and all times are coincident. The farther away — like where we poor bitches are — the more linear time appears to be."

I looked again at the Fire's-Eye. "But we're only looking at the center of the galaxy, not the universe."

"Right. But ours is the first and maybe the largest galaxy — at least according to quantum astrologers," Salvador said. "That part may require what your priests like to call a leap of faith. Because, how do you know where the center of anything is until you've been all around the edges?"

"Which we haven't...," I concurred.

"Which we haven't. But don't forget, either, that the Big Bang itself is supposed to have some kind of connection to black holes, or impossible black hole densities reaching conflagration or ignition points — something — anyway, you know black holes have wormhole, that is, time-bending qualities, or actually contain wormholes, so that the past and future are linked and mixed up in them…"

"Okay."

"The point is that a quantum astrologer is of the belief that he can see recorded in the Big Bang what has happened and is happening and will happen."

"And when we see the Fire's-Eye we're seeing —"

"We are seeing the center of our cosmos. As it was forty-five thousand years ago, since that's how many light-years we are from it. But since our galaxy is — supposedly — so near to the center of the universe, the Fire's-Eye, the Forge, whatever, is a close cousin to the older-than-ancient light of the Big Bang."

"…And what we experience as our future, but what the Universe just sees as what is, is there. From our perspective, *recorded* there…"

"Right."

"For those who can read it," I said. "Quantum astrologers."

"Yep."

I wondered why Master Salvador was telling me this. "And you, Master?"

"I, what?" I couldn't tell whether he found it amusing that I called him by his honorific.

"Are you a quantum astrologer? Can you read the Laws like your father?"

"My father broke off from the rest of our Affinity and founded his own Affinity. Which is about the worst blasphemy there is among techs and Godshouse practitioners. He taught his apprentices what he knew. That's where we *get* quantum astrology as a practice. And together my father and his astrologers paid for sight and for the knowledge of how to read what they saw. Course the apprentices paid more than my daddy, but that's the way he rolled: if Pops could get you to pay the price and let him enjoy the profit, that was how Pops made it happen."

This sounded a little bitter. I thought it best to steer him away from the subject of his father. "So, then… how much do you see?"

Ironically in answering, Master Salvador's eyes narrowed to slits. "If you represented being able to see all that's written in that record as a picture of one very large eye, then my father and his apprentices paid, in their blood and the blood and suffering of too many others, for a tiny, tiny splinter of that eye, a flicker of sight. As much as you see of a little spider skittering over the floorboards between rugs. As much as you see of the hind parts of a panther hightailing it out of danger. That much I can see. Forty-five thousand years, give or take, of the history of This World, up there, bright and tiny. And I don't mean forty-five thousand of, like, anything that would pass as a garden variety social *history*. I mean, like, some itty bitty moments strung together, little local bits of little local pieces of time. Like, if you're — you're what, a waiter?"

I frowned. "Mostly. I fill in for short order cook, too."

"Right. So if you're picking up an order for table two and pause to flirt with the cook for a minute, or gossip about some girl you both like, you're *there,* so you should be able to tell me what's happening. But real talk, if you perceive even a quarter of what's going on at that moment when you're actually there — everything you perceive about what the cook says and what you half-guess and half-sense from nonverbal cues what she might be feeling, everything you yourself feel, the source of all the sounds you hear, the thread of all the conversations around you, let alone the multitude of molecular processes going on inside your body and all around you — if you get even a quarter, hell, a fifth of that, you're perceiving a lot."

I nodded. Even listening to that was a bit overwhelming.

"Yeah, so I don't perceive nearly that much. When I say I can see the signs, the marks of some of what was done, even a little bit of what was felt, it's no more, and truthfully a lot less, than you get when you're actually on the scene, in the moment. I'm seeing signs and marks of *sweeps* of shit, and little pieces within the sweep of events. Because each movement creates its own ripple that writes itself, that leaves its scratch, in that divine light. Actually, what's visible are patterns of *darkness* or dimness *in* the light — but the shit is complicated, don't get me started. Anyway, what I can see I can't fully interpret. We got astrologers that have made a life's work out of interpreting the data that seers accumulate. And they ain't gonna finish, even with a sorcerer's lifespan."

Master Salvador's hand rested lightly on my shoulder. (I flinched at the contact. This was too similar to the posture of Sílvio, during that terrible interrogation — which, I could not forget, had also taken place in a "place" shaped by a sorcerer's mind.)

"So why'm I telling you this?"

I moved slightly, instinctively, just enough to affect Salvador's hand. His hand didn't fall, but slid down my back. I didn't like that. But then his hand was gone, which is where I wanted it.

"I don't know why," I answered him.

"Cuz when I and my father's affinity 'read' the Forge, one thing we see is that at some point the Wall comes down. We've known this. Just couldn't know when, either exactly or vaguely. It's all guess work, pinpointing the time, which is the most frustrating thing about the whole practice."

"Which might be the thing about the whole practice that most makes it useless," I heard myself say.

"Fair enough, cracka. But we still saw what we saw. We can see that the Wall will come down — I mean that it comes down. And we see that something or someone is a key part of the Wall coming down — someone or some *thing* we call a Breaker. Of course, this is all interpretation at the very edge of what's possible to know, at the point where interpreting is too close to invention to make anyone comfortable. We are translating flickers of light and darkness from thousands and sometimes millions and even billions of light-years ago, that's already old and fading when we see it, into *language*. Breaker could be Tunneler. It could be Builder. Opener. The interpretation process is by nature just fuckin' nonsensical..."

"Don't sugar coat it for me," I blurted. *"I'm* the Breaker? I'm responsible for bringing the Wall down! *That's* what I am? Some cosmic herald of doom?"

He nodded.

I couldn't stop myself from saying it, though I regretted it the moment it left my mouth. "I'd almost rather be a dream-slave."

"There's no guarantee the Breaker *isn't* a dream-slave," Salvador said — which was very disappointing to hear. Up till then I'd thought he was my best cheerleader for the "he's human" camp.

"Did you know I was this Breaker or Universal Can-Opener or whatever when Ydris rescued me in the park? Is that why you helped me?"

"We didn't know anything about you," Salvador said. "Ydris found you, and she brought you to us. You heard what she said about why she found you. She said she felt she had to hunt. I don't know any more than that about her motivations or why she does what she does. The Envoys follow their own compass." He paused, considering. "As time went on and we learned more about you — and especially when you seemed to learn how to fly just from whatever you absorbed dreaming or taking the Waters — I was reminded of what I'd seen and interpreted in the light of the galactic center." His face crinkled in a wince, his shoulders heaved in a shrug. "That's kinda what's funky about quantum astrology. Even when you get a warning, the fact that the timing of the event you're being warned about isn't clear means the warning doesn't do you that much good. But what it does do is help you know what you've experienced *after* the fact. It's taken me awhile, but now I know — or I'm pretty sure, anyway — that you are what I learned about years ago."

"Frigging hell," I swore. "And this — this is because I took the fucking Waters? I've done that, like, six or seven times!"

"Yeah, but this time you took the Waters, and then a threshold was crossed. Without any instruction, you stepped onto a higher plateau." I must have looked bewildered, for he said, "I mean, a higher level in working with the Unseen, with magic." He tried explaining again. "The Waters are not just the Waters for everyone. For those with certain proclivities — those who often go on to become saint-fathers, or sorcerers, or dream-techs —"

"— Or stark bloody insane," I barked.

Salvador gave this a tiny shake of his head. "Those who are sensitive, who perceive, or maybe even can make, a passage to the Next World. For *them,* an experience of the Waters can sometimes be an initiation. Seems like it was that way for you."

I held my head in my hands. I wasn't crying. I wasn't even emotional. I just felt like I needed to hold my head, or else it would fall off, overweighed with all the crap it had been filled with since I was crazy enough to say yes to Princess Isabel's invitation to work that bloody fête.

"But to be clear," Master Salvador continued, "to say the Breaker is *responsible* for the Wall is not accurate. Say he or she or they, or whatever" — this qualification made me nervous, even amongst all the other nervousnesses I was prey to at the moment — "*catalyzes* the Wall coming down. All the frenzied activity recently — especially taking the Water — it opened you up, pushed your mind out of the way long enough. Then, you crossed over. And this was a catalyst for the thinning of the Wall. Our clairvoyants agree on this. Your initiation, your crossing over, is linked to the fall of the Wall, the way a key is built for a lock. Crossing over functioned either as an incendiary device in the Wall, blowing the shit up, or as a lighthouse beacon in the fog, calling the Great Gods and their minions to us. Or both. Or neither quite."

Master Salvador took a breath. "This, as I think you can imagine, is pretty fuckin' curious to us. And here's something even more curious."

"Last of All Prophets Cristos!" I swore. "That's not the worst of it?"

"No, it isn't," Salvador said. "The Breaker — which, gotta say for full disclosure, some of the apprentices translate as the Betrayer, the Rebel, the Transgressor, the Undoer —"

"Oh, fine."

"Look, some astrologers translate it as the Muddy One or the Muddy Man. Betrayer's hella preferable."

I snorted. "The Muddy Man? What the hell does that — ?"

"It's a way to symbolize the transgression bit, the crossing boundaries stuff. Mud is dirt and water, earth and water — two classical elements, yada yada yada?"

I shook my head. "You know, where I come from, there are crazy people, *white* people whose skin color is like mine who call darker-skinned people like you *mud people*. And it's an insult."

"Oh right. Your 'race' shit." Master Salvador's guffaw winged into the air.

This mockery rather got my goose. "What's so funny? Like you don't have race down here?"

Salvador laughed a bit more before some thought stilled his expression. "Kinda, yeah, we do, but — it just doesn't matter the same way to us as it does to you." He looked thoughtful. "It *used* to matter, we know that from the histories. But at a certain point, more than a century before anything happened with traffic Between the Worlds, and way before dream-tech, the whole process of" — here he threw his arms wide and crimped his fingers in that annoyingly dramatic way we all do when we want to cast aspersions on the terms we're using — "*race formation,* et cetera, and of people organizing slavery around skin color and everything that went with it — that process got interrupted. For us, anyway. For all of Zilia, which is most of the continent."

Salvador was gazing at the stars, as though in reading them he could read the history to me — and I didn't know, maybe he could. "One of our forebears — I'm not talking a great-great-grandparent, I mean someone in the lineage of the teachings in magic I'm heir to, someone very powerful — she cast what's called the Foundation-spell. We don't know how she was able to do it, or how it worked to change the minds of millions of people — or why it didn't work outside Zilia. Part of the way the spell worked was to prevent everyone that it affected, and everyone descended from those it affected, from knowing exactly what happened. *And* from knowing exactly how things were before she cast the spell. That's why it's called the Foundation. It was like — starting over. You know all that goop your people used to like to talk about coming to Omeriga and making themselves anew? The *New* World, blah blah blah?"

I bristled again, but made a noise of understanding.

"Yeah, well, our ancestor, she made it so everyone here *had* to rebirth themselves, because they couldn't remember how things had been before. Not only that, the Foundation-spell did all kinds of crazy stuff — moved people physically around, so damn near everybody basically went to sleep one night, then woke up living someplace they didn't know, with some people they didn't recognize, and only a fuzzy memory of who their own families were. It wasn't like the garden of Eden your Ur liked to talk about, it wasn't like a tabula rasa. We weren't *innocent.* We were and are still human. We were still fucked up. But we forgot, for a minute, how racial division was supposed to work. You go to sleep lying on the ground in a wooden shelter with chains around your ankles; you wake up lying in a feather bed with a fully loaded rifle lying on the floor next to you. You know your name, and you know your skills, you know what you've learned to *do* — you just don't know how your name and how your skills relate to anyone else. Kids don't know who their parents are, parents don't recognize their children. When I learned about this, the teacher told me that one in four people woke up that day convinced that their body wasn't the right body — not the right look, not the right size, not the right gender or color. It was like, everybody was *physically* okay, everybody was healthy, nobody was without shelter. But the real deal? Everybody was homeless. You know what I mean? Social life — who was supposed to live where, and how resources were routed to some people and not others — it was mixed up for a long time. Some racialist ideas did eventually get started again, but they never became as — I don't know, *popular* as racism is with you folks up north. We were pretty isolated, too, with the mountains sealing us off to the north and east, the desert to the south, and the storms on the ocean getting worse and worse. Some say the Foundation-spell whipped up the storms, too."

"I guess I could see how something that—" I groped for the right description.

"Something that catastrophic, you mean," Salvador suggested.

"Yes," I agreed with some relief. This polite relief at not having to name some other nationality's misfortune was, however, just a disguise for more envy of the Zilians. At that moment, the idea of waking up without me or anyone else knowing who (or what) I was sounded divine. "I can see how that kind of social upheaval, that kind of mass forgetting, could certainly shake up your view of race."

"It did. And that's not even the craziest part. The spell made it so one whole generation of Zilians didn't have to *eat* to live."

"What?" I didn't believe him, of course. Not then.

"No, really! The spell transformed Zilians' bodies so that they processed energy almost the way plants do. Sunlight and water alone were all they needed. It was a gradual thing. All the other changes were sudden. With the eating and the food, it was, first, they didn't need to eat as much as they used to, then, a couple years later, they didn't have to eat at all. When it was all over, twenty or thirty years later, first, they or their children needed a little food when they hadn't needed food at all before. Then little by little over the course of a few years, people were back to eating like they had before the Foundation. That was probably the most genius, the most powerful part of the spell."

Salvador seemed a little excited. "See, that's the part nobody today can even fathom. Move people around, sure, it's hard to do, and impossible for us on the scale that she did it, but any practitioner can understand that theoretically. Mess up people's memories? Again, not nearly on that scale and not to that extent, but we do smaller versions of that shit all the time. But make it so you don't have to *eat* for twenty years? We don't have a clue how you do that." He paused to look directly at me. "But that's the key, isn't it? When you think about it. It's hard to force people to work for you at all, let alone slave for you, if you can't exploit their hunger."

It was hard to think of what he'd told me as anything other than a fable. So I asked the sort of question I used to ask as a child, when being told fables. "If they didn't eat, and they didn't have to work to eat, what did they spend their time doing?"

Master Salvador smiled. "They fucked a lot. They fought a lot. They made a lot of art. I don't think that generation constructed a lot of *buildings* or left an architectural style behind to imitate or anything, and they didn't get too far in cuisine innova tions either. And I don't think they were too into organized education. Definitely their governments were shit, and they didn't leave a very complete historical archive. But they sure painted a ton of paintings, they composed a hell of a lot of music, they staged a lotta plays — mostly about love and romance and sexual jealousy, those were their obsessions — and they sculpted every which way, and they went hog-wild with clothing fashions. Now that part, those twenty, thirty years of not having to eat, except for pleasure? That *was* a little like your Ur's Garden of Eden."

Salvador stretched and looked up at the stars again. "But really, man, I gotta say I never studied that part of the history very attentively. I mean, the Foundation-spell, the traditions and histories around *that,* I studied the hell out of. Everybody working the Unseen has to. But the race stuff, it just never seemed to be all that relevant. Maybe I should've, though?" He shrugged.

I could only blow a sigh. "Okay. But"—*fables aside,* but of course I didn't say that aloud—"the 'Breaker' or the 'Mud Man'..."—I let fly some air quotes of my own—"he brings down the Wall."

"Right."

"But. I don't wanna be the herald of death, or destruction, or whatever!" There was just no way, unfortunately, to purge that line of its whine.

Master Salvador decided to answer in the same foolish vein. "But you are, cracka, you are." He laughed.

Unable to think of anything else to do, I laughed with him.

We stood there together, laughing. Soon he was laughing so hard he had to stumble away and brace himself against the trunk of a tree.

It wasn't *that* funny, of course. But, I suppose, it was certainly that dire.

"What the hell do you want me to do with information like this?" I asked him.

Salvador's hand came back to my shoulder. I considered, then decided against pushing it off again.

"Just let what I've said sink in," Salvador advised me. "The only thing you need to really get right this moment is that you, by your nature—whatever that nature is or whatever it makes you—are connected to, and maybe the focus of, powerful energies that go way the fuck back. It's not about you meaning to do harm, or about you necessarily doing any harm. It's just how things unfold. Think of it as—you're part of nature. But not a mindless part, like a wave of ocean or a drop of rain. You're a part that gets to make choices. *You* have a part to play in how things turn out. *You* can influence the outcome. Which has already happened, of course, but we can't know that... Anyhow. That's why I'm gonna get you to the place that you're as powerful as you can be. That's why I'm introducing you to working with the Unseen, and why we're doing it right now. Tonight."

I dropped my face into my hands. "Fuuuck."

"And I promise you, Alexander," Master Salvador declared, "that I would never use you as I would use a slave. You are *not* just a weapon to me."

Of course, my ears picked out his *just* as an admission that he did in fact think of me as a weapon at least in part. Curiously (it's curious to me now, looking back) I did not heed this as a warning. After all, to be a weapon, certainly a powerful weapon in a war against gods, was *important.* A powerful weapon was special. And nothing — this is the curious part — no mortal danger or great ecstasy or joy could push me from the altar at which I waited, stubborn, consumed with fear, for fate to anoint me as special. I would have rather left my own fingernails, my own hands even, clinging to that altar than allow myself to be dragged from it, then.

But wait: Master Salvador was still talking. "Fact, I try my best not to use dream-slaves at all, even though I am a badass dreamtech. Sometimes I *have* to use one. But I promise you I never do it thoughtlessly. And I always fuckin' hate it."

"Why? Do you hate it because you think we — they — the dream-slaves — are sentient?"

Salvador looked troubled. "I don't know whether they are, or they aren't. I suspect they are." His hand dropped from my shoulder. After a moment he said, "I don't like using slaves because —" He hesitated, then an uneasy sigh seemed to leak from his mouth.

I recoiled with unease and with an unaccountable feeling of vulnerability — as though I were fifteen again and about to be taken into some embarrassing sexual confidence by a friend. I could almost hear the terrible admission in Master Salvador's heavy masculine voice: *I'm still a virgin!*

Of course, he didn't say anything like that.

"My mother was a dream-slave," he said.

In the false world made real to the senses that was this corner of Master Salvador's consciousness, the forest night was like a forest night anywhere on earth. It was full of sound — insect symphonies, wind wars, the complaint of padded paws or hard hooves on leaf and dirt, the questioning of the occasional nocturnal bird.

All such simulation now ceased.

For a moment after Master Salvador spoke, it seemed that the forest went white and blank. That flicker passed. But when I replied, I heard myself slightly echo in a dome of silence.

My voice was almost too eager. "How is that possible?"

"My father built her." The forest remained quiet. "My father was one of the greatest dream-techs of his generation. Some say the greatest ever. He was the one who weaponized the Wall of Storms, to hold the Great Gods at bay, keep them from invading the west. He's also the only slave-maker — as far as I know — to have built a dream-slave that so completely mimicked human DNA that she was able to sexually reproduce a child with her human Maker."

A tongue of breeze danced across my arm. My mind raced, but all I could articulate was another, "How?"

"She lived ten months. Just long enough. He built her to copy a human body, and he impregnated her. That's how."

I knew it was not my place to judge, but what he was saying sounded monstrous. "Why would he do a thing like that?"

Salvador sighed again. "To protect *me*. To have me — to *make* me, I guess you gotta say — and pass on the qualities of the dream-slave to me."

"What, like, magical ability...?"

"I am good at magic, and I didn't need to labor at learning it the way every other sorcerer and tech has to. But he didn't care about that so much. What he wanted was for me to be protected from possession by the Great Gods. The Great Gods, when They're able to manifest in This World, can possess anybody. And when They do, They completely consume you. Eat your ass up, spit you out, move on to the next vessel. Magic alone won't stop that."

"If that's so, what does... Oh! The Great Gods can possess *any*body, but they can't — !" I stopped. It still sounded monstrous to me.

"Dream-slaves are not alive — well, they are, obviously, but not in the same way. They have no souls, and can't be possessed. They're immune. They can't destroy the Great Gods — at least as far as we know — but the Great Gods can't destroy them either. They stalemate the Greats. The only dream-tech to ever fight the

Great Gods and live was my father, and he saw it. A dream-slave creation saved his life."

"Then, he meant to pass on the protection dream-slaves have to you," I said. "And you're—*half*-human and *half*-dream-slave?"

Salvador turned his face to me. "I don't know what I am," he said. The bitterness in his voice seemed to make the forest darken. I couldn't see past a few feet in front of me. "I'm an experiment. My father was fuckin' excellent at conducting experiments. And making slaves. And making weapons. As the result of an experiment, I'm, biologically, half human and half magically-mimicked-human." He went quiet for a moment, then said, "So you see, you and I may have something in common."

I was trying to figure out how I fit into this story. The man I'd seen in my fever dreams, the one who was captured in the hold of "the Black Ship," was that Salvador's father? And the woman naked on a rooftop, the one who came running back to the man—Salvador's father, I presume—who treated her so abusively: that was Salvador's dream-slave mother?

"You're immune to the Great Gods then," I ventured. "If they invade, you'll be okay. But you want to fight them because..."

"I *have* to fight them because of my mother!" Yes, now lightning curled overhead, and thunder trundled soon after. "Because she had a short *human* or part-way human life and I never got to know her, so that there would be something in This World to resist those fucking Gods. I am what I am, and I lost her, because of Them. I hate Them almost as much as I hate my fucking bitch-ass father." This last he said softly, without emphasis or variation in tone.

Salvador turned away from me now. That proud dark head, always so erect on his long neck, slumped between his shoulders. "I don't even know if I *am* immune to the Great Gods. Pops never got to complete his experiment. He claimed he *loved* me too much to risk it, in the end. I'm etsy-ketsy on believing that. Then again," another exhalation billowed up from his broad chest, "could be I hate those motherfuckers because that's part of the slave programming I inherited from *her.*"

I hadn't wanted to say anything, but that thought had occurred to me, too. If I was a dream-slave and had been programmed to, I don't know, kill the Prince of Norio or some-thing — and this story made me think it all the more possible that I was (and that scared me too much to focus on it, so my mind skipped away fast) — then certainly Master Salvador could have been programmed to fight the Great Gods, just as he was pro-grammed, or at least enabled, to be a powerful dream-tech and sorcerer. We might both be the puppets of our makers, whether those who made us did so biologically or magically.

And wasn't this the fate of all children of all parents, as well as the slaves who were made? The range of our choices charted for us before we were born, selected by the choices our makers made, the prisoners of a history that pre-existed us and that made our world and us in it?

By such philosophical musing I managed to distract myself completely from the fearful implications Salvador's story had for me.

"Are the Great Gods just evil, then?" I asked. We had been taught in Arlina that the Great Gods were not gods at all, but demons, opposed to the One True God, whose chosen people we of course were. "It doesn't sound like they want to exchange gifts or bargain with us the way the other — spirits — your sorcer-ers communicate with do."

Salvador intuited my train of thought. "Evil's a word your folks up North like to dig in with. The Great Gods are supreme predators. Before Pops weaponized the Wall — one experiment of his that *did* work, until now — it seemed like They were on Their way to turning every eastern continent into their own divine cafeteria. Whatever it is They're after, it ain't good, not for us."

"That makes them sound almost like they're animals," I said.

"Naw, we don't know Their motivation, good, bad, natural, or unnatural. It can't be that They need the food to survive, cuz the bitches've been around since This World began, and They obviously weren't eating folks till recently, or we wouldn't be here. My view? I studied these deities for most of my life. And my view is that They're much worse than we think."

"In what way...?"

"Look around you. When you see some people living like a king and ordering everybody else around, and some people so unlucky they're born sick as dogs and never eat in a day what the king eats for a mid-day snack. When you see bigger stronger people murdering or raping smaller weaker people. When you see some groups' life-chances half as healthy, half as wealthy, half as happy as some other groups'. When you see injustice. That's on Them. They did that. When They created This World, They did it wrong. They committed a crime so dire that even divine beings can't put it right. The Founder tried to change it, but she could only change it for thirty years, and only for Zilians. The Great Gods in creating This World condemned us all, all humanity, to damnation. When They eat us, They're just covering up the evidence. Or They're trying to make *us* pay the fine for what They did."

I frowned. "But that's so... upside-down. Human beings suffer because humans make awful choices. Because we *sin*. In Arlina we remember what Ur said. There was a paradise once, and our first ancestors were expelled from it and could never find their way back because they chose to ignore the commandments of the One True God."

Salvador would have none of this. "Northern superstition. And it was Ur's teachings that turned upside-down the truth that the ancients knew. Same truth that the Envoys who have come back to us from our own forgotten history know. Have any of your priests and archbishops and shit ever *met* your One True God? I'm sure Ur and your one other prophet Cristos from thousands of years ago did meet the motherfucker —"

I blanched and made the sign of the Three.

"Those bitches got lied to. They were probably being ridden their whole lives and didn't even know. Mr. 'One True' was just one of the many spirits and Spirit-Lords or Homely Gods that the saint-mothers and saint-fathers met a hundred-and-fifty years ago. Or maybe 'One True' is even one of the Great Gods that the Envoys knew so well, and despised. Or one of the Ones my father went to battle against. Either way, trying to put the blame on original sin or some shit is a massive fuckin' con."

My blood pressure was rising, but Master Salvador plowed on, heedless of my well-drilled aversion to heresy and blasphemy. "Yeah, and all that thou-shalt-do-this and don't-dare-fuck-except-with-the-man-on-top hippidy hoo-dah is nothing *at all* but the evidence of a seriously bad bargaining process. I bet even Mr. One True didn't get the shit he wanted outta that bargain. What does any god care what ya'll get up to when he's not ridin' you or you're not feeding him?" Salvador jabbed a finger at me. Theological passion, it seemed, had stirred his normal equanimity. "You're right, humans do make stupid choices. But our stupidity is a direct result of the treachery of the Great Gods."

It seemed cheeky to argue, ensconced as I apparently was in Master Salvador's own mind. My beliefs were my beliefs, and would not be shaken. (I thought.)

"Well, we won't settle the matter of the creation of the world tonight," I conceded. "If it *is* actually night. You still haven't convinced me why I ought to risk my life to fight the Great Gods. Did your father oppose them for the same reasons you do? Did he go to such lengths to keep them out of the west because he thought they'd committed some cosmic 'crime'?"

Salvador waved his hand. The sky brightened. Impending dawn?

"No. My father opposed the Great Gods because They tried to kill him and he barely escaped with his life. He saw Them kill thousands of people. And, rightly, he was afraid."

Then Master Salvador told me the story of how his father decided to make his mother. But he did not, and perhaps could not, tell the story as I shall tell it to you.

Salvador *gave* the story to me, as sorcerers affianced in each affinity of sorcerers commonly do — though it was the first time, for me.

To give a story is to gather the receiver of the story into one's own thoughts and emotions, one's fears, desires, and memories stretching beyond and behind the story given. To give a story in this way is an act of profound trust: for what secrets might I have learned in such a union of consciousnesses? (Indeed, I did learn many secrets, though of course not all; I was not with Master Salvador *as* him long enough to learn all.) It is, you will understand, an act so intimate that the congress of bodies seems merely its echo, its impoverished analog version.

The story of Salvador's mother — which was not even Salvador's own story, really, and thus must have been told to

Salvador himself by his father in the same mode that Salvador told it to me — is then, like the story I've recounted of Princess Isabel's conversations with Prince Amaro, a story that for the purposes of this memoir is out of sequence. I have to bracket it as a *construction,* a kind of false placeholder, at best a scaffold, for the events as they happened, which are perforce misconstrued by all storytelling and all mere reporting.

Backwards, then, I fly, on wings thin and fragile, and you with me. Backwards to one beginning among many we might choose. Just one of several meetings of egg, seed, and water from which the present emergency, and the rebirth of the so-called human, grew.

FERNANDO'S STORY

Date not known to me, but:
1997, late Octavius (the Month of the Exalted Moons)

The military transport carrying Lieutenant Colonel Brinen Malroy, Captain Elias Baker, Hieronymus-Theodoric, and Fernando Evandro Casiera had been circling low in the air above the city of Umasi, which lay on the western outskirts of the fertile greenlands that spread between the Enina River and the Greater Enina Lake. Black smoke sent twisting towers up into the bright, cloudless skies above Umasi. They saw cars and trees adrift in the air, as though snarled in the winds of a tornado. Mobs marched in synchrony through Umasi's streets, destroying buildings, overrunning tanks.

(I *knew* this! I remembered it from my dream —!)

The plane took a punch, and fell from the sky.

The long arm of the Great God called Domna Ra Zah.

(I remembered this from the dream, yes. The way I knew it was not *just* a dream was due to the way Master Salvador gave me the memory, as his father Fernando had given the memory to him: by wrapping him up in its folds, enmeshing him in it. So when I say Fernando, I could just as well say *I,* given how I accessed the story. For your sake — and especially for Yours — I'm simplifying.)

Neither the pilots nor any of their instruments, not even Hieronymus-Theodoric, saw, detected, or warned of missile fire, and there was no explosion. Fernando's senses expanded at the moment of impact, and it felt and even looked to him like a hand the size of a jetliner had struck its knuckles against the bottom of the military transport.

The sound of the impact broke some of their eardrums. The plane was upended, with passengers and crew tumbling through the suddenly de-pressurized interior like grains of salt in a tilted shaker. A moment later — a moment as measured in the dreadful elongated time of accidents and the end of life — the transport's mechanisms shut down, as though the plane had fainted.

Hieronymus-Theodoric was able to save Fernando, Lt. Col. Malroy, Capt. Baker and two others who happened to be nearby at the moment the slave's power embraced the five of them in what Fernando, the only one of them fully alert and awake during the descent, perceived to be a dimly lit sphere of oxygenated, dense but clear salt-laden fluid in which all of them floated as though in the womb again, quiet, soothed, until they gained the land six minutes later.

They alighted to earth gently, with the weight of a feather. The sphere dissolved, making a small but distinct sucking sound as it vanished. The humans' eyes blinked as they coughed up fluid and took in new breaths heavy with smoke.

Around them, near them, were screams, fire, explosions, people running, people pissing and shitting themselves in terror, people dying, buildings falling.

They stood amid moving death on the western edge of the city of Umasi.

In the ruination of Umasi, Brinen Malroy scrambled to find her coordinates. Her GPS wasn't functioning. Her phone was dead. A bullet, or bullets, whizzed into their midst. She flung herself out of what her instinct told her was the bullets' path.

But if the bullets were aimed at her, they missed. They struck Lt. Davies in the chest instead.

Davies like all of them wore body armor, but the wind was knocked out of him. He staggered and then crumbled. Brinen and Corporal Potter started to drag Davies's limp body out of the maze of rubble in the street into the nearest alley for something like shelter, while Capt. Baker fired back, wildly at first, but then with increasing steadiness, at ten or more invaders. These were a mélange of Negali, Gerians, Malê-landers — and *Arionese,* from the looks of them, Fernando thought — who had marched smartly from around the bend of the street onto their block, guns firing.

Fernando planted his feet and closed his eyes. With an effort that left his body shaking and his muscles spent, he broke the barrier Between the Worlds and let electromagnetism gush through the gap toward the invaders.

The invaders' guns fell uselessly from their fried fingers. H-T intensified the Next World's flow. After a moment the invaders began to catch fire, quickly, almost all at once. They burned, their bodies dancing and twitching, but they didn't scream or make a sound.

Fernando watched for a minute or more, to see if the invaders survived. Finally he turned away.

"I think I killed them," Fernando announced when he reached the alley. He sat heavily on the ground, tucking his knees beneath him. A smell of motor oil and of burnt and burning things — burning wood, burning paper, burning flesh — filled the narrow, grimed space. Empty balconies jutted from the buildings hovering above, looking as if they might fall to the street at any moment. But they offered shelter from the hot sunshine. "There will be more. Hieronymus has seen several more troops approaching this area."

"What, what should we do?" stammered Corporal Potter. There was too much fear in the Negalı soldiers, Fernando observed. As though they hadn't been trained at all, or had never been in combat. And perhaps they never had.

"Why doesn't your slave take us someplace else?" Elias blurted. "Why the fuck did he float us *here?*"

Fernando, with a flicker of thought, instructed Hieronymus to heal and revive Lt. Davies. "Hieronymus made a survival decision," he replied to Elias, "one in keeping with the duty I have to perform, which is to observe this invasion. But, I've seen enough. You're right. We should leave."

"What if — whatever it is — knocks us down while we're floating up in your slave-bubble the same way it knocked down the plane?" Elias persisted.

Hieronymus chanted over Lt. Davies. Brinen watched with a mixture of rapt curiosity and revulsion.

"Domna didn't knock us down when we descended under Hieronymus's power," Fernando answered, trying to sound confident. "And She was still there. I felt Her. It's a risk, but what are our alternatives?" He hated to admit it, but of course both Fernando and his second-self were already calculating whether Hieronymus would have the power to transport the five of them all the way back to Minakkra. Or whether he would have to cull some — or all — of them.

"We don't have time," Brinen said, voice rising. She had stopped watching Hieronymus, and her head was swinging around as she surveyed their position. "Get us out of here!"

Fernando felt he could *see* Brinen's desperation to reunite with her family. It was pouring from her mouth, as visible as breath in cold air.

He was determined to help her somehow, no matter what the as-yet-incomplete calculations ultimately revealed. He thought if he simply bent light around them so that the five of them couldn't be clearly seen, they could move far enough on foot out of town and out of the reach of Domna's army to take to the air again without fear.

But then Hieronymus alerted him, and no sooner had he turned his head than the possessed troops were upon them, pouring into the alley.

At a glance there were twenty infantry, marching four tightly abreast, but it looked like there could be more. Only their feet made a sound. They were each completely different in look, but the expressions on their faces were incongruously identical. Bright eyes, set mouths: the picture of impassivity yet somehow radiant with — exultation. Not vengeance or fury, or even hunger or craving. Just a fierce, fierce joy. For all their differing bodies they were each of the same mind, the same consciousness. Fernando wasn't sure what the others perceived, but he saw immediately the appeal of a surrender to such unity.

Of the four in front, one was an elderly woman pale enough to be from Arcady, two were burly Negali in Negalian uniform, and one was an adolescent with the dark features and red-caramel coloring of the Arionese, riding on a skateboard.

Absurdly, Fernando wondered: *Did he ride that skateboard all the way from Arion?* But there was no time for such stupid thoughts, the invaders moved too fast for that.

They marched in synchrony but evidently the divine mind that rode them all could engage in multiple activities simultaneously, for two of them, the elderly woman and the skateboarder, leapt at Brinen and Davies, who was still struggling to rise up from the ground. They swung their arms as though they expected to swat Davies and Brinen down. At the same time the two Negali soldiers started firing on the rest of them.

Their actions were at an inhuman speed. Elias, Potter, and even Fernando would already be riddled with bullets were it not for the reflexes of Hieronymus-Theodoric, which, with a wave of its hands, took away the bullets' speed.

The bullets clattered as they struck the ground and started rolling.

"Shield us all!" Fernando commanded as he saw more rows of invaders pushing behind the front four into the alley.

But the downside of a dream-slave, as no one better than Fernando knew, was and is that no matter the wondrousness of their feats, those feats are local, finite in space and time — as the slaves themselves are. The shield, which might have been magnetism or gravity or the force of Hieronymus's will impossibly made manifest — even Fernando didn't know for certain: he was without peer in making slaves, but no one truly understood how slaves' sorcery worked — held back new rounds of fire, and kept the ruffians away, as evidenced by the fact that there were now possessed troops pushing from the back, causing the front groups to stumble and even fall to their knees under the pressure of the bodies behind them.

But Brinen had been dragging Davies back out of harm, and Davies had been scrambling on his knees, trying to assist Brinen in saving him.

And so they were outside the perimeter of Hieronymus's shield.

Elias made as if to charge out from the shield's protection himself to rescue his fiancee, but everything happened more quickly than it takes to tell. Some of the invaders surrounded Brinen and

Davies, their coordination making it appear that a hood made of human bodies had drawn down over the Negali officers.

Fernando, with no help from Hieronymus, sent a short burst of electricity toward the old Arcadian and the Arionese skateboarder (too much might have fried Brinen and Davies, too) through a hole in the shield Hieronymus created and then closed in less than a full second. The Arcadian and the Arionese halted short, shook themselves like wet dogs, lurched a step and then pitched forward, probably breaking bones in their faces or at least getting a nasty clout to the sternum.

Too late: The damage, in whatever way it was wrought, was already done. Just as Domna's possessed creatures fell, two more rose from the earth to take their places: Brinen and Davies. The Negalian — or formerly Negalian — officers rushed at a speed neither had ever before sprinted, toward the exposed, unshielded rear of Fernando, Elias, and Potter. Their faces were terrifying in the intensity of their apparent happiness. The Arionese youth and the Arcadian elder, recovered from their falls, sprung up behind them.

Elias's scream joined more distant ones in the air as he struggled with and overcame his hesitation. He fired his assault rifle repeatedly at his wife-to-be.

He had shifted aim from her heart to her head by the time — immediately plus a moment-and-a-half — that Brinen, or the Brinen who was Domna Ra Zah now, reached him.

The rain of bullets entered Brinen's body, made holes, summoned blood, disfigured her flesh. And the holes closed, the blood flow stopped, the disfigurement was refigured, almost as soon as you'd seen it: faster even, since Fernando found himself having to remember that, yes, in fact he had not imagined that Brinen's lovely hazel eye had popped free from its socket and had splattered or been disintegrated, because looking at her now, her eye and the features of her face were restored.

Elias's rifle served to turn Brinen briefly aside, but that was all. Now she was choking the life out of poor Potter, he was sputtering and his hands were digging impotently at her hands firmly crushing his neck. And then in a snap, but with no such transitional sound, indeed no transition at all, Potter respired, no longer sputtering. He righted himself from his feet, which had been dangling and dragging while in Brinen's invincible grip, looking like a figure made out of rubber.

Then Potter turned to lunge for Fernando and Elias. Brinen was beside him, as was Davies. All three wore the same face in their dissimilar features — determined and exultant.

Hieronymus, as well it should, closed the shield around the three of them, so that they were once again, as they had been when they descended from the wreckage of the plane, embraced in a sphere.

The warriors of Domna Ra Zah pelted the shield with fire-power for several minutes, until, seeing this to be of little avail, they began throwing themselves against the shield, again, and again, and again, and again. Sometimes the shield hurt them, breaking shoulders, throwing arms out of sockets, smashing faces.

Or it killed them. Hieronymus electrified the sphere's exterior, or for a brief span the dream-slave set the sphere afire, and the invaders spun away in flames, and anyone too near caught fire as well. When that happened the fiery ones all quickly — but not unmessily — congregated together, clasping hands, and then they hurtled away marching at the ridden's inhuman speed, a phalanx of fire looking like some errant land-bound comet.

Perhaps Brinen, Davies, and Potter were among those who ran from the fray burning. Fernando wanted to keep track of them, especially Brinen. He felt he owed it to them to witness their deaths. But there were so many bodies and faces clashing against the thin transparent walls of the sphere that he lost them.

Hieronymus did not keep the shield permanently aflame because doing so would likely tax the slave's ability to maintain sufficient oxygen within the sphere. There was also a need, or a need that would all too soon become exigent, to conserve its sorcerous energies. The Great God could not breach the dream-slave's shield, but as long as they were sealed within it, neither Fernando nor Hieronymus could rend the veil Between the Worlds and call down the destruction of the four fundamental forces to eradicate the army.

Such was the nature of the slave's shield, Fernando guessed. He was learning as he went along, since he had never been in this situation before; when he had faced the Omerigans it was never in close combat, or assailed by such numbers. The shield was like a fine gossamer spun from the stuff of some other dimension, and, while in it, they were separated from This World though conjunct and visible to it; they were rendered of This World but not in it.

Ironic, Fernando mused. To have the world visible to one but not to be able to enter it without risking death — that was the eternal condition and dilemma of the Great Gods, and indeed of all the spirits of the Next Worlds: until and unless They found a human body and mind to ride.

Domna Ra Zah had found a way to ride hundreds, or thousands. Hundreds of thousands, maybe.

Mere shreds of sunlight entered the sphere now. The bodies of the ridden invaders were stacked three deep or more on all sides.

Elias Baker was babbling. Evidently the silent conversation going on constantly between Fernando and his slave left the captain feeling an increasingly desperate need for a comforting or explanatory word.

"What the fuck what the fuck what the *fuck!* It's your fault, you fucking killed my wife!!! Let me die, let me at least fuckin' die with her!!"

Fernando ignored the grieving man, unable to provide succor. There was no time now to coddle emotions, to deal with loss or fear or hurt.

What could they do?

They could remain here. Hieronymus never needed to sleep. But eventually Fernando and Elias would both have to eat and drink. In the sphere they were closed off even from the soil, which Fernando with his sorcery might have been able to fashion into sustenance — though such a spell required sunlight, Hieronymus reminded him. Hieronymus could certainly manufacture foodstuffs from his own being, but this would eventually detract from the strength of the shield, and it was unclear anyway whether a human being could survive on dream-slave ichor alone.

If Hieronymus could shift local gravity they might fly in the sphere, and get free.

But the presence of the Great God played havoc with all the four forces. Hieronymus tried to lift them, and tried again, but failed. Perhaps Domna's will was bearing down on them, holding them fast.

Elias was raving. Yet the solution had already been found. Fernando's second-self alerted him. *You/We already came up with it,* he said. *You just weren't paying attention.*

And then Fernando knew, as Hieronymus knew, and the decision was easy. There was no other feasible option.

Possession. The Great God craved to ride Fernando, but he must choose his own rider, and it would be an entity of his creation: Hieronymus. Hieronymus would repurpose its corporeal shell and down-convert entirely to the oneiric energy of which it was Made. Fernando would consume this energy — but he was already consuming it, the plan was instantaneous with its execution, for Hieronymus had infiltrated the shield at that moment with rapid decay, it had given the shield a kind of timer before its will ceased to make the bubble manifest, and at the same time Hieronymus's body had turned in on itself, a rapid imperceptible implosion. Hieronymus was a bright blue liquid now in a bright blue glass.

Elias turned away from the bodies crowded at the sphere to look at Fernando, puzzled and vaguely horrified.

Fernando tipped the bright blue glass to his lips, the movement incongruously elegant. He swallowed carefully, not gulping, and then he crumbled the glass, which was not, of course, actually glass, into his mouth and ate it.

Elias's look of confused horror transmogrified into disgust, and then to terror.

Fernando's brown eyes blazed bright blue, as did his lips, his nostrils, the tips of his fingers and ears, and the ends of his hair. He was Fernando-plus-Hieronymus now, for as long as Hieronymus could continue to exist in This World.

Long enough, Fernando hoped, to make his escape.

Now the shield gave way.

There was a loud *POP!* as the pane Between dimensions broke, and what had been two shifted again into one.

Elias screamed once more as the frantically pushing bodies of the now hundreds of invaders fell on them from above and surged into them from every direction. They were both crushed beneath the sea.

But Fernando's new slave-born strength brought him up to his feet as he shrugged off all the maniacal hosts of the God near him. He waved his arm, and with a flash of blue, waves of bodies broke before him. With another turn of his hand, they ebbed all around him, carried back, back, back as though by a powerful wind.

Fernando stood clear in the alley. The invaders—many of whom, he could see, he had just killed—were all flush against the walls of the buildings on either side as though plastered to them, or they were heaped in the street.

Elias was dead, his body looking not quite like a body, but like some mostly-two- and barely-three-dimensional version of itself, lying in the alleyway like Domna Ra Zah's destroyed soldiers.

Since it had likely been Fernando's new power that had killed Captain Baker at the same time it had slain all Domna's warriors within his sight, Elias now would probably never join Brinen in living-dead unity with the God. Fernando had robbed them even of that meager solace. The loss was tragic, and he would not be able to evade feeling it later—even if the amount of remorse and grief he would feel would never be adequate to account for the magnitude of what he had caused. But for now, he put this aside, consoled, or deceived, in the knowledge that the sacrifice was necessary.

Strange, Fernando thought: but the thought hummed in his head and echoed, and buzzed in his inner ears, so heavy were all his gestures, physical or mental, with power.

I feel more myself than I ever imagined I could feel. Three-souled. I am Three. Is this *what it is to be* truly *human...?*

Which thought was the strangest of all the things Fernando had thought and seen yet.

On another level of his consciousness, or perhaps, with one of his other two selves, Fernando stepped away from the illusion-world of the senses into the essence-world of psychic space-and-time.

He saw his own body there, giving off a soft penumbra of blue luminescence, like a firefly in the night.

He saw the Great God Herself. She was not only in all the yet-living bodies now climbing over the dead bodies at the end of the alley — and more who were breaking windows in the building above and leaping stories down to the street to stride rapidly towards Fernando's body. She was a shape Fernando could see, looming up above the buildings' roofs. Behind Her and through Her, he could see sky and cloud. In Her shape, which rippled with the passing of breeze, he saw mighty arms with biceps like hillocks, a necklace from which hung a hundred women's heaving breasts dripping with milk and honey, a mouth red and wide as a truck, and lightning brows crowning eyes of summer-pond-yellow.

Domna Ra Zah saw him seeing Her.

He felt Her displeasure, Her mounting wrath.

Submit!

It was the earth quaking when She spoke.

Submit to the will of Your God!

Fernando shaded his eyes that were not, in that space-and-time, truly eyes, but only the thought of them.

He returned again to This World.

In his body again, Fernando allowed the warriors to pull him into their arms. They were tentative at first, cautious of whether another inexplicable blast would emanate from him, but when they — or when the God — saw he wasn't resisting, they flung themselves at him as though he were some saint or prophet whose touch offered paradise. He surrendered to them, and to Domna.

But he did not submit. Domna's once-human creatures pulled and clawed Fernando. They tried to tear his limbs from his torso as they had torn asunder plaster and stone. Frustrated by their failure, they tried to rip his clothing from him. But somehow body and clothes were equally stubborn. They were unable to even cut off his breathing by piling on him or smothering him.

As one, Domna's horses ceased action. They stopped trying to crush him, unhanded him. They stood upright and stepped away. Watching them, Fernando felt sure that they were engaged in some interior process: thinking, considering, calculating, or maybe just listening to Domna Ra Zah.

Only a moment or two passed. In the distance, Fernando heard the screams and explosions of war rumbling on. Then, moving with their odd and impossible synchrony, several of the creatures lifted Fernando on their shoulders. They began to carry him away. He rode atop them without struggle, as though folded into a coffin or draped over a bier.

They were moving toward Umasi's port on the Enina River, Fernando sensed. It took him only a heartbeat, in his slave-augmented state, to understand that they were taking him to one of the Great Gods' Black Ships, which had so gruesome a reputation that until this very moment he had only believed them to be legends.

He was afraid of what would await him there. But only at first; only a little of him was afraid, the oldest, most juvenile part of him.

In just a few breaths, all three aspects of him settled into quiet confidence, a quiet sense of triumph, even. He, they, now understood something they had each observed in the melee, something they had calculated watching their own responses to events at the same time as they monitored and recorded all the information they could gather about the invaders. It was something the Great God Herself evidently did not understand.

Fernando Evandro Casiera was suffused with the energy and essence of Hieronymus-Theodoric, which Fernando himself had Made. And he knew now that the Great Gods could not ride, and could not destroy, dream-slaves.

ALEIXO'S STORY

2048, probably Primeiro (the Month of Bright Air)

Disentanglement from shared memory, with all its intimacy, is a tricky business, or at least it felt so to me.

There we all three were together, Master Salvador, me, and Fernando (who was himself, at that point in the memory, a kind of triple). And then gradually, but still too quickly for the process not to register with a shock — not to leave me gasping, coughing, head-achey, bewildered — we weren't.

I was me again, sitting on a chair. I didn't remember sitting down anywhere.

Salvador was sitting in his own chair alongside me. Our feet lounged bare on velvety grass, our heads and torsos were draped in the shadow of a tree's canopy while moons-light and starlight shivered across our legs.

It took a while to clamber up out of the dream. For now, it seemed it all *had* been a dream, rather than the visceral experience it really had been.

My head throbbed, in pain I thought at first, though I soon realized that I was actually still sifting through the information I'd been provided. My conscious mind was catching up, and it was struggling to collate all that I had felt, experienced, all that I had *been.*

There was the peculiarity, too, that I had returned to a *me* who didn't know *what* I was, and that I had emerged out of one man's memory into a physical space somehow manifested in or by the mind of that man's son.

That man's son who's half a dream-slave...

I had to start talking, otherwise my brain would sprout aneurysms.

"He — your father — was captured by the Great Gods? Or he allowed himself to be."

"Right..." Salvador sounded a bit dreamy and uncertain himself.

"And that means the, I don't know, vision, I had when I was in your apartment. Of the man being held captive in a, a 'Black Ship' —"

"Yeah. That was Pops. Playing possum for a while in their prison —"

"Why didn't he just teleport, or fly, immediately after he let the shield down?"

A shrug. "He wasn't sure he could. He needed a little time to get confident in his new abilities. Plus Pops wanted information, so he went along to see what he could see. Some creatures called The Shining Lords, or some such shit, which were probably avatars of the Great Gods or maybe just their servants, he was never sure, came along after the zombified soldiers took him to the river port. They scared the mess out of him."

The connections were rapidly knitting themselves together in my mind. "So, the *Shining Lords* took him to the Black Ship."

Salvador nodded. "He didn't find out exactly what the Black Ship was. He speculated that it was a vessel lying partly in This World and partly in the Next, where They could manifest. Or it was a machine that the Great Gods could use as a beachhead to get into This World and start riding folks to Their greedy hearts' content. From what he gave me of his memories while he was there, I guess when They captured him and started torturing him, They were trying to figure out why the hell They couldn't ride him like They could ride anybody else. Apparently, They just didn't understand dream-slaves. But he couldn't wait too long, cuz one, he didn't know if he could survive what They were doing to him. And two, he didn't know how long H-T would be a part of him. Since, you know, dream-slaves have a very finite lifespan. And good thing he got out when he did. They had zombies and Shining Lords all trying to get him. Like they were gonna dissect him, or — eat him. He had only so much of H-T's power left by then. Just enough."

It was then that another memory of Fernando's peeled open in my thoughts, rushing into my own memory —

... Down in the hold of the Ship, where it was no longer dark but bright, Fernando waited. He waited until the numbers assailing him — of the piercing light-creatures that called themselves Shining Lords, of the possessed former humans — crested above a thousand. Then two thousand. Their frenzy rose.

He was like a rock anchored to the bed of a river. The droplets of water lashed and lashed him, they even drowned him, but he was unmoved, he always resurfaced. He waited. Then when he thought the number that he could kill would actually make a difference, he *pushed* 360 degrees around him, with his body, with his thought, with all the breath and the semblance of breath within him.

The invaders' bodies crumbled, shattered, cracked, all at once, in a disarray that was like the chaos and devastation left by a tornado. The Shining Lords dimmed and dwindled into dark. What the consciousness riding them all suffered Fernando-Hieronymus could not tell, and did not tarry to observe. He lifted upward in a sphere of air (though in this state he did not really need to breathe). He tore through the walls or the barriers of the Ship, and he sped west on the wind, fleeing the divine wrath that beetled the skies and earth at his back.

My brain was moving fast enough to process it now. "So it was from that experience that he got the idea to Make a dream-slave he could have a child with. So that—"

"— So that child would be protected for the length of its *human* lifespan. That was his gamble, anyhow."

Salvador had hinted at this before, but now that it was clearer to me, I was troubled. "But why not Make dream-slaves that could, like, fuse with everybody? Wouldn't that be a more straightforward way to protect the populace?"

Master Salvador made a short laugh-like noise, and as soon as he did, I knew the answer. "You think them sum-bitches in his Affinity, in *any* Affinity then *or* now, would put all that work into Making enough dream-slaves to protect every member of the whole population of Zilia? What're you smokin'? It's not just any dream-slave that offers protection. It's the highly complex ones like H-T, or my mother. Those are the ones hardest to Make. The ones people pay millions of reais for. You think they'd give 'em out for free? You think my father would?"

"... Anyway, I guess if the dream-slaves fade so fast —"

"The better they are, the sooner they're gone. Usually," he added, glancing quickly at me.

"— Then it wouldn't be much practical protection in the long run," I said.

"No, it wouldn't. The best thing would be to keep the Great Gods *out.* So while he was conducting his little experiment — Making me — he was also figuring out a way to weaponize the Wall of Storms. The latter proved to be a successful experiment. Till you came along." Salvador exhaled. "We still don't know about whether the experiment that's me worked. But we damn sure will find out. Or I will. You have a choice about whether you're joining me."

I didn't want to make that decision yet, though.

Instead I said, "It seems like your father developed a very... intense relationship to your mother?" I remembered the odd tension between the man and the woman in my second vision: the taunts, the violence — the abuse, really.

"They did. At least that's what I get from the memories," was all Salvador said to this.

"What happened to your father?" I asked. "I thought dream-techs could live a long time."

"He was assassinated."

"By agents of the Great Gods?"

"By a rival Affinity, working in concert with some Godshouses. You never carry that much public power without being punished for it." He barked another unpleasant laugh. "It all worked out well for a lot of folks. An accord was reached between the major Godshouses and the dream-tech Affinities. Pops' Affinity was absorbed into the Affinity of Amaro's and Izzy's parents, and that Affinity was soon ruling what was soon an empire."

"Why didn't — couldn't his slaves have protected him?"

Salvador paused. "I'm sure he instructed them to. But they faded when he died."

This was news: it meant that if I were a slave, then my Maker must still live.

"I guess either whatever he told his slaves to do to protect him didn't work, or maybe they just didn't do what he told them," Salvador said, half to himself.

This sparked another thought. "Your mother was — in my dream or vision or whatever — very human-like. Very independent."

"She was."

"What I don't understand," I said tentatively, "is why *I* received those visions at all. Were you already sharing your father's memories with me while I was healing from the Vashi poison?"

"Not of my own volition, I wasn't. I think" — I felt Salvador lean toward me from his chair next to mine — "that this is what your special talent is. Whether you're a dream-slave, or a half-dream-slave like me, or an Opener or whatever the fuck you might be, it seems like what you do is *read*. You link with people, and you see or feel their memories. Like with what you told me about Isabel. You were seeing the life of one of her ancestors."

"Is that what I was doing?" I blurted.

"Now Reading," Salvador went on, "is a very special skill, one of the eight conjurors' disciplines and arts sorcerers used to teach way back centuries ago when the work was more secretive. Some of the Godshouses still teach those disciplines. It takes years for people to develop Reading. But *you,* you do that complicated shit in your sleep. I think even when you flew, you were just picking up stray info from Ydris about how to do it. Now, somebody who can Read and then up and mimic an *Ifah's* powers —"

"A what?" Then I remembered. "Oh, the Envoys' people..."

"Somebody like that, cracka, is a brotha I want riding in my crew."

Master Salvador paused, but I could almost hear his anticipation, I could *feel* without seeing the brightness of his eyes trained on me. "I notice you haven't responded to my invitation yet."

When I said nothing, he added, "I'm gonna teach you at least the rudiments of working with the Unseen, whether you join me or not. Assuming you want to know, that is."

Oh really...? I thought.

If I understood everything I'd heard thus far since the night Princess Isabel and the odious Sílvio had interrogated me, then my next question, however impertinent and cynically suspicious it would sound, had to be answered.

"Isn't it the case that whoever teaches his student sorcery binds that student to his lineage? So, if I let you teach me working with the Unseen, then aren't I joining you anyway, whether I want to fight Great Gods or not?"

Master Salvador smiled — not in a very reassuring way, I have to say. "True. If you're an ordinary human being who gets taught sorcery by the saint-mother of a Godshouse, you become part of her lineage. The way they tell it, it's like putting a new grape on an old vine. If you get initiated by a dream-tech, you become part of his or her Affinity. The point of bringing you into the lineage has nothing much to do with binding you or enslaving you or anything, though. Each Godshouse has its own longstanding agreements with particular members of the Homely Gods, and dream-tech Affinities have established their own particular safe pathways Between the Worlds. If you work with the Unseen *without* the protections of agreements like that, or don't travel on found and guarded pathways, you have about a 98% chance of being completely possessed by one of the many spirits waiting to catch some unwary doofus that takes a stroll in the Between. Then you get ate, cracka. At best you become some spirit's slave for the rest of your life, no matter what power you get out of the bargain."

This didn't mollify me. "But whatever the *intent* of the bond is, it's still a bond, and you still become your teacher's subordinate. Right?"

"For ordinary people, yeah!" Salvador boomed. I thought he was enjoying this, that he relished the chance either to outfox me or convince or reassure me, or all three. "It don't stay true forever, but for a term, yeah, you Mr. Ordinary Person are the saint-father's or the dream-lord's novice, and you do what saint-daddy or dream-papa says to do. But I doubt that applies to *you*. Not to somebody who *might* be a dream-slave, who *must* be an Opener, and who can Read like a pro high-saint-papa without ever having played in the bush league."

It was too much to process, I felt. Surely Salvador was just flattering me to get his way, and probably he like anyone adept at manipulating people could recognize and play on what was after all my very ordinary and very childish wish to be "special."

But I didn't get any intuitive sense that he was deceiving me, or that his intent was to find a way to dominate me. Wouldn't I, shouldn't I, have *sensed* if he were playing me?

I hemmed and hawed and tried to trip him up with more of what I pretended was rapier logic. But the die was cast. It was better to be Salvador's student rather than Princess Isabel's: she wanted me dead, and if not dead, she wanted me well-smashed beneath her thumb, while Salvador just wanted me to fight in a war I might actually be equipped to survive (but which, on the other hand, might kill me, too...).

Plus, if I were a dream-slave, then Salvador as a half-dream-slave might be like my kinda cousin or some such, and he might, just might, have my back, when Isabel absolutely wouldn't.

Of course, I was in love with Isabel. But unrequited love was obviously no good guide to this kind of decision-making.

And, childish wish or not — and it was in fact a childish wish, a stupid wish, I admit it — I just couldn't forego the opportunity to be special in the eyes of someone who, clearly, was special himself.

I was ready to accede, had all the words to the pledge *I will call you dream-daddy* percolated to a high boil in the back of my throat.

Just then Lilia entered.

With her, I saw dawn creeping over hills that looked like they were miles away.

She glanced at us both over the top of her phone, which she was thumbing with some urgency. How was it possible to have a working tablet-phone inside Master Salvador's mind?

Lilia said good morning to her teacher — her master. "It looks like the Winged Serpent has put out a wide all-points alert on our friend." She stuck her chin in my direction but didn't bother looking at me. "They're not keeping it in-house anymore. They've alerted everyone, including the postal service, that Aleixo is a menace to public safety, and his whereabouts should be reported." Now she did look at me. "The good news is, they want you alive. 'Under no circumstances kill,' the directives say."

"Interesting," Master Salvador said. He rose from his chair — the better to think, I supposed — and as he stepped away the chair faded back into the gray dawn air of the jungle. "Guess our trick with the doubles didn't work. You pick up anything about them?"

"Not a thing," Lilia said.

"Damn. It'll be tough when we get back to Norio, if they're on high alert for us."

"Can't we just hide out here?" I made an effort, rather valiant if I may say so myself, not to sound panicked.

"I don't want to stay here forever," Salvador answered. "War to fight, remember? But we gotta go anyway, if I'm going to teach you two Unseen work."

"Why can't you do that here?" I asked — hoping a little that this was a subtle way of saying I'd signed on to being his student, without formally having to say, *Yes,* Master *Salvador, I agree to be your bitch.*

"Here we're kinda Between-Worlds-slash-not. Roughly speakin', there's three types of Between/not spaces. There are mind-spaces, like this one. If you start working magic here that isn't my magic but yours, you'll have an effect on my mind. I'm not lookin' to deal with shit like that. Nobody with sense would. Second type are spaces plucked out of time, like where Isabel took you to. But those pretty much have to be in the past, and if you learn magic in those time-ripped spaces, then when you come back to gravitational time — when you come back to the present — there's a gap in time between when you learned the magic and when you use it in This World, a gap you haven't actually experienced, but which will have an effect when you're in the present. Stuff could have happened between when you learned and when you use: skills could have atrophied, certain areas of your power-set could have gotten out of control — errors will definitely have crept in. It's just the way magic works. So that's no go too."

"Okayyy," I said.

Lilia cut in. "That leaves spaces built into the actual Between Worlds but connected and anchored in This World. Those are the only safe spaces for instruction in sorcery — assuming they're properly sealed."

"Those third-type spaces," Salvador said, "can and usually are built with protections against predacious spirits, and they're built so that time flows at a different rate once you pass through the doorway. You learn sorcery best in those spaces because you can spend three years getting through the basics, but only an hour or a day would pass in This World."

I jumped ahead of them. "I take it, then, we're going back to the Fraids clinic?" I shuddered at the thought, as though I were preemptively infected.

But we weren't going back to the clinic.

The plan of escape had always been to take us out of the Winged Serpent's reckoning to someplace where we couldn't be traced — Salvador's mind-space fit the bill nicely — and then to re-enter Norio in a safehouse, where we would be hidden in plain sight, as it were. We took what Lilia and Salvador insisted on calling the "back-door exit" from Salvador's mind-space refuge.

And we went, of course, to 7097 Candido Constanti, an address that I had previously conjured without understanding why. Now I knew that I had plucked the address from Master Salvador's mind, just as I had plucked his father's memories from him. I had *Read* him, evidently, without any intention, desire, or plan of which I was aware.

It took less time to leave Salvador's mind-space behind and return to a physical space than it takes to write of it. (This is yet another disadvantage of having to communicate by writing.)

I did have a sufficient moment, however, to reflect a bit upon the signal peculiarity — I considered it an irony, when I should have recognized it as revelation — that my gift, my special-ness, was that I was often, without intention, immersed in thoughts and memories and experiences not my own. Though I do not think of myself at all as a shrinking personality, the jarring take-home message of my last conversation with the Master was that what made me unique and powerful (what made me *me,* then) was that I was often, by any common-sense measure, being some-one else.

I was Princess Isabel, though I did not yet know to what extent. I was Master Salvador's father, Fernando, and even his mother, the dream-slave. I was Salvador himself, or at least some of his thoughts were my thoughts. I was even an Envoy of the ancient other-human Ifah.

I cannot pretend I took this knowledge in stride. It frightened and unsettled me. (It unsettles me still.) It unsettled me in ways that the word fails to describe unless we define it via imagination of a physical state: it was the state of inability to walk or move steadily or willfully because the earth is shaking in an earthquake, or the boat you're walking on is being tossed on the high seas.

I was convinced now.

I could not be and was not, after all, human.

ALEIXO'S STORY

2048, Primeiro (the Month of Bright Air), probably Terça

At 7097 Candido Constanti we were somewhere in a back room, or so I presumed. We passed into a simple box-like space, with a colorless carpet running from blank stucco wall to blank stucco wall. Three-hundred-square meters, maybe? There was no window, but there were several foldout chairs facing a larger, far more comfortable-looking chair in the room.

Naturally I headed for the comfortable chair, but Lilia hissed at me. That woman really didn't like me, I finally realized, though I hadn't the slightest idea why. She yanked me by the arm over to the wooden-slat foldout chairs.

Master Salvador angled his long body into the comfortable chair (it sat rather low to the ground) and propped his feet up on one of the uncomfortable ones Lilia and I sat on.

The three of us sat in silence, just long enough to make me anxious again.

I was about to raise my hand like a kid in grammar school when Master Salvador suddenly demanded, "What is the source of magic?"

My rising hand fell to my thigh with what seemed to me a cartoony sound-effect. My mouth opened, then closed. I had no idea.

"The immortal soul," Lilia, teacher's pet par excellence, took to the spirit of competition with relish.

Fortunately, Master Salvador was unimpressed. "What makes you think that?" he shot back.

Lilia glanced at the glowing face of her phone, but then saw Master Salvador frowning. She tucked the phone away between her thighs on the chair, and in a strong voice explained, "The soul is the one phenomenon we know of in This World that transcends it. The existence of the soul is the universal. Almost everyone in all the world, of all peoples, has experienced it. The presence of a consciousness never gone except when you're asleep — and then it dreams. In moments of fear or excitement, a voice that you hear and might wonder because everyone else nearby clearly doesn't hear it, its tone is so clarion. Or, in illness and fever, the memory of floating above our bodies, trying to speak to the flesh packets that pay us no heed. The ability to do something in a moment of high stress, when your life is in danger, that you didn't think you could do, or you couldn't do in the time that you had. These things are reported by every science and art. In every known language there is a word for it: we call it the soul. As this is universal and non-physical, and as work with the Unseen exists, that means that it must proceed from the soul." Lilia tried to conceal her insecure little inhale at the end — she must have run out of breath yapping — but I saw the crack in her confidence, and felt a frisson of pleasure.

"Well reasoned," Master Salvador said smoothly. His voice was pitched low and quiet. "And that is what educated people tend to think. It's true that the soul is universal. All of the teachings of Aleixo's people's prophet, Ur, were built on the foundation of that idea. But Ur wasn't right about magic, and you aren't right either, Lilia. Sorcery has nothing to do with the soul. Not fundamentally. In fact, the soul is the one piece of This World that magic can't do much of anything about. The soul is mostly beyond the reach of magic. That's why one limit of all practitioners' ability is that we can't raise the dead."

"Well, what's the right answer then?" Lilia switched from eager pet to petulant malcontent at circuit-breaker speed.

My mouth was open again, but this time sounds were coming out, even before I knew what they meant. Which might have been because of my soul, operating beyond the consciousness in exactly the manner Lilia was talking about. Or because of dream-slave programming.

"The source of magic is the link between parallel planes of reality, This World and the Next."

Master Salvador's body lifted a fraction higher from the soft recesses of his comfortable chair in surprise. "High five to Aleixo. Is that knowledge, or a guess?"

Though I often don't know the answer to questions put to me, I can usually be counted on for a flip reply. "Why can't it be both?"

He laughed warmly. (I could feel Lilia's hate like a spike of heat.)

"Whichever it is, you're right. When we fought Izzy's agents and the Silvar, how could I use gravity and magnetism to beat them? I couldn't have affected the gravity of this earth. That's not possible, except maybe for the Great Gods. So, what did I do? I took a piece of gravity from a world, a universe, where gravity is thicker and stronger than it is on our world. I stole just the tiniest piece, the way you pinch salt. Not much more, because if it were more, and if you could do it every which way that easy, who knows what damage it could do. I could break a hole in the earth so wide whole cities could slide into it. Or I might rip the planet from its orbit."

"What did Lilia do?" I asked. I meant to be inclusive and make sure Lilia didn't feel left out or stupid, because even if the woman hated me, she was hot, and I wanted her to at least be open to the infinitesimal probability that one day she might be willing to sleep with me. Of course, I was making the wrong move if that was my goal. I spoke to Master Salvador, when I should have asked her directly.

"I used a magical device," she spat out, not needing to add, *you fucking idiot.*

"She did," Master Salvador said. "I built that device, and it's a kind of interface with the source of magic. It's a bridge. Now it requires skill to use it! Not anybody can just pick it up. Lilia's gifted that way." I glanced over to see if she felt something other than patronized. She didn't: even though her eyes were on our teacher, they had just enough width to give me a mean side-eye.

Master Salvador continued, "See, all possible universes coexist, but they each vibrate on their own frequency. These frequencies decohere from one another, so ordinarily we can't get into contact with another reality. But that tablet-phone I built for Lilia operates on the same principle as dream-slaves, and the same principle as magic, period. It harmonizes a little. It pings at a frequency like the Next World — which is shorthand for one of many possible next-door realities. A regular bridge, a stable bridge, theoretically would need a huge fuckin' expenditure of some kind of energy source. Out in space you get a bridge only with a black hole. But a sorcerer learns to open a tiny, tiny, tiny connection between this reality and another. When a sorcerer does that, when she creates a little harmony, what we like to call the Archway Between — all that's just shorthand shit, mystical hoo-hah — the Between is ripped, and energy is released: that is, the four fundamental forces: gravity, electromagnetism, and the two forces at the nuclear level."

All of this, at least put so simply, was new to me. Our savants speculated about such matters in the north, but they didn't *know* anything. There were no practitioners of magic in Arlinas and Ork or the rest of Omeriga as there were in the south. As I listened, though, I felt as if I were re-visiting a country I'd forgotten I once lived in — like watching a movie you saw so long ago you'd swear you never saw it, but as the villain plants the seeds of doubt in the mind of the poor heroine whose fortune he intends to swindle, you know already what his next step will be, and what she'll do to resist, even if you don't know for sure how the story turns out.

Was this an effect of my dream-slave programming, or my human soul? Both?

I floated easily in the current of Master Salvador's lecture, as though I were still sharing his mind-space.

If consciousness were so pure, he said, so fully imbued with what it perceives and was nothing of the nothing that it is, but only the substance of the world in which it lives, then it could be a reflective surface. Then like a mirror in which you see what is behind you, not what is in front of you, a lens where what is here is actually what is there (and what is there is here), consciousness would slip, waywardly, from This World to the Next. With a nudge of will — tricky, though, to have the will, but to let it dissolve as soon as it arises — such a consciousness opens the way to the Other Worlds.

"This is the old path, the so-called Pure Path," Salvador told us.

The Pure Path is achieved by nothing more than the magnificence of the human mind altered by the refining fire of discipline. First along this path a novice sorcerer would perceive alternate realities closely attuned to this reality.

"These would be the echoes of the past, and possible futures," Salvador said. "The basic shit — I don't mean to pooh pooh the shit, it's important shit, maybe the most important shit for most people — but it's the information you get from what y'all up north call a psychic reading, and what we here used to call getting your shells read by a saint-mother."

On this quest of knowledge, small apertures between This World and the Next open. They open in your own mind, but their effects, their gifts and curses, may be felt outside the mind's eye or the heart's touch. With practice comes skill, and with skill a direction for these effects can be chosen, a shape for them can be sought.

"Though those old school sages always say, you don't choose a shape, the shape chooses itself," Master Salvador added. "The funny thing is, that's exactly what any dream-teach Maker will tell you about Making a slave."

So, for example, he said, an assassin could with skill direct fire at the body of a victim, or electricity, etc. Or the assassin might try a less blunt instrument, though one equally bloody and probably more painful to the assassinee: he might choose to open a window, a little space, in the body of the victim — say, the chest cavity — which connects to the Next World. This would damage the internal organs of the victim, obviously, but because every time one makes a passage beneath the Archway there is some kind of resulting channeling of forces, the assassin would need to harness that force to some localized effect, like a flash of light, if he had a really delicate touch, or, more likely, a nearby explosion that might kill the victim on its own. "Or the assassin could double-down," Salvador mused, "and in addition to opening the gap in the vic's body he could direct the weak nuclear force of decay into the vic at the same time, which would mean that if the hole was something that could be, say, sutured, then you'd still be giving the vic cell-breakdown and probably a hella vicious cancer."

"That's horrid," I said, moved to loudness. "Why are we talking about using magic for such horrible things?"

Master Salvador laughed again. "I like your soft heart, Aleixo. I'm talking ugly because, one, we *are* going to be using magic for some horrible shit. We're going to war, ain't we? But two, this example illustrates a larger issue. Magic has a price, often a fuckin' destructive price, unless you become highly skilled — or, unless you work with the safety provided by those who've walked the path before you. The biggest danger is to you the sorcerer — and probably to anybody unlucky enough to be a short distance from you. You can obviously see that even on the Pure Path, if you're looking into Other Worlds and shit, and opening holes Between, the *least* thing that could happen is you could go crazy."

"At higher skill levels, you could do more creative things," Lilia offered.

"Yeah," Master Salvador agreed. "At upper levels of skill, you could open apertures to work as shields. That would involve opening a 'hole' so that whatever threat coming toward you, whether it's a bullet, or a knife, or your enemy's magical burst of energy, it either meets the force of energy at the point of opening in front of your body — though obviously this is dangerous for the reasons I've already said — or it 'falls' into the hole. Now, a shield meeting a *shield* might nullify both: a hole meeting a hole. *Or* it might begin a chain reaction that creates a whirlwind of force — again with potentially catastrophic effects. That's if you're fighting other sorcerers. But it can also come into play with fighting gods."

At this point our teacher got rolling. "Then at even higher greater skill levels, you really shape the forces released by opening a passage under the Archway. You draw on gravity lines or magnetic lines to move items in This World, which is telekinesis. You bring over into This World specific forms of energy, not the fundamental four, that maybe only exist in alternate realities — like instead of electromagnetism or strong nuclear reactions, you bring vapors that put an embodied being to sleep, or that prematurely age or deform a body. Et cetera. Then you could take these arcane wacky-universe forces and smelt them into objects that bear whatever properties those forces have in their native reality. Like you could make a sword that cuts through material as dense as iridium, or a piece of jewelry that spreads good feelings wherever it goes, or a house that is a physicalized intelligence. Of course, *that* involves shaping a living consciousness — what you'd call a 'demon,' Aleixo. And living entities work their own wills and can be dangerous. They'd need to be bound to your will or under the credible threat of your immediate destruction of them or dismissal of them from This World."

There was an obvious question. "Is that how dream-slaves are made?"

Master Salvador's lips pursed. "Mm, same principle, different practice. And where you 'go' for a dream-slave is very specific. We go to the World of Dreams, or what us techs prefer to call the oneiric plane, and we're the only ones who know the pathways to get there and get back safely."

"Saint-mothers can't find the way to the oneiric plane? Or find Homely Gods to help them there?" I asked.

"Good thinking." Master Salvador's compliment turned up the dial of Lilia's hatred, I could feel it. "They've tried. Very unsuccessfully. Fatally unsuccessfully."

Lilia headed off our lovey-dovey one-on-one with her own question. "What about telepathy?"

"Telepathy is movement Between. Opening a passage under the Arch always facilitates movement Between, either as thought or other forms of energy, or in physical form. Thought-form is easiest. The sorcerer shapes a thought-form, that thought-form steps into the Next World, then steps back at another point into This World where the object of communication is, and transmits thoughts, then carries the reply back. Or the two meet in the Next, exchange, and go back and report. You can get so there's not too much time-lag doing that. There's a whole lotta thought out there, though, so it's pretty easy to get lost trying to Read some particular person's thought. That's why it's easier when two skilled telepaths talk to each other. Or when you have a special talent for Reading."

I shifted subjects quickly for Lilia's sake. "That sounds like you could teleport, too. But your father acted like that was —"

"Moving in physical form is not the way to go," Master Salvador corrected me. "In physical form either you get torn apart by the forces involved in opening the aperture as you try to come back to This World... or worse, you get enslaved by the Powers. Look, first rule, and the most important one. You need protection doing anything Between. Anything. You have to follow the roads already marked out or already agreed to by your predecessors. Otherwise: well, one way or another, you are gonna have to be a slave to a teacher, or to one or many of the gods, or both, to work the Unseen. Without this service you remain only a psychic, not a sorcerer. You can perceive, but you can't do much. You can't *shape,* you can't *choose,* you can't *effect.* And if you are slave to a teacher, you're not really a slave, you're a student and a novice, and you'll be free one day. As long as the teacher is ethical. If you're a slave to one of the gods, you're toast. Powerful toast, maybe, but burnt bread just the same."

He did not let us dwell on the irony of this. He continued explaining that the price of opening the way Between is that there are consciousnesses or entities in the Between or from the Next World who will prey upon you: destroy you, torture you, use you, possess you, or ride you for a time. There is no complete taxonomy of what awaits in the Between. There are no thorough descriptions or names for what or who they are, and no categories which link one to another in any reliable way, he warned.

"All we know is that there are many and that they are hungry, or else that for them what we call malice is as defining of existence as breathing."

With two exceptions, he added: The Homely Gods, the spirits whom the first practitioners long before history began knew and bargained with, and worshipped, before ever a sorcerer opened the way to the Next World. The Homely Ones have a long association with the generations of their worshippers, and have developed, Salvador speculated, something of a symbiotic relationship with them. The Homely Ones offer protection from exploitation by any other spirits, and this is why the first practitioners to survive exploration of the Between were devout members of Godshouses.

The Homely Gods could provide little or no protection from the Great Gods, however. The Greats were the second exception.

The Great Gods, Salvador said, may or may not be inhabitants of the Between, although They can sometimes be found there. "Usually the Great Gods are busy winging in the ionosphere, or riding their worshippers in the orgy They make when They manage to manifest in This World," he said. "They do seem to want to manifest more than the average god-spirit. For reasons we don't know They have a harder time getting into This World than the Homely Gods or lesser spirits do. Always have, for millennia."

"Why do they want to?" I asked without thinking.

Salvador and Lilia both looked at me, unreadable. I quickly surmised I was supposed to answer my own query. "I guess... well, you said They're supreme predators, but They don't need to feed to survive. What, They want to manifest in This World just to — enjoy human misery?"

"May be. May be," Master Salvador mused. "Maybe it's not the misery that They want so much as the control. Misery's easier to control than contentment or happiness. That was Pops' guess, anyway." He rose from his chair and stretched out his legs, as though the little time he'd been sitting were too much sloth to be tolerated. "Anyway, there's like a whole book of history twice as thick as your Testaments of Ur, Aleixo, that describes all Their efforts to get down here and ride us, and all the ways and times They failed. Then," he snapped his fingers, "They figured it out! But soon as They did, the Wall of Storms, courtesy of my Pops, stopped Them cold — until recently."

"Now" — Salvador indicated he was switching tacks — "all this is a lot easier if you're working with slaves. Dream-slaves don't have to follow these rules. They're not in any danger in the Between. The Greats can't kill them. And they can shape forces — they *are* forces, in a way — with a delicacy no human of the highest skill-level can. That's why the Affinity that Makes the best dream-slaves runs the world." Another quick shift. "I'm gonna go in the next room and get some water. Y'all want some?"

I demurred. I just wasn't thirsty, probably because we'd been drinking (though drinking what, exactly?) in Salvador's mind-space not very long ago.

But Lilia hadn't been with us drinking, and so when she also said she didn't want any water, I knew the competition between us was still going strong.

Why? What were we really competing for?

I kept my face turned from her because I didn't want to see all that hostility. But it occurred to me: maybe I could Read her...?

I hadn't ever done it deliberately before. I hadn't even known I was doing it.

But supposedly I had a talent for it.

I figured: open your mind and think of Lilia.

I got nothing. Nothing besides, maybe, an image of her body that was none too calming, and that didn't seem likely to lead me in the direction of her thoughts.

So then I figured — maybe her phone? It was a device that was like, but not quite exactly, a dream-slave. Dream-slaves have implicit telepathic links to their Makers, and devices like this might have a link to a skilled User, which Lilia, according to Master Salvador, was. So maybe...

I looked long and hard, not at her, but at the face of her tablet-phone.

She had it sitting in her lap now. Its blue light — a very slave-like light — was soft and steady. Blue. Flickers of other colors: red, green.

I closed my eyes and saw all the colors, saw the light. It filled my thought, for just a moment.

And I was *in.*

Just like that. Simply.

I tried not to be giddy about it. I tried to just listen.

"The trick," I remembered Master Salvador saying, "is to have the will, but to let the will dissolve as soon as it arises."

(Which was strangely easy. Disturbingly easy. Did I possess no true will, was that why it was so uncomplicated, so greased-smooth, to be able to release it so effortlessly...?)

What I was *in* was not exactly words I heard or even read — certainly not the paragraphs of words I've produced for you below — but more a combination of words and images and memories nested in memories, and feelings streaming beneath other feelings. I have no option here, however, than to render what I was in, in words. With apologies then for the artifice, this is "where" I was—

LILIA:

How the fuck did I *sleep* through these two mother-fuckers exchanging fucking *memories* and becoming bestest boyfriends forever all of a sudden? Smarmy piece of shit. I swear to Ayayá, he better not want him, or I will fucking climb out of my skin!

(Now that *was* in fact all in words. I briefly surfaced to wonder, *What the fuck is she talking about? Is she worried I "want"* Master Salvador? *Hells no, bitch.*)

I know why I slept through it. I sleep hard after a job. Sleep hard—maybe sleep wrong is more true. Working intensely with these slave-devices takes something out of me. Afterwards I can hardly stay awake long enough to brush my teeth and get my clothes off. I fall into sleep fast, and later it's difficult and shitty trying to wake up, as if the second my eyes shut, I sink down into a black hole left by what the job has taken from me, and it's a long, hard climb to come back up again.

I hate it. I don't like not dreaming. I like my dreams. I need my dreams, good or bad. Without them I don't feel right.

Sometimes I wonder, after I manage to wake up, is *this* what it's like for a powered-down slave? Blank, black inside, like an empty jar waiting to be filled? And yet just enough of you is there, just enough to yearn for something to fill you up?

The whole thing freaks me out. Nobody, not techs, not saint-mothers, not even Silvara and Vashi consultants, understands this talent I have for communicating with slave-devices. Least of all me. It's just something I do, something my brain is wired for, I guess. Slave-whisperer they call me, as a joke. Sometimes I think it's an insult, as if there's something low or distasteful about working with slaves or slave-devices rather than Making them.

It was my slave-whispering talent that brought me to Master Salvador's attention. Master Salvador doesn't think there's anything low about me or my talent. Now, as a result of being able to work with slaves, I get to work with him.

I think he's interested in the fact that being a slave-whisperer means I can fix slave-devices if they suddenly run off their programming and pose a danger. I can take them down if they need to be taken down. Most people don't even have any idea there's a use for slave-whisperers, because they don't know that slaves malfunction. And the higher-ups aren't gonna let them know either, because folks might start panicking and stop buying slaves, and then where would we be?

But I wanna do more than just *work* with him: sexy mother-fucker... damn!

Whatever. I get it. I understand why the Affinity paid me excessively and put me under lock and key with a psychic loyalty oath. (But Master Salvador broke the oath, with ease. Because he's just that damn good. He didn't ask me to swear one to him, either. Although now, since I'll be his *student* —)

The Affinities need to keep me and my talents on the down-low. I get it, but I hate it — and maybe what that really means is that I hate my talent...? Like maybe *I* think it's low and distasteful?

That could be why it felt good at first, when my brother Arielo called and woke me up. It was crazy that he could even call, since we were in Master Salvador's mind-refuge. But the slave-device Master'd Made for me routed the call right through. It wasn't too worrying because nobody could trace it no matter what, not in there. It was kinda cool, actually. I think the device could do that because of *me,* not because of Master Salvador. It was *my* skill that made it possible. And it was cooler still for me to ask Arielo what time it was where he was calling from, which of course he thought was nuts, but, just as I guessed, it was late morning at his place in Taleza, and not even dawn yet in the mind-refuge.

The phone was on its third flight of rings, he told me, and so he knew to keep calling because the only thing that would explain my not taking his call was that I must have finished another of my gods-forsaken jobs and was in the sinks again, he said. Except of course I would have, under ordinary circumstances — ignored his call, that is. Because Arielo pisses me off.

But this morning I was actually happy he called, I was even happy he was going on and on about Mom, and then about how pleased he was to be able to quit his job because of the fact that I was making so much money I could provide for the whole family. Not that we really have to work much anyway, Arielo said, trying to mitigate his gratitude — unless it got so big it would choke him, I guess, the bitch. But I love him. And I was happy to get that call and have him rattle on, because the call brought me out of the dark and sometimes — every time, to tell the truth — I'm afraid I'll go under and not come back up again.

Plus, it's good to know normal life is going on, even if I have little or no part of it.

So he was telling me for what must really and truly have been the fourth time — Arielo's one of those types who never seems to notice how much they repeat themselves — about his wedding in two months and his man and how good everything is, how much of a stud his fiancé Gabriel is, and how hot and muscular. As if I need the reminder; Gabriel's just a hunk of hairy golden-honey goodness. To look at, anyway. I don't know how much fun it would be to have to talk to him for more than five minutes and like, smell his farts every day. Arielo was telling me for the fifteenth time what a fat big dick Gabriel has, and how it fills and stretches him just the way he likes it — just the way *any* one who likes men would like it, that's how Arielo put it, the bragging presumptuous ass — and how Gabriel likes to fuck him hard and kiss him hard at the same time and that he does it so fiercely Arielo's swimming in his sweat afterwards and then Arielo smells like Gabriel, and he loves that, smelling his man once he's gone and feeling the soreness in his body of Gabriel's having been inside him, and...

(And I'm kind of blanking out at that point, because even though it's my role to play the good girl once my brother gets going with his slut-talk, I like that shit, too, and gods know, it's been too long for me since I felt it like that. Maybe I should rent one of those hot slaves — or maybe pay for one to look like Master Salvador...? Now *that's* an idea.)

... And then he was talking about Gabriel's money, because once they're married, he'll no longer need my family money anyway, "Gabriel's bank account is as prodigious as his other endowments," and ha ha ha, in fact the one seems to plump in proportion to the other.

And I'm listening but not exactly listening, and that's when — oh, shit.

(*Master Salvador returned. Her mind was quiet. For a moment —*)

Fuck! Despite the baggy fit of his clothes, you can tell that body's *tight.*

While I'm supposed to be attuning myself to the rhythms of the cosmos and the flickering presence of the spirits, here I am lusting after my teacher. It looks as though he can tell, the way he smirks at me when he says (in a voice that's rough and sexy, though the intonation is precise and pedantic):

"You work with the Unseen one of three ways. I grew up around my Pops's Affinity, and they were the government, so I learned to appreciate acronyms. Take out your phones and record this shit. Abe — spell it A. I. B. Next, I. A. B., or Ibe. And then somewhere on another line, write down in bold red letters, FUCKED, cause that's what the third way is. Since this is a crash seminar in magic, we like the question-and-answer method — or I do, cuz unlike many teachers in the world, including those torturing long-winded motherfuckers who taught me, I get tired of listening to my own fucking voice all day long. Does anyone know what the acronyms stand for?"

I wish the white guy next to me would stop trying to impress everybody. Anyway he's probably a slave, although I can't tell yet —

(As I'm thinking this I'm also thinking but kinda not actually *thinking,* more just concentrated way-sprung *looking* at Honored Master with his shoulders like coat hangers and the way he's folding his long torso and longer legs into the tight space of the chair he's in, and I'm *thinking* that every dream-tech who works with the Unseen must be skinny — and skinny guys have big ones, my brother always said. And he should know, the whore. But I love him.)

— so thinking all that I missed part of the stupid white guy's stupid-ass answer, but I hear the rest.

"... A spontaneous initial awakening to the presence of the Next World is what characterizes most of those who practice in the Houses of the saint-mothers. Those who work with techs or under their direction generally are Ibe, however —"

Where does this white bitch *get* this shit? It *has* to be slave-programming. Has to be —

"Yeah yeah yeah." Honored Master waves his hand and shuts pale-and-irritating right up. Honored Master Salvador has hellacious long fingers, and a big-ass palm. "Given that dirty provincial street scum and half-breeds like you two are not born to the magical purple like our Princes, or to church and monastery like our great revered brethren in the Houses of the Saints, you have no choice but to follow the plebeian ways of I.A.B.: you are *i*nitiated first, *a*wakened second, and *b*onded third. Although" — he pauses to kick away the chair his feet were propped up on — "some technical affinities prefer the efficient to the elaborate, and endeavor to accomplish all three steps in one fell swoop." He stands. All nearly seven feet of him. "And that, my pussies, is how we gon' fly here."

Shit! The way he says pussyyyy, *dayamn!*

Honored Master's lips are big and wet and suck-suck-suckable.

I remembered this, and remembered it for a long time. Your memories are focused on little meaningless details this way when you're traumatized —

At that point I wrenched my way out.

I mean I wanted to withdraw smoothly, but when Lilia switched like that into past-tense, as though she had leapt in one bound to the other side of a river we were about to ford and was looking backward, every instinct screamed, *Get Out!!!* (Surprising, that instincts should in any way govern actions taken in the psychic realm while telepathically eavesdropping...)

Because one does not try to anticipate being on the other side of something you refer to as "trauma," unless you expect something ugly imminently. I figured it would be better to be in my own head for the next disaster.

It wasn't a clean break, though. For a moment I lingered in Lilia's thoughts, particularly her perspective on me, and I fought with her perspective in my own mind, the way, in your fantasies, you spend more of your mental time and energy than you'd ever admit for fear of being exposed as insane, administering really devastating, immensely clever put-downs to people who've disrespected you.

Though I should have been trying to find the thread back to home, I lost my way: *the "stupid white guy"? The "stupid white guy"?* The stupidity part I easily hurdled—I'm not stupid, I knew; or maybe I am, but only time will prove it, not some Rioca chick's half-baked judgments.

But my *color?* Very few people ever called me "the white guy" back home in Arlina. There I was usually a "mixie" or "half-white." Or sometimes, among old-school idiots (of whom one finds a high incidence in jail, I'm sorry to report), I was a "ginger nigger."

And Lilia wasn't much darker than I. It was a curious thing, to see and observe me and my color as other than the way I observed or narrated it, through the eyes of others. Especially where it, me, was not only some alien thing, but a desirable alien thing: for mine was the color of *sarará* that the Prince fancied, and so, too, maybe, did Master Salvador—or at least Lilia worried that he did. What is that color? Not the white of unmarked notebook paper or salt, but a white of smoke and dusk. A white that might accompany a smell of light musk. An ivory like the burnt rim of charcoal—

Such was the seesaw of Reading and telepathy.

Once I was really out, long enough to, one, congratulate myself on having successfully achieved a feat of magic, and, two, to remember to start bracing for whatever trauma was about to ensue, I caught the tail-end of Master Salvador's lecture-slash-rant.

"... It has to be a complete destruction, a complete ripping-apart. I mean, not *complete,* but almost complete. It has to be trauma, capital-T. The initiator doesn't *really* do it to you. But you do really experience it: usually someone else's trauma, as though it were your own."

Hang on. What?

"Sooo," Master Salvador summed up whatever I had not been listening to when I was eavesdropping on Lilia's thoughts. "The choice is usually between experiencing a profound assault on your person. Or the extinguishing of your life. That's your choice. Either way, I'm the one beating the shit out of you, and the one bringing you back from the dead."

A reflex I was surprised I'd had time to develop made me listen for Lilia's mental reply. But now I heard nothing, and she didn't speak either. So it was up to me to articulate, "Wh-what?"

Master Salvador looked a tad impatient. "Initiation, awakening, bonding, all in one step. That's what we have time for. So what's it gonna be? Fucked down or killed?"

Lilia spoke now. "I'll take a killing." She gave a grimaced smile. "So that I can have you the right way later." (But she didn't actually say that. I "heard" it in her thoughts, from which, it appeared, I had not yet fully disentangled.)

Master Salvador's face, even the stance of his body, was a paradigm of masculine inscrutability. "Okay."

"Wait, you mean you're going to kill her?" I said, alarmed now that the obvious had cold-clocked me. "For real? To the death?"

"Yeah. But I'll bring her back, it's just—"

"I'll take being beat the shit out of. The, uh, fuck down." I could hardly believe the words coming out of my mouth. And in fact they sounded pretty tinny, as though there were no lungs behind them. Probably everything in me was constricting to protect my hitherto never-violated orifices I was offering up in exchange for instruction in the ways of magic.

(Though it did not escape me that the Prince had expected to get up in those orifices, and likely would have done, had I not escaped. Was the anticipated career of catamite what made it so easy for me to make this choice?)

Salvador nodded. "Fine. Let's go."

Salvador escorted me from the room. I looked back at Lilia, thinking some kind of farewell was in order. But she was busy with her phone, and may have been — probably was — deliberately ignoring me.

Beyond the room was a comfortably wide corridor with high ceilings. It was well-lit, and an expensive-looking runner carpet stretched over its wooden slat floor. A mural that looked more like street graffiti blazed across the wall on one side — a warrior, Motherlander by the looks of him, with a fretful stormcloud of hair, but wielding a long, elegantly arced sword, and encased in the layered crabshell-upon-crabshell armor of ancient Ponese knights, faced down an unseen opponent with a tense ferocious stare, against a backdrop of a red sun and tree branches blossoming in pink. On the other wall, a muted, conservative pattern of geometric doodles.

There were several doors on either side of the hallway, all closed. As I couldn't quite see how the corridor ended — a bright halation seemed to sit like a fog bank at the limit of my sight — I had a clear impression that despite the cramped, bare bones accommodations of the room we three had been in, 7097 Candido Constanti was a spacious abode.

We entered the fourth door on the left. This room, too, was sadly free of anything that might render it gracious, but unlike the other it was large. In fact, it looked like an apartment all on its own. There was a kitchen (no pots, dishes, or other signs of use anywhere in evidence) with a pass-through window in the wall to a broad expanse that, had there been any furniture, was probably a combination dining room and living room, off of which dark doors led to other rooms.

Master Salvador told me to wait, and not to leave the room under any circumstances.

I asked for something to drink or eat. He told me it was better that I do neither.

So I waited, standing around alone in a suite.

I wandered over to the windows.

They were blackened. Light creaked through the seams around the edges of the frames, and through splits where the paint had buckled.

A glance through the darkness into more gray darkness in the nearest rooms did not offer encouragement, either.

I was beginning to compare this to my stint — now so long ago, it seemed — in Princess Isabel's dungeon before she whisked me off beyond the prosaic confines of "gravitational time."

I waited, with misery and anxiety creeping above the water-line, for about an hour, maybe more.

Finally, the door swept open, and Master Salvador returned.

He didn't say anything, so I did. "Did you... is Lilia *dead?*"

Salvador made a sound combining a sigh with a grunt. "She died." His slow enunciation implied an ellipsis.

Wizards are horribly infuriating people.

"Now," he said, with just the slightest quirk of a smile, "you."

I anticipated perhaps sitting cross-legged on the floor with thumbs and forefingers joined calmly at their tips, and being led in a trance-inducing chant.

Instead, my teacher took a step toward me that, had it been less quick, ought to have given me warning of what followed.

He clocked me, hard.

As I staggered to the side from the blow and clutched my jaw — feeling those odd reverberations of pain: the shocking impact combined with radial waves eddying out from the point of contact — Master Salvador ducked behind me, grabbed my wrist and twisted my arm behind my back, and tripped me in rapid succession. Already off-balance, I tumbled to the floor, but Salvador was both breaking my fall and guiding me, since by the time I crashed down on my knees, he was already there on his, kneeling on one knee to my side like a wrestler on a mat awaiting a whistle. He pushed roughly against my back, and I lay awkwardly prone, face-down. He caught my neck in the crook of his arm. I smelled his sweat. I felt him straddle me.

My buttocks clenched immediately. Was this how it was going to happen? I saw no evidence of having been draped in an illusion.

But he didn't rip my pants down. He dug two fingers through the curls at the back of my head until he was touching my skull.

I heard him whispering words I couldn't make out.

I saw a light rise in the dark room — a bluish light, growing brighter and brighter —

And then I was gone.

Not entirely.

Enough of me remained at first to be able to feel, to know, that the telepathic link Salvador forced on me had been established too easily. That was what Salvador thought, anyway. I "heard" him think it. *What sort of person can be so easily linked to?*

Surely someone not truly a person.

But this was the last thought I had as Alexander Dion Hyypia, for a while.

ALEIXO'S STORY,
but also Daiane's

*Aleixo: 2048, Primeiro (the Month of Bright Air),
probably Terça / Daiane: 2023*

I should say, the last *clear* perception of myself as myself that I had for a time.

I became someone else: my memories became her memories, her actions, her needs, her desires, her fears my own. I became Daiane da Pessoa.

Daiane's story, which is also the story of my initiation, was intertwined with — or perhaps it too was the same as — the story of Salvador's safe-house apartment, about which I now learned considerably more than I might have wished.

The history of how the venerable six-story building at 7097 Candido Constanti Street became the dormitory and practice grounds for Master Salvador's students in sorcery is one of those common stories. The kind of story you see re-told in grisly detail every week on the tabloid screens of your tablet-phone, or rendered into low-budget drama-of-the-week 2-D tableaux on your entertainment visors or your 3-D hologlobes. Interestingly, it is a kind of story that richly-endowed newswatch programs who use dream-slaves as anchors or reporters usually omit.

Salvador heard the story because he was always on the lookout for useful properties in the city that he could purchase on the cheap. 7097 was just the sort of buy he avidly sought: a tall, colonial villa, with one of those classic baroque façades. It was clarion red, and the sea-wave-curved balustrades of its four long balconies were lifted up from the plaza floor, as though on the tips of gods' fingers, by a row of high arches and delicate columns. Deep porticoes burrowed beneath, providing shade from the brutal Norio sun, with ample space to rent to food vendors or even hourly restaurants.

The best of 7097's amenities, the best, at least, for Master Salvador's purposes, was that all floors of the building opened onto dimensional portals.

7097 appeared in city real estate listings touting a discounted price because of the circumstances surrounding the building's desertion by human inhabitants the previous summer. The City owned the property, just as it owned thousands upon thousands of buildings in the hundreds of nondescript urban and suburban neighborhoods that covered the hills, valleys, and micro-climate zones stretching across the bowl beneath the Atlas Mountains. Since '75, when dimensional-nesting had been first devised, these properties were able to comfortably and cheaply (and by comparison with the rest of the empire, luxuriously) house an exponentially large number of renters.

The most powerful and successful of the dream-tech Affinities, with that expansive noblesse oblige which had prompted them to build fountains for free distribution of Water to Rioca citizens and pilgrims from the empire, rented out these high-capacity spaces in old buildings like 7097, at rates so low that every previous generation of Zilian ancestors since colonial times would have indentured their firstborn children to secure them. Rents were considerably lower than Norio's monthly minimum-income dole, which meant idle persons could live like kings — or at least, like the kings' wealthy ministers.

Such bargains, some prominent saint-mothers and saint-fathers warned, could not be resisted, and doubtless would come with a high cost to the peace of the previously indigent idlers' souls.

Why, the suspicious and the skeptical wondered, would the City charge so little for its space? Magic was not inexpensive, at least not if measured in personal risk. What did the City fathers in their wealthy Affinities hope to gain by such profligacy? *Were* the apartments a species of indenture, and by renting them *did* the City illegally gain secret slaves, of a human kind?

And where, the voices of warning asked, did the food come from for these people?

Everyone possessing any knowledge of the history of magic in the world — which is to say then, any citizen of Norio — knew the ancient Elleni story about the young goddess kidnapped by the god of the dead, who, during her luxurious captivity in the underworld, nibbled six pomegranate seeds proffered to her, and thus was condemned for eternity to abide in the underworld as her captor's wife four months of every year.

Might not the food provided in these City domiciles have some equally sinister purpose? Some food was certainly purchased with the plentiful remainder of their monthly dole after the pitiful rent was paid, yet City-property people ate and dressed rather too well for that modest financial windfall to explain.

"We get their food from local farmer's markets," the City fathers explained. "We pay for the food out of our funds, and it just so happens it's easier to teleport the food into our renters' kitchens than to organize deliveries." Renters did, they pointed out, have to cook their own meals.

(To the confusion of many, despite numerous investments without apparent profit such as these homes for the indigent, the City coffers were overflowing. Of course, on this point as on others, the skeptics went astray. The City's treasury was full for one good reason: governments, corporations, and people of wealth all over the western world were willing to pay a great deal of money to acquire the services of dream-slaves. Dream-slaves were made nowhere in the world other than Norio. The City's tax base benefited enormously from this monopoly; and this is to say nothing of the profits of sale gained by the dream-tech Affinities that were the City's de facto government, and the empire's de jure government.)

If, indeed, the abundance of cheap housing and its contradiction with Norio's seemingly eternal budgetary surplus were the elements of a conspiracy to suborn men's souls — or, perhaps, as one muckraking tabloid newscaster constantly inveighed, part of an elaborate plot to provide test subjects for sinister experiments conducted on tenants in their sleep in which their superfluous internal organs were excised for later sale — the renters of 7097 were oblivious to these perils.

The five floors above the level of the portico at 7097 held two apartments each. In '79 the City ordered the demolition of dividing walls between what had been a rabbits' warren of dumpy hovel apartments with scarcely a single working toilet and shower per floor, and directed architects and contractors to reshape the building's old bones into more capacious domiciles.

As this process neared completion, before the last new walls had been fully plastered, and before any doors had been bolted to doorframes, a duo of third-level dream-techs whom the City Manager had hired from Sirius One Affinity arrived on the premises. These techs were, it was reported, not eminent in their field. Hence they had advanced no higher than the third level, but they were certainly competent and came with the full confidence of their Affinity, which was known for the efficiency and elegance of its works throughout Norio.

The Sirius One duo wore the floppy shapeless tracksuits and hoodies of their class. To the construction workers staring openly at them, the two looked dangerously unprotected from dangling wires and as-yet unsecured roof-beams.

After some words of cursory greeting to whoever stood nearest them, and after a short series of mysterious movements that appeared to be an eruption of physical tics, or an odd, coordinated dance, the two zipped up their hoods so that their faces and heads were completely covered in dark navy blue. Then, concealed within the cotton chambers of their clothes and sightless — at least in the physical sense — they began to conduct the secret work that is known only to the initiates of the dream-tech guilds.

To the contractors and the City manager present, it looked as though the two practitioners — the clothes were too baggy to tell what gender they might be, a fashion choice frowned upon by most Rioca, who were all for body-hugging and body-revealing clothing — were doing nothing other than blindly bumping into the walls. But the techs were searching out openings, groping to find Archways into the spaces between This World and the Next, apertures between the manifold dimensions of reality.

The majority of such Archways are exceedingly tiny, and wink in and out of existence with maddening irregularity. But they can be stabilized and widened by the dream-techs' craft. The portals dream-techs find are portals into nothing, not This World or the Next. This of course is to the good, since just any old passage between dimensions will take you someplace you likely don't wish to go, where you would be found — and have done to you very unpleasant and probably fatal things — by entities which you surely wouldn't choose to meet (presuming you are in your right mind).

But when these Archways are reshaped by learned workers of the Unseen, the workers shape the nothingness that lies beyond the Archways, in the manner and according to the intent of the shapers. And the shapers at 7097, like those in so many other places in the City, saw fit to mold this potential-rich nothing into habitable space, into kitchens and baths and rooms with every useful amenity, into large rooms with high ceilings and even windows which, by some mysterious displacement of space and time, looked out onto the sunstruck cobblestones of the plaza outside or out to the jagged restless sea of building upon building that eddied around and behind 7097.

The rich and near-rich, of course, have eminent techs who shape on the other sides of such Archways meadows with rolling hills, lily-strewn ponds, and unicorns prancing in an unchanging gold and violet twilight or beneath the watchfulness of triple moons and even triple suns. But this was 7097 Candido Constanti Street, a City property, and what you got was about a mile of extra square footage in each apartment consisting of clean, pretty rooms (which, however, you would have to clean on your own, without the help of the elfin dream-slaves the rich had to serve them), none of which impinged upon the adjoining buildings or was visible from the outside.

Before Salvador's purchase of the building, 7097 Candido Constanti Street, Suite 1A, was the residence of an entire Ponese village, population two-hundred-and-nineteen. The villagers' erstwhile residence had been devastated by an earthquake, and, having been told by the Ponese government that the land where their ancestors had lived for centuries was condemned and would be permanently evacuated, they renounced their citizenship in desperation and pique, and, following rumors of transformation and success, relocated to Norio. (Pon, in case You don't know, lies on the other side of the Eastern Ocean's Wall of Storms, allowing easy air-and-sea travel between there and Zilia.)

After several years a significant portion of the Ponese villagers had yet to find good work in the City. On many a morning you would see the men troop out across the plaza to stand futilely along the roads in hopes of being picked up for day jobs, which increasing use of slave-labor had rendered largely redundant. Their labor, however, was no longer necessary to provide either shelter or food after the intervention of Sirius One Affinity, for 7097, Suite 1A, now provided these in abundance, at a fully practical rent.

1B at that time housed a large extended family, the flock of them born and raised in Norio, each adult employed, the children all in school, and all their noses very much in the air when colliding schedules forced them to jostle in the elevator with any of the Ponese. The upper four floors were rented by: other large families (2A, 2B, 3A, and 4B), some less and some even more haughty than those in 1B; a collective of terminally unrecognized sculptors, dancers, actors, playwrights, and video artists (3B); and a group of young men and women of fluctuating membership (4A and 5B), all of whom actually lived in wealthier neighborhoods closer to the beaches, but who kept the two apartments for intermittent debauches and, when struck by acute ennui, as spaces in which to collaborate on half-brained schemes to become crimelords by challenging the Vashi crime gangs that terrorized the environs of Barrier Street seven blocks to the east.

7097 Candido Constanti Street, Suite 5A, on the top floor with windows that could glimpse the sea between nearby buildings, was where Daiane Iracema da Pessoa lived with her seven children, ages six to sixteen, who had five different fathers. The da Pessoa family was the smallest of all those in the building, and thus they had more room to enjoy in 5A than they needed.

Daiane was not a young woman, nor had she the good fortune that rich and middle-class folk had to drink the ichor of dream-slaves in order to prolong her youth. But like many a Rioca, she took the Waters fairly frequently, and so her forty-plus years looked the way twenty-plus looked in Arlina and other outlands.

Before Salvador's purchase, Daiane had lived in Norio for twelve years, and in 7097, 5A for two. The language of the City was her native tongue, and the 2-D and 3-D entertainments that filled her dreams were made in and about Norio and its citizens.

But she was not born in the City, and thus was not a true Rioca. She hailed from a little town called Linfe, in the backland province of Raisminas.

The tenants of 1B looked down on Daiane fully as much as they scorned the pale Ponese — except for one of the younger men in that family, João. João was the same age as Daiane's eldest children (twins). He sometimes moseyed upstairs to steal twenty minutes with Daiane in one of the many rooms no one in Daiane's family used, and Daiane found him to be so excitable and so soft-skinned — a delectable combination — that she did what she probably should not have done.

By the time João began his moseying, Daiane had already taken many lovers, and with each new beau she further sloughed off the layers of stupidity and bigotry with which a girlhood in benighted Linfe had provisioned her.

In the care of the City of Norio, no woman need marry a man, nor even attach herself to a man. She did not need to be pretty for a man, or interesting for one, or to pretend interest in their idiot obsessions. The City provided for Daiane's needs and for the needs of her children. So, freed at last of the past, Daiane had cultivated a practice of fucking men only because she enjoyed their bodies, or the way they smelled, or the softness of their skin and the stunning femme fullness of their lips.

João was twice endowed in these qualities (skin *and* lips), and thus irresistible. If it troubled her that he was the age of her own eldest children and that his family thought she was a peasant or worse, then the trouble was not enough to dispel the pleasure of those moments of glory when she ogled the creamy golden skin of his buttocks, strangely and excitingly darker than his dusk-ivory skin (*so João's color was* my *color — when I was still Aleixo*). Or the pleasure she had when she watched — as she liked to do, insisting that João do her from behind as she crouched on all fours in front of a wall-length mirror — his muscles ripple as he lost control inside her, and when she felt him hitch against her body as though flinching from a blow, and she heard him cry out, "Goh-zaaahh!" in the curious atavistic cry of rapturous Rioca, who sometimes speak the primal language Atinya rather than plain Gaish at the moment of orgasm.

As a result of these little glories and multiple twenty-minute trysts, Daiane was carrying the child she and João had made together at the time of the events in this story—the events in which Daiane and I were one.

Neither Daiane nor I was aware of incubating little Daiane-slash-João, however. Perhaps if she/I had—well, no. It was the pre-City past that Daiane had so successfully and determinedly carved away that led to events as they transpired—indirectly, of course, not by way of cause-A-effect-B. Rather, the past functioned as a kind of brining process, whereby Daiane, via ill fortune, via both the viciousness and the indifferent kindness of strangers, and via everything she needed to do to overcome these forces more powerful than herself, became expertly seasoned and tenderized for the meal of some hungry and malicious god.

Daiane's hometown Linfe, and the impoverished past-self Daiane that Linfe had shaped, lay some two hundred miles away from the coast, southwest of Santos, the great old colonial city which long ago had been Zilia's proud capital. Linfe was nearly as old as Santos but partook of very little of the elder city's regional pride, being by imperial standards very backward.

With a population edging close to one hundred thousand but never quite achieving that milestone, Linfe was dominated by three old families, as it had been since its foundation in the mid-sixteenth century. These esteemed clans, comprising an economic class wholly to themselves, owned most of the land in the area. They provided entertainment for everyone else, during the long empty years of the town's barely notable history, by letting their meaningless rivalry for a supremacy that no one beyond the town's borders would ever acknowledge erupt into occasional gunfights or fierce primitive football matches ending in fatalities. Or, more recently, the families' warfare advanced via rounds of spectacularly grisly and inventively cruel magical assassinations, such as impaling a rival on an imported elephant tusk that flew through the marketplace to unerringly pierce said rival's stomach, or death-by-nonce-gallows, where a rival emerged from a restaurant plumped with alcohol and excess gas only to find his legs kicking against the air and his throat violently constricted as he came to hang, by no visible means, fifteen feet above the earth.

There was a common conviction, shared by citizens from the very top of Linfe society all the way to its bottom, that life was cheap. People were born and people died in one way or another, and while it was tolerable for you to think your own existence was important, you certainly couldn't expect anyone else to think so — unless, that is, your family name was Alencar, Moritz, or Galba. The Alencars, Moritzes, and Galbas for nearly two centuries owned slaves (humans) whom they worked to death in gem mines and on coffee plantations. Subsequently — after human slavery was abolished by a stroke of the then-empress's pen — they had, with a ruthless talent for deceit and an utter lack of moral compass bred into the families over several generations, maintained the freed population in penury as sharecroppers and day-workers. Daiane's ancestors counted among that faceless, unthanked mass. Her ancestors had later been factory workers when light industry made its way to the Raisminas region, and Daiane's parents and their parents had been service industry and slave-support workers after the light industry factories at last shuttered.

Daiane's head rose above the muck of this unvarying march of years only because she was pretty. There were many pretty girls in Linfe, but Daiane happened to have a certain sort of prettiness — a complexion more cream than coffee, verging in deepest winter on fair, and she had silky black hair blacker than the face of the river at night, which contrasted with her skin in a way that drove Gilberto Alencar, most eligible bachelor of the Alencar clan, to utter distraction from the moment he saw her.

A girl with parents like Daiane's could in no way resist the seduction of a young man with parents like Gilberto's, and indeed it scarcely occurred to her, or indeed to her parents, to resist at all. Her mother hoped that Daiane might really please Don Alencar, and become a bona fide mistress.

Alas, predictably Gilberto grew bored with Daiane's charms, and predictably too the precipitous decline of his affections coincided with the untimely departure of Daiane's menstrual courses.

These events were followed by the discovery of her pregnancy. Daiane's pregnancy did not, as Daiane and her mother both speculatively hoped, evoke in Gilberto or his family any surge of paternal or familial regard. The Alencars were keen to have their new relative aborted despite Daiane's insistent demurrals.

Alencar's pleading became demands, which became commands, then threats. The Alencars' collective wishes to see the fruits of Gilberto's poor match unharvested were so keen that a botched midnight home invasion conducted by Vashi bandits supposedly passing through Linfe randomly (but of course hired by the Alencars) tragically resulted in the death of Daiane's stepfather, who tried heroically to fight the Vashi and was exsanguinated for his trouble, then torn asunder. This was followed by the death of Daiane's mother, who put her own body in harm's way as Daiane made her escape.

The three Vashi home invaders did not pursue the fleeing girl. In the rush and thrill of violence, they forgot that it was Daiane whom they had been paid to target. (Though they had not been paid enough; the Alencars were notorious cheapskates.) These Vashi were not skilled thugs, but merely young ruffians only recently passed over the Bridge Between Worlds, quite new to their fleshly incarnations, and so intoxicated by the blood they drank from Daiane's stepfather and the thrill of ripping his corpse to pieces — *How funny he looks without this piece!* and, *What do they do with* these?, the late-arriving police overheard the Vashi saying — that they just sat on the front stoop giggling till they were arrested. (The police shortly lost custody of the Vashi, since jails in Linfe were inadequately equipped to hold beings of non-human strength, not to mention the Vashi's capacity, for a few hours after having fully fed, to render themselves intangible and thus walk unimpeded through merely ordinary walls.)

Daiane's mother's sacrifice bought Daiane's escape in the dark pre-morning hours. Then, after an interminable interval that found her wandering the deserted streets suppressing cries of grief and paroxysms of dread as she waited, barely able to tolerate breeze across her skin, for the cold touch of Vashi on her shoulder, she was at last assured she had not been followed. The dawn found Daiane begging at the doorstep of Fausto, one of her mother's uncles-by-marriage (the sister he'd married had died of Fraids).

Daiane spent two days hiding in Fausto's quiet, unassuming, and unfrequented domicile, her family's equivalent of a safe-house. When the way seemed clear, in consultation with her great-uncle, Daiane left town.

Linfe was not situated on the ley-lines running from coast to hinterland, and so had no stations connecting to the short-range teleportation hops of the national throughway. Quite possibly a ticket for such transport would have been difficult to scrounge from the members of her family, anyway, who after all were quite bereaved and had plenty of their own travails to occupy them.

So Daiane took the airship to Santos.

This was a sensible destination. Santos was the greatest and largest city of the north, and insofar as justice or governance had prevailed in the hinterlands of the empire after the Great Collapse and subsequent Revolution a century-and-a-half prior, backland Linfe owed fealty to the Two Dukes of Santos (Upper and Lower). True, it was unlikely that either of the Dukes would seek justice against the Alencar family for Daiane's stepfather's and mother's deaths. The young regime trod lightly on the pre-rogatives of the old, even if former measures of distinction like mere money had been rendered nearly superfluous in the New Era. Nevertheless, the cities of the empire were generous to their poor: the ducal offices might well be prevailed upon to offer Daiane a cash compensation for the murders, or perhaps even the temporary services of a dream-slave, if they deemed her sufficiently distressed.

The airship to Santos was a dirigible inflated by natural gases and driven by unnatural alchemical processes. By the '70s such dirigibles were widely considered a safer mode of air travel than fuel-powered electric airplanes, since the electromagnetic disturbances created by the transformation of the Wall of Storms into a weapon had led in the '00s and '10s to an unprecedented number of airplane crashes. But Daiane had never flown in any vehicle, and the prospect was therefore terrifying.

Daiane boarded the airship in haste and disarray, nervously watching through the porthole windows lest a carriage full of Vashi assassins ride up on the tarmac to storm the plane. She could not shake the memories of their long, crooked teeth bared, the light glancing off the liquid poison dripping from their gums so that the enamel seemed to gleam and glow, the red on the insides of their white lips visible as the thin rubbery lips smacked closed and pursed open like jellyfish bodies.

Daiane shuddered in her seat on the airship, remembering. She was none too sure of her fellow passengers either, who for the most part looked like seasoned travelers, indifferent to her, but who might just as easily be in the Alencars' service.

But Daiane strapped herself in, breathed deeply as she had been taught, and prayed, as she rarely ever did, to the Lord of the Crossroads, to the Iron Warrior, and to the Lady of the Sea, who were the only gods she truly knew. (Just so You who are unfamiliar know, these three are Homely Gods, not Great.) Flight from Linfe and Raisminas was the biggest thing Daiane had ever done, and it had happened because of the worst event of her life. She understood that her plight was a test of her character, and it seemed a sound conclusion that the piety she had so long neglected ought to be dredged up and presented to the universe now that a New Daiane was required.

Throughout her existence to that point Daiane had fancied herself an optimistic person, fun-loving, humorous, even frivolous, in the way that girls are encouraged and expected to be, especially pretty girls in the backlands where the old traditions were (and often are) still cherished. Now she had lost her mother. Thus the gods had chosen to tell her that she must take up the mantle of womanhood, and that she was a girl no longer. She had a child to bring into the world, and protect, and raise. This also was a way the gods chose to speak, and the message was the same. She was without family — she had no relatives where she was going — and without a man, without even a girlfriend. Responsibility. Self-reliance. Caution. Watchfulness. Reverence for the gods. These were now to be the cornerstones of who she must become. Her old lifestyle would have to be forsaken. What was necessary to protect her unborn child and her remaining family by fleeing must trump all that she had believed or known in the past.

This beginning of Daiane's new life proved to be not auspicious. The gods' messages, if indeed they were sending any, were garbled. Daiane's great-uncle Fausto had insisted the airship was the safest way for her to leave Linfe — she would get farthest fastest that way — but Fausto didn't know, and Daiane certainly didn't, that the *physical* safety record of airships was not proof against dangers of a psychic nature.

It so happened that Daiane was fleeing to Santos at the time of that city's celebration of the Return of Our Lord of the Happy Ending. This was Santos's most famous municipal festival and its largest, in which tens of thousands if not hundreds of thousands began the morning by cleansing the steps of the Godshouses, and ended the day convulsing in trances and ecstasies of dance, devotion, and heaven-raising, which brought all normal business, not only in the city but in the suburbs and towns roundabout for many miles, to an exhilarated halt. The celebrations effect a glorious cessation of routine, a kind of collective municipal magic that brings about, for an hour or a day only, the cessation of time itself, wherein each supplicant of the Gods, afloat in a wet, rich, loamy Nothing created by the citizenry's assiduous efforts of step-cleaning and mind-cleansing, has an encounter, empty of thought or desire, with Divinity.

Santos as you probably know is a raptly devout city, boasting, so its partisans claim and no one has bothered to dispute, at least one Godshouse for every four residential homes. The calendar of Santos is at a variance with everywhere else, replete with festivals and holidays of such feasting and orgy that the folk of Santos are said to be drunk half the year, to have developed stomachs of iron for digesting all the festivals' rich ceremonial meals, and not to really know for certain who their fathers are, since half their mothers are priestesses and saint-mothers who accept the touch of the gods while in the throes of deepest worship. And the citizens of Santos worship strange gods — they *say* they are the same gods as the Homely Gods worshipped (that is, if anyone worships) throughout the empire, but the citizens of Santos give the Homely Ones different names, and paint and sculpt their effigies differently.

All of which is to say that Santos is a city brimming over with workers of the Unseen.

These things Daiane had heard before, even if she had failed to consider the consequences of them for her travel plans. She heard these old saws repeated once more by the flight attendants in the aisles, bays, and corridors of the airship, who were very smug and very mmhmm-just-like-I-*told*-you after the captain announced that the ship would not be able to land in Santos and would have to re-direct some five hundred miles south to Norio.

"The entire atmosphere surrounding the city and its environs in at least a thirty-mile radius is extremely disturbed," the captain explained to the passengers.

Meaning, as the flight attendants further explained and the captain did not, that pilots upon flying into the area might slump over catatonic at their stations and be able to do nothing more than drool on their instruments as the dirigible rolled out to sea and into the Wall, or they might crash into other wayward dirigibles, or, as had happened so frequently back in the 'oos that news of the crashes were suppressed, into mountainsides. And the passengers themselves might be direly affected. Suicides, acts of violent rage, and spontaneous combustions had afflicted small private airships in the past during this time of year.

But then why was the flight scheduled at all? Why didn't they land somewhere fairly close to Santos, like Searide or Jilhius or Vador? Why weren't the pilots magically or psychically shielded? Couldn't they have brought a saint-mother on board to ride on the flight, who could disperse all the bad psychic phenomena?

These were the questions Daiane found herself near-babbling at the criminally amused flight attendants, who shrugged, much like most of the seasoned passengers, who appeared to find the serials playing on their tele-visors of far greater import than the announcement of their diversion far south.

"But isn't this a flight to *Santos?*" Daiane demanded. "Why wasn't it better planned?"

Well, it was a flight to Santos, and it wasn't.

Daiane, being a backland yokel, did not yet understand that the availability of magic as a resource — which no one in their right mind would speak out against given that its discovery had lassoed the western world back from disaster's brink — depended on many things, but primarily it depended on the structures and edifices built by those who possessed the gifts and know-how to mine it. These were rigs and pipelines, as it were, made up of various components, including elaborate visualizations and ritual sacrifices, but most prominently composed of a great patchwork of ironclad promises made to any number of entities whom some call gods or the Homely Ones, whom others call demons or spirits, and whom the dream-techs call lesser-order entelechies.

Amongst these promises, those made by the ruling Affinity of Norio, queen of all cities and master of the world, were of the highest importance.

Norio has long been devoted above all to Manja, Lady of the Sea. This was the same Lady of the Sea who for inscrutable divine reasons of Her own had taken hold of ships crossing from Old World to New and thrown them off course thousands of times, casting them ashore in lands — and times, and dimensions — far-flung from their intended destinations. Since the time that the Storms which were the Lady's most treasured toys had been pirated for the empire's protection (that is, when the Wall became a weapon in 1998), Manja had demanded other compensation: which meant that dream-techs of the ruling Affinity of Norio were enjoined to misdirect a small but not insignificant percentage of airship flights and watership voyages, and even some dream-slave buses, away from their planned routes to diverse locations throughout the empire. A small percentage of that percentage was diverted to Norio itself, Manja's favorite city. Such percentages were recalculated annually at the occasion of the Lady's Festival of the New Year.

As luck, or the Homely Gods, would have it, Daiane's flight fell within the ambit of one of Norio's promises to Manja. Happily Daiane's airship did not waft away to Stralia or West Couver, for then she would have been marooned by lack of funds needed for a return flight in alien lands where they did not speak her language. Instead, fortunately, she was marooned in Norio.

But also, not so fortunately.

Daiane emigrated to Norio, not Santos. And though Santos too is a vast city of dangers and delights, it did not possess a sixth-floor apartment at 7097 Candido Constanti Street, with these particular dimensional portals, faultily constructed by the otherwise wholly competent techs of Sirius One Affinity.

Daiane to her credit — but perhaps ultimately to her detriment, for the ways of the gods are obscure, and what they wish of us, and how we succeed or fail in their tests, is unknowable — took the mishap of her flight's diversion in such stride as she could. She reasoned that Norio was as good a place to hide from the wrath of the Alencars as Santos.

(Which was true, but sadly also irrelevant in the end. The fact was — a fact not uncovered till after the story's conclusion — that Alencar and his family had no intention of pursuing Daiane. They hadn't even intended to kill Daiane or her family members. They did hire the three newly-incarnate Vashi youth, and their directive to the Vashi was that the young goons *terrorize* Daiane particularly and the family secondarily, that they put the fear of Alencar in them, so that Daiane would either abort her vile pregnancy and shut up as they wished, or at worst, leave town as she actually did. The Vashi youths, as I've noted, botched the operation. The family chief, Don Claudio Alencar, retaliated by halving the Vashi's pay. Thus, the Alencar endeavored to correct the error of their miserliness, which had led them to purchase the services of untrained and untrustworthy enforcers, by saving some more money. Don Claudio did however see to it that one of the local Godshouses paid Daiane's aunt Camila — Daiane's mother's bereaved sister — and Daiane's great-uncle Fausto reasonable death benefits. Naturally this was done with the greatest care for the Alencars' anonymity.)

In Norio, Daiane found haven in a Godshouse charity dormitory, as many penurious refugees who arrive in the City do. After a seven-month period in which she took up odd jobs that paid neither badly nor well, as a waiter and as a salesgirl in a quickslave convenience store and as a secretary's assistant, Daiane gave birth to twins in one of several maternity wards run by the City, Armando and Amelie.

Daiane had taken Water for the first time soon after arrival in the City, at the insistence of one of the novitiates attending her in the charity dormitory. Having thereby received a vital baptism while they were in the womb, Daiane's twins were healthy, vigorous, and in full possession of their faculties, without any of the deficits that a mother undergoing the great stress Daiane suffered might have unwittingly passed on to her children.

As I *was* Daiane in the course of learning and observing her story, I took quite an interest in my first-borns, Armando and Amelie, and can't stop myself from saying a bit more about them here. (In fact, I've written some stories about their later life that are not included in this memoir.)

Armando and Amelie had a tender fondness for their often-wayward mother. But due to her waywardness they grew up untamed, short-tempered, and inclined toward imperiousness. On the other hand, these perhaps were inheritances of their Alencar father, whom they never met. They certainly received their portion of the Alencar look, which in both fraternal twins was a long neck and a prominent bent nose like a hawk's beak.

These avian characteristics aroused in many who encountered the twins as they grew older a focused attentiveness. Those primarily attracted to women thought the neck an ideal of femininity, while those primarily attracted to men thought the nose an ideal of masculinity. (Those attracted to both characteristics, and to both twins, either fled from the room or tried to get drunk enough to propose elopement and a polyamorous tri-marriage.)

Such attentions taught the children to be charismatic, and eventually they acquired a clutch of followers, would-be suitors, admirers, hangers-on, and outright fanatics who trailed them like paparazzi. This was a difficult to manage phenomenon. For the resolution of their difficulties the twins eventually decided to found their own Godshouse together. Their House was dedicated to Zili, a wayward and voraciously sensual member of the Homely Gods, whom they selected in honor of their mother — and a deity from whose protection and guidance their mother might have benefited, had Daiane known anything about Her.

Alone among the family, the twins lived to ripe ages (I prophesy here, for the events I'm building up to took place only fifteen years ago, and the twins are still alive at the time of this writing): 219 for Amelie, 224 for her brother Armando. This longevity they owed to becoming proficients in working with the Unseen. Alas, too late for Daiane. In the course of their many deeds, the twins sowed much havoc and caused no small amount of heartache for the many people unlucky enough to become enamored of them.

Prior to visiting romantic cruelty on a score or more of disappointed lovers (thus carrying on the Alencar legacy amongst people who had never heard of Linfe and would never travel there), Armando and Amelie were forced to navigate the rough waters of Daiane's motherhood. Both their navigation of Daiane's maternal shortcomings, and Daiane's shortcomings themselves, owed much to the succession of men who bedded Daiane — I should say bedded, as well as tabled, floored, sofa-ed, car-hooded, stairwelled, and basemented her/me.

On the afternoon that the most dire events of Daiane's life occurred, she was visiting her latest lover, Narciso.

Latest, however, may not be the best adjective. One might justifiably espy little packets of moral judgment being parachuted into that choice of word, especially since — yes, it is a tad confusing, and it was for me when I first learned it, checking my own Daiane memories against the evidence of my Daiane-eyes — Narcisco was *not* and is not the (also-young) man João whom I mentioned before. In the word *Latest,* then, eager for its bow to be untied and its wrapping to be torn free, there lies an unspoken accusation of slutty behavior, with an imputation (at least, I'm sure, in the minds of readers from my homeland — and probably in the minds of You bunch of sex-hating Puritans from Your sex-hating Puritan world) of low self-esteem and a high venereal disease quotient — the latter of which would be a misapprehension even if the former were true, since the healers of the Saints' Houses and the astonishing success of slave-medicine have all but eliminated the incidence of even the most intractable sexually transmitted diseases, not only in Norio, but in all of Zilia.

This is to say nothing of the fact that many Zilians now found their sexual satisfactions in orgies under the influence of Water, which provided a barrier to disease, or sated their needs under the ministrations of utterly pliable and completely satisfying sex-slaves that could be cheaply purchased for an hour or some longer term. No sex-slave carried any disease, and many simulated orgasm — if one desired this of one's slave — by showering their owners with a hyper-hygienic ejaculate which instantly killed all strains of syphilis, gonorrhea, hepatitis, and immunodeficiency virus. The sexual economy had evolved since Master Fernando's day, and precisely in the way that his many human lovers feared.

From Daiane's perspective — which you must remember was, at the moment that I was becoming acquainted with it, actually *my* perspective — Narciso, who was short, slight of build, body-hair-less, copper-colored, and square-jawed, was in no way a lover whom Daiane/I would ever have narrated as her usual type. Narciso was sweet and tender and smart and articulate and thoughtful and roughly-passionately-demandingly-skillful in sex, and he was a revelation to her — they'd met cruising online — because of the purity of his personal smell: like fresh-baked bread, like sun-baked earth, like, well, like youth itself (he was fourteen years her junior), which rendered him in the legendarium of her life a bearer of ambrosia. This impression was buttressed by the taste of his kisses, which utterly lacked the hint of mouthwash or toothpaste but nevertheless were unfailingly clean and bracing and healthy. It was in the arms of this paragon, this paradise in the form of a person, that Daiane spent that fateful afternoon, and he was why she was not at home.

Narciso lived on Valentini Street on Neymar da Silva Jr. Plaza in an apartment building similar to that of 7097 Candido Constanti, but a good twenty minutes' walk distant. He worked in advertising sales for a start-up Affinity (the Affinity consisted of two dream-techs, Narciso, and five other support staff, all heady with dreams of their future success). Narciso worked long hours, but that day he had a free couple of hours, having taken a break in his workday to go to the gym for the first time in two weeks — and so Daiane anticipated Narciso was going to smell especially like himself that day, making her all the more eager to take advantage of the unusual daytime opportunity to get at him.

It was not at all, therefore, low self-esteem that led Daiane to take this *latest* lover, but something closer to its opposite. She felt, for the first time in some time, that she *deserved* such a young, virile, and good-smelling lover with a bright future awaiting him. João, though younger of course than Narciso, was an occasional, relatively-unskilled fuck and not a *true* lover like Narciso (Narciso and Daiane had been "dating" for three weeks). And, alas, João was unambitious in the extreme despite his family's pretensions. And he smelled entirely like the soap he used.

Yes, it is true that at this time Daiane was pregnant with João's child. But she didn't know she was. (I must say I suspect, or rather I felt myself as I/Daiane flounced off to my tryst with Narciso of the Liquor Saliva and the Fresh-Baked Skin, that even if I'd known I was pregnant, I wouldn't have stopped seeing Narciso. I couldn't have resisted Narciso if I tried.)

Thus, Daiane was not at home, and had left her two youngest, Marcelo and Maria — also twins, please note — in the care of their elder siblings Amelie and Armando — who were, of course, being sixteen then, "attentive" only in the most desultory form that the notion of attention can be applied without completely disintegrating into its absence.

Not, it should be emphasized, that Daiane being home with her children would necessarily have made a significant difference. It might have — but her presence would only, I suspect, have postponed the inevitable.

Had Daiane been home, she might have been watching Marcelo, and thus prevented him from sticking his fingers into the black hole in the sink of one of the apartment's three kitchens.

But probably Spice Mouth would have got to Marcelo, or one of the other younger ones, anyway.

Daiane returned from her tryst with Narciso — which, for full disclosure, must be reported to have been just as incandescent as she had fantasized it would be: in fact, her fantasies were clearly inferior to the full living richness of the experience, and she was still sniffing her fingers and catching whiffs of the cascades of Narciso's scent as beautiful surprises as she walked down the hall and to her door, when she found apartment 5A at 7097 Candido Constanti in an uproar.

The commotion that had set the household on its ear in Daiane's absence was explained to her primarily by Armando and Amelie, and their tale was supplemented by the other surviving children, Caterina and Carlos.

Maria was dead. Vasily was gravely wounded, but might well survive (he did). And Marcelo, poor Marcelo, was lost.

"What? What?" Daiane repeated imbecilically.

Incongruously, a volley of Narciso-scent wafted from her exposed neck into her nostrils, bringing back for the briefest, briefest second an exquisite memory — which she snuffed in doubled horror.

According to Amelie and Armando, the tragedy's first act began when six-year-old Marcelo, behind everyone else's back, went to play with the garbage disposal.

The elder twins were incorrect about this. The problem had actually started months before when the dream-techs of Sirius One Affinity expanded the tiny space of 5A, and had not done the job as well as they had in other apartments in the building.

The elder twins were also deliberately misleading their mother about Marcelo's deceitfulness. Marcelo had not gone behind Armando's and Amelie's backs at all, but had wandered through the apartment's many, many rooms, utterly emancipated from his siblings' distracted babysitting. Amelie and Armando were engrossed in playing *Heaven's Rage XII* in the 3-D environment that filled the games room, and which crowded out the other children with the tall winding stairs, haunted passages, and crenellated parapets looking over a sheer drop into a moat of spikes which were chief features of the game's 3-D ducal fortress. Here at last was the powerful Casket of Souls whispered about and killed for in *Heaven's Rage I-XI,* the possession of which would give players a nigh-insurmountable advantage in the quest to defeat Dis the lord of Death in subsequent editions of the game. The Duke of Second Heaven, a ruthless rebel in league with the Morningstar, had pilfered the Casket, and now his fellow demons were fighting claw and wing to keep Amelie and Armando (who was right behind her) from obtaining it, a battle sure to draw the attention of the Light Lord and bring a platoon of warrior angels descending upon them all in wrath —

In such circumstances there was scant attention for Marcelo, who was confused by the lights and the morphing environment in the games room. And so he buggered off.

Maria followed him but got lost, which Marcelo himself did too. Marcelo ambled down 5A's main corridor with a vague thought of finding the stairs to the roof deck where other children from 7097 his age might be playing. Then, for some reason, the dull crack-of-dawn gray interior of one suite of rooms snagged Marcelo's interest. (This was the very room I had waited for Salvador in, and might still have been physically in, for all I knew.)

This — the piquing of Marcelo's interest — surely was a work of the devil, or at least the devil that exists in every young child's mind. For there was no good reason to go into that dry soulless apartment-within-the-apartment, unless you meant to do something you ought not to, like write obscenities in crayon on the wall or pee into the deep pile of the carpet.

Whatever the reason, which could never thereafter be ascertained since Marcelo was not there to recall it, Marcelo entered the suite.

The boy did not move toward the window to get a look at 7097's inner courtyards as you might guess he would. As you would guess, he did not linger in that offensively boring, featureless open space that the words "living room" or "grand room" could not be applied to (indeed, had you dared employ them, those words would have leaped screaming from the top of a tall building to their deaths rather than tolerate the association with that god-awful hideous nadir of interior non-decoration).

Instead, Marcelo tottered — he was six, and not impressive for his age in physical coordination — into the kitchen area, which though equally blank as the other rooms boasted the relative excitement of countertops, cabinets, a pass-through to the empty environs beyond, and a pantry.

Pantries always appealed to Marcelo. The sheer volume of *stuff* made his pulse race. Marcelo found very little of interest in this particular pantry, however, because this third kitchen, apart from its use as a place of surplus storage, was nearly as abandoned and empty as all the other rooms in the apartment-within-the-apartment. Marcelo wandered therefore to the sink, and, taking advantage of the stool left in the corner between the sinkside countertops and the wall of cabinetry uninterrupted by a pass-through, he —

"The stool?" Daiane's voice rose as she became more frightened by the story. "What stool?"

It may strike you otherwise, but this was a reasonable question. The rooms were mostly unused and certainly unfurnished. So, who had brought in a stool?

No one had. No *one,* that is, if by "one" we refer, as anybody would when using the word "one," to humans, Silvara, or Vashi. Or even if "one" refers to a dog or a cat or some other animal.

No: the stool had been materialized from elsewhere, from the break between the manifold dimensions that practitioners of dream-tech and sorcery call The Between.

7097 Candido Constanti was, as I said, built with a myriad of dimensional Archways intended to expand its space. Expansion into The Between, and construction of tangible commonsense-reality three-dimensional habitations in The Between, can be undertaken without limit, for the dimensions are infinite in number. But the larger the simple commonsense-reality habitation, the greater the need for proper sealants against leakage or, worse, against entry from that which lies Between. It was incumbent upon the dream-techs of Sirius One Affinity to apply adequate sealant, as one ought to board up one's windows when hurricane winds come sweeping in from the ocean. The dream-techs had fulfilled their duties as they should in the rest of 7097. But, to great misfortune, they had not done so in 5A. There the boarding-up had not been completed, and, for want of a nail, as it were, Daiane's family was decimated, if not destroyed.

A stool had been materialized at the behest of one of the many entities that lie Between, one that had evidently been observing Daiane's family in their private lives and wished to join in the fun. We remain unaware what this entity might have called itself, or what kind or order in which it could be classified. Probably it was without name in its long existence of oozing across the broken panes of the murky kaleidoscope Between Worlds. Even nameless, though, it was hungry like so many such half beings for novel experiences to flavor the gruel of its uncounted millennia.

This entity made a stool — itself something of a feat, for you can be sure the entity in its natural state possessed neither height nor limbs, and would not have conceptualized anything like a stool unless such a conception were the fruit of long close observation. And the stool was there enabling Marcelo to stand on it, and standing on it, enabling him to lean over the sink, and leaning over the sink, enabling him to stare, stare, stare at the hole in the center with its down-sloping black rubber, like a backwards awning concealing secrets of an irresistible nature.

Marcelo had seen a garbage disposal in the other two kitchens, kitchens that saw some use, in the vast apartment. He had been warned away from them. (These were simple electric disposals, of course. Only the homes of the well-off have environmentally friendlier slave-conducted disposals, which consume and reprocess waste with minimal fuss and zero danger.)

But now there was no one to warn him off. And in fact, there was something — not, remember, some*one* — to egg him on.

Marcelo, with the aid of the infernal stool, was just able to flip on the switch that caused the blades of the disposal to whir and clatter. As always, he was mesmerized by the sound, by the sheer energetic rush of it, so unlike home sounds and so very like big strong powerful things out there in the world. The sound beckoned to him, as for so many of us the sound seems to beckon, the gnash and growl of hidden metal becoming a kind of slip of the tongue in the mind which says, "Stick your finger in and see." Such an entreaty, such a seducing call like the calls of Sirens of myth, wormed its way into Marcelo's six-year-old thoughts, and coiled themselves around his little immature brain like a constricting python. Not that, being six years old, he had much defense against impulse anyway.

And so — now Amelie and Armando did not of course know all this; I interpolate based on information subsequently gleaned — Marcelo dipped his fingers in.

The scream bellow howl of Marcelo's pain jackknifed into the hollows of the suite, and died immediately.

Maria, just outside in the hallway, heard it. Armando and Amelie, engrossed in their game, didn't notice what they'd heard, taking it for some effect of the martial action taking place on the cloud-clotted borders between Second and Third Heaven.

Marcelo obviously would have kept screaming, and would have retracted his hand, too.

But already Marcelo was no longer Marcelo. The entity, evidently needing only the severing of some body part as its entryway, had entered Marcelo's flesh now as surely as it had already taken hold of the boy's thoughts, and in mere seconds utterly overthrew Marcelo's mind and soul.

The entity let the chewing of the blades go on for a bit. The pain took some time to register as the indication of a threat to survival — and time itself was new. Single-point-of-view duration was a shock to the entity, as was the immense wildness of being encased in bone, jelly, blood, and water, and the very notion that survival was something one ought to give consideration to. Eventually the entity withdrew Marcelo's mangled hand from the disposal, and, with no more than a ricochet of its bouncing will, it stanched the bleeding so that the survival of its new body was ensured, and it reknit some semblance of appendages that were like but unlike fingers — and which were, as you may imagine, very disturbing for anyone other than what was now Marcelo to see.

Thereafter in all things when you picture Marcelo you should see him with one good strong hand — as good and strong as a plump six-year-old hand can be — and one hand with dangling, twisted strips of flesh below the knuckles like so much chewed-over and play-molded strawberry gum.

This was how Maria saw her brother, her twin. Were she older — she also was six — and living in another era, she might have fainted. As it was, she ran away, too frightened, shocked, unseated, and bewildered even to scream. But she got lost again, and did not find her older brother and sister as she intended. Possibly this had something to do with the entity, which for some span after its incarnation could scarcely exhale without casting a spell of some kind, and was warping time and shredding up space willy-nilly as it got the hang of human-like existence.

Meantime — the simultaneity of all events was something the entity was well acquainted with — Marcelo-the-entity began by finding the one half-stocked cabinet in the kitchen. He walked along the countertops, opening them one by one, and found stuff that might have fascinated Marcelo if Marcelo were still present. The entity which had possessed the child — the entity which had squeezed out the essence of who Marcelo had been as you or I might squeeze the milk from a cow's teat, and which then drank the essence of Marcelo in terms of personality, deportment, memories, and all those ineffable qualities attributed to spirit — ate the contents of a bottle of maple syrup. (It considered eating the glass bottle, too, but guessed that this might be difficult for its new body.)

It marveled at the sensation of taste, and of stickiness in its bizarre orifice, and of difficulties and satisfactions in the muscular machinations of swallowing.

"But that's not unusual," Daiane insisted. Half in and half out of shock, her mind was lively enough to believe that if she could argue against what she was being told, then the commotion would be undone, and perhaps whatever had happened to Maria would reverse itself.

Well yes, Daiane relented immediately, it was *unusual,* to be sure. But little Marcelo did have quite a sweet tooth.

The entity now incarnate in Marcelo's body did not choose to eat syrup out of loyalty to the now-defunct Marcelo's tastes and preferences, however. With the syrup done, Marcelo ate the contents of a carton of salt, and some nutmeg, and powdered garlic and crushed basil leaves and vanilla extract and guava extract and dried raisins and dried cayenne pepper and black peppered almonds.

Hence in subsequent adventures the entity became known as Spice Mouth.

It was an orgy for the entity. The tastes themselves were perhaps not so interesting once it had got the hang of each one, and then too one taste seemed to drive out the other, so that taste itself hardly seemed such a fun arrow to possess in one's quiver. But the *sensations* — the illusion of rises and falls in temperature, the internal heat and burning feelings, the gargling in the throat, and the coughing and the convulsions of the inner organs (the intestines and stomach, though the entity had no words for these), and above all the farting and then the shitting (completed right there in his clothes and right there on the countertop): these were glorious, and the entity had to raid all of the cabinet to achieve more of this sensorium.

But since this was a surplus spice cabinet and not the cabinet Daiane kept well stocked (she prided herself on her skills as a chef), Spice Mouth soon ran out of spices, and perforce sought other sensations.

Spice Mouth climbed down from the countertop on the stool, padded across the floor, and — well, perhaps it caught Maria's scent, since though the sense of smell itself was new, that sense had been well exercised by the plethora of tastes he'd just indulged himself with, and, Marcelo's body was suffused with the entity's otherworldly energies and abilities. Thus the creature could *smell* human life, and was drawn to it as surely as it had been drawn to the lives of Daiane's family from its skulking grounds Between.

Scenting her, Spice Mouth went after Marcelo's twin.

It found her down the hall, dizzy and thirsty and looking for a water-tank in one of the other kitchens, one better lit and better stocked, but still not the main kitchen Daiane used, and thus not the kitchen where the water-tank the kids could draw from at will was kept.

Maria was so affected by the disorienting spells wafting unintentionally (at least for now) from Spice Mouth's mere presence in This World that she felt vaguely wobbly when Marcelo entered the kitchen. As he drew near her, her dizziness got worse.

Maria saw something, but it was not her brother. It was some sort of blob. It was a blob with legs. With multiple legs sticking out from its ovalish sides. It was — Maria was terrified of spiders, and so she screamed, loudly. (Loudly enough that the elder twins, in a suite down the corridor, this time did distinguish the scream from the stereophonic sounds of *Heaven's Rage*. They paused, annoyed...)

Spice Mouth smacked Maria on the face with his chewed-up hand and she cried out again. The slap was an impulsive inspiration, just something to do, not necessarily having anything to do with her, just an action motivated by Spice Mouth's interest in its new body. Plus, there was something about the sight of the girl and her poor comportment of her own body, which she certainly ought to have had better command of than Spice Mouth had of his, that affected Spice Mouth. The effect she had on him felt new. It was a horripilation that later, with the benefit of greater experience, he was to attribute to irritation.

Marcelo Spice Mouth hit Maria again, perhaps harder, perhaps softer, it was not measuring the intensity of the blows, not at first, not until it learned that the harder blows got the wilder shrieks. For it was the sounds she made that hooked its interest in the girl, whom otherwise, not being in any clear way connected to Spice Mouth's marvelous new body, the being would have ignored, or destroyed.

These sounds were so unlike the analogous protestations of pain or suffering made by entities and hapless interlopers in the Next World. For in that spirit world the pain of one's enemy or one's prey is what we in this world would call psychic, and is not distinguishable from the environment — the "air," if you will, the medium — in which the suffering occurs. One knows the enemy suffers because one experiences their suffering, one is not separate from it.

Maria's water flowing from her eyes, and her bruises and above all her making noises, seemed not expressions of any genuine experience, but rather seemed to be make-believe, a stratagem of feint to throw Marcelo off so that Maria could counter-attack. The very nature of her shrieks seemed to say to Spice Mouth, *I am distant from you and it is so obvious that I feel nothing that I have to pretend I do.* For certainly Spice Mouth didn't feel anything — except the sting and dull impact on his fist (or his — nubs) of her flesh meeting and rebounding from his flesh, a sensation Spice Mouth shortly put aside in favor of beating her with instruments such as kitchenware, spoons and forks and pots and then knives, which worked best.

As time went on Spice Mouth began to see that these declamations of pain on Maria's part were not, in fact, feints. Something did rather seem to be happening to the thing making all the noise.

And then the noises, which at first had only been a curiosity, began to seem to Spice Mouth very interesting and very appealing in themselves. Which brought on something else new: the aesthetic. He sought as much of these sounds in as many varieties as he could.

Now the blood — that was a disappointment. Again the *taste,* when he sidled up to her wounds and waved off her ineffectual flopping slaps to gnaw on, say, the gash on her — hmm, what is it, yes, the thing on which her face stands, her headstand, her *neck* — when he gnawed on her neck, there was no spice or heat or zing in the taste, it was all metal. All metal and stars, that's what one tasted. And one got quite enough of things *metallic,* if little else, in the Next World.

The screams and pleas and whines and tears and cries and snot-missiles, though: those were choice.

Maria was dead when, after too long a delay, Armando and Amelie found their little sister in kitchen number two, lying on the floor as though flung there from a height, amid streaks and spills of drying blood. Her body and features were a mass of purplish swellings, of bumps, bruises, and welts.

At first, they didn't recognize her. But she was dead, and what is almost as awful as her dying like that, alone, frightened, being murdered for sport by something that looked to her like a giant spider made out of shadow, is that in this story I heard as it was told to Daiane, and in Daiane's own feelings which were mine, too, Maria is herself little more than a shadow, without claim to any more story than her story's end, as though she were just a red mark in destiny's ledger. The elder twins were too horrified by what they saw to fully or even partially recognize and account for the life that had been lost, and for what they'd lost in its losing. Daiane too, aware enough to be horror-struck as she listened, was not able and not willing yet to push even an inch outside the capsule of her own horror to *feel* anything of what she'd been told. Maria might have been no more than a bloody handprint you find on a windowpane: you recoil — what in heaven's name is *that* doing there? — but the handprint is unconnected to cause or other effect. It is just a disquieting mystery.

Later they all felt the loss. Much later, when shock, and the subtle influence of the creature's exhalations which fouled all perception and affect for some time yet to come, had both withdrawn their leaguer.

Now the story marched on with its other horrors, for when the twins found Maria, Marcelo was not there. The entity had wandered off and found Marcelo's older brother — a robust eleven-year-old, Vasily — as well as thirteen-year-old Carlos and fourteen-year-old Caterina, who were all three engrossed in the shows currently running on each of their entertainment visors as they lay sprawled on the floors and couches of one of 5A's most-used rooms, a living-room/dining-room combination with high ceilings and sparkling plaza views (though 5A did not physically front on the plaza).

Having discovered the aesthetically pleasing results of fleshly violence against the living (against the dead the effects were not so keen, which was why he'd left Maria on her own to experience the boredom of the being-dead part), and for some reason carrying a midsize iron skillet in his one strong hand, Spice Mouth set upon the nearest of the three siblings.

This was Vasily, who saw something out of the corner of his eye but assumed it was a problem in his visor's data-stream feed. Spice Mouth smashed the skillet directly on Vasily's arm.

Vasily of course screamed, and now beyond the edge of his visor he saw not a shadow but Marcelo. Although the bones of Vasily's arm were fractured and he was in more pain than he'd ever felt, Vasily ripped off his visor with his unaffected hand and pushed himself off the couch, driven by that particular outrage felt when your little brother whom you routinely torment, tease, and injure, has the utter gall to lay his hands on *you* as though he's not going to get six kinds of ass-kickings in response.

Vasily clutched his bad arm with his good one, but he kicked viciously (and off-balance) at little Marcelo-Spice-Mouth, who was unprepared for such a response, and went down at roughly the same time as Vasily's imbalance and violence caused Vasily himself to fall back onto the couch cushions.

This made the couch skid, which drew the attention of Caterina, lying pig-in-the-mud happy up to that point on her back on the floor — she hadn't heard Vasily's scream, or noticed anything till that point, but now she flipped open her visor and ripped out her earpods, and saw the results of the short melee, and rolled up onto her knees by way of getting up to give both her stupid brothers a lesson in respecting the house.

But now Spice Mouth was kicking Vasily as he lay on the couch — he let the skillet clatter to the floor — and added to his kicks that extra special knife-like twist of psychic jab that the average entity of the Between is never without in a fight. Naturally neither Caterina nor Carlos, who had now flipped open his visor from his perch on the arm of another smaller couch a few feet away, were aware of the psychic dimensions of the scuffle, though it puzzled them that Vasily was clutching his head and that it looked as though his nose might be bleeding, when all these terrible kicks — which rained down with more force and at greater speed than they would have previously attributed to little Marcelo — were hitting Vasily's legs and crotch.

A succession of ugly violent mini-events — small because they were administered by so small a person, though the results were significant — ensued.

(*At which point I wrenched myself out and back for as long as I could, thinking,* screaming *as much as it is possible to scream in one's thoughts, WHY? Why do I have to be in this poor woman's head and listen to this and watch this and know this? Why do I have to have any idea what this repulsive evil entity is thinking and feeling?*

And then it was completely clear. Maybe Master Salvador heard my scream and replied.

Why? Because this is you getting beat the shit out of and fucked DOWN, bitch.)

Suffice it to say that in due course Vasily would have gone the way of his little sister Maria, had not Armando and Amelie, following the trail of mayhem, come upon the scene and, though bewildered, commenced to wrestle Marcelo down. Marcelo-Spice-Mouth shrugged them off easily and got back to beating Vasily, and when they rushed at their brotherish thing again, this time with Caterina and Carlos helping, it whirled on them in a fury and gave as many of them as it could a terrible punch to the thigh or the face or the stomach, and all of them terrible headaches. But just as they were thrashed, at least for the moment, Spice Mouth ran away, probably overwhelmed by the volume of perceptions and sensations.

(Vasily survived, although he ended up in the hospital for a week, and his arm in a cast for months, and he never was able to produce healthy enough sperm to father children without the assistance of slaves.)

After Marcelo exited, the other siblings set about nursing their wounds and their throbbing heads (Vasily just lay there drooling, inattentive to attempts to rouse or aid him) and trying to make sense of things. They were at these tasks for a bit — perhaps five minutes, perhaps twenty: time continued to move in strange fits and starts — when their mother Daiane entered the great room, flush with sexual contentment that rapidly receded the further she traveled into the disturbed depths of 5A.

And now there she was, staggered by the story her children — her surviving children — were telling her.

She couldn't, she wouldn't, go see the body. Maria's body.

Daiane lurched away even from her surviving children's presence. She couldn't look at them, not just yet. Just to look and to know they were the ones who hadn't died, hadn't been consumed. Just to. It was

(But her mind was in shards. *Our* mind was in shards. I cannot report it to you now as I truly felt it then, with her.)

Vasily needed care. Armando bent himself groggily to the task, not knowing what to do or what exactly he was doing, but just moving and touching and bandaging while speaking in hushed and soothing tones. Carlos and Caterina, immobile, watched Vasily.

Then Amelie charged into action following her mother, who had suddenly reached the front door of 5A and was picking up speed as she tried to break free from the confines of hell.

But another circle of the inferno awaited.

Beneath the barrel ceiling of the top-floor landing where both apartments received their visitors, smoke rose. The large ornate wooden door to 5B, a close copy of the seventeenth-century original with its stiff carvings of jungle scenes and metal-hatted explorers, had been blown from its hinges, and lay askew upon the veined limestone tiles of the landing.

A fire Daiane and Amelie couldn't see was evidently responsible for the smoke, which was quickly thickening inside the space where the door used to be.

One screamy shout, short but hair-raising, pirouetted into the pristine calm beyond the broken door, and quickly died.

Daiane couldn't go in, and she couldn't turn back to see Amelie, whom she knew was behind her. So she leaned toward the open doorway and coughed. Then she bellowed, with a voice so strong it amazed her, "Marcelllllloooo!!!!"

There was a pause. Noise that neither Daiane nor Amelie had recognized they'd been hearing until they stopped hearing it, ceased.

Then there was a new noise in the quiet. Of someone, something, shoving pieces of furniture out of its way. The door collapsed away from its remaining hinge with a complaining shudder.

The child pushed its way through the smoke, or seemed to reshape the smoke into the familiar child's body. Slender and neat and little-boy pretty.

Spice Mouth looked at Daiane out of Marcelo's eyes, and Daiane looked back at Spice Mouth.

But she could only see her son. Only him.

This was why she did nothing when he pushed her down to the limestone tiles on her back and began arranging her legs to suit him. This was why, as he sought to stab her in the orifices available to him with his six-year-old penis and made rude lascivious noises and muttered off-kilter comments he obviously thought were sexy but which sounded instead like instructions one might overhear in a puppy obedience class (it was all new to Spice Mouth; really he was just trying to grasp for himself the recent experience he smelled on her), Daiane did not resist and did not cry out.

She was being violated by a demon, but the demon was her son. All she could feel — or all she would allow herself to know of all her feelings — was love for her son, and sorrow for him. So the tears, which did begin to flow, were lamentations for her son, who was once so sweet and who now was not; her son who was not even there, but still somehow was right there, on top of her, being hurt even as he tried to hurt her.

She wouldn't take her eyes off his eyes. She couldn't. She had to help him. She had to help the boy, her littlest boy, the boy who'd survived but whom she'd failed to save.

Amelie rushed at the two bodies, her hands claws, her mouth fanged and shrieking imprecations. In aspect she had become ursine, and some damage surely was going to be done. But Daiane waved her daughter off frantically — though perhaps Daiane's protests and her desperate hands and pleading tear-filled eyes were less effective than the barrage of winds Spice Mouth hurled at the girl, which sent Amelie tumbling back toward the door of 5A and settled her quite painfully on her narrow behind.

Daiane tried to soothe Marcelo. She tried to arrange her face in something like a nurturing parental smile. Tentatively, she stroked his back.

(And really, the child's penis was so small and not even hard, so she barely felt it, and despite the creature's intent, Spice Mouth wasn't *hurting* her, not physically... I have to say however that this thought didn't cross Daiane's mind. This was me thinking and feeling with her, and — since I was holding on still to the coarse man I had been — fleeing from feeling with her and as her.)

Amid the churning of its host's fleshy-bony-strange-things-called-hips and the not-fully-welcome sensations accompanying these movements, Spice Mouth sensed something.

Another presence. Another presence *with* it, Marcelo, and Marcelo's mother.

Spice Mouth prickled. How dare — it! How dare this other thing interfere! This was *its* experience, not the intruder's! The effrontery!

Spice Mouth yanked Marcelo free from Marcelo's mother.

It squinted, but it didn't really see with Marcelo's eyes what and who it was that dared horn in on its fun, that dared oust it from the body that (it now sensed) had birthed its host: the scavenger thing attempting to supplant it was — a homunculus. A little flesh packet scarcely ensouled, a child not yet formed.

This was, you see, João's child.

Such rudeness called for chastisement, cried out for correction.

Spice Mouth sliced open Daiane's belly using his fingernail, which, with an inspired thought, it caused to lengthen and sharpen to do the job. (It wished it had come up with this idea for the boy's penis, which had been bitterly disappointing as a weapon.)

A muttered spell of silence and stillness kept Daiane quiescent as it cut the C in her flesh. Blood gushed and muscle and guts flopped out. The guts looked to it like dying fish hauled from the water onto a boat's deck, or so its search of Marcelo's memories suggested.

It was no surgeon, Spice Mouth, and sliced cavalierly without regard for damage to any organs, and so Daiane was going to die.

We were going to die. In no moment of the life I'd shared with her up till this moment had I felt more clearly that she and I were one, were indistinguishable, than in those elongated minutes of stinging-wire burning-rack pain, and of a horror and revulsion that almost — almost — was worse than the physical suffering. We were going to die, and in death throes we were knit together, two threads in the same seam.

Perhaps our synchrony was due to a new correspondence in our positioning. For as endorphins erupt to blunt the pain of the moment of the body's death, the soul rises up and looks down on its incarnate self, similar to the way I had been (it seemed like always) at once a part of Daiane and yet the observer of her experiences.

A thread like a stream of powder ran between the top of Daiane's head and her soul which we both were. It looked like a stream of sandy particles twisting in an ascending helix in the space Between life and death.

I saw the particles ignite, as a lit fuse burns. Where it burned the particles were consumed. It burned from the middle outward, towards both Daiane's head and Daiane's hovering soul.

On earth, in the tangible Seen world, an elevator door sighed open, and a host of people clamored out.

From the vantage point of the Between where Daiane and I both partly dwelt, retreating with the rest of Daiane's soul, everyone except Daiane, including the new arrivals, seemed mere shadows, outlined with a dim glow, and yet possessed of clean, clear attributes as though each of them were characters in an epic poem of the ancient Elleni.

Armando had come, fear-straddled, green sickness of heart, and so had Caterina and Carlos, the brethren of the choir, who affirmed and condemned what they beheld according to the first notes sung by their leader (who was Armando). Others crowded in: neighbors— Fedelia of the closed purse and closed eyes, Tomas trembler, Gilberto of the reflex rage when he doesn't know what to do.

Amelie lay hurt, throbbing heart of grief.

As the sea parts in myth, each of these presences gave way to the last presence, which shone through the gray scrim of the Between like a star in a man's shape.

This, I later learned, was Jonas Pedro Almaguer. He was one of the initiated in Xanxo the Justiciar Godshouse, a young but promising member of that collective of practitioners, for whom the saint-mother had high hopes.

Bright. Bright Jonas was with power. Jonas Pedro had been passing through the plaza below when he felt the anguish on the sixth floor, and perceived the seeping wound in space and time there. He had come up to investigate.

Jonas Pedro did not possess third-level skills like the Sirius One Affinity techs, but no one could fault his raw, unblemished force and the strength of his music.

Light flowed in waves from him; it spun around his body like the rings of Cronus.

Sound, brassy and percussive, rayed through all the space around us, and glass cracked, and the elevator cables shuddered.

With Jonas Pedro's coming, Marcelo's body bucked as though in a seizure, and its knifing finger retracted in some way that made the creature that looked like an injured boy cry out in pain.

Spice Mouth fell numb and cold and blind, itself now the victim of silence and stillness. Jonas Pedro couldn't banish Spice Mouth from Marcelo's body, but he could imprison the demon there unable to move or act, at least for a while.

Daiane was dying. Her body was aware of nothing, and the only eyes that could see were the eyes of us, her soul.

But Jonas Pedro sang, and her body's damage reversed itself. Guts crawled back inside, torn flesh soldered to its neighbor.

Daiane screamed and writhed, and would have run or even crawled if she were able, so painful was this healing. But she lived, and would live.

I/we saw the stair of dust between her head and us thicken and congeal till it was a rope. The rope ringed our necks and wrists — for the soul imagines it is a body and holds that shape, at least in the moments of dying — and we were tugged and corralled downward, downward, until we and Daiane-the-body could no longer perceive the difference between us.

"Come back to us, lady."

It was Jonas Pedro, his voice singsong, words more chant than sentence. "Come back, come back."

But when Daiane came back, I was no longer with her. I was with Master Salvador.

I lay curled in a ball on the floor, sobbing, until the fact that it was my voice sobbing and my tears I felt on my cheeks so shocked me that I stopped, and opened my eyes.

The first thing I saw was Master Salvador's boots.

I refused to look up, but I felt him bend down and sensed his knee slant above my head as he stroked and patted my heaving back, tenderly.

ALEIXO'S STORY,
Also a Little of Daiane's

*2048, Primeiro (the Month of Bright Air),
probably Terça through Sábado*

When I was well enough to hear it, Master Salvador told me how when he'd purchased 7097 Candido Constanti, as you might expect, everyone had already moved away in haste and distress, except for the rich boys in 4A, who after all didn't really live there full-time.

After he bought the place and became aware of his purchase's history, Salvador tracked Daiane down. She and the surviving kids were living with Narciso in a modest two-story walk-up far away, where some of the worst shantytowns used to be but which now had clean, small, modern homes.

The City had never accepted even partial responsibility for the tragedy of 7097, but they paid Daiane a decent bimonthly stipend so that some degree of justice could be seen to be more or less done.

Spice Mouth in the interim had become infamous as a much-feared freelance thug. In Marcelo's body it wreaked havoc for fun on a catholic selection of victims when it wasn't carrying out assassin jobs for the gangs (mostly Vashi, but humans, too) who hired it. Mostly it was known for breaking its way into bars and clubs Marcelo was too young to enter and whose bouncers and ticket-takers it punished mercilessly, after which it could be found amid the carnage at the bar contentedly smoking cigars and tossing back shots to drown fistfuls of prescription narcotics.

The authorities hadn't been able to capture it.

Salvador did. He captured Spice Mouth and expelled the entity from Marcelo's now-undead body. It was only after Salvador had dressed Marcelo's decayed corpse up as decently as he could and presented Daiane with the body to bury that he was able to convince her to let him give her the title to one of his other properties in the city. She lived there now, not far from Blon, taking care of Vasily, while Amelie and Armando were off on their own studying with Xanxo House. Caterina and Carlos had left — run away, Daiane said — some time before. Even Salvador hadn't been able to find them yet.

"I think they left Zilia," he speculated. "You can understand why. The trauma and all. But they may be back someday..."

Spice Mouth — the entity, not the child — was currently encased in a six-by-six-inch cube that Salvador kept in a cabinet of collectibles.

"So."

Master Salvador was smiling. We were having tuna and egg sandwiches on thick, fresh-baked bread. He was sitting across a small round café table from me on the rooftop deck of 7097. The weight of his elbows on the table rocked it.

A little lion-monkey, golden-bodied and proud-maned, crawled up and down his arm picking at the leavings of his plate, and occasionally snatching more than its due. Was this creature the Master's familiar? I wondered, but I felt no urgency to find an answer.

"So, you have been initiated and bonded — to me, of course," he continued. "I'm pretty sure you were *already* more or less awakened before we started. You've learned the fundamental art, which is the art of giving over, the Art of Surrender. Now we can start practicing combat spells and making weapons-slash-slave-devices fierce enough to kill gods. And all the fun shit."

I nodded.

"It *is* fun for me," Master Salvador added after a moment — as though he'd been weighing whether to tack this bit on. "So you know who you hitched your wagon to. I *am* a warrior. I'm all about the fight. That's good when there's something to fight, and we do have a hell of a fight in front of us. But..." He smiled. "Sometimes a warrior can't stop fighting. And when that happens, not just the enemy can get hurt. I just want to be clear."

I wasn't sure he had been. He seemed massive beside me, like some great bear crouched beside my little hen self.

The sun felt extra hot, or else I myself felt dry and sapped. Finally, I murmured, "Okay."

If I was well enough to hear the latest news in the story of Daiane (whom I could not yet fully distinguish from myself — nor, in honesty, have I ever completely disentangled us; you have been reading her voice as much as mine, all along), I was apparently not so well that we could commence immediately with the fun shit.

I don't remember the next span of time, which probably comprised a couple of days. I don't remember those days even now, traveling back magically through time via access to the memories we don't know we have. Nothing happened, I'm sure. I ate well, sometimes with Master Salvador and sometimes alone. The food appeared when I needed it either way. I slept well, but only in short bursts, no more than three hours at a stretch. I spent other hours on the roof deck looking down on the plaza and out at the metropolis engulfing us. Or I sat where it seemed pleasant to sit. I spoke little. My mind grew quiet. Or quieter. Words and worries washed away, and my brain seemed content to take note of what I saw and the sensations of my body. Or, maybe, or maybe also, my brain could not or would not, for that time, allow itself to take in more than the brief, physical present. I breathed in, I breathed out. Nothing more. It was enough, then.

A couple of days later, I was feeling more energetic. My mind, at any rate, was up and at its usual thrusts, feints, and parries, dueling with itself or with other versions of me.

Had my experience with — in? — as? — Daiane proved that I could not be a dream-slave?

Or had it proved that I must be?

I seemed to recall something Salvador had told me that might shed light on the question. I say *seemed* because I did not remember when or why he said this to me, whether in his penthouse apartment that night (which seemed so long ago), or within the haven of his mind, or here, on the roof, where I was sitting and thinking.

"The others of course don't understand," I remembered him saying. (What others?) "A dream-slave is by its nature dead. I mean, it's not *alive* like humans are. Thus, for a slave, to die is not to do or to change anything. At most it is to elaborate upon what is already fact."

I *had* died, though, right? Or something like it. Surrender.

Something unspeakable had happened to Daiane/me, to us. But no. That was the Arlinian in me rushing to its familiar labels, no longer suited to the new. What happened was *not* unspeakable. It was something few would ever choose to speak, or to share, yes. Not in Arlina certainly, where the shame of being violated muzzles victims more than it ever does violators or the fascinated, repulsed bystanders who quiver to ask you, "But how did it feel...?" You wouldn't speak of it, you couldn't speak of it, other than indirectly, fleetingly. In the past tense, distanced.

That was Arlina. That was me, myself alone. This was Norio, and Daiane and I were intertwined now. What we endured, and what we knew or thought we knew because of what Daiane and I had endured, we shared with each other. And now I, we, have shared it with *you,* and You as well. I have spoken the not-unspeakable, at least in writing.

Something happened. It was done to us, but we were there, we were not merely acted-upon, we were present. It did not obliterate us, not then, not now.

Something awful happened, for which neither awe nor horror are adequate responses.

Surrender.

And it had certainly changed me.

Except I wasn't certain how.

Lilia came up to the roof. It was the first time I'd seen her since — since she went off to die.

Perhaps it was due to her skill at applying a particularly good brand of moisturizer, but Lilia looked very fresh and vibrant. You certainly couldn't tell she'd been dead recently.

She spent a few preliminary moments chumming with me. Even hugged me, although it was a quick hug and she used only one arm. She sat down next to me. I was on a bench that ran across the side of the roof opposite to the plaza. It aimed toward the sea, but you couldn't see the sea because of the buildings blocking the sightlines.

Lilia sighed. I tensed slightly. She turned to me. "So he beat the shit out of you, huh?" Lilia looked at me through slits.

I said, "Yeah."

I got the feeling it was the "fucked down" way of describing my initiation that really intrigued her. Like she was wondering, completely against her better judgment, but unable to stop herself, if maybe Master Salvador's dick was somehow involved, and if I'd gotten any of it. I wanted to say, *Hells no.* And, *Even if it* had *been sexual, it wouldn't have been at all what you think it would be, believe me.*

I also wanted to say that it seemed likely to me that whatever her experience of being killed and resurrected had been, she had learned exactly what I had learned, and in this we were the same, so there was no need for envy, or even for curiosity.

Everywhere I go, everything I've done, it's always the same. We hunger. Even I. Still. Like the scream of that child we all were once, that hungry child, left in the dark in its crib or swaddled in its mother's arms, with toothless mouth stretched so far the arc of its lips enclose the whole earth and could swallow oceans. Nothing is enough, nothing will satisfy it, the emptiness is greater than myself, greater than the vain attempts to fill it, the emptiness and its need is all. I am a mote in the black needful maw of that emptiness, which is me though it is also mine, which swallows me though the taste on the tongue and the sustenance is my own. That hunger is all: that hunger to connect, to be with and even to be others, to *belong,* at last and as it was in the beginning, in the world that is my home and where I am never not a stranger.

This story is the same story: as it always is, everywhere in the world.

But I didn't say anything. I just looked at her. And I'm sure she knew what I would have said if there were any need to say it.

Eventually Lilia left. And when she left my thoughts came a bit clearer.

The wonderful thing was that I had lived others' lives: Daiane's, Fernando's, even, to an extent, Isabel's and Lilia's and Salvador's. I had lived them and survived them, and somehow in my doing so I felt (in defiance of logic) that they too had survived even if they had died, that they had triumphed, through the wedding of their lives with mine.

It was a lovely feeling. And it was a feeling inherent to who and what I am — whatever that is, whether dream-slave or human, or neither.

I felt at peace, certainly for the first time since I'd seen Princess Isabel in East Park Seven. Probably for the first time ever.

This peace lasted for perhaps twenty minutes.

Twenty minutes later, I was summoned to 5A, to one of the more sumptuously done up rooms, not that I had time to think about that, other than that the view below of the plaza was magnificent. Lilia was looking out the window and when I came in she glared over her shoulder at me.

"We've got incoming!" The word brought out all Lilia's contempt and disgust. I had an intuition these feelings weren't for the "incoming," but for me.

"Incoming?" I asked, walking slowly towards the window. "Agents?"

"Agents. Armed forces." Master Salvador stood perfectly still, and his voice was inflectionless.

"How?" I asked once I joined them.

Below in the plaza there was a throng of armored slave-sedans, and scores of soldiers and police, and still more police clearing people out of the way. There were one or two people with megaphones in their hands and they talked to one another milling among the press of people.

The crowd and chaos was as though an outdoor concert were going to be held in the plaza, or a political speech given.

Indeed, as though there was indeed going to be a speech, I saw Prince Amaro. He sat on the hood of a large black limousine, his thick muscular arms folded. Princess Isabel walked up to him.

They bent their heads together, and then they both looked to the window I was looking out of.

And there were slaves. Not just the ordinary slaves, not just the slaves whose bodies were the armored cars, or which carried the vehicles, or that served as rocket launchers (yes, there were rocket-launchers, aimed directly at my forehead, it seemed). *Real* slaves. Affinity-made, high-magic dream-slaves. Six of them I counted. The odious Sílvio among them. I was able to tell now which human-looking things were slaves, and which were not. I could *see* the power rolling off them like halation.

"They've found us," Master Salvador said quietly.

"It's *him!*" Lilia spat.

"Lilia, I've told you to let this jealousy shit with Aleixo go! I'm not into fellas!"

If it were possible for eyes to roll so violently you might fear they were going to rocket out of someone's head and hit you, that's how Lilia's eyes rolled. "I'm not speaking from jealousy, you moron, I'm speaking from logic! *They* must have a way of tracing *him!*"

Master Salvador considered this. I was weirdly calm; not non-plussed, calm. I might have been a daisy in a field on a windless afternoon.

"I don't understand," Salvador said slowly, "why they haven't attacked. Why they're not at least making demands. They're just gathered there."

"They're giving you time to make a move," Lilia agreed. "Why would they do that?"

Master Salvador grunted. "Well, I am making a move. Not one they expect—I hope. Help is on the way."

This would be Ydris, I assumed—or knew, as though I could read (as I had done before, after all) Salvador's thoughts. The Prince and the Winged Serpent would probably expect the Envoys not to involve themselves in an open confrontation. Ydris had saved me when I'd gone up to the Fountain and witnessed the taking of the Waters, but the Winged Serpent agents hadn't been openly declared then. Maybe the whole reason they were gathering out in the plaza as though preparing for a pitched battle on some medieval meadow was because they wanted to keep

Ydris out of it. They assumed she wouldn't intervene, wouldn't show her hand. They were wrong, about that, at least.

I scanned the crowd, calm. I was only observing. Salvador and Ydris would handle things. I didn't fear for myself, or for them.

There were some people in the crowd who didn't look like the Prince's people, or Winged Serpent people, or police, or slaves.

Beside Sílvio there was a Silvar: skin so pale a shade of blue it was nearly parchment-white, tall as all Silvars are, but not clad in threatening reavers' armor, instead wearing a parti-colored doublet and silken black hose. I couldn't tell the gender. Silvar are like that. There was only one of them I could see. But there were three Vashi. They were hiding themselves beneath the portico on the far side of the plaza, but two times I saw one or more of them emerge briefly into the sunlight, which glinted on the porcelain sheen of their plastic facemasks.

Someone else who looked out of place stood near the Prince's limousine, a short woman with a scarf over her high pile of hair. Her back was turned to 7097 and she was talking to one of the Prince's entourage, a slave that I didn't recognize but which was shaped into a muscular shaven-domed circus performer in a leopard-print wrestler's singlet. They made a strange couple. The slave looked like a joke — but of course those are the most dangerous sort.

The woman talking to it began to unwrap the scarf from her head. Her hair was a rich saffron gold, elegantly coiffed.

Elegantly, that is, for women in my homeland. One rarely saw women, especially rich women, wear their hair that way here.

Now the woman turned to face 7097. A graceful smile was on her lips. Each of her movements was the exemplar of gracefulness.

I noted the features of her face. I blinked. Then I stared.

Slow was my movement. It was movement out of time. I see that now, looking at my hand as it lifted from my side and traveled through the air: I had stepped Out — just for a moment. Less than a moment, even.

Back Inside again, time flowed: I grabbed hold of Master Salvador's sleeve. "My mother!" I said.

"What?"

"My mother is here! There, in the plaza! With the Prince!"

"Your…" Salvador looked at me then looked out at the crowd below. "Your mother."

"Whose mother?" Lilia asked, still — perpetually — irritated.

"Ah, I see," Salvador said. *"That's* why they're not doing anything. They're waiting for you to jump. They expect you to come to them…"

My mother!

My mother was with the Prince?

Great wings passed between the plaza floor and the sun, casting the plaza not into shadow but into a scattering of wild color, of inhuman brightnesses and twilight lulls of grey.

So light behaves when it passes through the wings of an Ifah.

Two Ifah. Both Envoys rode the wind above us, swooping down, Ydris and another.

I recognized the other though I had never spoken to him before. When I last saw him, he'd not even been moving, or alive. He had been the pitch-black sculpture that stood in the living room of Master Salvador's apartment, where I'd jumped from the balcony railing. I'd only kept the image of it in memory, I realized, because Ydris had been caressing the statue.

As the Ifah flew, everyone in the plaza covered their faces. Though not, I saw, the slaves, who stared steadily, even balefully, skyward.

When the light cleared — the confusion of which left all the humans, even those of us inside the building, all blind for a second or two — the soldiers and police raised their guns but did not shoot.

I saw my mother in the crowd. She was standing apart from the Prince's muscular leopard-suited slave now.

My mother saw me seeing her. She pointed a finger at me. Her gun finger.

When she was sure she'd seen me see her, she shot her finger-gun, and as she shot it she was smiling the most incongruous smile. Her face looked as though she were offering me positive encouragement at a spelling bee.

She spoke, too, or at least she mouthed words. Somehow it seemed that behind glass and wall I heard every word, next to my ear. "Now! Now is the time, my wondrous darling child. Now do what the One True God and I made you to do!"

For this I could find no reply.

Instead, events supplied it.

One of the two Ifah screamed a war cry. Not Ydris, I think. The other one. He too was a warrior, I could tell. The fierceness of his face, the fury of his voice, showed it. The sound affected all who heard his cry, awakening in us knots of nerves and engrams at the bases of our brains, memories none of us knew we had, memories older than history. Memories of warning, and loathing, and above all of terror.

We all covered our heads, remembering for the first time a time when all humankind were slaves.

It was strange. And from strange, matters soon passed into even wilder country. Because this was no culmination, no final finding or revealing or answering, but only the beginning of my learning who I was and am, and what we all have been, are now, and will be in the future. It was only the start of the war that would break all This World (and Yours, too) into the pieces that lie at our feet.

www.ingramcontent.com/pod-product-compliance
Lightning Source LLC
Chambersburg PA
CBHW050123030726
47505CB00007B/2003